The Random House Book of *Horse Stories*

The Random House
Book of
Horse
Stories

Edited by
Felicity Trotman

Illustrated by
Victor Ambrus

Random House 🏠 New York

Compilation copyright © 1996 by Felicity Trotman.
Cover art copyright © 1997 by Robert Gant Steele.

All rights reserved under International
and Pan-American Copyright Conven-
tions. Published in the United States by
Random House, Inc.,
New York. Originally published
in Great Britain as *Horse Stories*
by Robinson Publishing Children's
Books, an imprint of Robinson
Publishing Ltd., in 1996.
Copyright details for individual
stories appear under the
Acknowledgments, on pages 405-406.

Library of Congress Catalog Card Number: 96-70234

ISBN: 0-679-88530-7

http://www.randomhouse.com/

Printed and bound in the EC

3 5 7 9 10 8 6 4 2

Contents

Contents

Introduction

ELIZABETH LINDSAY

I have always loved horses. When I was tiny, I strayed from my parents and wandered into a stable where a giant dapple-gray creature towered above me. This is my first memory of meeting a horse, and I thought it the most wonderful creature I had ever seen. I have felt the same about horses ever since. Many is the time I have watched a group of friends gallop across a field, manes flying, tails tall plumes behind them, bucking, twisting, exploding with energy and power. Yet for all this vivacity when running free, horses are the gentlest of creatures and can become true partners, engaging wholeheartedly in whatever we humans might request of them.

For thousands of years these powerful animals have played a crucial part in our lives, carrying us speedily and safely on their backs. They have heaved our cannons and our carts, taken us to war and to market, pulled our plows and borne our loads with willingness and generosity. We have told stories about them, imagining them as enchanted and magical, and they have brought a special mystery to these myths and legends.

It is only in recent times, with the development of motor vehicles, that horses have assumed a less essential role, but they have not faded from our lives. There

are still places where heavy horses work, and more
people than ever ride for pleasure and watch or take
part in many different equestrian sports: racing, event-
ing, showjumping, and endurance riding—sports as
exciting for the horses as for the riders.

In *The Random House Book of Horse Stories* we gallop
across time and country, from the myths of ancient
Greece to stories set in the present day; some are
magical, and some, like the story I tell, contain real
and ordinary events. I hope that you enjoy reading
this impressive selection and that it adds further to
your knowledge of and pleasure in this remarkable
creature.

One of Those Funny Little Mishaps

ELIZABETH LINDSAY

In this story, Kate has to cope with an emergency. It's based on a misunderstanding, but she acts responsibly— and then finds that she's misunderstood Gemma, the new student at the riding school. This story, by the author of the "Midnight Dancer" series, is based on an actual incident.

Gemma, the new girl, walked into the yard. She must have been dropped at the end of the drive, for Kate hadn't heard a car. She saw her out of the corner of her eye and ducked out of sight behind the stable door. Firefly stretched his neck down and blew at Kate, interested as to why she was suddenly on her knees.

"Go away, Fly," Kate said, gently pushing him. She fought a feeling of dislike. Her mother, who owned and ran Brockwood Riding School and Livery Stables, was always warning her about politeness to clients, and Kate usually did her best. But there was a certain haughtiness about Gemma Hardwick that made being civil difficult, although Starlight, her pony, was sweet.

Peering over the stable door, Kate saw Gemma disappear into the tack room and stood up, rubbing the back of her hand against Firefly's muzzle. Then, with a couple of rasps against the curry comb, she slid the body brush down Firefly's neck. She brushed and brushed until the pony's dark coat gleamed.

"Excuse me!"

Kate almost jumped out of her skin.

"Why's this Brockwood Stables disk thing been fixed to my saddle?" Pouting slightly, Gemma peered into the gloom of Firefly's stable. "Only there's no one around to ask."

"Oh," said Kate. "Mum puts those on all the saddles. Just in case there's an accident. It's so people will know who to get in touch with. She'll ask you to put a name and address label in your riding hat as well."

"I've no intention of having an accident," said Gemma. "Just a nice quiet ride." She paused. Kate sensed her uncertainty and waited. "I don't suppose you fancy coming with me, do you?"

"I can't. Not until Mum gets back. There's no one here but me at the moment."

Almost as if she had not heard, Gemma asked, "Where is Starlight? He's not in his stable."

"In the paddock," said Kate.

"Oh, yes." Gemma swung on her heel and walked off, no doubt to fetch a head collar. Kate knew she had an inbuilt bias against people who were rich enough to pay someone else to look after their horses. Nevertheless her feelings did a little seesaw and she went from irritated to sorry. Gemma, she suddenly realized, was lonely. Kate made a mental note to be nicer.

She was lining up buckets in the feed store prior to making up the evening feeds when Gemma led Starlight from his stable, tacked up and ready to go. Kate crossed the yard to the girl and her gray pony, automatically stretching to hold down the offside stirrup leather when Gemma mounted.

"Where are you going?" she asked.

"For a ride." Gemma looked surprised by the question.

"I'm not being nosy. It's just in case," said Kate. "You are going out on your own."

"I always go out on my own."

"All the more reason for saying in what direction." Then realizing that Gemma would probably not know the best places to ride yet, Kate suggested Beacon Hill. "It's pleasant up there at this time of the evening," she said, and gave her directions.

Gemma mumbled what might have been thanks and turned Starlight, who was impatient to go. His hooves clattered brusquely across the concrete of the yard. Kate watched their retreating backs before glancing at her watch to wonder vaguely what was holding up her mother. She should have been back by now. With a sigh she returned to the feed bin to try and find the mislaid scoop.

By the time the telephone rang Kate was seriously fed up. She had brought in the horses that were stabled overnight and fed them, and was in the process of topping up water buckets. It was too bad. She had wanted to ride herself, besides which she had a mountain of homework. At this rate it would be dark before she got indoors, and she hadn't even had time for tea. She ran to the extension in the tack room, ready to wail her list of complaints to the caller, whom she expected to be her mother.

"Hello; Brockwood Riding Stables." Only it wasn't Mum. It was a woman driver who had found a gray pony trotting along the lane toward her approaching car.

"I've tied it to a field gate. It seemed quite happy to

be caught. I noticed the address disk and thought I'd better ring you. I'm at the phone booth in the village."

"Yes, yes, thank you." Kate was suddenly flustered. "Where was this gate again?" The woman described the lane that led to the bridle path for Beacon Hill.

"Is there anything else I can do?" the woman asked.

"You didn't see any sign of a rider?" Kate asked hopefully.

"No, there was no one in sight. I did look."

"I'd better get out there," Kate said. "Thank you very much." She flung the receiver back on the hook and ran into the yard. "Don't panic," she told herself. But already her imagination had raced Gemma into tragedy and she saw her lying somewhere on Beacon Hill unconscious. She quickly thought things through and decided to ride her mountain bike up the lane to collect Starlight. She'd dump the bike and ride the pony up Beacon Hill to find Gemma. As to leaving the yard unattended, she didn't have any choice. This was an emergency. She ran back into the tack room, rummaged for a scrap of paper, and wrote: "Mum, Gemma Hardwick fallen off. Have gone off to Beacon Hill to find her. Kate." She pulled on her hard hat and sprinted to the barn for her bike.

Five minutes later she was pedaling up the lane toward the bridle path. There were two field gates along the lane both inset into the hedge off to the right. To her left the ground was raised but unfenced, a great stretch of common land from the middle of which Beacon Hill grew into a craggy peak. Her tires hummed as she stood on her pedals and pushed. There was no pony tied to the first gate. Kate, panting with effort, propelled herself on up the slope to the next. Behind her a horn tooted. Turning around, Kate saw a car stop by the gate she had just passed. The horn tooted again. There was no doubt it was her attention the driver wanted. Kate swung around. A woman hung out of the car window.

"I tied it to here!" she shouted. Kate coasted back down the slope. As she drew closer the woman asked, "You are from the riding school, aren't you? I guessed by the hat."

"Are you sure it was this gate?" Kate asked. "There's another farther up."

"Quite sure."

Kate's heart sank. Her next dreadful thought was that someone had stolen Starlight.

"Thanks," said Kate. "Only I must go on. I've got to find Gemma, the rider. Something may have happened to her."

"It's getting dark," said the woman. "Don't let anything happen to you. Do you think you should phone the police?"

"I don't know," said Kate. "I think I ought to keep looking while it's still light. If I don't get back Mum'll get a search organized."

"Well . . ." said the woman doubtfully. "I'm not sure you should be going off on your own."

"I'll be fine," said Kate. "Don't worry. Thanks for all your help."

She swung her bike around and set off up the narrow lane, pedaling hard, before the woman could stop her. There were acres of ground to cover before it got dark. Now she wished she had brought Firefly. It was going to be much harder searching Beacon Hill on a bike.

By the time Kate bumped exhausted down the bridle path the light had almost gone, she was hoarse from calling, and her eyes were tired from scanning every hump and dip. She'd had no luck at all although she had ridden all over the hill. But, as she well knew, Gemma could have ridden anywhere. The last bit of the path was sunken almost to the lane. She put out her feet to steady herself, pushing to stay upright as her tires bit into the sand. She was glad when she reached the lane and could coast downhill, resting her tired muscles. She was filled with a sense of failure and distress at having to tell her mother what had happened. The breeze blew in her face and she slowed to turn and cross the bridge onto the bottom lane. The evening air was chilly and now that she had cooled she felt goose pimples grow on her arms. She turned into the drive past the Brockwood sign and automatically pedaled around the potholes. In the fields on either side the ponies were blurred shapes in the fading light.

Kate arrived in the yard with a screech of brakes. The lights were on but the yard was empty. Her mother's Discovery was parked by the wall, but there was no hustle and bustle of people organizing a search. Everything was just, well, normal. Kate dumped her bike against the wall. Mum must have missed the note.

"Mum!" Her mother came out of the tack room, smiling a greeting! "Mum, didn't you get my note?"

"I did, dear, but all's well." And she pointed across the yard to Starlight's stable. The door opened, and Gemma came out, carrying her pony's tack. Kate's jaw dropped.

"What are you doing here? I thought you were lying unconscious somewhere on Beacon Hill."

Gemma grinned weakly, a sort of apologetic grimace.

"Sorry," she said.

"Sorry!" said Kate. "I've just biked miles looking for you. For goodness' sake, what happened? Why are you all right?"

"Now, now, Kate," said her mother, sensing an explosion. "Let Gemma explain." She took Gemma's tack from her. "I'll hang this up for you." The address disk tinkled against the metal D ring on the saddle as Kate's mother hoisted it onto her arm and disappeared into the tack room.

"Well, go on, then," said Kate, bad temper welling up.

"I took your advice about the ride. It seemed a good idea," said Gemma. She brushed something, Kate couldn't see what, off her sweatshirt. "Only when I turned up the bridle path and rode along that sunken bit, I wasn't really paying attention. Sort of looking around at things. So I didn't see the large black dog charge us until after Starlight reared up. It was the only way he could turn, and the dog really frightened him. I wasn't ready for it."

"OK, OK, so you fell off."

Gemma pressed her bottom gingerly. "I'm going to have a wonderful bruise." Kate gave Gemma a look that meant, Get on with it. Gemma did. "The dog chased Starlight and he galloped off. Then it ran back and started licking me. Its owner was ever so apologetic. I said she should keep her dog under control and she said she was trying, only it was young."

"The usual excuse," said Kate. "And?"

"And I ran after Starlight, back down the path and along the lane. I guessed he was coming back here. Then I found him tied to a gate. He seemed fine, so I thought, well, he really ought to go straight back up

that bridle path in case he gets a thing about it. I never ever thought that the person who tied him up would see the address disk and call you. I never ever thought that you'd come after me. If I had I would have come straight back. But when I was on Beacon Hill I saw I could ride back through the woods to the other end of the village. So I missed you. I'm really, really sorry." Tears welled up into Gemma's eyes. "You'll never want to be friends with me after this."

Kate looked down at her feet and let out a long sigh. Then she looked at Gemma's distraught face and laughed. It was a wry little chuckle, but she was beginning to see a lighter side to what had happened. Gemma looked at her questioningly.

"It's all right," said Kate. "I'm going to think of this as one of those funny little mishaps." Gemma's face was a picture of grateful relief.

"I'm supposed to be walking home but I think as it's got so late I'd better call my mum for a lift," said Gemma. "Will that be all right?"

Kate relented completely and smiled.

"It can't have been much fun falling off."

"Oh, I don't mind."

Kate surveyed Gemma's backside, which even in the half light showed obvious signs of being in contact with the ground. "Your mum will when she sees the state of your jodhpurs. You've got a brown streak across your bottom."

"Do you think I could get it off with a damp cloth? I really don't want her to know I've fallen off. She worries, you see."

"Yeah. Come indoors and I'll make you a drink. Do you collect horse posters, by the way?"

"Yes, I do."

"Cool. We can do swaps."

The White Knight

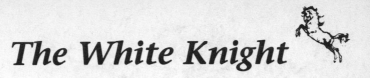

LEWIS CARROLL

Alice's Adventures in Wonderland and Through the Looking Glass, and What Alice Found There *have been popular ever since they first appeared, over a hundred years ago. This extract comes from* Through the Looking Glass, *where Alice finds a back-to-front world, full of chess pieces. In the real world, knights were strong and brave, and rode chargers into battle. In the looking-glass world, things are a bit different. . . .*

At this moment her thoughts were interrupted by a loud shouting of "Ahoy! Ahoy! Check!" and a Knight, dressed in crimson armor, came galloping down upon her, brandishing a great club. Just as he reached her, the horse stopped suddenly: "You're my prisoner!" the Knight cried, as he tumbled off his horse.

Startled as she was, Alice was more frightened for him than for herself at the moment, and watched him with some anxiety as he mounted again. As soon as he was comfortably in the saddle, he began once more "You're my—" but here another voice broke in—"Ahoy! Ahoy! Check!"—and Alice looked round in some surprise for the new enemy.

This time it was a White Knight. He drew up at Alice's side, and tumbled off his horse just as the Red Knight had done; then he got on again, and the two

Knights sat and looked at each other without speaking. Alice looked from one to the other in some bewilderment.

"She's my prisoner, you know!" the Red Knight said at last.

"Yes, but then I came and rescued her!" the White Knight replied.

"Well, we must fight for her, then," said the Red Knight, as he took up his helmet (which hung from the saddle, and was something like the shape of a horse's head), and put it on.

"You will observe the Rules of Battle, of course?" the White Knight remarked, putting on his helmet too.

"I always do," said the Red Knight, and they began banging away at each other with such fury that Alice got behind a tree to be out of the way of the blows.

"I wonder, now, what the Rules of Battle are," she said to herself, as she watched the fight, timidly peeping out from her hiding place: "One rule seems to be that, if one Knight hits the other, he knocks him off his horse, and if he misses, he tumbles off himself— and another Rule seems to be that they hold their clubs in their arms, as if they were Punch and Judy. What a noise they make when they tumble, just like fire irons falling into the fender! And how quiet the horses are! They let them get on and off them just as if they were tables!"

Another Rule of Battle, that Alice had not noticed, seemed to be that they always fell on their heads, and the battle ended with their both falling off in this way, side by side: when they got up again, they shook hands, and then the Red Knight mounted and galloped off.

"It was a glorious victory, wasn't it?" said the White Knight, as he came up panting.

"I don't know," Alice said doubtfully. "I don't want to be anybody's prisoner. I want to be a Queen."

"So you will, when you've crossed the next brook," said the White Knight. "I'll see you safe to the end of the wood—and then I must go back, you know. That's the end of my move."

"Thank you very much," said Alice. "May I help you off with your helmet?" It was evidently more than he could manage by himself; however, she managed to shake him out of it at last.

"Now one can breathe more easily," said the Knight, putting back his shaggy hair with both hands, and turning his gentle face and large mild eyes to Alice. She thought she had never seen such a strange-looking soldier in all her life.

"Now help me on. I hope you've got your hair well fastened on?" he continued, as they set off.

"Only in the usual way," Alice said, smiling. For a few minutes she walked on in silence, every now and then stopping to help the poor Knight, who certainly was not a good rider.

Whenever the horse stopped (which it did very often), he fell off in front; and whenever it went on again (which it generally did rather suddenly), he fell off behind. Otherwise he kept on pretty well, except that he had a habit of now and then falling off sideways; and as he generally did this on the side on which Alice was walking, she soon found that it was the best plan not to walk quite close to the horse.

"I'm afraid you've not had much practice in riding," she ventured to say, as she was helping him up from his fifth tumble.

The Knight looked very much surprised, and a little offended at the remark. "What makes you say that?" he asked, as he scrambled back into the saddle, keeping hold of Alice's hair with one hand, to save himself from falling over on the other side.

"Because people don't fall off quite so often, when they've had much practice."

"I've had plenty of practice," the Knight said very gravely. "Plenty of practice!"

Alice could think of nothing better to say than

"Indeed?" but she said it as heartily as she could. They went on a little way in silence after this, the Knight with his eyes shut, muttering to himself, and Alice watching anxiously for the next tumble.

"The great art of riding," the Knight suddenly began in a loud voice, waving his right arm as he spoke, "is to keep—" Here the sentence ended as suddenly as it had begun, as the Knight fell heavily on the top of his head exactly in the path where Alice was walking.

She was quite frightened this time, and said in an anxious tone, as she picked him up, "I hope no bones are broken?"

"None to speak of," the Knight said, as if he didn't mind breaking two or three of them. "The great art of riding, as I was saying, is—to keep your balance. Like this, you know—"

He let go of the bridle, and stretched out both his arms to show Alice what he meant, and this time he fell flat on his back, right under the horse's feet.

"Plenty of practice!" he went on repeating, all the time that Alice was getting him on his feet again. "Plenty of practice!"

"It's too ridiculous!" cried Alice, getting quite out of patience. "You ought to have a wooden horse on wheels, that you ought!"

"Does that kind go smoothly?" the Knight asked in a tone of great interest, clasping his arms around the horse's neck as he spoke, just in time to save himself from tumbling off again.

"Much more smoothly than a live horse," Alice said, with a little scream of laughter, in spite of all she could do to prevent it.

"I'll get one," the Knight said thoughtfully to himself. "One or two—several."

The Pony Club Camp

C. NORTHCOTE PARKINSON

Every pony dreams of a little girl of his own—so when Daisy Dedleigh-Sirkett gets engaged, and decides to close down the Dundreary Riding School, the ponies decide that this is their chance to act. They will choose the children they would like to have. This story, which tells how some of the ponies achieve their ambition, comes from Ponies Plot *("A book about children written for ponies . . . there should be a copy in every loosebox"). It was written down by C. Northcote Parkinson from stories told to him by his friends Fairy and Spice. When he was not talking to ponies, C. Northcote Parkinson was a professor of history, a journalist, and a writer. He was also famous for discovering that work expands until it fills all the time available for it.*

By the time of the Melbury Horticultural Show, which happens in May, several of the ponies had gone to a new home. Unbeatable went, inevitably, to Clare Rounding. Prune we already know about; he found a fine new stable at Windfall Orchard. For young Jennifer any pony was better than none; or so she thought for the first few weeks. Brighty was to go to Sally Bopwith, who wanted a second pony (spoiled child that she was). Dunblane, the last pony any sane person could want, was in fact one of the earlier ones to go, being acquired as a birthday present for Diana

Dashwood. How Diana's aunt, Mrs. Bifocal, could ever have thought Dunblane a suitable mount for Diana must remain a mystery. That is nevertheless what happened and it would be hard to say which was the more embarrassed, the girl or the pony. The aunt was alone in believing that her choice represented an astute stroke of business. Diana, for her part, thought that the old lady must be completely dotty; which, as a matter of fact, she is. Diana rechristened Dunblane The Dismal Dumpling, and that was soon the name by which he was known. But of all the ponies at the Dundreary School, the most unlucky was poor Mischief. And here again we are faced by an apparently hopeless problem. Why, in heaven's name, should Mrs. Overwaite have chosen Mischief as the right pony for Deirdre? To this question I have no answer. All we know is that the arrangement was made and marked the beginning of a most unpromising partnership.

It was at the Melbury Show that the ponies still with Daisy met those who had already found another stable. All the Pony Club was there and it was a great opportunity for gossip. Each wanted to know how the others had fared. There was also talk about the Pony Club Camp, which always happened in August. And, more immediately, there were the actual events to discuss; which pony had done well or badly, and what the chances were of Unbeatable winning the highest number of points. So far as that went, Unbeatable had at least nothing to fear from Mischief. By the last day of the Show that pony's heart was ready to break.

"Hard luck, Mischief! You were a good fourth, mind you, and there *might* have been a rosette going. I had a yellow rosette once when *I* was fourth—'Reserve'— you know. Well, we can't win every time, can we?"

Dunblane, the pony now known as The Dismal Dumpling, was, as usual, making matters worse. Mischief had just come back to the collecting ring after the junior jumping event, won (of course) by Unbeatable, with Clare Rounding.

"I didn't think Deirdre was being particularly helpful. But for her, old horse, you might have been third. That's what *I* thought, anyway, and several of the other ponies said the same. Did I ever tell you about the time *I* was third?"

"Yes, Dumpling, you did," snapped Mischief. "Often! And no one would know, from the way you tell it, that it was in the leading rein class, with four ponies entered and one of them scratched."

Mischief spoke bitterly, choking back a sob. It was bad enough to come in with eight faults. But to be treated as a fellow duffer by this Dumpling creature turned gloom into agony.

"No need to be rude," replied Dumpling. "I was only trying to cheer you up."

The two ponies stood hitched to the rail while their two small girls had left the ring. Mischief's handicap was that sacklike creature Deirdre Overwaite, who had gone to buy herself some candy floss. As for Dumpling's partner, Diana Dashwood, she had run off to cry behind the tent devoted to Garden Implements. For her, and for Mischief, the day had been disastrous.

"You'll do better next year," Dumpling continued unfeelingly. "If Paleface, say, were to go down with glanders, you might be third, with a green rosette, which I myself have had only once."

"And if all the other ponies were to drop dead, *you* would win the sash of honor," said Mischief. In no other circumstance, to be sure, would such a result

19

have been likely. Dumpling was, in every way, the Pony Club Bore. But Mischief's chances, with Deirdre up, were little better. This wretched child would never give him sufficient rein; and each attempt at a fence ended with a jabbed mouth and another pole on the ground. Hopeless in the saddle and not much better in the stable, Deirdre was the subhuman equivalent of the Dismal Dumpling. So poor Mischief was literally saddled with a sausage-shaped, mouth-jabbing, and selfish child, the joke of the Pony Club. To make matters worse, she proposed to take him to the Pony Club Camp.

The camp that year was to be at Mickleby Moorside. The ponies would be in a paddock, the girls in tents, and the meals served in Farmer Woodcock's barn. The organizing committee members would be Miss Helena Nutshell, Major Bastable (who charged, you will remember, with the Light Brigade) and Mrs. Kewside, who would see to the catering. They could expect a visit from the Commissioner, The Hon. Mrs. Hark-Forrard, and there was pretty certain to be that film on the Ponies of Paraguay. For a lively pony like Mischief some of the games would have been rather fun; nor would he have minded the all-day trek or the Visitors' Day. But what could he do in partnership with Dreary Deirdre? She would oversleep and they would be late for inspection. She would fail to slacken the guy ropes and the tent pole would fall on her. She would have forgotten her raincoat and might catch cold when it drizzled. There would be a line of smashed fences, with Major Bastable muttering that there had been less damage at the storming of the Malakoff. There would be Miss Nutshell screaming *"Will* you *make* your pony canter?"* while Deirdre tugged at the reins.

Finally there would be the return to the pony lines with Dumpling saying, "Hard luck, old horse! A bit out of sorts today? I have the same trouble sometimes. Did I ever tell you about the time when . . .?"

The camp was very much what Mischief thought it would be, but Mrs. Harriet Hark-Forrard, who appeared on the second day, shook up the morning session by calling, "Change ponies!" She did not say who should change with what, but Diana was on Mischief before most people had so much as looked around. There was a scampering and a squealing and a lengthening and shortening of stirrup leathers, in the midst of which Deirdre, wandering aimlessly around, found a riderless pony. It was Dumpling and she managed, at the third attempt, to place herself in the saddle. A minute later the ride moved off, circled left, circled right, quitted stirrups, and were told to trot. There was a mutual sympathy between Deirdre and Dumpling. Here, the girl felt, was a pony which would never do the unexpected—would never, for preference do anything at all. She felt, for the first time, confident and safe. Dumpling, for his part, felt relieved to be rid of Diana, a girl who was always urging him to jump ditches and fences, scramble up banks, and wade through streams. Deirdre, now, was less demanding. She expected him to trot when the others did, and even canter when the time for cantering had apparently come. But that was all she expected and more than she got. For Deirdre the pony Dumpling began to show a tolerance bordering on affection.

Between Mischief and Diana there was, by contrast, a real romance. It would seem that they had been friends from the beginning of time. Each knew what the other was thinking and anticipated what the other would do. It was not a question of riding or being ridden; they floated together in a golden haze, danced to the music of the trumpets which no one had actually blown.

"What do you think you are doing?" asked Miss Nutshell sarcastically.

"Really, child!" protested Major Bastable.

But Diana did not even hear them, and Mischief's hooves were not touching the ground. Each had lived for this moment of discovery, the finding of the perfect partner. Each knew that separation might follow, that they might never come together again, that the minutes they had must be lived as if they were the last. Sharing their brief heaven, they behaved very badly indeed. "Get that pony under control!" shouted the Crimean Major. "You are upsetting the whole ride!" wailed Mrs. Hark-Forrard. "Stop that circus act, Diana!" screamed Miss Helena Nutshell. So annoyed was the Major with Mischief's prancing about that he did something he should not have done. He tried to bring Mischief back to earth with his whip, used quite smartly on the pony's rump. Unfortunately, his wrath was more impressive than his eyesight. His whip fell on the wrong pony—on the wretched Dumpling, who happened to be standing where Mischief had been a few seconds before. The crack of the whip was enough to bring Mischief under control. It was from the back of a perfectly behaved pony that Diana made her apologies. "I'm so sorry, Mrs. Hark-Forrard. This pony is a little fresh." But the committee members were not listening. They were gazing in blank surprise at a moving object in the distance—a dwindling speck, which was passing from the middle distance into the background, out of the background toward the horizon, over the horizon

and out of the picture. It was Dumpling and Deirdre, moving as neither had ever moved before.

Reading the last two sentences I feel that I may have misled the reader, giving Dumpling a turn of speed he could not possibly have had. In point of fact, his gallop was nothing remarkable. It came as a surprise, nevertheless, to those who knew him best; which is why they stared after him at a moment when they could perhaps have tried to head him off. It also came as a surprise to Deirdre, who clung to his mane, staying somehow in the saddle until such time as he should choose to halt. It was a good twenty-five minutes before that idea occurred to him, and they had by that time covered some four or five miles. Miss Nutshell finally came up with them near Bingley Common, where Deirdre was in the pond and Dumpling grazing calmly on the bank. By the time they were all back in camp, Deirdre had the symptoms of a nasty cold. She was put to bed in the farmhouse with a hot drink and a hot water bottle.

Back in the pony lines, Dumpling made the most of his adventure. "Actually," he explained to the other ponies, "I am not at all keen on this riding school routine. I do better, really, in a point-to-point. Take this morning's run, for example. I dare say one or two others here could have equaled my time over the given distance—some could, others couldn't—but would any other pony (I ask myself) be as fresh as I am at the end of the day? Stamina, that is what so many ponies lack! Good to look at, some of them, keen to jump, but show them the open country, the far horizons—and where *are* they?" At that moment, before he could answer his own question, poor Dumpling collapsed in a heap and lay there until morning. Completely exhausted, he stayed in the pony lines for the next three days, having his breakfast in bed and telling all visitors, in a feeble voice, that his life was drawing peacefully to its close.

With Deirdre and Dumpling on the sick list, it was inevitable that Diana should ride Mischief. She was still riding him when Visitors' Day came, with a display for parents and friends. On the previous evening Diana had a talk with Deirdre, who was recovering but not expected to compete. Diana came straight to the point by proposing that they should swap ponies.

"I get on well with Mischief," she said, "and you are far happier on Dunblane." (She was careful to use the pony's real name.)

"All very fine," Deirdre replied, "but Mischief is a far better pony."

"Mischief is more promising *as a show jumper*," Diana admitted. "But aren't you forgetting your own cross-country performance on Dunblane? Do you know what I thought at the time?"

"No, Diana, do tell me," pleaded Deirdre.

"I thought that you would do well in a three-day event!"

"No—*really*?"

"You were splendid. I'll never forget how you kept in the saddle. Hill and dale, hedges and ditches—you took 'em all in your stride."

"Well, I did come off in the end . . ."

"Ah," said Diana, "but that was miles away, after you had been galloping for hours."

"I didn't know," admitted Deirdre, "that old Dumpling had it in him."

"Nor did I!" said Diana eagerly. "The fact is, I have not got the best out of that pony. It needed a better rider to show what he is really capable of."

"Oh, no!" protested Deirdre. "You are far better than I am!"

"Well, I'll admit I thought I was. But I realize now that Dunblane has great possibilities—with you! *I* could never do much with him, but *you* understand his character."

"Nice of you to say so . . . All right, Diana, let's swap! Your parents and mine will be here tomorrow. It can all be fixed then, before the display!"

The exchange was agreed without much argument, and the display was a great success. Mischief was an easy winner in musical gates and pushed Firefly (ridden by Rachel Rossetti) to third place in the obstacle race. Then came the jumping event, which had always meant an easy victory for Unbeatable (and Clare Rounding).

But Mischief sailed effortlessly over every jump and there was a final jump-off between the two. Twice the jumps were raised and then—to everyone's surprise— Unbeatable refused at the brick wall. Three minutes later Mischief did a last clear round and received the blue rosette. The happiest girl that day was Diana and the happiest pony was Mischief. Deirdre had been terribly useful giving out the programs, and Dumpling had been ridden in turn by the younger brothers and sisters. That evening, back in the pony lines, he told the other ponies about it. Not every pony, he pointed out, has the patience for this sort of work.

"It's a sort of knack," he admitted, "which a few ponies have. The tricky part is when you have walked across the paddock and have to go back again. To circle round smoothly, so that the child doesn't fall off, is something of an art. There's more in it than you might think. Even *before* that, there can be a crisis—we had one this afternoon. There is a point, half-way (or *nearly* half-way) across the paddock, when the child realizes that its mother has been left behind at the starting line. This is called, technically, the point of no return. Well, that was where the trouble began. I had sensed it coming, mind you. One develops a sort of instinct as the result of experience. But for that, things might have been serious. It occurred to me at the time that a rosette for saving life would have been a nice gesture. Did I ever tell you, Mischief, about the time I was third . . .?"

But Mischief wasn't listening. Diana was patting his neck and stroking his mane and saying, "You are the most wonderful pony in the whole world!"

Overhearing this, Dumpling muttered, "There's no accounting for taste!"

Gulliver Meets the Houyhnhnms

JONATHAN SWIFT

Lemuel Gulliver is a ship's surgeon. His adventures in Lilliput, where ordinary people are tiny and he is a giant, and in Brobdingnag, where the inhabitants are giants and he is minute, are famous—but here is part of another adventure in which, now a ship's captain, he is marooned by his crew on an island ruled by horses. There are other creatures there—the dirty, savage Yahoos; and it is a shock to Gulliver to discover what the Yahoos really are.

Jonathan Swift was an Irish clergyman, who did not like the way politicians behaved. His book Gulliver's Travels *(from which this extract comes) was published in 1726. It was written not as a novel, but as a satire, poking rather savage fun at some of the silly things politicians did. Writers could be punished—sometimes even imprisoned— for satires, so to protect himself, Swift had his manuscript left on a London publisher's doorstep in the dead of night, when he was safely in Ireland.*

Upon the ninth day of May, 1711, one James Welch came down to my cabin, and said he had orders from the Captain to set me ashore. I expostulated with him, but in vain; neither would he so much as tell me who their new captain was. They forced me into the longboat, letting me put on my best suit of clothes, which were as good as new, and a small bundle of linen, but no arms except my hanger*; and they were so civil as not to search my pockets, into which I conveyed what money I had, with some other little necessaries. They rowed about a league, and then set me down on a strand. I desired them to tell me what country it was. They all swore they knew no more than myself, but said that the Captain (as they called him) was resolved, after they had sold the lading, to get rid of me in the first place where they could discover land. They pushed off immediately, advising me to make haste for fear of being overtaken by the tide, and so bade me farewell.

In this desolate condition I advanced forward and soon got upon firm ground, where I sat down on a bank to rest myself and consider what I had best to do. When I was a little refreshed I went up into the country, resolving to deliver myself to the first savages I should meet, and purchase my life from them by some bracelets, glass rings, and other toys which sailors usually provide themselves with in those voyages, and whereof I had some about me; the land was divided by long rows of trees not regularly planted, but naturally growing; there was great plenty of grass and several fields of oats. I walked very circumspectly for fear of being surprised or suddenly shot with an arrow from behind or on either side. I fell into a beaten road, where I saw many tracks of human feet, and some of cows, but most of horses. At last I beheld several animals in a field, and one or two of the same kind sitting in trees. Their shape was very singular and deformed,

*Hanger = little sword

which a little discomposed me, so that I lay down behind a thicket to observe them better. Some of them, coming forward near the place where I lay, gave me an opportunity of distinctly marking their form. Their heads and breasts were covered with a thick hair, some frizzled and others lank; they had beards like goats, and a long ridge of hair down their backs and the foreparts of their legs and feet; but the rest of their bodies were bare, so that I might see their skins, which were of a brown buff color. They climbed high trees as nimbly as a squirrel, for they had strong extended claws before and behind, terminating in sharp points hooked. They would often spring, and bound, and leap with prodigious agility. The females were not so large as the males; they had long lank hair on their faces, nor anything more than a sort of down on the rest of their bodies. The hair of both sexes was of several colors—brown, red, black, and yellow. Upon the whole, I never beheld in all my travels so disagreeable an animal, nor one against which I naturally conceived so strong an antipathy. So that thinking I had seen enough, full of contempt and aversion, I got up and pursued the beaten road, hoping it might direct me to the cabin of some Indian. I had not gone far when I met one of these creatures full in my way, and coming up directly to me. The ugly monster, when he saw me, distorted several ways every feature of his visage, and started as at an object he had never seen before; then, approaching nearer, lifted up his forepaw, whether out of curiosity or mischief I could not tell. But I drew my hanger and gave him a good blow with the flat side of it, for I durst not strike him with the edge, fearing the inhabitants might be provoked against me if they should come to know that I had killed or maimed any of their cattle. When the beast felt the smart he drew back and roared so loud that a herd of at least forty came flocking about me from the next field, howling and making odious faces; but I ran to the body of a tree and, leaning my back against it, kept them off by waving my hanger. Several of this cursed brood, getting hold of the branches behind, leaped up in the tree, from whence they began to throw nuts on my head after the manner of monkeys. However, I escaped pretty well by sticking close to the stem of the tree.

In the midst of this distress I observed them all to run away on a sudden as fast as they could, at which I ventured to leave the tree and pursue the road, wondering what it was that could put them into this fright. But looking on my left hand, I saw a horse walking softly in the field, which, my persecutors having sooner discovered, was the cause of their flight. The horse started a little when he came near me, but, soon recovering himself, looked full in my face with manifest tokens of wonder. He viewed my hands and feet, walking around me several times. I would have pursued my journey, but he placed himself directly in the way, yet looking with a very mild aspect, never offering the least violence. We stood gazing at each other for some time; at last I took the boldness to reach my hand toward his neck with a design to stroke it, using the common style and whistle of jockeys when they are going to handle a strange horse. But this animal, seeming to receive my civilities with disdain, shook his head and bent his brows, softly raising up his right forefoot to remove my hand. Then he neighed three or four times, but in so different a cadence that I almost began to think he was speaking to himself in some language of his own.

While he and I were thus employed, another horse came up, who, applying himself to the first in a very formal manner, they gently struck each other's right hoof before, neighing several times by turns, and varying the sound, which seemed to be almost articulate. They went some paces off, as if it were to confer together, walking side by side backward and forward, like persons deliberating upon some affair of weight, but often turning their eyes toward me, as it were to watch that I might not escape. I was amazed to see such actions and behaviors in brute beasts, and concluded with myself that if the inhabitants of this country were endued with a proportionable degree of reason, they must needs be the wisest people upon earth. This thought gave me so much comfort that I resolved to go forward until I could discover some house or village, or meet with any of the natives, leaving the two horses to discourse together as they pleased. But the first, who was a dapple gray, observing me to steal off, neighed after me in so expressive a tone that I fancied myself to understand what he meant, whereupon I turned back and came near him to expect his further commands, but concealing my fear as much as I could, for I began to be in some pain how this adventure might terminate; and the reader will easily believe that I did not much like my present situation.

The two horses came up close to me, looking with great earnestness upon my face and hands. The gray steed rubbed my hat all round with his right forehoof, and discomposed it so much that I was forced to adjust it better by taking it off and settling it again; whereat both he and his companion (who was a brown bay) appeared to be much surprised; the latter felt the lappet of my coat, and, finding it to hang loose about me, they both looked with new signs of wonder. He stroked my right hand, seeming to admire the softness and color: but he squeezed it so hard between his hoof and his pastern that I was forced to roar, after which they both touched me with all possible tenderness. They were under great perplexity about my shoes and stockings, which they felt very often, neighing to each other and using various gestures not unlike those of a philosopher when he would attempt to solve some new and difficult phenomenon.

Upon the whole, the behavior of these animals were so orderly and rational, so acute and judicious, that I at last concluded they must needs be magicians, who had thus metamorphosed themselves upon some design, and, seeing a stranger in the way, were resolved to divert themselves with him; or, perhaps, were really amazed at the sight of a man so very different in habit, feature, and complexion from those who might probably live in so remote a climate. Upon the strength of this reasoning I ventured to address them in the following manner: "Gentlemen, if you be conjurers, as I have good cause to believe, you can understand any language, therefore I make bold to let your worships know that I am a poor distressed Englishman driven by his misfortunes upon your coast, and I entreat one of you to let me ride upon his back, as if he were a real horse, to some house or village where I can be relieved. In return of which favor I will make you a present of this knife and bracelet" (taking them out of my pocket). The two creatures stood silent while I spoke, seeming to listen with great attention; and when I had ended, they neighed frequently toward each other, as if they were engaged in serious conversation. I plainly observed that their language expressed the passions very well, and their words might, with little pains, be resolved into an alphabet more easily than the Chinese.

I could frequently distinguish the word "Yahoo," which was repeated by each of them several times; and although it was impossible for me to conjecture what it meant, yet while the two horses were busy in conversation, I endeavored to practice this word upon my tongue; and as soon as they were silent, I boldly pronounced "Yahoo" in a loud voice, imitating, at the same time, as near as I could, the neighing of a horse, at which they were both visibly surprised, and the gray repeated the same word twice, as if he meant to teach me the right accent, wherein I spoke after him as well as I could, and found myself perceivably to improve every time, though very far from any degree of perfection. Then the bay tried me with a second word, much harder to be pronounced; but, reducing it to the English orthography, may be spelled thus, "Houyhnhnms." I did not succeed in this so well as in the former, but after two or three further trials I had better fortune; and they both appeared amazed at my capacity.

After some further discourse, which I then conjectured might relate to me, the two friends took their leaves, with the same compliment of striking each other's hoof; and the gray made me signs that I should walk before them, wherein I thought it prudent to comply till I could find a better director. When I offered to slacken my pace he would cry "Hhuun, Hhuun." I guessed his meaning, and gave him to understand, as well as I could, that I was weary, and

not able to walk faster, upon which he would stand awhile to let me rest.

Having traveled about three miles, we came to a long kind of building, made of timber stuck in the ground and wattled across; the roof was low and covered with straw. I now began to be a little comforted, and took out some toys, which travelers usually carry for presents to the savage Indians of America and other parts, in hopes the people of the house would be thereby encouraged to receive me kindly. The horse made me a sign to go in first. It was a large room with a smooth clay floor, and the rack and manger extending the whole length on one side. There were three nags and two mares, not eating, but some of them sitting down upon their hams, which I very much wondered at, but wondered more to see the rest employed in domestic business. They seemed but ordinary cattle. However, this confirmed my first opinion, that a people who could so far civilize brute animals must needs excel in wisdom all the nations of the world. The gray came in just after, and thereby prevented any ill-treatment which the others might have given me. He neighed to them several times in a style of authority, and received answers.

Beyond this room there were three others, reaching the length of the house, to which you passed through three doors opposite to each other, in the manner of a vista. We went through the second room, towards the third. Here the gray walked in first, beckoning me to attend. I waited in the second room, and got ready my presents for the master and mistress of the house. They were two knives, three bracelets of false pearl, a small looking glass, and a bead necklace. The horse neighed three or four times, and I waited to hear some answers in a human voice, but I observed no other returns than in the same dialect, only one or two a little shriller than his. I began to think that this house must belong to some person of great note among them, because there appeared so much ceremony before I could gain admittance. But that a man of quality should be served all by horses was beyond my comprehension. I feared my brain was disturbed by my sufferings and misfortunes. I roused myself, and looked about me in the room where I was left alone. This was furnished like the first, only after a more elegant manner. I rubbed my eyes often, but the same objects still occurred. I pinched my arms and sides to awake myself, hoping I might be in a dream. I then absolutely concluded that all these appearances could be nothing else than necromancy and magic. But I had no time to pursue these reflections, for the gray horse came to the door and made me a sign to follow him into a third room, where I saw a very comely mare, together with a colt and foal, sitting up on their haunches upon mats of straw, not unartfully made, and perfectly neat and clean.

The mare, soon after my entrance, rose from her mat, and coming up close, after having nicely observed my hands and face, gave me a contemptuous look; then, turning to the horse, I heard the word "Yahoo" often repeated betwixt them; the meaning of which word I could not then comprehend, although it was the first I had learned to pronounce, but I was soon better informed, to my everlasting mortification, for the horse beckoned to me with his head, and repeating the word "Hhuun, Hhuun," as he did upon the road, which I understand was to attend him, led me out into a kind of court, where was another building at some distance from the house. Here we entered, and I saw three of these detestable creatures whom I first met after my landing, feeding upon roots and the flesh of some animals, which I afterwards found to be that of asses and dogs, and now and then a cow dead by accident or disease. They were all tied by the neck with strong withes fastened to a beam; they held their food between the claws of their forefeet, and tore it with their teeth.

The master horse ordered a sorrel nag, one of his servants, to untie the largest of these animals and take him into the yard. The beast and I were brought close together, and our countenances diligently compared, both by master and servant, who thereupon repeated several times the word "Yahoo." My horror and astonishment are not to be described when I observed in this abominable animal a perfect human figure. The face of it, indeed, was flat and broad, the nose depressed, the lips large, and the mouth wide. But these differences are common to all savage nations, where the lineaments of the countenance are distorted by the natives suffering their infants to lie groveling on the earth, or by carrying them on their backs, nuzzling with their faces against the mother's shoulders. The forefeet of the Yahoo differed from my hands in nothing else but the length of the nails, the coarseness and brownness of the palm, and the hairiness on the backs. There was the same resemblance between our feet, with the same differences, which I knew very well, though the horses did not, because of my shoes and stockings; the same in every part of our bodies, except as to hairiness and color, which I have already described.

The great difficulty that seemed to stick with the two horses was to see the rest of my body so very different from that of a Yahoo, for which I was obliged to my clothes, whereof they had no conception. The sorrel nag offered me a root, which he held (after their manner, which we shall describe in its proper place) between his hoofs and pastern. I took it in my hand, and having smelled it, returned it to him again as civilly as I could. He brought out of the Yahoo's kennel a piece of ass's flesh, but it smelled so offensively that I turned from it with loathing. He then threw it to the Yahoo, by whom it was greedily devoured. He afterward showed me a wisp of hay and a fetlock full of oats, but I shook my head to signify that neither of these were food for me. And, indeed, I now apprehended that I must absolutely starve if I did not get to some of my own species; for as to those filthy Yahoos, although there were few greater lovers of mankind at that time than myself, yet I confess I never saw any sensitive being so detestable on all accounts; and the more I came near them the more hateful they grew while I stayed in that country. This the master-horse observed by my behavior, and therefore sent the Yahoo back to his kennel. He then put his forehoof to his mouth, at which I was much surprised, although he did it with ease and with a motion that appeared perfectly natural, and made other signs to know what I would eat; but I could not return him such an answer as he was able to apprehend; and if he had understood me, I did not see how it was possible to contrive any way for finding myself nourishment. While we were thus engaged I observed a cow passing by, whereupon I pointed to her and expressed a desire to let me go and milk her. This had its effect, for he led me back into the house, and ordered a mare-servant to open a room where a good store of milk lay in earthen and wooden vessels, after a very orderly and cleanly manner. She gave me a large bowl full, of which I drank very heartily, and found myself well refreshed.

About noon I saw coming towards the house a kind of vehicle drawn like a sledge by four Yahoos. There was in it an old steed, who seemed to be of quality. He alighted with his hind feet forward, having by accident got a hurt in his left forefoot. He came to dine with our horse, who received him with great civility. They dined in the best room, and had oats boiled in milk for the second course, which the old horse ate warm, but the rest cold. Their mangers were placed circular in the middle of the room, and divided into several partitions, round which they sat on their haunches upon bosses of straw. In the middle was a large rack with angles answering to every partition of the manger; so that each horse and mare ate their own hay and their own mash of oats and milk, with much decency and regularity. The behavior of the young colt and foal appeared very modest, and that of the master and mistress extremely cheerful and complaisant to their guest. The gray ordered me to stand by him, and much discourse passed between him and his friend concerning me, as I found by the stranger's often looking on me, and the frequent repetition of the word "Yahoo."

I happened to wear my gloves, which the master-gray observing seemed perplexed, discovering signs of wonder what I had done to my forefeet. He put his hoof three or four times to them, as if he would signify that I should reduce them to their former shape, which I presently did, pulling off both my gloves, and putting them into my pocket. This occasioned further talk, and I saw the company was pleased with my behavior, whereof I soon found the good effects. I was ordered to speak the few words I understood, and while they were at dinner the master taught me the names for oats, milk, fire, water, and some others, which I could readily pronounce after him, having from my youth a great facility in learning languages.

When dinner was done the master-horse took me aside, and by signs and wonders made me understand the concern that he was in that I had nothing to eat. Oats in their tongue are called "hlunnh." This word I pronounced two or three times, for although I had refused them at first, yet upon second thoughts I considered that I could contrive to make of them a kind of bread which might be sufficient, with milk, to keep me alive till I could make my escape to some other country and to creatures of my own species. The horse immediately ordered a white mare-servant of his family to bring me a good quantity of oats in a sort of wooden tray. These I heated before the fire as well as I could, and rubbed them till the husks came off, which I made a shift to winnow from the grain; I ground and beat them between two stones, then took water, and made them into a paste or cake, which I toasted at the fire, and ate warm with milk. It was at first a very insipid diet, though common enough in many parts of Europe, but grew tolerable by time; and having been often reduced to hard fare in my life, this was not the first experiment I had made how easily nature is satisfied. And I cannot but observe that I never had one hour's sickness while I stayed in this island. 'Tis true I sometimes made a shift to catch a rabbit or bird by springes* made of Yahoo's hair, and I often gathered wholesome herbs, which I boiled, or ate as salads with my bread; and now and then, for a rarity, I made a little butter, and drank the whey. I was at first at a great loss for salt, but custom soon reconciled the want of it, and I am confident the frequent use of salt among us is an effect of luxury, and was first intro-

* Springes = traps

duced only as a provocative to drink, except where it is necessary for preserving of flesh in long voyages or in places remote from great markets; for we observe no animal to be fond of it but man; and as to myself, when I left this country it was a great while before I could endure the taste of it in anything that I ate.

This is enough to say upon the subject of my diet, wherewith other travelers fill their books, as if the readers were personally concerned, whether we fare well or ill. However, it was necessary to mention this matter, lest the World should think it impossible that I could find sustenance for three years in such a country and among such inhabitants.

When it grew toward evening, the master-horse ordered a place for me to lodge in; it was but six yards from the house, and separated from the stable of the Yahoos. Here I got some straw, and covering myself with my own clothes, slept very sound.

Munchausen's Mounts

RUDOLPH ERICH RASPE

Fantastic journeys have always been a popular subject for storytelling, and Baron Munchausen's travels are among the most farfetched and amazing ever written. His name has become a byword for tall tales—just read these two adventures featuring horses, which come from The Singular Travels, Campaigns, *and* Adventures of Baron Munchausen, *and sample Raspe's outrageous invention yourselves! There really was a Baron Munchausen, who was not pleased to become famous in his own lifetime as the hero of these stories—but the author was good at getting into trouble. Rudolph Erich Raspe had an international reputation as a scientist, but he had to leave his own country, Germany, because of a scandal caused by his debts. He ended up helping to modernize the tin mines in Cornwall. He wrote his stories about Baron Munchausen in English, and they were first published in Oxford in 1785.*

I set off from Rome on a journey to Russia, in the midst of winter, from a just notion that frost and snow must of course mend the roads, which every traveler had described as uncommonly bad through the northern parts of Germany, Poland, Courland, and Livonia. I went on horseback, as the most convenient manner of traveling; I was but lightly clothed, and of this I felt the inconvenience the more I advanced northeast. I went on: night and darkness overtook me. No village was to be seen. The country was covered with snow, and I was unacquainted with the road.

Tired, I alighted, and fastened my horse to something like a pointed stump of a tree, which appeared above the snow; for the sake of safety I placed my pistols under my arm, and lay down on the snow, where I slept so soundly that I did not open my eyes till full daylight. It is not easy to conceive my astonishment to find myself in the midst of a village, lying in a churchyard; nor was my horse to be seen, but I heard him soon after neigh somewhere above me. On looking upward I beheld him hanging by his bridle from the weather-cock of the steeple. Matters were now very plain to me: the village had been covered with snow overnight; a sudden change of weather had taken place; I had sunk down to the churchyard whilst asleep, gently, and in the same proportion as the snow had melted away; and what in the dark I had taken to be a stump of a little tree appearing above the snow, to which I had tied my horse, proved to have been the cross or weather-cock of the steeple!

Without long consideration I took one of my pistols, shot the bridle in two, brought down the horse, and proceeded on my journey. [Here the Baron seems to have forgot his feelings; he should certainly have ordered his horse a feed of corn, after fasting so long.]

He carried me well—advancing into the interior parts of Russia. I found traveling on horseback rather unfashionable in winter, therefore I submitted, as I always do, to the custom of the country, took a single-horse sledge, and drove briskly toward St. Petersburg.

* * *

I have always been as remarkable for the excellency of my horses, dogs, guns, and swords, as for the proper manner of using and managing them. I remember with pleasure and tenderness a superb Lithuanian horse, which no money could have bought. He became mine by an accident, which gave me an opportunity of showing my horsemanship to a great advantage.

I was at Count Przobossky's noble country seat in Lithuania, and remained with the ladies at tea in the drawing room, while the gentlemen were down in the yard to see a young horse of blood that had just arrived from the stud. We suddenly heard a noise of distress; I hastened downstairs, and found the horse so unruly, that nobody durst approach or mount him. The most resolute horsemen stood dismayed and aghast; despondency was expressed in every countenance, when, in one leap, I was on his back, took him by surprise, and worked him quite into gentleness and obedience with the best display of horsemanship I was master of. Fully to show this to the ladies, and save them unnecessary trouble, I forced him to leap in at one of the open windows of the tea-room, walked around several times, pace, trot, and gallop, and at last made him mount the tea table, there to repeat his lessons in a pretty style of miniature that was exceedingly pleasing to the ladies, for he performed them amazingly well, and did not break either cup or saucer. It placed me so high in their opinion, and so well in that of the noble lord, that, with his usual politeness, he begged I would accept of this young horse, and ride him full career to conquest and honor in the campaign against the Turks, which was soon to be opened under the command of Count Munich.

I could not indeed have received a more agreeable present, nor a more ominous one at the opening of that campaign, in which I made my apprenticeship as a soldier. A horse so gentle, so spirited, and so fierce—at once a lamb and a Bucephalus—put me always in mind of the soldier's and the gentleman's duty! of young Alexander, and of the astonishing things he performed in the field.

We took the field, among several other reasons, it seems, with an intention to retrieve the character of the Russian arms, which had been blemished a little by Czar Peter's last campaign on the Pruth; and this we fully accomplished by several very fatiguing and glorious campaigns under the command of that great general I mentioned before.

Modesty forbids individuals to arrogate to themselves great successes or victories, the glory of which is generally engrossed by the commander—nay, which is rather awkward, by kings and queens who never smelled gunpowder but at the field days and reviews of their troops; never saw a field of battle, or an enemy in battle array.

Nor do I claim any particular share of glory in the great engagements with the enemy. We all did our duty, which, in the patriot's, soldier's, and gentleman's language, is a very comprehensive word, of great honor, meaning, and import, and of which the generality of idle quidnuncs and coffeehouse politicians can hardly form any but a very mean and contemptible idea. However, having had the command of a body of hussars, I went upon several expeditions, with discretionary powers; and the success I then met with is, I think, fairly and only to be placed to my account, and to that of the brave fellows whom I led on to conquest and to victory.

We had very hot work once in the van of the army, when we drove the Turks into Oczakow. My spirited Lithuanian had almost brought me into a scrape: I had an advanced fore-post, and saw the enemy coming against me in a cloud of dust, which left me rather uncertain about their actual numbers and real intentions: to wrap myself up in a similar cloud was common prudence, but would not have much advanced my knowledge, or answered the end for which I had been sent out; therefore I let my flankers on both wings spread to the right and left, and make what dust they could, and I myself led on straight upon the enemy, to have a nearer sight of them: in this I was gratified, for they stood and fought, till, for fear of my flankers, they began to move off rather disorderly. This was the moment to fall upon them with spirit; we broke them entirely—made a terrible havoc among them, and drove them not only back to a walled town in their rear, but even through it, contrary to our most sanguine expectation.

The swiftness of my Lithuanian enabled me to be foremost in the pursuit; and seeing the enemy fairly flying through the opposite gate, I thought it would be prudent to stop in the marketplace to order the men to rendezvous. I stopped, gentlemen, but judge of my astonishment when in this marketplace I saw not one of my hussars about me. Are they scouring the other streets? Or what is become of them? They could not be far off, and must, at all events, soon join me. In that expectation I walked my panting Lithuanian to a spring in this marketplace, and let him drink. He drank uncommonly, with an eagerness not to be satisfied, but natural enough; for when I looked around for my men, what should I see, gentlemen! The hind part of the poor creature—croup and legs—was missing, as if he had been cut in two, and the water ran out as it came in, without refreshing or doing him any good! How it could have happened was quite a mystery to me, till I returned with him to the town gate. There I saw, that when I pushed in pell-mell with the flying enemy, they had dropped the portcullis (a heavy falling door, with sharp spikes at the bottom, let down suddenly to prevent the entrance of an enemy into a fortified town) unperceived by me, which had totally cut off his hind part, which still lay quivering on the outside of the gate. It would have been an irreparable loss, had not our farrier contrived to bring both parts together while hot. He sewed them up with sprigs and young shoots of laurels that were at hand; the wound healed, and, what could not have happened but to so glorious a horse, the sprigs took root in his body, grew up, and formed a bower over me; so that afterward I could go upon many other expeditions in the shade of my own and my horse's laurels.

For "Cow," Read "Horse"

DONALD LIGHTWOOD

The Houyhnhnms whom Gulliver met in the earlier story are noble, dignified horses. The horse in this story isn't even real—but it certainly conveys its message about the right way to treat a horse. A scary story, and one to make you think!

The town hall dressing-room was freezing as the cast of *Jack and the Beanstalk* tried on their costumes for the first time.

"Has the cow come?" asked Patrick, the director.

Jenny nodded and pointed at a hamper. She was the wardrobe mistress and had a mouthful of pins.

"Good," said Patrick. "Where are the kids? They can try it on."

The stage manager found them. George was helping the bass guitarist set up and Kay was watching the girl dancers rehearse.

"I wanted to be a Beanette, not the back end of a cow," grumbled Kay.

"It suits you," said George.

"It's all right for you, at the front."

"Not when I've got you behind me, it isn't," he retorted.

"Stop squabbling, you two," snapped Patrick. "You should think yourselves lucky to be in the pantomime."

"Daisy the cow," muttered Kay.

"One of the most important characters," said Patrick. "Right, Jenny, let's try it on." He opened the hamper and she took out the costume and held it up by the head.

Patrick stared at it. "That's not a cow. . . ."

"It looks like a horse to me," said Jenny.

"That's ridiculous!" cried Patrick. "We can't do *Jack and the Beanstalk* without a cow!"

"There's a note in the hamper."

Patrick read it. "Listen to this. *'Dear Dramatic Society, Sorry, I haven't got a Daisy left. Everybody seems to be doing* Jack *this year. But so you wouldn't be stuck, I've sent the enclosed. At least it's got four legs. Good luck with your show.'*"

"Will I still have to moo, Patrick?" said George.

"Be quiet," said Patrick. He thrust the note at Jenny. "Get that fool on the phone."

"I can't, it's Sunday afternoon."

"But we open in two days' time."

Jenny dropped the horse costume on the hamper. "Then we'll just have to change the cow into a horse."

Patrick gazed at it in disgust. "What about the story? Everybody knows Jack takes Daisy the cow to market to sell her."

"People don't care about that," said Jenny with a shrug. "All they want is a good laugh. After all, what have a bunch of skinny little dancers got to do with the story?"

Patrick stamped his foot and cursed. "Very well, get them to try it on. I'm going to see if we can alter the script."

*   *   *

50

"Put the legs on first—they're like trousers," Jenny told the children. "Now for the body. You get into the head first, George. Kay, when he is in place, hold his waist and I'll pull the back end over you."

"What do I do with my arms?" asked George's muffled voice.

"I'm not sure," said Jenny. "Lose them inside somewhere."

The back legs started to walk.

"What're you doing?" cried George.

"Practicing," answered Kay.

"I'm not ready."

Jenny clapped her hands to get their attention. "Try Daisy's funny little dance that you practiced with Patrick."

The horse raised his head and looked at her.

"Come along—'One, two, hop,' wasn't it?"

With a snort the horse cantered out of the dressing-room and into the hall. The chairs had not yet been set out and he galloped around. Taken by surprise, the band stopped rehearsing and applauded. Patrick looked down from the stage.

"Well, at least you can move in it," he shouted to them. "Take it off and we'll go over the changes in the script."

"I'll never remember all that," said Alan, sitting in his costume in the dressing-room.

"It's as bad for me," protested Louisa, who was playing Jack.

"Nonsense," said Patrick firmly. "For 'cow,' you say 'horse.' And for 'her,' you say 'him.' Simple."

"You don't have to do it," said Alan, pulling on his wig.

"Oh, and for 'Daisy,' you say 'Neddy,'" Patrick added. "A very sparky Neddy, if I may say so," he went on to the two children. "Well done. I would have preferred a cow, of course. But I must say you're a jolly good horse."

"Neddy?" said George. "That's a rotten name."

"It makes him sound like a donkey," said Kay.

She glanced at George. They hadn't spoken to each other since they'd got out of the costume. He had a puzzled look on his face.

"Brilliant," said Alan sarcastically. "Except that Daisy is supposed to be a dozy and lovable old cow."

"It'll be all right," said Patrick. "Neddy can be just as dozy and lovable. The kids in the audience will adore her. . . . I mean, him."

"Patrick," said George. "I don't think he's like that."

Patrick gave him a tolerant smile. "Neddy will be whatever we want him to be. Just as Daisy was."

"He's not," said Kay.

"Not what?"

"What you said Daisy was," she told him.

Louisa spoke impatiently. "You can't alter Daisy's character."

"I'll take care of this, Louisa, if you don't mind," said Patrick. He spoke to Kay and George. "I know it's thrown you, not getting a proper Daisy. I'm sorry. But if we all pull together I'm sure Neddy will be just as funny."

"It's not that," said George.

"I'll tell you what we'll do," said Patrick. "We'll run through all the cow scenes before the rehearsal. OK? Onstage in twenty minutes. I'll tell the others."

Standing backstage, waiting to get into the horse costume, George and Kay began to feel extremely nervous.

"Have you ever been hypnotized?" she asked him. He shook his head. "Neither have I, but I bet that's what it feels like."

He nodded. "It was peculiar. Like it wasn't me telling my legs what to do."

They regarded the costume. Neddy's glass eyes looked surprisingly bright in the semidarkness behind the scenery.

"Come on you two, hop in," said Jenny. "Patrick's waiting."

"Jenny," said Kay. "I don't feel very well."

"Nerves," said Jenny. "Everybody gets them."

"Me too," George told her. "I think I'm going to be sick."

"Look, we've got enough problems, without you two adding to them. Now, in you get."

*   *   *

In the hall the leader of the band called out to Patrick. "Do we still play 'Daisy, Daisy' for the entrance, now that it's a horse?"

"Yes," Patrick told him. "But try to think of something else for the dress rehearsal. Stand by, everyone. George and Kay, you can do the same little dance we worked out for Daisy. Just wait till Louisa leads you on. Right, off we go."

Waiting in the wings, Louisa heard the band start and took hold of the rope around Neddy's neck. He shook his head and snorted. She cried out in surprise, almost missing her entrance cue. She dashed onstage, trailing the rope behind her. "Come on Dais— Neddy!" she cried, in her hearty Jack voice. "She . . . *he* won't come, boys and girls," she said to the audience. "Will *you* help me to call Neddy? Good. Now, I'll count to three, and you all shout . . ."

The horse raced onto the stage and the rope snapped tight, pulling Louisa off her feet and dragging her until she let go. Patrick's voice bellowed over the music, but Neddy paid no attention to him and continued to gallop around the stage. Louisa rolled herself into a ball, to avoid being trampled on like a fallen jockey in the Grand National.

"Stop, stop!" Patrick yelled from the front.

Neddy cocked his head, neighed, and galloped offstage. But he didn't stop in the wings. The people in the hall heard him carrying on down the side corridor. Patrick ran out of the hall and found the horse in the foyer by the main door.

"What in heaven's name are you two playing at?" he shouted.

Jenny joined him and helped George and Kay out of the costume. They stood dazed, by a show poster

54

promising fun for all the family.

"I don't mind the odd joke in rehearsal," Patrick went on. "But that was ridiculous. You know time's against us."

"What happened?" said Kay.

"Ask *him*," said Patrick, pointing an accusing finger at George.

"*Me?*" said George, unsure of what was going on. "Why are we out here?"

Patrick opened his mouth, but before he could explode, Jenny interrupted. "Leave it to me, Patrick. It's a new costume. They can't see or hear very well inside. Give us five minutes. I'll check it out."

Back in the dressing-room George and Kay stood gulping glasses of water.

Jenny had the horse draped on her sewing table. "Now, show me where it feels uncomfortable."

"Nowhere, really—at my end," said Kay.

George shrugged. "Mine's OK," he told Jenny.

She frowned and inspected the costume. "I know these things can be quite claustrophobic. Even make you dizzy."

"It's a bit warm," said Kay. "That's all."

The door burst open and Louisa stormed in. "*Very* funny," she said angrily. "I warn you, if you ever do that again—"

"Calm down, Louisa, I'm sorting it out," Jenny told her, ushering her back through the door.

"What's her problem?" asked George.

Jenny stopped still. "Don't try to be smart. Wrecking a scene at this stage of the show is not very clever."

Kay sighed and sat down. "I didn't think it would work. I told Patrick."

"What?" asked Jenny.

"Trying to make him stupid, like Daisy," Kay went on. "Horses aren't like that. I'm not surprised he objected."

Jenny looked at her, but Kay seemed to be quite serious. Jenny took a deep breath and spoke to George. "Can you see where you're going—when you're inside?"

"I suppose so," he replied.

"You're doing this on purpose, aren't you?" Jenny snapped.

"Doing what?" George asked, in genuine surprise.

"Being awkward," Jenny said. "Well, there are other people in this show who do need help with their costumes."

She went out and left them alone.

"Did we really do what they said?" Kay said.

"We must have," George replied.

The horse's head was propped up on the table. Kay fondled its ears. "Anyway, I like horses."

"They beat cows." He hesitated. "Kay, do you still want to do it?"

She ran her finger down the horse's nose. "I suppose so. It's funny, I have a feeling we've got to. Now."

"I know what you mean," he said, as a tense excitement began building up in both of them.

The rest of the cast found excuses to wander into the hall to see the next Daisy scene re-rehearsed. Nobody said anything, but they were all curious to see what would happen after the last time.

Patrick had given his directions to the actors and the curtain opened on Jack, his mum (the Dame), and Neddy. They were grouped outside a cutout of their cottage. Alan, as Dame, spoke first.

"Oh Jack, what'll we do? I was going to give you fish and chips for your tea. But the cat has filched the fish, and the mice have spiflicated the spuds."

"Never mind, Mum. I'll buy something from the shop."

"But I've got no money. We're destitute."

Jack clicked his fingers. "I've just had a brilliant idea."

"Oh, I always knew sending you to school would turn out to be a wise investment."

"I'll sell Neddy and get some money."

The Dame threw her arms up in horror. "What! Dear old cuddly Neddy?" She turned to the audience and they joined in with a long, sad, "Ahhh . . ."

The horse snorted.

"See, Jack. He's crying," the Dame went on.

Jack put his arm around the horse's neck. "I'm sorry, Neddy. . . ."

The horse swung his head and clonked Jack on the jaw.

"What the—" cried Louisa in her own voice.

"I can't bear it, Jack," said the Dame, bursting into tears and pulling out a large spotted hankie. She mopped her own eyes and went to do the same for Neddy. He bit the hankie and held on. The Dame tugged, but he wouldn't let go.

"You see, Jack, poor old Neddy's upset," said the Dame.

"So am I," Jack responded, rubbing his head and trying to pat Neddy again. The horse lashed out with a back hoof at Jack's shin.

"You're unsettling Neddy, Jack."

"Neddy can drop dead, as far as I'm concerned,"

said Louisa in her own voice.

"What?" said the Dame, not recognizing the line.

The horse shook his head, flung away the hankie and reared on his hind legs with a loud neigh.

The cast watching in the hall gasped.

Immediately the scene onstage became like a chase from an old-fashioned silent film. The Dame and Jack dashed about wildly, trying to escape the pursuing Neddy. But each got butted, and the Dame's quaint little cottage was sent flying.

Patrick and Jenny ran up onto the stage and flung themselves at Neddy like cowpokes in a Western rodeo. Alan joined them, grabbing on to the horse's tail. Together they wrestled Neddy to the ground.

George and Kay had to be taken out of their costume. It seemed they had both fainted. They were carried to the dressing-room and revived with cups of tea.

Alan looked at them and scratched his head. "I don't believe it," he said. "That horse knocked me for six. It was so strong."

"Patrick, if those two are going to be the horse, you're going to have to find another Jack," said Louisa. "It's an outrage. I refuse to go on with them. They're ruining the show."

"Well?" said Patrick. "What have you got to say for yourselves?"

"Where's the horse?" said George.

"Onstage. Where you went berserk."

"Is he all right? I remember being pulled down," said Kay. "I hope he's not hurt."

"They're having us on," said Louisa. "Look at them. It's a big joke to them."

"I don't think it's as simple as that," Alan told her. "That horse reared up on its hind legs."

"Well?"

"Well, look who's in the back end: Kay."

Everyone stared at her—a ten-year-old girl, who was small for her age.

Patrick cleared his throat. "George, Kay, do you know what happened?"

"He was upset," they said together.

"That's right," Patrick went on. "He's supposed to be—like Daisy—because Jack's going to sell him."

They shook their heads. "It wasn't because of that," said Kay. "Horses aren't like that."

"They're dignified," said George.

"For heaven's sake!" cried Louisa. "We're talking about a pantomime costume, not a racehorse."

"Just a moment, Louisa," said Jenny, and spoke to George. "When I asked you if you could see out of the skin, you didn't give me a proper answer. Could you see out?"

George shook his head. "I can't remember."

"But there's a gauze panel in the neck," said Jenny.

"Is there?" he said.

The people in the dressing-room exchanged puzzled looks. Nobody spoke. The winter wind rattled the windows.

Patrick broke the silence. "Kay remembered being pulled down. Surely you can remember something?" he asked George.

The boy thought for a moment. "I think I can. But it wasn't anything I saw. More what I felt."

"Go on, what was it?"

"That I didn't like it."

"What?"

"Being made to look stupid."

The room became silent again. Patrick started to speak, but he stopped. He couldn't think of what to say. The December cold began to eat into the cast. Only the two children were unaware of the chill. Sitting in their T-shirts and shorts, they seemed to be glowing with warmth.

Odd sounds suddenly came from the stage. People looked around, wondering who it could be. Everyone in the show was crammed into the dressing-room.

People leaped up and rushed out onto the stage.

"Neddy's costume." someone cried.

It was no longer there.

"Look . . ."

The exit door was open at the far end of the hall. Patrick and Jenny jumped down from the stage and ran the length of the hall and through it into the foyer.

The front door was open, banging in the wind.

Patrick looked out. It was turning dark. "I don't believe it. Someone's stolen the horse costume." He shook his head in astonishment. "Why would anyone do that?"

"Shut the door!" cried Jenny. "Please, shut it— quickly."

He did so, and she slammed the bolt home. Patrick took her arm. "Jenny, what is it?"

She stood pale and trembling. "I don't think it has been stolen." She went on in a strained voice. "Patrick, remember how the children behaved, how they talked about the horse? Something seemed to enter into them—take them over—when they put it on. Like one of those spirits. What do you call them—poltergeists? How else did they become so strong?"

"What are you saying?"

"I'm not sure, but poltergeists are supposed to reveal themselves through children. It was as if George and Kay knew what a horse would think and feel." She looked concerned. "I hope they're all right."

"Jenny, we're talking about a comic costume," said Patrick.

"Exactly—something that's as insulting to a real horse as it's possible to be."

"But that's crazy!" he exclaimed. "And costumes don't just disappear." He groaned. "Now I've got to think of a way of doing *Jack and the Beanstalk* without a cow *or* a horse."

She wasn't listening to him. "George was right. Horses *are* dignified creatures. Don't ask me how, but we've been warned not to make fools of them."

He stared at her, anxious to convince himself she was wrong. "That costume has been stolen, that's all there is about it," he said, trying to make his voice sound firm.

Jenny shook her head slowly. "I wish it were," she said.

Left alone in the dressing-room, George and Kay began to shiver in the cold.

Bonny's Big Day

JAMES HERRIOT

A warm, happy story about another dignified horse—Bonny the old cart horse—and her adventures at the Darrowby Show. James Herriot worked as a country vet in Yorkshire, and all his stories are full of love for the animals, people, and countryside that he knew well.

One sunny morning in early September, I drove to see old John Skipton at Dale Close Farm since he had telephoned to say that one of his cart horses was lame.

As I got out of the car, the untidily dressed figure of the farmer came through the kitchen door of Dale Close. John always seemed to look like a scarecrow, and today was no different. He was wearing a tattered buttonless coat, which was tied round his waist with string. His trousers were much too short and, as he hurried toward me, I could see that he was wearing socks of different colors—one was red, and the other was blue.

By working very hard when he was a young man, Mr. Skipton had saved enough money to buy his own farm with its handsome stone house. He had never married, and because he was always so busy looking after the sheep and cows on the hill, bringing in the harvest from the fields, and picking the apples in the orchard, he had been much too busy to worry about himself—which is why he was always dressed in such very old clothes.

"The horses are down by the river," he said in his usual gruff manner. "We'll have to go down there." He seized a pitchfork and stabbed it into a big pile of hay, which he then hoisted onto his shoulder. I pulled my large gladstone bag from the car and set off behind him.

It was difficult to keep up with the farmer's brisk pace, even though he must have been fifty years older than me. I was glad when we reached the bottom of the hill, because the bag was heavy and I was getting rather hot.

I saw the two horses standing in the shallows of the pebbly river. They were nose to tail, and were rubbing their chins gently along each other's backs. Beyond them, a carpet of green turf ran up to a high sheltered ridge, while all around clumps of oak and beech blazed in the autumn sunshine.

"They're in a nice place, Mr. Skipton," I said.

"Aye, they can keep cool in the hot weather, and they've got the barn when the winter comes."

At the sound of his voice, the two big horses came trotting up from the river—the gray one first, and the chestnut following a little more slowly, and limping slightly.

They were fine big cart horses, but I could see they were old from the sprinkling of white hairs on their faces. Despite their age, however, they pranced around old John, stamping their enormous feet, throwing their heads about and pushing the farmer's cap over his eyes with their muzzles.

"Get over, leave off!" he cried.

He pulled at the gray horse's forelock. "This is Bonny; she's well over twenty years old." Then he ran his hand down the front leg of the chestnut. "And this is Dolly. She's nearly thirty now, and not one day's sickness until now."

"When did they last do any work?" I asked.

"Oh, about twelve years ago, I reckon," the farmer replied.

I stared at him in amazement. "Twelve years? Have they been down here all that time?"

"Aye, just playing about down here. They've earned their retirement."

For a few seconds he stood silent, shoulders hunched, hands deep in the pockets of his tattered coat.

"They worked very hard when I had to struggle to get this farm going," he murmured, and I knew he was thinking of the long years those horses had pulled the plow, drawn the hay and harvest wagons, and had done all the hard work which the tractors now do.

"I noticed that Dolly was a bit lame when I came down with their hay yesterday," he said. "Lucky I come down each day."

"You mean that you climb down that hillside every single day?" I asked.

"Aye—rain, wind, or snow. They look forward to me bringing a few oats or some good hay."

I examined Dolly's foot and found an old nail embedded deep in the soft part of her foot. I was able to pull it out quite easily with a pair of pincers, and then gave her an antitetanus injection to eliminate any risk of later infection.

Climbing back up the hill, I couldn't help thinking how wonderful it was that old John had made the long journey to see the horses in all weathers, every day for twelve years. He certainly loved those great animals.

A thought struck me, and I turned to him. "You know, Mr. Skipton, it's the Darrowby Show next Saturday. You should enter the mares in the family pets class. I know they are asking for unusual entries this year. Perhaps you should take Bonny since Dolly's foot will be a bit sore for a few days."

The farmer frowned. "What on earth are you talking about?"

"Go on," I said. "Take Bonny to the show! Those horses are your pets, aren't they?"

"Pet!" he snorted. "You couldn't call one of those great big clodhoppers a pet. I've never heard anything so silly."

When he got back to the farmyard, he thanked me gruffly, gave me a nod, and disappeared into his house.

The following Saturday, it was my duty to attend Darrowby Show as the vet-in-charge. I had spent a pleasant time strolling around the show ground, looking at the pens of cattle and sheep, the children's ponies, the massive bulls, and the sheepdog trials in the neighboring fields.

Then over the loudspeaker came the following announcement: "Would the entrants for the family pets class please take their places in the ring."

I was always interested in this event, so I walked over and stood by the secretary, who was sitting at a table near the edge of the ring. He was Darrowby's local bank manager, a prim little man with rimless spectacles and a porkpie hat. I could see that he was pleased at the number of entrants now filing into the ring.

He looked at me and beamed. "They have certainly

taken me at my word when I asked for unusual entries this year."

The parade was led by a fine white nanny goat, which was followed by a pink piglet. Apart from numerous cats and dogs of all shapes and sizes, there was a goldfish in its bowl, and at least five rabbits. There was a parrot on a perch, and some budgerigars having an outing in their cage. Then, to an excited buzz of conversation, a man walked into the ring with a hooded falcon on his wrist.

"Splendid, splendid!" cried Mr. Secretary—but then his mouth fell open and everyone stopped talking as a most unexpected sight appeared.

Old John Skipton came striding into the ring, and he was leading Bonny—but it was a quite different man and horse than I had seen a few days before.

John still wore the same old tattered coat tied with string, but today I noticed that both his socks were the same color and on his head, perched right in the center, was an ancient bowler hat.

It made him look almost smart, but not as smart as Bonny. She was dressed in the full show regalia of an old-fashioned cart horse. Her hooves were polished and oiled; the long feathery hair on her lower limbs had been washed and fluffed out; her mane, tail, and forelock had been plaited with green and yellow ribbons, and her coat had been groomed until it shone in the sunshine. She was wearing part of the harness from her working days and it, too, had been polished, and little bells hung from the harness saddle.

It quite took my breath away to look at her.

"Mr. Skipton, Mr. Skipton! You can't bring that great thing in here. This is the class for family pets!" cried Mr. Secretary, leaping up from his chair.

"Bonny *is* my pet," responded the farmer. "She's part of my family. Just like that old goat over there."

"Well, I disagree," said Mr. Secretary, waving his arms. "You must take her out of the ring and go home."

Old John Skipton put on a fierce face and glared at the man. "Bonny *is* my pet," he repeated. "Just ask Mr. Herriot."

I shrugged my shoulders. "Perfectly true. This mare hasn't worked for over twelve years and is kept entirely for Mr Skipton's pleasure. I'd certainly call Bonny a pet."

"But . . . but . . ." spluttered Mr. Secretary. Then he sat down suddenly on his chair, and sighed, "Oh, very well, then, go and get into line."

So John turned and led Bonny to a place right in the middle of the other competitors. On one side of them was the little pink piglet, and on the other side a tortoise. It was a most curious sight.

The task of judging the pets had been given to the district nurse, who was very sensibly dressed in her official uniform to give her an air of authority. Judging this class was always difficult, and when she looked along the line and kept seeing the great horse, she knew it was going to be very difficult indeed.

She looked carefully at every competitor, but her eyes always came back to Bonny. All the rabbits were very sweet, the falcon was impressive, the dogs were charming, and the piglet was cute—but Bonny was *MAGNIFICENT!*

"First prize to Mr. Skipton and Bonny," she announced, and everyone cheered.

As the rosette was presented, a man came to take a photograph for the local newspaper. It looked as though the great horse knew all about her prize as she posed there, dignified and beautiful. John, too, stood very erect and proud—but, unfortunately, every time the photographer clicked the camera, Bonny pushed the bowler hat over the farmer's eyes.

It was the mare's way of showing her love, but I couldn't help wondering how the picture would come out.

After the show, I went back to Dale Close to help John "undress" Bonny—and I went with him down the hill to the field by the river.

As we approached, Dolly came trotting up from the river, whinnying with pleasure to see her friend and companion again.

"Her foot is quite healed now," I said, noting the horse's even stride.

In the gentle evening light we watched the two old horses hurry toward each other. Then, for a long time, they stood rubbing their faces together.

"Look at that," said old John, with one of his rare smiles. "Bonny is telling Dolly all about her big day!"

Show Time

SANDY RANSFORD

Another story about a show—a horse show, this time. What happens if you love horses but don't have one? Lizzie Brown has no pony of her own, but she can do plenty to help the owner of her riding school, when she is showing horses. Then an unlooked-for opportunity comes her way. . . . The author is particularly fond of Arabian horses and has shown her own.

I'd been looking forward to Ashbury Show for weeks. I don't quite know what it is about shows, but there's something about all the preparation and then seeing gleaming ponies prancing over smooth, vanilla-scented turf and knowing you've had a hand in making it all work that makes me feel very happy. We'd spent all day yesterday at Foxearth Stables working really hard—and now, on the morning of the show, it was raining. Not just any old rain, but the really serious stuff, coming down in buckets. It had been pouring half the night, too, because I'd woken up and heard it, so the ground would be turned into a quagmire and Saffron's white socks would be black sludge, and as for Moonlight . . .

Not that they were my ponies, you understand. I didn't have a pony. I'd always wanted one, and when we moved down here from London for Dad's job I'd thought maybe I'd manage it. But things had gone dramatically wrong. Dad had left Mum and me, and Mum didn't earn enough working in the local hospital to pay for ponies, she said. Still, I'd found a lovely place to ride (we couldn't afford riding, either, but Mrs. Hemingway let me ride in exchange for work) and I spent all my spare time here. It was a combined riding school, livery stable, and organic farm, and to me it was heaven. Mrs. Hemingway—she let us call her Alison, despite being quite old (at least forty, my mother said)—had an Arab stallion and bred a few ponies herself. Saffron was one of hers, a splendid half-Arab chestnut mare, 14.2 hands high with four white socks. She was a lovely, bouncy ride, though a bit big for me, which is why Moonlight was my favorite. Moonlight also had some Arab blood, but was mostly Welsh. Dapple gray, like a rocking horse, she was 13.2 hands high and belonged to a rather wimpish girl called Isobel Hetherington, who kept her at livery. Isobel was riding her today in the 13.2 hands high class, but Alison said Moonlight lacked impulsion and wouldn't do well. I'd ridden her myself in the evenings after school, for Isobel went to a weekly boarding school and could only ride on weekends, and she was a heavenly ride, positively floated over the ground.

"Lizzie! Stop moping!" My mother's voice broke in on my thoughts. "Remember, rain before seven, fine before eleven! And if you want me to get you to Foxearth by eight o'clock you'd better be ready in five minutes, because I'm leaving then."

I looked sadly down at my clean boots and jodhpurs. I know it's daft if you're only grooming, but I do like to look the part when I go to a show. Still, I supposed I could carry my boots in a bag, put on my wellies, wear a raincoat, and hope I didn't get *too* muddy and let the ponies down. Somehow you feel you do when you're scruffy yourself.

Amazingly, Mum was right. By the time we were unloading the ponies a watery sun was making the drenched grass sparkle with jewels. The ground was still pretty sodden, though.

"It'll be quite slippery in the ring," Alison was saying to Sarah, who was riding her own sweet little dark bay gelding, Cobnut, in the 12.2 hands high class, and was the first of our lot to compete. "Careful not to take the corners too sharply when you're cantering."

It was quite a big class—I think there were twenty-five ponies altogether—but Sarah managed Cobnut beautifully. He went very well and was pulled in fifth in the first line up. Each of them did an individual show, and the pony who was third, an eye-catching bright bay who was cantering nicely around the ring, suddenly took off, bucking madly, when given the signal to gallop. His rider only just stayed on, and got a round of applause for eventually stopping him, but she was moved right down the line after that and Sarah moved up to fourth.

She did a beautiful show, cantering circles quietly and steadily on the right leg, and when I went in to rub Cobnut down when the ponies were unsaddled I congratulated her. "It's not over yet," I said. "You may well move up further—Cobnut's a lovely straight mover." He trotted out in hand very well and sure enough, when they were doing their final walk around while the judges conferred—the most nerve-racking moment of all, I think—they pulled her in second, behind the most perfect little chestnut which had gone so well she was an obvious winner right from the start.

"Well done," I shouted as Sarah rode out of the ring beaming, with the red rosette fluttering on Cobnut's bridle. "I told you they'd move you up."

"Come on, Lizzie, help get Moonlight ready. The 13.2s are in the collecting ring and she's still got a tail bandage on."

Alison sounded cross. I'd thought there was lots of time because the local hounds were parading between the two classes, but I'd forgotten you have to be ready in the collecting ring before you go in the main ring. I whipped off the tail bandage and gave Moonlight's lovely silver tail a final brush-out. Isobel, looking nervous but so elegant in her expensive riding clothes, was already up. They pranced off toward the collecting ring, and I eyed the competition.

The main problem, I thought, was a tall girl with long, sticklike legs, who was really too big for her bay pony, but she rode him beautifully and he went like a dream. Then there was a rather fat girl on a very showy chestnut, and a determined-looking boy on another gray. As they filed into the ring, I asked Alison what she thought Moonlight's chances were.

"If Isobel can keep her up to the bit, she should do well," she replied. "But the trouble with Isobel is that she forgets she's got legs and Moonlight either slops along half asleep or wants to whiz off if she's in the mood."

The walk, trot, and canter on one rein went quite well; then they changed the rein to canter the other way around the ring. Moonlight got bunched up with a lot of other ponies, but just as Isobel was extricating her the heavens opened again. Right in front of Moon-

light a man opened one of those huge, brightly colored golf umbrellas. As any self-respecting pony would, she shied, along with one or two of the others there. All would have been well, except the showy chestnut with the fat rider interpreted this as a signal to be off, and Moonlight, giving a buck and jinking to one side as she did so, followed suit. Isobel, unfortunately, did not, and went splat into the mud, her cream breeches and navy jacket resembling Moonlight's New Zealand rug. Alison shot into the ring to catch Moonlight, and Mrs. Hetherington rushed to the aid of her daughter, who was still sitting on the ground and rubbing her leg. I was just wondering if I should call the St. John Ambulance people to come and help when Alison led Moonlight up and hissed at me, "Quick, get up there and take her back in." She grabbed a jacket and hat from the back of the box. "Put these on, and ride that pony."

"But," I began, "I can't ride her in there. I've only pottered around in the school at home, I don't know what to do in the ring."

"You've watched plenty of times. Just pretend you're at home, trying to make her go as well as possible— and use your legs. Keep her going forward and collected. If Isobel had done that she'd still be on board."

I felt more scared, and more excited, than I'd ever done in my life. But as soon as I was in Moonlight's saddle I felt at home. I gathered up the reins and applied my legs lightly to send her forward into the ring, where order was beginning to be restored after the chaos. They'd even had an announcement on the loudspeaker about not opening umbrellas when horses were going past. We cantered around on the left rein and then, at a signal from one of the ring stewards, slowed to a sedate walk while the judge decided in what order to pull us in.

As expected, the tall girl on the bay was first. Then came one I hadn't noticed before, a liver chestnut with a flaxen mane and tail. Then the grim-faced boy on the other gray, then the showy chestnut, then another bay, a dark bay, an almost black pony, another chestnut—then me! Yes, they actually signaled to me to go in, I wasn't last.

While those higher up the line did their show I tried frantically to think what to do. They'd want to see her canter on both legs, though I didn't think we could do a figure-of-eight with a flying change. They'd also want to see her both collected and extended—at least, I remembered Alison saying that one evening when we'd pretended to be at a show in the school at home. I decided to do a circle at a collected trot, extend the trot across the diagonal, ride a right-hand circle in collected canter, come back to a trot and change the rein to a left-hand circle in collected canter, then extend the canter right around the ring, and finally stop (if I could!) and rein back. By the time I'd worked all this out I realized the steward was waving his hat at me rather impatiently, and it was my turn. Not sure if I could remember what I'd decided, I walked forward.

I was never quite sure what happened during the next few minutes. They seemed like a dream, they seemed to last hours, and they seemed to be over before I'd started. Moonlight went well. Some of our transitions were a bit untidy, but her collected canter felt marvelous, and we *did* manage to stop after belting around the ring, and did a reasonable rein-back. As we returned to our place in the line I realized the spectators were clapping—they were applauding *me*. I felt quite unreal—especially when the steward stopped me from returning to my former position and waved his hat toward third place—after the bay and the liver chestnut, and before the grim-faced boy and the showy chestnut. I'd missed the bay's show, being too anxious to work out my own, but Alison later told me they cantered on the wrong leg and the pony got all flustered and kept chucking its head about, so it didn't go too well.

The first two ponies were already unsaddled and being led out in hand when Alison rushed in with the grooming box. "You rode her beautifully." She beamed. "All you must do now is run fast so she can trot freely in hand. She's got a better trot than either of those two up in front."

I felt an absolute fraud as I led Moonlight out. Everyone seemed so competent, and I didn't know what I was doing. And to add to my confusion, the judge seemed to be a lady dressed in a blue suit and flowery hat who looked as if she were at a school prize-giving, and had no connection with horses. Amazingly, she smiled, which banished thoughts of school. I walked Moonlight down the ring, turned when the steward told me to, and ran back like mad, giving Moonlight a free rein to trot out. Distantly I heard more applause. The judge smiled again. "Some Arab blood there, I imagine?" I grinned stupidly, nodded, and walked back to the line.

Watching what the others did, I saddled up again and got on, and stood waiting for what seemed an age while everyone did their in-hand bit. At last we were told to walk around again.

Suddenly I realized the steward was waving his hat at me rather frantically, so I walked in to the center and stopped. There was no one else there! Then the bay with the tall girl came beside me. "Well done!" she smiled. "You rode her beautifully, especially after that mishap."

I stuttered my thanks, not quite sure what was happening, and then there was the flowery-hatted judge pinning a blue rosette to Moonlight's bridle! "You've got a lovely pony there; she could go far." She smiled. "Congratulations."

Had we really won? Me, Lizzie Brown, and this lovely pony who belonged to someone else? We led the final canter around the ring and out to the waiting friends and parents.

"Well done, Lizzie!" shouted Alison. "I knew you could do it!"

"I can't believe I have," I replied, thinking what an amazingly wonderful day it had turned out to be, after all.

But that wasn't quite the end of it. When Mrs. Hetherington came up to congratulate me and tell me Isobel wasn't too badly hurt, she said the following amazing words: "Lizzie, you and Moonlight look like a natural partnership. So Isobel and I wondered if you'd like to show her for us for the rest of the season. She's entered for quite a few shows, and if she does this well may even qualify for the national championships at Olympia, Alison tells me. What do you think? Would you like to?"

Trying not to sound too eager, in case she thought me impolite, I stuttered my thanks. But I know I had a great big grin on my face as I replied, "I can't think of anything I'd like better."

The Splendid Reality

PATRICIA WRIGHTSON

Andy Hoddel is different from other boys. When an old tramp offers to sell him Beecham Park Racecourse for three dollars, he manages to find the money. Then he really believes he has bought it. His friend Joe knows how hurt Andy will be if he ever discovers how he's been taken in— but how can he persuade Andy that the racecourse isn't his? Even the people who work there called him the owner. This story is a chapter from I Own the Racecourse! *by Patricia Wrightson, a well-known Australian author. Beecham Park is a trotting course, where the two-wheeled carriages known as sulkies are raced.*

In the evening of that day, Andy set out for his favorite spot on the cliff. He was dreaming that perhaps he really would go to the races, as he had told the cleaners in the morning. Perhaps, tonight, he would come down from his dark perch on the cliff and plunge into all the brilliance and noise below. The thought of it made him breathe hard, as though he had been running. It was one thing to own the racecourse in a quiet way, watching it and talking to the men who worked there. It was quite another thing to go striding into the middle of it under all the lights, where crowds of people could stare at him. Andy was going to sit on the cliff and dream about it.

Cars were flowing in rivers down Blunt Street and Wattle Road, spreading over the flat ground near the course, and banking up into all the streets and lanes above. All the white-coated men were at their busiest. "No, no!" they shouted to flustered drivers. "You won't do it! Forward again . . . now, back . . . back . . . now, around—keep going!" Horse floats went slowly down the hills. Buses, waddling among the lighter traffic like elephants, went down to join the herd in their own parking area. The sky was a mysterious glowing gray made up of violet, lilac, and faded rose. Over the rim of Blunt Street, a neon sign that stood above the city made sharp green flashes against the glowing gray.

Andy went quietly through his little alley and down to the rocks of the cliff. He sat there, looking at the lighted stage below and the crowds that were already drifting there; and he dreamed of himself drifting among them. He didn't hear anyone coming until someone arrived beside him on the rocks.

"Shove over," said Joe, pushing onto the ledge.

Andy's voice was full of pleasure. "Hey, it's you, Joe! Plenty of room here, Joe. Did you come to watch?" The toy figures of the bandsmen marched on the track, and the music came up to them. "Good, isn't it?" said Andy with simple pride.

"Not bad," said Joe cautiously. He had waited for Andy and followed him here, away from stray dogs and silently scornful Irishmen, slipping off while the O'Day boys were finding customers for their backyard parking space. He had a difficult job to do, and he was going to watch every word with the greatest care. He sat beside Andy, quietly watching while the silent, shabby racecourse put on its hidden truth of color and life.

82

"I bet they're making a mess," said Andy happily. "She was cleaned up good this morning, *I* know. I helped." He looked sideways at Joe in the gathering dusk, to see if he was impressed. Joe shifted uneasily on the rock. "They got two lots to clean up this time," Andy went on, "so I gave 'em a hand."

The voice from the amplifier spoke, heralding the first race. The crowd began to wash along the rails or drain away into the stands. The band disappeared. Andy gave a cry of delight.

"The horses! See the horses!"

The horses and silk-clad drivers went by, and Andy's heart went with them, snatched away under the golden lights, whirling around the track. Joe watched with him, while the great voice sang and the signals flashed; until the race broke and fell apart into flying units, and Andy's heart returned to his body.

"Dogs are all right," said Andy, breathing deeply. "Only horses are better."

"Do you like the horses best?" asked Joe. "Best of the whole show, I mean?"

Andy thought about it. "I might do," he said at last.

"But they're not yours, are they? You don't own the horses?"

Andy shook his head solemnly. "They're none of 'em mine. I know most of 'em, though."

"But you don't own them. They're not part of *your* show. What do you like next best? The dogs?"

"Dunno," said Andy, sounding a little confused. "I reckon the dogs are pretty good."

"Do you own them?"

"'Course not," said Andy, beginning to grow impatient. "You know I got no dogs."

"So you like the horses and dogs best, but you don't

own them. What else do you like, then? What's the next best?"

"See the numbers going up," said Andy, sliding away from these pointless and bothering questions. "It's a big night, *I* know. All those people, that's why it's a big night. Hey, Joe, did you ever see such a big night? I reckon there's thousands, don't you? Thousands of people."

"Is that what you like next best?" said Joe relentlessly. "The people? I suppose you don't reckon you own *them*?"

Andy laughed. "You must be crazy, Joe! Nobody owns people." He laughed again.

"All right," said Joe tensely. "So we've got that far, then. You don't own the horses, or the dogs, or the people. You don't own the cars and buses, either, do you? You don't own the money, or the men that do the sweeping. . . ." He stopped to take a breath, and to force himself to calm down. "I don't see how you own much at all, do you? Nothing very good, anyway. All the best parts, you don't own them at all. I mean, you said so yourself."

"I never said I did!" cried Andy stormily. "I never said any of that—the horses—the dogs . . ." He struggled with the words that came crowding into his mouth. "I told you—all I said—I said *I bought Beecham Park!*"

"Steady on, boy," said Joe. "I'm trying to work it out for you, see? I mean, if you don't own any of the best bits, it doesn't matter much, does it? What's the good of Beecham Park without the horses and dogs and people? What do you want with it, without that?"

"But they're *there!*" cried Andy. He thrust fiercely with his hand at the scene below. "Can't you see 'em? *There* they are."

84

"Put a sock in it, Andy—listen, can't you? Of course I can see them. I can see them just as good as you, and I never reckoned *I* owned Beecham Park. So what's the difference if *you* don't own it, either? You can see it, just the same as me. What's the difference if you own it or not?"

"I don't know if it's any difference," said Andy. He sounded hopeless and sullen. "I just own it, that's all."

"Don't kid yourself, boy. *I* don't own it, and I'm looking at it, too. You don't own it either, not really. That old chap was just kidding, to get your money out of you."

"You don't know nothing—you wasn't even there! It wasn't kidding—not like that game you play with the gasworks and the Manly ferry and all of that. You never owned that stuff, *I* know. You never bought it at all, not like me. You don't want me owning Beecham Park, that's all it is."

"Andy—Andy, boy. If it was mine, I'd give it to you. But it's not real, boy. You'll find out you've got no Beecham Park and no money either, just nothing. You've got to know what's real, or they'll take it all from you. Look, will you ask your mum? Will you listen to her? She'll tell you the same."

"What does she know? She wasn't there, no more than you." Andy tried for more words, choked, and tried again. "I got gardens down there, with flowers and that onionweed. They're mine. I grew that onionweed. . . ."

"Three dollars is a lot to pay for a bit of onionweed. Is that all you've got?"

Andy struggled to his feet. "Come on," he said fiercely. "I'll show you." He started off, scrambling and tumbling down the cliff with an agonized, clumsy speed. Joe hesitated for only a second, then went climbing and sliding after him. He mustn't lose Andy, now that they had come so painfully far in this fierce, wrestling argument. He hoped that it might be finished, once and for all, tonight.

They reached the pavement of Wattle Road, behind a line of parked cars. Across the road there were lights, parked buses and groups of people. Andy loped along on the darker side, with Joe following, until he reached the corner of Blunt Street. They both paused there, waiting for a chance to cross; and that was when Mike O'Day saw them from the other side of Blunt Street.

Mike was wandering aimlessly, alone and out of sorts. Terry and Matt had gone off to the workshop together as soon as the yard was full of cars, and without inviting Mike to join them. Mike knew they were baffled by the disagreement between himself and Joe. He didn't blame them, for he was baffled, too—but it hurt, all the same. He missed Terry, and he missed Joe. When he saw Andy and Joe across the street, he almost turned back. Then he saw their faces. He frowned, and walked across the street toward them.

"Hi, there," said Mike. "Going somewhere, Andy boy?"

Andy scowled at him. "You coming, too? Come on, then. *I'll* show you."

"Good show," said Mike, shooting a hard look at Joe and receiving one in return. They both followed Andy across Wattle Road to the turnstiles of Beecham Park, where he hovered for a moment.

Groups of people were clustering about the turnstiles or drifting through them, giving up their tickets as they went. Andy wandered along the row, looking at the faces of the men on the turnstiles and drawing back when anyone else came near. At last he made a dart at one of the turnstiles and spoke to the man in charge.

"You know me, mister?"

The man gave him a friendly nod. "Hello, it's the owner. Coming in to have a look, boss?"

Andy nodded. Then he jerked his head at Mike and Joe who stood close behind, uncomfortable but determined. "These others are coming in too. They're my friends."

The man hesitated. "Friends, are they? Well, I don't know. It's different with you—and we don't sell tickets to kids, of course—but I don't know if I can let half the kids of Appington Hill come through, without they come with their parents. Can I, now? That's not reasonable, boss."

Andy considered. "I never said that," he pointed out. "These two, that's all I said. I gotta show 'em. Half the kids of Appington Hill, I reckon that's not reasonable. I only said these two."

"Well . . ." said the man. He took his hand from the turnstile. "I'm not having any trouble with your dads, that's all. I never saw you."

They pushed between the wire barriers. Joe muttered, "Thanks, mister," as he passed.

"Don't try it next week," the man warned him. "Tonight you're with the owner, that's the difference."

Again Mike looked hard at Joe, and Joe frowned back.

They came through a narrow passage from the turnstile, and they all stood still. Even Andy had never seen Beecham Park like this before. At first they hardly saw the drifting crowds, the boys selling programs, the rows of little windows where people were placing bets. In front the ground sloped down to the blazing oval of the track with a pool of darkness inside it. From here the darkness looked much blacker than it did from above; there was only a glimmer here and there from the cars parked inside it. Beyond this circle of darkness and brilliantly lit track rose the big grandstand on the other side of the course. Its shape outlined with strings of lights, it seemed to float in a magical way above the course, the long rows of seats mounting tier above tier. The boys stared at it for a long moment, floating there against the rose-gray sky. When Andy turned to his friends, the driven look had gone from his face. It glowed again with the enchantment of the racecourse.

"I said I'd show you," he said simply. "There's more than onionweed."

He wanted to show them the onionweed too, and the bookmakers' stands, and the room where his broom was locked away with the others; but wherever they turned there was the excitement of race night snatching Andy away. Joe and Mike followed him from place to place, half dazed with listening and looking.

"There's my gardens—can't get around, they've locked the gate. I never knew about that gate. See, Joe? That cuts her in half, that does. See where they get their money, Mike? See, Joe? The bookmakers . . ."

They listened to the bookmakers and watched the crowd placing bets. There were men in sports jackets, women in floating frocks and sparkling brooches; there were men in crumpled shirts and shorts, and women who might have stepped straight out of their kitchens. There were babies in prams, and small children wandering among the crowds. A man with a bruised face was led off by a policeman.

"The band—see them, Mike?"

They watched the band marching and playing on the other side of the track. There were two very small bandsmen, two who looked very old and feeble, several with red stripes on their dark blue trousers, and several others with gold braid on their sleeves. They were a mixed lot. No one seemed to listen to them. There were young couples who stared at everything, people who walked primly in order to be stared at, men and women staring vacantly at nothing, and bored children who wanted to go home.

"I'll show you where I did the sweeping. . . ."

They walked along the white rails toward the shabby old stand on this side of the track. There were glasses of beer standing on posts, and white light beating down on the gritty surface of the track. They reached the place where the ground rose above the leveled track, and stood against the rails looking down.

"They'll come real close," said Andy solemnly. "We'll see them all right."

A car came slowly around the track and stopped below the spot where the boys hung over the rails. A man got out. He was an expensive-looking man in a sleek suit and a wonderful bowler hat. He disappeared below the rails, and the car drove on without him.

"A car always comes," said Andy, puzzled. He leaned out as far as he dared, craning to see. Then he burst into loud, surprised laughter and drew back. "You know what, Joe? Hey, Mike, you know what? He's got a little seat that he sits in, all by himself! I never knew that!"

"Shush!" said Joe; but Mike was leaning out to look. Sure enough, there was a small seat built into the bank. The expensive-looking gentleman sat primly perched below the rails and above the track.

"He's there to see that nobody cheats," Mike guessed. Andy laughed heartily.

Horses and gigs began to appear on the track, and a voice came from the amplifiers. A crowd came pressing around the boys, pinning them to the rails, waiting silently. Mike, Joe, and Andy looked along the track, waiting for the horses to come.

"Mysterious Stranger," chanted the amplifiers. "Black Velvet—My Conscience—Lucky Jim . . ."

"I know him!" cried Andy. "I know a lot of 'em."

The crowd stirred. With a rustling and drumming the horses sprang into view, spread wide across the track. Powerful, beating forelegs, deep, straining chests, and rolling eyes, they hurtled along the track straight at the boys. The three of them hung silent and breathless on the rails, with the crowd packed around them. The voice from the amplifiers chanted on. A man waved a glass and called, "*Come* on, fellers, *come* on," as if he were tired of arguing with the drivers. Cockaded heads high, the fierce horses passed. The drivers in their shining satin were perched above whirling wheels. The horses swung toward the inner rail and flowed in a dark stream around the curve.

"*Come* on, fellers," pleaded the man with the glass.

The stream of horses flowed by on the farther side of the track. Here and there, voices shouted to them as they passed. Then they were coming again in a great, strong rush, driving forward so that the boys could scarcely breathe.

"Aw, *come* on, fellers."

Around the track again, and a string of red lights flashed as they passed the big stand. The amplified voice grew frenzied and was almost drowned by the roaring of the crowd. They went by like dark thunder, whips flashing and drivers' faces grim; and around the track the roar of the crowd traveled with them. This time a white light flashed, and the horses went flying separately, slowing and turning one by one. The race was over.

The crowd began to break and separate. For a moment the three boys stood where they were in silence. Then Andy turned with a dreaming face and was surprised to see Joe and Mike. He laughed and said, "I forgot."

"Don't blame you," said Mike. "That was really something."

Andy chuckled happily. "Don't you reckon it was really something, Joe?"

"Sure, I do—but you don't own the horses, do you, boy?"

"He's not talking about the horses," said Mike shortly. "He's talking about the race."

"That's right," said Andy. "That's what I said. The race."

Joe and Mike looked darkly at each other. Andy was watching the track.

"Here's that car. I bet the man's going back in it." He craned over the rail. "He's got off his little chair. . . . There he goes."

Mike said, "Come on—we'll have some chips from that stall. My shout, Andy. You brought us in."

Andy chuckled shyly, and they went to the stall. They had to wait while two or three other people were served.

"That's where I did the sweeping," said Andy. "Hey, Mike, did you know I helped sweep her out this morning? There's a place behind here for the brooms, only they're locked up now. Mine and all." Mike hadn't heard about the sweeping, so he explained again. "They liked having the owner down, *I* know."

"Oh," said the woman in the stall, "so *you're* the owner, are you?" The other customers had gone, and she was smiling broadly at Andy. "I heard you were down tonight. After your rent, eh?" She reached across to a shelf and gave Andy a large bag of potato crisps. "That do?"

"I got no money," said Andy, hesitating and looking at Mike.

"That's all right," said the woman. She was young and plump, with a mass of yellow hair swathed and looped around her head. "You don't have to pay. That's the owner's rent for the stall."

Andy laughed with surprise and pleasure. "I never knew," he told her, and stood chuckling while Mike bought two more bags for himself and Joe.

"Look, boy," said Mike when the young woman was serving another customer, "it's been great, and thanks for bringing us, but I reckon we better go now. We have to get home. Coming?"

"All right," said Andy. "We can come anytime. I don't have to pay, see. I'm the owner." He followed Mike and Joe out through the big roller door that was opened between races.

Mike and Joe walked with him in silence to his own street. Andy went dreamily, full of warm content. He had gone boldly into his racecourse when it was alive, and it had been quite wonderful. His friends had gone with him and seen it all. Now they knew.

"See you," he said, nodding good night, and went loping away in the dark behind a wall of parked cars.

Mike turned on Joe. "Well?" he said sternly.

"Well, what?" said Joe, almost choking with anger and despair. When Mike didn't answer he burst out angrily: "I nearly had him till you came along, pulling his leg like the rest of them. I hope you're satisfied, that's all. I nearly had him talking sense."

"*Your* sort of sense," said Mike in the same cold, precise tone that Terry used when he was angry. "It seems to hurt pretty bad. I didn't like that, Mooney. I didn't think you'd do that to Andy."

"Do what? Try and get him out of a mess, do you mean? That's one thing *you're* not doing, anyhow, O'Day. *You* don't have to blame yourself."

"I haven't seen anything I *can* do—or you, either. What's the *good* of upsetting him like that? What's the use of you telling him one thing when the whole of that mob down there keep showing him you're wrong?"

"I'm *not* wrong. So they can't be showing him, can they?"

"Haven't you got a brain in your head, Joe Mooney? You're so sure that you know everything and poor old Andy's just a lunatic. Can't you shift out of your own light and have another look? Can't you see that *Andy Hoddel owns Beecham Park*?"

Mike turned on his heel and strode off, leaving Joe staring after him in the dark.

The Horse and the Colt

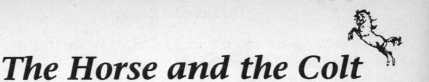

JEAN-PIERRE CLARIS DE FLORIAN

Fables are very short stories with animal characters and a moral at the end. This form of storytelling is very old; some of the most famous fables were told by Aesop, a slave in ancient Greece. Jean de La Fontaine, a Frenchman, is also famous for his fables. Jean-Pierre Claris de Florian, another Frenchman, is much less well known, but he wrote fresh and amusing fables. This one is taken from his book of fables, published in 1792.

Unacquainted with the iron sway of tyrant man lived a venerable Horse, who had been left a widower, with an only son; he reared him in a meadow, where the streams, the flowers, and the inviting shade offered at once all that was requisite for happiness.

Abusing these enjoyments, as is customary with youth, the Colt stuffed himself every day with clover, fooled away the time on the flowery plain, galloped about without an object, bathed without requiring it, or rested himself without being fatigued.

Lazy and fat, the young hermit grew weary, and became tired of wanting for nothing; disgust soon followed; and, seeking his father, he said to him, "For some time I have not been fit; this grass is unwholesome, and kills me; this clover is without smell; this water is muddy; the air we breathe here attacks my

lungs; in short, I shall die unless we leave it."

"Since it concerns your life, my dear son," replied his parent, "we will instantly take our departure." No sooner said than done—the two immediately set off in search of a new home.

The young traveler neighed for joy; the old one, less merry, went at a sedate pace, taking the lead, and made his child clamber up steep and arid mountains without a tuft of herbage, and where there was nothing which could afford them the least nourishment.

Evening came, but there was no pasturage; and the travelers had to go to bed supperless. The next day, when nearly exhausted by hunger, they were glad of a few stunted briars. This time there was no galloping on the part of the Colt; and after two days, he could scarcely drag one leg after the other.

Considering the lesson sufficient, the father returned by a road unknown to his son, and reconducted him to his meadow in the middle of the night. As soon as the Colt discovered a little fresh grass, he attacked it eagerly. "Oh! what a delicious banquet! What beautiful grass!" he exclaimed. "Was there ever anything so sweet and tender? My father, we will seek no further; let us not return to our old home—let us take up our abode for ever in this lovely spot: what country can equal this!"

As he thus spoke, day began to break; and the Colt, recognizing the meadow he had so lately quitted, cast down his eyes in the greatest confusion.

His father mildly said to him, "My dear child, in future remember this maxim: He who enjoys too much, is soon disgusted with pleasure; to be happy, one must be moderate."

Zeus and the Horse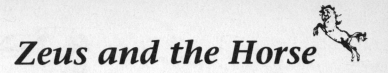

GOTTHOLD EPHRAIM LESSING

Another fable—a very short one, in which the proud horse learns a lesson. Maybe, though, Zeus was rather unfair to camels? Gotthold Ephraim Lessing was a German, who published his book of fables in 1759.

"Father of Animals and Men," said the horse, approaching the throne of the god Zeus, "they want me to be one of the most beautiful of thy creatures adorning the earth, and my self-love tells me that I could be this. But aren't there various parts of me that could be improved?"

"What, then, dost thou think could be improved in thee? Speak; I will learn," said the good god Zeus, smiling.

"Perhaps," continued the horse, "I should be swifter if my legs were longer and more slender; and perhaps a long swan's neck would be not unbecoming; a broader chest would increase my strength; and since thou hast decreed that I should carry thy darling—Man—I might well have a ready-made saddle for the rider."

"Certainly," said Zeus. "Just be patient for a moment!" And assuming a serious expression, he spoke the word of creation. Dust particles spun together, life moved them, and there beside the throne stood—the ungainly camel.

The horse saw it and shuddered.

"Here is thy ready-made saddle," said Zeus, "a swan's neck, and a chest broader than thine. But dost thou truly wish to have a camel's shape?"

The horse, still quivering, gave no answer.

"Go," continued Zeus. "This time, learn thy lesson without being punished. But every now and again, new creature, thou shalt cause the horse to recall with remorse his impudence." Zeus cast a lingering glance at the camel. "For the horse shall never look on thee without a shudder."

The Wild White Horses

JOYCE STRANGER

This is a very sad story—but it has a happy ending, too. Joyce Stranger trained as a biologist, specializing in animal behavior. She has always enjoyed animals, and has been writing splendid stories about them for more than thirty years.

It was Christmas Eve.

The world was alight with excitement. Children fretted at the slowly passing hours. They made plans and bought presents, and huddled in corners, glowing, as they whispered secrets. Parents glanced at each other with meaning in their eyes. Strange-shaped parcels, gaily wrapped, were hidden in odd corners and put on high shelves, and tucked into drawers, insecurely masked by piled shirts or underwear.

The excitement spilled into the seething last-minute streets, where, at night, bright lights glittered. From every lamppost angels danced. Unicorns, splendid in silver and gold, shone above the slowly moving motorcars. Children gazed skyward at giant crowns, jeweled with glory, and Santa Claus sat on his sleigh, his reindeer lifting their antlers high above Market Street.

Shop windows were hung with tinsel, and snow covered the floor inside, while mannequins, in their

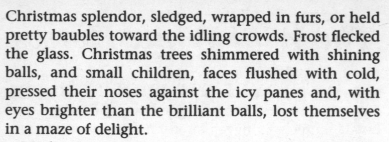

Christmas splendor, sledged, wrapped in furs, or held pretty baubles toward the idling crowds. Frost flecked the glass. Christmas trees shimmered with shining balls, and small children, faces flushed with cold, pressed their noses against the icy panes and, with eyes brighter than the brilliant balls, lost themselves in a maze of delight.

Market Street was a solid mass of people, homeward bound, hurrying to the bus station and the railway station, anxious to get home, away from the cold, to start preparing for the next day, the greatest day of all, for feast and for fun and for the early present-giving. Few of them noticed the three Gypsy girls with their long black tangled hair and brown faces and bright patched shawls of orange and green and blue, clutching their baskets. The girls had saved their money so that they could come to Manchester to shop and to see the big city for the first time, and moreover, see it in all its Christmas splendor. They were in no hurry and going nowhere and had all the time in the world. They looked up at lights that dazzled along the street, and looked down at mock snow and fake frost on shop-window floors, and looked in at every scene set to attract and excite them, unaware that this was to lure the people inside and help them spend their money. They had no money left to spend, nor did it occur to them to be envious.

They walked through Piccadilly Gardens, where luminous plaster owls lurked in the trees and goblins peeped from the bushes, enchanting the children, and colored lights hung, unusual exotic winter fruits, from slender branches. They paused to look at a snow house and a snowman, seeming more real than snow itself. They crossed the road, moving with the throng, unnerved by traffic that snarled and fought its way down the main roads and turned off at every corner, often balked by the mass of pedestrians attempting to cross from side to side, eyes on the lights above them and not on the streets in front of them. The Gypsy girls were thin and ragged and undernourished but laughter was never far from their mouths, and their merry voices and quick movement caught many eyes as they moved through the busy throng. Their world today was an infinite satisfaction, as brave and colorful as any Gypsy's wildest dream. The girls asked for nothing and expected nothing. It was enough to look, to caress with every glance, to fold the glory and wonder away in the mind where it could remain. At a later date they would bring it from their treasure house and revel afresh in the color and excitement and brilliance of a world to which they could never belong and whose splendor they could only admire from outside.

It began to snow. Large flakes drifted slowly through the air, and the city dirt was masked in shining white. Flakes settled on hair and cheek and shoulder, drifted down onto the side street barrows of gold and green fruit, and on those which were massed with yellow and red tawny flowers. The stragglers hurried, anxious for warm fire and tea and television set. Children wailed, hungry and fretful. The girls watched them and smiled. There were small ones at home, inside the brightly painted caravans. They, too, were preparing for Christmas. They did not want to hasten back. They would wait and see the nighttime crowds and sleep, huddled together for warmth, in some arched doorway, or perhaps, if they were lucky, find a deserted hayloft outside the city. They had shopped for Christmas. Romaine had bought her mother a shining brooch, a beautiful thing of glass and beads, the cluster as bright as any real gem in any jeweler's window. She held it in her hand, wrapped in tissue paper, more precious than diamonds. Sarina had found a tinsel scarf that would brighten her married sister's hair. Both her parents were dead, and her sister looked after her. She had also a bag of tiny sweets for her baby niece. Anita had found a fluffy horse, all of four inches high, made of white brushed-up felt, with a curled black wool mane and bright black eyes and nose. A minute scarlet saddle added an air of gaiety. Her little sister would love the toy.

The girls turned into a side street. The high walls closed together and the lights were gone. They had entered a black canyon, lit by the soft glow from one lamp, which illuminated the falling flakes. A black and white timbered building cast its shadow on the cobbles and loured against the dark as it had when Shakespeare was a boy. The windows glowed gold, and voices from the public house spilled into the darkness. The girls moved to catch the warmth from the doorway and savor the smell of frying chips that came from the kitchen.

It was then that they saw the pony; he was tethered to a post. A creamy pony with gold mane and tail, trembling with cold and weariness and hunger. His large wise eyes shone with tears caused by the icy wind that cut into him. The girls stopped.

Anita put her arms about his neck and leaned against him. She was warm and she smelled of comfort and love, and his tired, tense body relaxed. He was not used to kindness. Her small hand fondled his mane.

"He is just like my pony. See?" she said, and held the toy up to the light. The pony huffed at her.

He was a gentle creature, and life was wearying for him. He found the world a frightening place.

His master drove a cart. Each morning the cream pony was caught, groomed roughly and carelessly, and put between the shafts, where he stood, dejected, until a whip was laid spitefully across his shoulders.

His hooves were painful, needed paring, and he clip-clopped along in shoes lacking a nail, so that often he was lame, but not lame enough for his master to know or care.

Sometimes a bright balloon was tied to his harness, to attract the children who swarmed on his route. He hated it. He hated the flabby feel and the bat, bat, bat against his neck when he trotted, and even worse, the terrifying bang when some boy, grinning with mischief, punctured it with a pin, or a man pushed a glowing cigarette butt against it.

He hated the days spent dragging a cart that became heavier and heavier as the hours went by; and the evenings standing in the rain and mud in the seven-acre field where the grass grew thin and spare and thistly and the food his master gave him was sparse and stale.

He longed for lush green grass, for the feel of summer meadow, rich with buttercups, beneath his tired hooves, and the dip and trickle of running water, remembered dimly from a time long ago when freedom had been his. Freedom to gallop under a summer sun, to roll in long, clean grass, and stand swishing his tail against the flies, fetlock deep in cool clear water where tiny fish arrowed in darting flight brushed against his legs, tickling them.

The pony had often stood with his head over the gate, longing for a human to stop and give him a kind

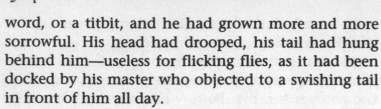

word, or a titbit, and he had grown more and more sorrowful. His head had drooped, his tail had hung behind him—useless for flicking flies, as it had been docked by his master who objected to a swishing tail in front of him all day.

Slowly the years had passed. The pony had wilted, finding no pleasure in living. How should he? His days were spent trotting on hard roads, the whip ever ready to flick at his shoulders. At night he had grown too tired to run in the seedy field. Sometimes he had watched the moon slide over the sky, and leaves, moon-flecked, shiver in the wind.

When the wind had blown he had turned his tail to it and stood patient, feeling the strange unseen creature ruffle his hair and tease his mane, tangling it even more. He had longed for someone to brush the grit from his coat and smooth the jagged tangles in mane and tail, and he had sighed more deeply as the years went by.

He had also longed for company. Another pony to lean against, and lick in friendship; to run against, and to call joyously when he had come back from the streets at night.

He had nothing.

Now he looked at the girls, feeling the friendship that radiated from them, warming him. He leaned his head against Romaine, who was standing in front of him, crooning to him as no one had crooned in his life before, and he pushed her gently, wishing he could communicate both his gratitude and his need.

Snow was drifting over them. The pony shook his head, hating it. He yearned for food, for warmth, for love and for kindness, for an owner who would groom him and soothe him and comfort him, for a warm stable and for hay that smelled of summer, and not of damp and mold.

Romaine put both her arms around him and he turned his head and nuzzled her with velvet lips. His brown eyes gazed at her, wishing that he could be hers, that her gentle hands might always stroke his coat and play with his mane, that he might be free forever of the rumbling jolting cart that dragged behind him uphill and chased after him downhill and always hurt his back. He longed to be free of the confining chafing harness that made him sore, and of the hateful batting balloon.

"We ought to do something about him," Romaine said.

Sarina and Anita looked at her. The alley-way was dark, light from the street lamp spilling onto the pony's head. The cart, piled high with old clothes, with tires, with bits and pieces once treasured and now discarded, was in deep shadow. They gave the pony a last kiss each, then one by one they crept under the old clothes, making no sound, showing neither face nor arm nor hand.

The man came out of the public house, stumbling and swearing. He fumbled at the reins and when the pony did not acknowledge him, slapped its neck. The pony breathed sadly and softly and dropped his head lower. He did not want to start again, did not want to pull the heavy cart, did not want to clop over the cobbles, with the wind knifing at him. The snow had turned to rain, which had just begun to fall, wetting him.

The man clambered onto the cart, tugged at the reins, and slashed with his whip. The pony moved, heaving with his shoulders, feeling the weight of the cart. The wheels gripped and began to turn.

They walked out of the alley and into the main traffic. Cars sped past him, and a policeman looked at him sourly. He was holding up all the traffic behind him. Horns sounded, and men glared at him when they found room to pass. Children looked back, seeing not an old and shabby pony, but a dream horse, piebald and beautiful, his head looking toward them, mild-eyed, the gay balloon a banner at his neck, the man a figure of mystery, as he drove through the night.

The rain, which had succeeded the snow, turned once more to sleet, and finally to snow again. Huge wet flakes drifted down and the trees were masked and shone in the lamplight. The world turned from everyday to fairytale magic and houses lay secret under whitened roofs, and hedges and roads alike were smooth and beautiful. The thud of the dragging hooves was muffled, and the pony slipped, and stopped. The flicking spiteful whip drove him on again.

The girls, warm under the old clothes, but almost stifled by the dust and stuffy smell of them, peeped out through the cracks, and watched the world they knew change. In the fields where the caravans stood, there would be even more beauty, for all the daytime mud would be hidden, while the silent snow turned the trees to Christmas glory.

They clopped on. The traffic was less. Most people were home by now, and the road beyond Fallowfield station stretched broad and quiet. The shops were closed, some of them lit for Christmas, so that trees and tinsel and shining baubles glittered invitingly.

It seemed a long journey to the girls, and even longer to the pony. He thought of food, hung in bags for him to tug, of grass, long and green and luscious, of water, and of sunshine and warmth. He shivered. Other creatures would spend the night indoors, but his only shelter was a shed without a door to it and with only half a roof and with the floor sodden. He had little protection from the weather. If he was lucky there might be some moldy hay bought cheap because it was useless to anyone else. He would have to dig through the snow and nose out the grass that remained in the muddy field. He was cold and he was hungry and he was tired. His hooves dragged but the whip stung his neck again, so he speeded his pace. Once he got the man home the cart would be removed and the chafing harness hung on the wall and there would be a little moment of peace before the galls that chafed him began to hurt again, and hunger remind him of his misery.

When they reached Didsbury they turned by the church and came into a tiny lane that the girls had never seen before. It was part of the old village, hidden away between the houses, a memory of long ago when there had been fields and trees, and the mist that still straddled Fog Lane in autumn and winter had come from the low-lying fields now succeeded by rows of houses.

Anita caught a glimpse of the lane and the name at the end of it: Paradise Meadow.

The meadow was small, hardly big enough to keep a pony, but here there was a ruined shed and a five-barred gate and beside the meadow was an old house, tumbledown and decrepit, long ago condemned but for some reason forgotten by the authorities.

The man left the horse and cart for a moment and went inside to light his fire so the Gypsy girls slipped

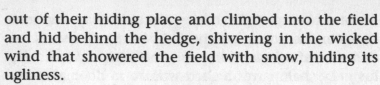

out of their hiding place and climbed into the field and hid behind the hedge, shivering in the wicked wind that showered the field with snow, hiding its ugliness.

The man came back. His fingers were clumsy with drink and pulled and tugged at the buckles. He was cold, and he kicked the unresisting pony in temper, wanting to be by his fireside and safe with his bottle of beer again. He had neither wife nor child to comfort him.

At last the pony was free and the man pushed him into the shed and flung hay at his feet. There was not much and it was not good, but the pony had no choice. He began to eat. The man left the cart and went indoors and the girls watched as the light went on in the decrepit house, and his shadow fell across the thin curtain, as he settled himself in his chair and kicked off his boots before the fire that now blazed, logs burning brightly.

The girls went to the shed. The pony saw them come and lifted his head, and made a tiny whinny of welcome.

"Hush," Sarina said and rubbed his soft muzzle, and put her arms around his neck. She felt the galls on his back.

"He has harness sores," she said angrily.

Anita, who had learned the art of healing from her grandmother, felt with her soft fingers.

"No one has taken care of him, ever," she said passionately. "That man is wicked. We ought to teach him a lesson."

"How?" Sarina asked, but Anita did not know.

Romaine had vanished, and only her footsteps showed in the snow. Anita and Sarina waited, and

Anita picked out the better pieces of hay and gave them to the pony, and he held his head toward her and rubbed against her dress, to show how much he loved her company and appreciated not being alone.

The slender ghost of a moon slipped up the starry sky and magic spilled over the field. The girls looked at the new-made world, reveling in its beauty. They loved beauty. Their eyes shone, and their small bodies, leaning against the pony, one on either side, warmed him and comforted him, and happiness filled him. He sighed deeply, this time with joy.

Anita took her comb and began to tease it through his mane, her fingers gently pulling at the tangles. He bore it patiently and she whispered to him as Sarina fed him.

"I will make you beautiful. You will be the most beautiful pony in Manchester. Your coat will shine and your mane and tail will be silken soft and your hooves will be polished and everyone will turn to look at you."

The moon was brighter now. The stars hung in the sky, far away, overhead, deep in outer space, and the world whirled on, and Sarina took her sharp knife and began to pare the overgrown hooves, her hands so gentle that he scarcely felt them as she brought him comfort. It was a job that she had often done before for her own ponies.

Anita took a dry wisp of hay and began to rub the dust from the pony's coat. She slapped him gently and the clouds of dust flew around them, and she had to stifle a sneeze. She looked anxiously toward the cottage but all was dark. The man had gone to bed and they were safe for the time being.

"No one has ever groomed him," she said, and she

worked to shift the dust and grime and the mud around his legs. He stood patiently, knowing that he would feel better when she had finished.

Romaine came back, drifting on the wind like a snowflake herself, so silent that she made the other girls jump as she spoke.

"There were some apples on the tree in the old orchard, left from autumn," she whispered. "The pony can feed on them. And I found some hay in the corner of the farmyard at the end of the lane. No one will miss it."

The hay was fresh and the pony ate it greedily. He had never fed so well before, not for long ages, longer ago than he could remember, when he was a colt in a green field and the world was new and young and exciting and he could race on smooth turf and chase with his mother.

It was very long ago. He had raced, he remembered, running against other horses on a wide racecourse, when he was only two years old, but his untried muscles rebelled and his legs were strained and the tendons stretched and he had been sold at an auction to a girl who rode him occasionally and kept him in a big field, and then forgot him.

He had been sold again; this time the man bought him, and ever since he had dragged the cart over the streets and come home at night to the tiny field and waited uncomplaining for day to dawn again.

Sometimes children gave him apples and old ladies gave him carrots: sometimes the sun shone and he savored the warmth and sometimes there was green grass on the verges and the man let him graze, knowing that it saved money in the end. His thoughts slipped through his mind, pictures without words, memories of people's faces, and of voices that spoke to him, and of weather.

"I have one other apple," Romaine said. "The Apple of Peace and Freedom that was given to me by my grandmother's grandmother long ago. It keeps fresh forever."

Sarina and Anita looked at her.

"Shall I give it to him?" she asked.

Their eyes were troubled. They looked at the pony, at the coat that would never shine again and the hooves that would never trot fast again. He was old and his wind was broken and his legs were knobbly and worn with age and hard work, and he would never know comfort again. Only the lonely desolate field and the man who drank too much and swore too much and who used the whip too often and did not give him food or water, or comfort, or company.

"Give him the apple," Sarina said, and her hand stroked the soft neck, and the pony wondered why her eyes suddenly filled with tears.

He took the apple, and ate it. Nothing had ever tasted so wonderful. Nothing had ever brought such a feeling of well-being. It was sweet and firm and refreshing and it gave him strange ideas. He lifted his head. Dim memories of far places came to him, of rolling moors where birds called shrill and sweet, and rabbits ran and other ponies cantered, tossing their manes, knowing nothing of roads and carts. The girls, hand in hand, downcast, slipped into the lane, each one kissing the pony as she passed. Silent, they turned for home.

The moon was high and the wind was wild, a rushing ecstatic wind that brought with it the scent of the sea, faint and faraway, of driftwood and seawrack and the tossing tumbling waves.

Bewitched by the girl who gave him the apple, the pony nosed open the gate. He stared for a moment into the rustling dark. It was so long since freedom had been his. He was not aware that there had been magic in the apple.

He turned into the lane, pushing through brambles and bracken on to a hill. His familiar world had mysteriously vanished and he was in a land beyond time. Uphill to woodland, where the turf was soft and cool and kind, and where there was grass, grass such as he had never tasted, long and green and clean and cool and sweet-smelling. He browsed, shadowy beneath a tree, savoring delight.

The grass gave him new energy. He turned and pricked his ears, wary, listening. A rabbit, bounding under his hooves, startled him, but he knew it did not threaten his safety. He sped over the turf, alone in the windy night, trotting faster than he had ever trotted, racing against the wind.

He began to canter. The night and the wind excited him and the soft ground, kind to his hooves, was tempting, so that he fled through the windy dark leaving the town and the seven-acre field and the world's unkindness far behind him.

Somewhere, he did not know where, he was joined by other ponies, long-legged, cream-colored, very like himself, manes and tails silken with loving care, and satin coats shining. Now that the girls had groomed him, he was as beautiful as they.

They called to him, and he answered, lifting his voice in joyous ecstasy, a long neighing call that challenged the moon, and brought answering neighs from the ponies running beside him.

They were almost flying, a frieze of cantering beauties, speeding over the moors. They leaped a running brook where water sparkled, gemlike, under the gleaming light, and sped on, tiny divots of turf flashing up behind the urgent hooves.

The pony raced with them, all tiredness forgotten. Now and again one of his companions brushed against him and it was good to feel the warmth and solidity of a companion of his own kind. He could see the splendid creatures all around him, so that there seemed to be hundreds of cream-colored ponies on the moors.

Then they were dropping toward the sea and the sea smell was a wild excitement and he could remember—how, he did not know—the sting of salt, the surge and roar and thunder of green waters and the wild exotic fury of the rolling waves.

They plunged through a pine wood, the needles kicked up behind them, the birds just awakening, shouting angry calls as the flying bodies sped among the trees.

The cliffs were before them, raking into the sky and, beyond them, the world was a maze of white water as the wind piled the sea to seething fury, and the waves hurled themselves against the rocks and broke high in cascading fountains of white, lacy foam that glittered in the light of the newborn sun.

They were at the edge of the cliffs. They were leaping over, cream ponies dropping from the sky, dropping into the thunder and the foam and fret of the flashing, tumbling sea, bodies arched and beautiful.

The pony did not hesitate. He leaped with his companions, felt the sudden impact of water, the clean coolness, the soothing welcome that told him that, after a lifetime of misery, he had come home.

He was strong, he was powerful, he was gleaming with glory, swimming into the sunrise, calling his kind.

He was power, he was strength, he was beauty, and the years of toil and misery were nothing, and he swam to a life of rousing wonder, of wildness and foam and fret, with his companions, the wild, white horses of the sea.

Far away in a muddy distant field, surrounded by houses that gloomed, and smoke that poured from grimy chimneys, a man whipped his leg and cursed, as he found the body of his dead pony, lying in the mud beside the half-open gate.

The White Horse of Zennor

MICHAEL MORPURGO

Zennor in Cornwall is the setting for an exciting tale of a great white horse that comes to the rescue of Farmer Veluna and his family, when it looks as though they will lose their home and their land. Cornwall is a land of magic and legend, so it's not surprising that there's an unexpected twist at the end of this tale. Michael Morpurgo is a prize-winning children's author. He also owns a special farm in Devon where schoolchildren can stay and help with all the work.

The family had farmed the land in the Foage Valley at Zennor for over five hundred years. They had been there, it was said, ever since Miguel Veluna first crawled ashore half drowned at Porthzennor Cove from the wreck of his galleon off Gunnards Head. As soon as he could make himself understood, so the story goes, he married the farmer's daughter who had just nursed him back to life; and with her came the farm in the fertile valley that runs down from the north coast to the south with the high moors rising on either side. Through the generations the Velunas prospered, sowing their corn along the sheltered fields and grazing their hardy cattle on the moors above. They became tough and circumspect, as are all the farmers whose roots lie deep in the rocks and soil of Penwith, the last bastion of land against the mighty Atlantic that seeks with every storm to subdue the peninsula and to rejoin the Channel a few short miles to the south. Over the centuries the family had survived famine and disease, invasion and depression; but now the Velunas were staring ruin in the face and there seemed no way forward for them.

Farmer Veluna had been a joyful soul all his life, a man of laughter, who rode high through the fields on his tractor, forever singing his heart out, in a perpetual celebration that he belonged where he was. His joy in life was infectious, so that he spread around him a convivial sense of security and happiness. In business he was always fair, although he was thought to be overgenerous at times, not hard enough a man according to some of the more craggy moorland farmers. But no one in the parish was better respected and liked than Farmer Veluna, so that when he married lovely Molly Parson from Morvah and produced a daughter and a son within two years, everyone thought it was no more than he deserved. When he built a new milking parlor some of his friends shook their heads and wondered, for no one could recall a milking herd on the land before; but they knew Farmer Veluna to be levelheaded and hardworking. No one doubted that if anyone could make it work he could, and certainly everyone wished him well in his new venture.

For several years the milk flowed and the profits came. He built up the finest herd of Guernsey cows for miles around, and there was talk that he was doing so well that he might take on more land. Then, within six short weeks he was a ruined man. First the corn harvest failed completely, a summer storm lashing through the valley breaking the ripened corn and flattening it to the ground. The storm was followed by weeks of heavy drizzle, so that not even the straw could be salvaged. But the cows were still milking and the regular milk check was always there every month to see them through. Farmer Veluna was disappointed by the setback but burned off the straw when he could and began to plow again. He was still singing on his tractor.

Then came the annual ministry check for brucellosis* the outcome of which had never worried Farmer Veluna. It was routine, no more than that, so that when the two vets arrived at his front door some days later it never even occurred to him that they had come about the brucellosis test. The vets knew him well and liked him, for he was good to his stock and paid his bills, so they broke the news to him as gently as they could. Farmer Veluna stood in the doorway, his heart heavy with foreboding as they began to tell him the worst.

"There can be no mistake?" he said. "You're sure there's no mistake?" But he knew he need not have asked.

"It's brucellosis, Farmer, no doubt about it; right through the herd. I'm sorry, but you know what has to be done," said one of the vets, putting a hand on his shoulder to comfort him. "It has to be done today. The ministry men are on their way. We've come to help." Farmer Veluna nodded slowly and they went inside together.

That afternoon his entire herd of golden Guernseys was driven into the yard below the dairy and killed.

* A highly contagious disease that kills calves before they are born.

Every cow and calf on the farm, even one born that same morning, was slaughtered; and the milking parlor stood silent from that day on.

In the weeks that followed the disaster every tractor and salable machine had to be sold for there was the family to feed as well as the other stock, and an overdraft at the bank that Farmer Veluna had to honor. It was not much money to find each month, but with little coming in, it soon became apparent that the pigs had to be sold, then the geese, and finally the beloved horse. All that was left were a few hens and a shed full of redundant rusting machinery.

Each evening the family would sit around the kitchen table and talk over the possibilities, but as the situation worsened the children noticed that it was their mother who emerged the stronger. The light had gone out of their father's eye; his entire demeanor was clouded over with despair. Even his jaunty, lurruping walk had slowed, and he moved aimlessly around the farm now as if in a daze. He seemed scarcely even willing or able to consider any suggestions for the future. His wife, Molly, managed to persuade him to go to the bank to ask for an extension of the loan, and for a new loan to finance new stock and seed; but times were hard even for the banks and when both were refused he lapsed into a profound depression that pervaded every room in the house.

Friends and neighbors came with offers of help, but he thanked them kindly for their generosity and refused them politely as they knew he would, for he was above all a proud man from a proud family and not accustomed to accepting charity from anyone, however dire the necessity.

Desperately Molly urged him on, trying to release

him from the prison of his despair, believing in her heart that he had it in him to recover and knowing that without him they were lost. The two children, meanwhile, sought their own consolation and relief up on the high moors they knew and loved so well. They would leave the house and farm behind them, and climb up to the great granite rocks above the village where the wind blew in so fiercely from the sea that they could lean into it with arms outstretched and be held and buffeted like kites. They would leap from rock to rock like mountain goats, play endless hide-and-seek, and tramp together over the boggy moors, all the while trying to forget the threat that hung over them. Their walks would end often on the same rocking stone above the Eagle's Nest, a giant slab of rounded granite as finely balanced as a pair of scales on the rock below, so that if they stood on opposite ends they could rock it up and down like a seesaw.

Here they were sitting one early autumn evening with the sun setting fire to the sea beyond Zennor when they saw their father and mother climbing up through the bracken toward them. Unusually, they were holding hands, and that signified to both children that a decision might have been reached. They instinctively sensed what the decision was, and dreaded it. Annie decided she would forestall them.

"You needn't tell us," Annie said to them as they climbed up to sit down beside the children on the logan stone. "We know already. There's no other way, is there?"

"What do you know, Annie?" said Farmer Veluna, the first words either of the children had heard him utter for more than a week.

"That we're going to sell the farm," she said softly,

almost as if she did not wish to hear it. "We're going to sell the farm and move away, aren't we?"

"I won't go," said Arthur, shrugging off his mother's arm. "I won't. I was born here and I'm going to stay here. No one is going to make me move."

He spoke with grim resolve.

At nine, he was a year younger than his sister, but at that moment he seemed suddenly a great deal older. He was already as tall as Annie, and even as an infant others had recognized in him that strong Veluna spirit.

"We shall have to sell, Arthur," said his father. "We've no alternative. You need money to run a farm and we haven't got any. It's that simple. Everything we had was in the cows and now they're gone. I'm not going to argue about it; there's no point. We shall have to sell up and buy a smaller farm elsewhere. That's all there is to it. There's other farms and there's other places."

"Not like this one," Arthur said, and turned to his father, tears filling his eyes. "There's no place like this place and you know it. So don't pretend. You told me often enough, Father: you told me never to give up, and now you're giving up yourself." Farmer Veluna looked away, unable to give his son any answer that would convince even himself.

"That's unkind, Arthur," said his mother. "You mustn't be unkind to your father, not now. He's done all he can—you know he has. It'll be all right. It'll be the same. We shall go on farming, but in a smaller way, that's all. It's all your father can do; you must see that Arthur."

Annie turned to her father and put her arms around him, as much to comfort herself as to comfort him. It seemed to do neither.

Farmer Veluna stroked his daughter's hair gently.

"We shall be all right, Annie," he said. "I promise you that. Don't worry, I'm not a man to break my promises. You know that, don't you?"

Annie nodded into his chest, fighting back her tears.

"We'll see you back at home, children," Molly said. "Don't be long now. It gets cold up here when the sun's gone."

The two children sat side by side and watched their parents move slowly back down the hill toward the farm. The girl and boy were so alike to look at that many people considered them to be twins. Both had their parents' dark shining hair, and their skin stayed dark even in the winter. They had few friends besides each other, for there were not many children of their own age on other farms around about, and so they had spent much of their life together, and by now sensed each other's mood intuitively.

"Annie," Arthur said finally when he had wiped the tears away from his cheeks. "I couldn't live anywhere else, could you? We have to find a way to stay here, because I'm not going. I don't care what Father says, I'm not going."

But Annie was not listening to her brother, for she had been distracted some moments before by the sound of a distant voice from behind her, perhaps from the direction of the Quoit. She had thought it might be the wind at first, moaning through the stones. She put her hand on her brother's arm.

"Listen," she said. And the voice was still there, clearly discernible now that Arthur had stopped talking. It was more distinct now, and although they could as yet make out no words, they could tell that someone was calling out for help. They leaped from the rocking stone and ran down the track into the heather and bracken of the high moor, homing in all the while on the plaintive cry that came to them ever more urgently from across the moor. They could hear now that it came from the ruins of the old count-house, and they slowed to a walk as they approached, suddenly uncertain of themselves.

"Help me, please help me"—clearly a man's voice, a man in pain; and no longer a shout into the wilderness, but a plea directed to them.

"Can you see anyone?" Annie said, clutching Arthur's arm in fright.

"I'm down here, over here in the ruins. Oh, for pity's sake, come quickly." The children climbed slowly down into the ruin itself, Annie still holding on to her brother, and at last they found what they had been looking for.

Lying in the corner of the ruined old count-house, propped up against a granite pillar, was an old man, but no ordinary man, for he was smaller even than any dwarf. But unlike a dwarf's, his features were in perfect proportion to his size. He was roughly clothed in heavy tweed trousers and a black moleskin jacket. He had wild white hair and eyes as blue as the sea. He lay with one knee clasped to his chest, and the children saw that clinging grotesquely to his foot was a rusty leghold trap.

"A Knocker," Annie whispered, and she stepped back in alarm, dragging Arthur back with her; but Arthur wrenched himself free and stood his ground.

"I know that," Arthur said, speaking loudly, for he felt it was rude to whisper. "There's nothing wrong with Knockers. They won't hurt you, 'less you hurt them. Isn't that right, sir?"

"Quite right, young fellow," said the old man

crisply, "and anyway, since I'm pinioned here with
this confounded trap, there's not too much danger of
my hurting you, my girl—now, is there?"

Annie shook her head vigorously but was not convinced.

"And since you're here, I wonder: Would it be too
much trouble to ask you to help me out of this thing?
I would have done it myself if I could, but I'm a wee
bit little to pull the spring back and if I move, my leg
burns like hellfire. Confounded farmers," he went on,
wincing in pain, "they're still trapping, you know, but

it's not as bad as it was. In the old days my father told me the whole moor was littered with them—rabbit traps, bird traps, fox traps, all sorts. You couldn't go out at dark, you know, for fear of putting your foot in it, so to speak. This is an old one—been here for years I should think—but there's still some of them at it. I've seen them. I know everything that goes on. Confounded farmers."

"I'm a farmer's son," said Arthur defensively, crouching down to examine the trap, "and my father wouldn't use leghold traps. He says they're cruel, and anyway they're not allowed anymore."

"Quite right," the Knocker said, straightening out his leg for Arthur. "I know your father. He's a good man. Know you two as well—seen you often enough springing around out on those rocks. Didn't know I was watching, did you? 'Course it's a shame about your farm, but that's life. Swings and roundabouts, ups and downs. It happens."

"You've watched us?" said Annie, who had plucked up enough courage at last to come closer. "You've seen us up there?"

"'Course I have," said the Knocker. "We know everyone for miles around. It's our job to know what's going on; that's what we're here for. Now look, children, can we continue this discussion after you've set me free, if you don't mind. My leg's throbbing and I'll bleed to death if you don't help me out of this soon."

Rust had stiffened the spring so it took Arthur and Annie some time to prize open the jaws of the trap far enough for the Knocker to withdraw his boot. He fell back to the ground in a faint as the boot came clear. By the time he came to, some minutes later, he found the children had taken his boot off and were kneeling over him bathing his ankle with a wet handkerchief. He lifted himself onto his elbows and smiled up at them.

"That was kind of you," he said. "I'm surprised you didn't run away; most people would have, you know. I think you must know about us. Someone must've told you. But you didn't know we bled, did you?"

Arthur shook his head. "No, but everyone's heard about you," he said, "although no one really believes in you anymore. But ever since my mother told us all about Knockers and little people and all that, I've always thought that if you were true then you'd live up here on the moor or maybe down the mines. There's nowhere else for you, is there?"

"I still don't think I should really believe it," said Annie, tying the handkerchief in a tight knot, "if I wasn't touching you, I'm sure I wouldn't."

"The leg will be fine now, right as rain, good as new," said the Knocker.

His pale face was deeply lined with age and there was a kindness and a wisdom in his face that both the children trusted instinctively.

"Thank you," he said as the children helped him to his feet.

He shook them each solemnly by the hand.

"Thank you both very kindly. I don't think I should have survived a frosty autumn night out here on the moor. I'm old, you see—and even Knockers die when they get old, you know. It's so nice to find people who'll talk to us. So many people just run away, and it's such a pity, because there's nothing to be frightened of."

He hobbled unaided around the ruined count-house, testing his leg, before returning to the children.

"No broken bones, I think. All's well that ends well, as they say."

"Will you be all right now?" Arthur asked. "We ought to be getting back home now. Father said we should be off the moor by dark."

"Quite right. Wise man, your father," the little Knocker said, brushing off his moleskin jacket and pulling it down straight. "After all, you never know who you might bump into up here. The place is full of spriggans and pixies and nasty wee little folk and even," he whispered low, "even the odd Knocker or two." And the three laughed together as old friends might do over a confidential joke. "But before you go, children, I have to thank you properly. One good turn deserves another, tit for tat, you scratch my back, I'll scratch yours, and so on. I want each of you to close your eyes and tell me your one dearest wish. You have to say what you'd most like in all the world. Ask and you shall have it. Annie, you're first. Come on now."

Annie did not have to think for long.

"A horse," she said, her eyes squeezed tight shut. "We had to sell our horse, you see, because Father needed the money for the farm. I've always wanted a great white horse."

"Keep your eyes closed," said the Knocker. "Keep them closed, both of you, and don't open them until I tell you. Now you, Arthur. What is it that you'd most want in all the world?"

"I want to stay here on the farm," said Arthur slowly. "I want my father to be happy again and to go singing on his tractor. I want the animals back and the farm working again like it used to."

"That's a lot of wants," said the Knocker. "Let's see what we can do now."

130

He chuckled aloud, and his voice seemed more animated now.

"You know, children, I haven't had the chance to do this for donkey's years. I'm so excited, I feel like a little Knocker all over again. You wished for the horse, Annie; and you wished for the farm back as it was, Arthur. How you do it is up to you, but you'll find enough seed corn in the barn when you get back home and you can use the horse as you wish. But after a year and a day you must bring the horse back here to me and leave twelve sacks of good seed corn back in your barn to repay me. Do you understand? Remember, be back here by dusk a year and a day from now."

"We'll be here," said Arthur.

"Promise?" said the Knocker.

"We promise," they said solemnly.

"You should be able to manage everything by that time with luck, and I'll see you have enough of that. All right, children, open your eyes now."

In place of the little Knocker stood a giant of a horse, towering above them, a brilliant white from mane to tail. He looked down at the children almost casually, swished his tail, shook his head with impatience, and then sprang out over the ruined wall and onto the open moor, beyond where he stood waiting in the bracken for the scrambling children to catch up.

Arthur had never been fond of horses. They seemed to him to be unpredictable creatures, and he had always steered clear of them. Anyway, as a budding farmer he had no use for any animal that was not productive. But Annie had enough confidence and experience for both of them, and she caught the horse gently by the mane and stroked his nose, speaking softly to him all the while. Within a few minutes they were both mounted on the great white horse and were trotting down the hillside and into the farmyard, where the chickens scattered in panic at their approach. The noise brought Farmer Veluna and Molly running out of the back door, where they were faced with the terrifying spectacle of their two children perched precariously upon a massive white stallion of at least seventeen hands. The horse snorted in excitement, tossing its head and pawing the yard, sending sparks flying along the cobbles into the dark.

Arthur told their story breathlessly. With the evidence of the horse before their eyes and the obvious sincerity in Arthur's voice, it was difficult for his father or mother to harbor any doubt but that the story was indeed true. Certainly they knew Arthur had a wild and fertile imagination and was impetuous enough at times, but with Annie sitting astride the horse in front of him, laughing aloud with delight and adding her own details from time to time, both Farmer and Molly were very soon completely convinced.

"Look in the barn, Father," Arthur proclaimed with absolute confidence. "The little man said there'd be enough seed in there to make a start. We can save the farm, Father, I know we can. The seed will be there, I'm sure of it. Have a look, Father."

Farmer Veluna crossed the yard on his own and opened wide the great barn doors. They saw the light go on, bathing the yard in a yellow glow, and they heard a whoop of joy before Farmer Veluna came running out again. He was laughing as he used to laugh.

"Well, I'll eat my hat," he said, and stuffed the peak of his flat cap into his mouth. Annie and Arthur knew then they had found their father again. "We have a horse and we have the seed," Farmer Veluna said. "There's all my father's old horse-drawn equipment in the old cart shed, and I think I know where I can find his old set of harness. It's up in the attic, isn't it, Molly?" But he did not wait for a reply. "It may be a bit small for this giant of a horse, but it'll stretch. It'll fit—it's got to fit. Course, I've never worked a horse, but Father did and I watched him years ago and followed him often enough in the fields. I'll pick it up; it shouldn't be too difficult. We've got a chance," he said. "We've a chance, children, a sporting chance."

And from that moment on there was no more talk of selling up.

Plowing started the following morning just after dawn. The ground was just dry enough, the earth turning cleanly from the shares. The horse proved tireless in the fields. They had sold every bale of hay, so he had to pick enough sustenance from the cold wet autumn grass; but that seemed to be enough for him, for the horse plowed on that day well into the evening, and came back for more the next day and the next and the next.

It was clear at the outset that the horse had an uncanny instinct for the land. He knew how tight to turn, what speed to go, without ever having to be told. When his father tired, Arthur could walk behind the plow and simply follow the horse down the furrows and around the headlands until the job was done. If he stumbled and fell in the furrows, as he often did, the horse would wait for him to regain his feet before leaning again into his harness, taking the strain, and plodding off down the field.

Within three weeks all the corn fields along the valley were plowed, harrowed, and drilled with barley. Word spread quickly around the parish that Farmer Veluna was laughing again and they came visiting once more to stand at the gate with him and admire his miraculous workhorse.

"No diesel, nothing to go wrong; he'll plow the steepest land on the farm," Farmer would say with expansive pride. "Built like a tank, but gentle as a lamb. See for yourself. Arthur can manage him on his own—and he's only nine, you know. Have you ever seen anything like it?"

"Where the devil did you get him from?" they would ask, because they had heard all kinds of rumors.

And he would tell them the story of the little Knocker man on the moor who had come to their rescue, but no one believed him. The farmers among them laughed knowingly at the story and told Farmer Veluna to pull the other one; but they did not press him, for they knew well enough that a farmer will never disclose the source of his good fortune. But at home their wives knew better, and the story of the amazing white horse of Zennor spread along the coast like thistledown in the wind. But in spite of their skepticism all their friends were delighted to see Farmer Veluna his old self again, and they determined to help him succeed. So one winter's night in the Tinners' Arms they got together and worked out how they might help the Farmer back on his feet whether he wanted their help or not. They knew he was proud, as they were, so that any help had to be both anonymous and unreturnable.

So it was that on Christmas morning when Farmer Veluna and his family returned home after church, they found their yard filled with milling animals: three sows and a boar, half a dozen geese, five cows with suckling calves, and at least twenty-five ewes. Puzzled and not a little suspicious, Farmer Veluna phoned all around the parish to find out who owned the wandering animals that had converged on his yard, but no one seemed to know anything about them and no one claimed them. He was about to contact the police in Penzance when Arthur and Annie came running into the kitchen, their voices shrill with excitement.

"The barn," Annie shouted. "It's full, full of hay and straw."

"And there's feed," Arthur said. "Sacks and sacks of it, enough to last us through the winter."

"It's that Knocker again," Farmer Veluna said, and the children believed him; but Molly, with a woman's intuition, knew better but said nothing.

The winter was long and hard that year, but with the sounds of the farm all around them again and the winter corn shooting up green in the fields, Farmer and his family were more than content. The white horse wintered out in a sheltered field behind the old granary. He grew a long white shaggy coat so that he seemed even more vast than ever. Whenever he was not needed hauling the dung cart or carrying hay bales out to the cattle on the farm, Annie would ride him out over the moor and down through the fields to the cliffs. He was, of course, far too big for her to control, but she had no fear of horses and found that no control was needed anyway. A gentle word in his ear, a pat of encouragement on his great arching neck, and he would instantly do what she wanted. It was not obedience, and Annie recognized that; it was simply that the horse wished to please her. He would go like the wind, jump any ditch or fence he was asked to, and seemed as surefooted on the hills as a goat. But it was on one of these rides that Annie first discovered that he had an inclination to make his way toward the cliffs, and once there he would stand looking out to the open sea, ears pricked to the cry of the wheeling gulls and the thunder of the surf against the cliffs. He was always reluctant to turn away for home, calling out at the last over his shoulder and turning back his ears as if expecting some kind of reply.

After just such a ride Annie finally decided upon a name for the horse. No name seemed to have suited until now. "He'll be called Pegasus," she declared, and no one argued, for she had become vehemently possessive, scolding both Arthur and her father if they worked him too hard on the farm or did not look after him as well as she thought they should have done. She groomed him regularly every morning and picked out his feet. She it was who toweled him down after work and rubbed in the soothing salted water so that the harness would not make him sore. She was passionately proud of him and would ride tall through the village when she rode out with the hunt, soaking in the admiration and envy of both riders and spectators alike. There was not a horse in the parish to touch him, and even other horses seemed to sense it, moving nervously away whenever he approached. There were some who doubted that any horse could jump just as well as he could plow, but when they witnessed his performance in the chase any doubts vanished at once. Where others pulled aside to find a lower hedge or a narrower ditch, Pegasus sailed over with apparent ease. He outpaced every horse in the field, and Annie used no whip and no spur, for none were needed. He was, she said glowingly when she got back home, as strong as any tractor, as bold as a hunter, and as fast as a racehorse. Pegasus had become a local celebrity, and Annie basked in his reflected glory.

With the spring drying out the land Pegasus turned cart horse once more and was hitched up for the spring plowing. Farmer Veluna had enough seed for two small fields of oats, and Pegasus went to it with a will; but both Arthur and his father now noticed that the horse would pause, ears pricked, at the end of the furrow nearest to the sea; and it was quite apparent that the furrows going down the hill toward the cliffs in the distance were sometimes plowed more quickly and therefore less deeply than the furrows leading back to the farmhouse.

"Most horses speed up on the way back home; that's what I thought," said Farmer Veluna. "Can't understand it, doesn't make sense."

"But you can't expect him to behave like an ordinary horse, father," said Arthur, "'cause he isn't an ordinary horse. Just look at him, Father, he'd plow this field all on his own if you let him. Go on, Father, try it, let him do it."

Farmer Veluna let go of the plow more to please his son than anything else and allowed the horse to move on alone. As they watched in amazement the plow remained straight as an arrow, and inch-perfect in depth. Pegasus turned slowly and came back toward them, his line immaculate and parallel. Arthur and his father picked the stones out of the furrows as evening fell while Pegasus plowed up and down the field until the last furrow was complete. Then they ran over the field toward him to guide him around the headlands, but Pegasus had already turned and was making the first circuit of the field. At that moment both Arthur and his father finally understood what Annie already knew, that this was a miraculous creature that needed no help from them or from anyone.

Annie fitted in her rides whenever she thought Pegasus was rested enough after his work, but as the blackthorn withered and the fuchsia began to bud in the early summer, Pegasus was more and more occupied on the farm. At the end of June he cut a fine crop of sweet meadow hay, turned it, and baled it. He took cartloads of farmyard manure out into the fields for spreading. He cut thistles and docks and bracken in the steeper fields up near the moor. Hitched up with a great chain, he pulled huge granite rocks out of the ground and dragged them into the hedgerows. In the blazing heat of high summer he hauled the water tanks out onto the farthest fields, and in August harvested the corn he had drilled the autumn before.

The barley crop was so rich that summer that Farmer Veluna was able to sell so much to the merchants that he could buy in more suckling cows and calves, as well as his first ten milking cows, the beginnings of his new dairy herd. As autumn began the milking parlor throbbed into life once more—but he had not forgotten to keep back twelve sacks of seed corn that he owed to the little Knocker.

The sows had farrowed well and there were already fat pigs to sell; and some of the lambs were already big enough to go to market. The hens were laying well, even in the heat, and the goslings would be ready for Christmas.

But in spite of the recovery and all it meant to the family, the mood of the farmhouse was far from happy, for as the summer nights shortened and the blackberries ripened in the hedgerows, they knew that their year with Pegasus was almost over. Annie spent all her time now with him, taking him out every day for long rides down to the cliffs where she knew he loved to be. Until dusk each evening she would sit astride him, gazing with him out to sea, before turning him away and walking slowly up Trevail Valley, through Wicca Farm, and back home over the moor.

When the time came that September evening, a year and a day from the first meeting with the Knocker, Annie and Arthur led the horse by his long white mane up onto the high moors. Arthur wanted to comfort his sister for he could feel the grief she was suffering. He said nothing but put his hand into hers and clasped it tight. As they neared the cheesewring rocks and moved out along the track across the moor toward the ruined count-house, Pegasus lifted his head and whinnied excitedly. There was a new spring in his step and his ears twitched back and forth as they approached the count-house. Annie let go of his mane and whispered softly. "Off you go, Pegasus," she said. Pegasus looked down at her as if reassuring himself that she meant what she said, and then trotted out ahead of them and down into the ruins until he was hidden from their view. The children followed him, clambering laboriously over the walls.

As they dropped down into the count-house they saw that the horse was gone and in his place was the little old Knocker, who waved to them cheerily. "Good as your word," he said.

"So were you," Arthur said. "Father is a happy man again, and it won't be long before we'll be milking fifty cows, like we were before. Father says we'll be able to afford a tractor soon."

"Where's he gone?" Annie asked in a voice as com-

posed as her tears would allow. "Where's Pegasus gone?"

"Out there," said the Knocker, pointing out to sea. "Look out there. Can you see the white horses playing, d'you see their waving manes? Can you hear them calling? Don't be sad, Annie," he said kindly. "He loves it out there with his friends. A year on the land was a year of exile for him. But you were so good to him, Annie, and for that reason he'll come back to you this one night in every year. That's a promise. Be here up on the moor and he'll come every year for as long as you want him to."

And he does come, one autumn night in every year, as the old Knocker promised. So if you happen to be walking up towards Zennor Quoit one moon-bright autumn night with the mists hovering over the valley and the sea shining below the Eagle's Nest, and if you hear the pounding of hoofbeats and see a white horse come out of the moon and thunder over the moor, you will know that it is Annie, Annie and the white horse of Zennor.

The Chimera

NATHANIEL HAWTHORNE

The white horse in the last story was called Pegasus by the children. This is the story of the original Pegasus—the flying horse who, in a myth of ancient Greece, helped to overcome a dreadful monster. Nathaniel Hawthorne was an American who wrote two famous books retelling Greek myths and legends. This story is slightly abridged from the original version, which appears in The Wonder Book.

Once, in the old, old times a fountain gushed out of a hillside, in the marvelous land of Greece. And, for aught I know, it is still gushing out of the selfsame spot. At any rate, there was the fountain, welling freshly forth and sparkling in the golden sunset, when a handsome young man named Bellerophon drew near its margin. In his hand he held a bridle, studded with brilliant gems and adorned with a golden bit. Seeing an old man, and another of middle age, and a little boy near the fountain, and a maiden, who was dipping up some of the water in a pitcher, he said to the maiden, "Will you be kind enough to tell me whether the fountain has any name?"

"Yes; it is called the Fountain of Pirene," answered the maiden.

"I thank you, pretty maiden, for telling me its name.

I have come from a faraway country to find this very spot," said Bellerophon.

The middle-aged country fellow (he had driven his cow to drink out of the spring) stared hard at Bellerophon and at the handsome bridle that he carried in his hand.

"The watercourses must be getting low in your part of the world," remarked he, "if you come so far to find the Fountain of Pirene. But have you lost a horse? I see you carry the bridle in your hand, and a very pretty one it is. If the horse was as fine as the bridle, you are much to be pitied for losing him."

"I have lost no horse," said Bellerophon, with a smile. "But I happen to be seeking a very famous one, which must be found hereabouts, if anywhere. Do you know whether the winged horse Pegasus still haunts the Fountain of Pirene, as he used to do?"

But the country fellow laughed.

Pegasus was a snow-white steed, with beautiful silvery wings, who spent most of his time on the summit of Mount Helicon. He was as wild, and as swift, and as buoyant, in his flight through the air, as any eagle that ever soared into the clouds. There was nothing else like him in the world. He had no mate; he had never been backed or bridled by a master; and for many a long year he led a solitary and a happy life.

In the summertime, and in the beautifullest of weather, Pegasus often alighted on the solid earth, and, closing his silvery wings, would gallop over hill and dale for pastime, as fleetly as the wind. Oftener than in any other place, he had been seen near the Fountain of Pirene, drinking the delicious water, or rolling himself upon the soft grass of the bank. Sometimes, too, he would crop a few of the clover blossoms that happened to be sweetest.

To the Fountain of Pirene, therefore, people had been in the habit of going (as long as they were youthful, and retained their faith in winged horses), in hopes of getting a glimpse of the beautiful Pegasus. But, of late years, he had been very seldom seen. Indeed, there were many country folk who had never beheld Pegasus, and did not believe that there was any such creature. The country fellow to whom Bellerophon was speaking chanced to be one.

And that was the reason why he laughed.

"Pegasus, indeed!" cried he, turning up his nose. "A winged horse, truly! Why, friend, are you in your senses? Of what use would wings be to a horse? No, no! I don't believe in Pegasus. There never was such a ridiculous kind of a horse-fowl made!"

"I have reason to think otherwise," said Bellerophon quietly.

And then he turned to an old gray man, who was leaning on a staff and listening very attentively, with his head stretched forward, and one hand at his ear, because, for the last twenty years he had been getting rather deaf.

"And what say you?" inquired Bellerophon. "In your younger days, I should imagine you must frequently have seen the winged steed!"

"Ah, young stranger, my memory is very poor!" said the aged man. "When I was a lad, if I remember rightly, I used to believe there was such a horse, and so did everybody else. But, nowadays, I hardly know what to think, and very seldom think about the winged horse at all."

"And have you never seen him?" asked Bellerophon of the girl.

"Once I thought I saw him," replied the maiden, with a smile and a blush. "It was either Pegasus, or a large white bird, a very great way up in the air. And one other time, as I was coming to the fountain with my pitcher, I heard a neigh. Oh, such a brisk and melodious neigh as that was! But it startled me, so that I ran home without filling my pitcher."

"That was a pity!" said Bellerophon.

And he turned to the child.

"I suppose you have often seen the winged horse?"

"That I have," answered the child. "I saw him yesterday, and many times before."

"Come, tell me all about it," said Bellerophon.

"Why," replied the child, "I often come here to sail little boats in the fountain. And sometimes, when I look down into the water, I see the image of a winged horse, in the picture of the sky that is there. But, if I so much as stir to look at him, he flies far away, out of sight."

And Bellerophon put his faith in the child, who had seen the image of Pegasus in the water, and in the maiden, who had heard him neigh so melodiously, rather than in the middle-aged clown, or in the old man, who had forgotten the beautiful things of his youth.

He hunted about the Fountain of Pirene for a great many days afterward. He kept continually on the watch, looking upward at the sky, or else down into the water, hoping that he should see either the reflected image of the winged horse, or the marvelous reality. He held the bridle, with its bright gems and golden bit, always ready in his hand.

Now you will, perhaps, wish to be told why it was that Bellerophon had undertaken to catch the winged horse.

In a certain country of Asia, a terrible monster, called a Chimera, had made its appearance, and was doing more mischief than could be talked about between now and sunset. This Chimera was nearly, if not quite, the ugliest and most poisonous creature, and the strangest and unaccountablest, and the hardest to fight with, and the most difficult to run away from, that ever came out of the earth's inside. It had a tail like a boa constrictor; its body was like I do not care what; and it had three separate heads, one of which was a lion's, the second a goat's, and the third an abominably great snake's. And a hot blast of fire came flaming out of each of its three mouths! Being an earthly monster, I doubt whether it had any wings; but, wings or no, it ran like a goat and a lion, and wriggled along like a serpent, and thus contrived to make about as much speed as all the three together.

With its flaming breath it could set a forest on fire, or burn up a field of grain, or, for that matter, a village, with all its fences and houses. It laid waste the whole country around about and used to eat people and animals alive, and cook them afterward in the burning oven of its stomach.

While the hateful beast was doing all these horrible things, it so chanced that Bellerophon came to that part of the world, on a visit to the king. The king's name was Iobates, and Lycia was the country which he ruled over. Bellerophon was one of the bravest youths in the world, and desired nothing so much as to do some valiant deed, such as would make all mankind admire and love him. In those days, the only way for a young man to distinguish himself was by fighting battles, either with the enemies of his country, or with wicked giants, or with troublesome dragons, or with wild beasts, when he could find nothing more dangerous to encounter. King Iobates, perceiving the courage of his youthful visitor, proposed to him to go and fight the Chimera, which everybody else was afraid of, and which, unless it should be soon killed, was likely to convert Lycia into a desert. Bellerophon hesitated not a moment, but assured the king that he would either slay this dreaded Chimera, or perish in the attempt.

But, in the first place, as the monster was so prodigiously swift, he thought that he should never win the victory by fighting on foot. The wisest thing he could do was to get the very best and fleetest horse that could anywhere be found. And what other horse in all the world was half so fleet as the marvelous horse Pegasus, who had wings as well as legs, and was even more active in the air than on the earth? A great many people denied that there was any such horse with wings, and said that the stories about him were all poetry and nonsense. But Bellerophon believed that Pegasus was a real steed, and hoped that he himself might be fortunate enough to find him; and, once mounted on his back, he would be able to fight the Chimera at better advantage.

And this was the purpose with which he had traveled from Lycia to Greece, and had brought the beautifully ornamental bridle in his hand. It was an enchanted bridle. If he could only succeed in putting the golden bit into the mouth of Pegasus, the winged horse would be submissive, and own Bellerophon for his master, and fly whithersoever he might choose to turn the rein.

But it was a weary and anxious time, while

Bellerophon waited and waited for Pegasus, in hopes that he would come and drink at the Fountain of Pirene. He was afraid lest King Iobates should imagine that he had fled from the Chimera. It pained him, too, to think how much mischief the monster was doing, while he himself, instead of fighting with it, was compelled to sit idly poring over the bright waters of Pirene, as they gushed out of the sparkling sand. Well was it for Bellerophon that the child had grown fond of him, and was never weary of keeping him company.

If it had not been for the little boy's unwavering faith, Bellerophon would have given up all hope, and would have gone back to Lycia, and have done his best to slay the Chimera without the help of the winged horse. And in that case poor Bellerophon would at least have been terribly scorched by the creature's breath, and would most probably have been killed or devoured.

One morning the child spoke to Bellerophon even more hopefully than usual. "I know not why it is, but I feel as if we should certainly see Pegasus today!"

And all that day he would not stir a step from Bellerophon's side.

But, when he least thought of it, Bellerophon felt the pressure of the child's little hand, and heard a soft, almost breathless whisper: "See there, Bellerophon! There is an image in the water!"

The young man looked down into the dimpling mirror of the fountain, and saw what he took to be the reflection of a bird which seemed to be flying at a great height in the air, with a gleam of sunshine on its snowy or silvery wings.

"What a splendid bird it must be!" said he. "And

how very large it looks, though it must really be flying higher than the clouds!"

"It makes me tremble!" whispered the child. "I am afraid to look up into the air! It is very beautiful, and yet I dare only look at its image in the water. Bellerophon, do you not see that it is no bird? It is the winged horse, Pegasus!"

Bellerophon caught the child in his arms, and shrank back with him, so that they were both hidden among the thick shrubbery which grew all around the fountain. Not that he was afraid of any harm, but he dreaded lest, if Pegasus caught a glimpse of them, he would fly far away, and alight in some inaccessible mountaintop. For it was really the winged horse. After they had expected him so long, he was coming to quench his thirst with the water of Pirene.

Downward came Pegasus, in those wide sweeping circles, which grew narrower and narrower still, as he gradually approached the earth. The nigher the view of him, the more beautiful he was, and the more marvelous the sweep of his silvery wings. At last, with so slight a pressure as hardly to bend the grass about the fountain, or imprint a hoof tramp in the sand of its margin, he alighted, and, stooping his wild head, began to drink. He drew in the water with long and pleasant sighs and tranquil pauses of enjoyment; and then another draft, and another and another. And when his thirst was slaked, he cropped a few of the honey blossoms of the clover.

At length Pegasus folded his wings and lay down on the soft green turf. But, being too full of aerial life to remain quiet for many moments together, he soon rolled over on his back, with his four slender legs in the air. It was beautiful to see him, this one solitary

creature, whose mate had never been created, but who needed no companion, and, living a great many hundred years, was as happy as the centuries were long. The more he did such things as mortal horses are accustomed to do, the less earthly and more wonderful he seemed. Bellerophon and the child held their breath, because they dreaded lest the slightest stir or murmur should send him up, with the speed of an arrow flight, into the furthest blue of the sky.

Finally, when he had had enough of rolling over and over, Pegasus turned himself about, and, indolently, like any other horse, put out his forelegs, in order to rise from the ground; and Bellerophon, who had guessed that he would do so, darted suddenly from the thicket, and leaped astride of his back.

Yes, there he sat, on the back of the winged horse!

But what a bound did Pegasus make when, for the first time, he felt the weight of a mortal man upon his loins! Before he had time to draw a breath, Bellerophon found himself five hundred feet aloft, and still shooting upward, while the winged horse snorted and trembled with terror and anger. Upward he went, up, up, up, until he plunged into a cloud. Then out of the heart of the cloud, Pegasus shot down like a thunderbolt, as if he meant to dash both himself and his rider headlong against a rock. Then he went through about a thousand of the wildest caprioles that had ever been performed either by a bird or a horse.

He skimmed straight forward, and sideways, and backward. He reared himself erect. He flung out his heels behind, and put down his head between his legs, with his wings pointing right upward. At about two miles' height above the earth, he turned a somersault, so that Bellerophon's heels were where his head should have been, and he seemed to look down into the sky, instead of up. He twisted his head about, and looking Bellerophon in the face, with fire flashing from his eyes, made a terrible attempt to bite him. He fluttered his pinions so wildly that one of the silver feathers was shaken out, and, floating earthward, was picked up by the child, who kept it as long as he lived, in memory of Pegasus and Bellerophon.

But the latter (who was as good a horseman as ever galloped) had been watching his opportunity, and at last clapped the golden bit of the enchanted bridle between the winged steed's jaws. No sooner was this done than Pegasus became as manageable as if he had taken food, all his life, out of Bellerophon's hand. It was almost a sadness to see so wild a creature grow suddenly so tame. And Pegasus seemed to feel it so, likewise. He looked around to Bellerophon, with tears in his beautiful eyes, instead of the fire that so recently flashed from them. But when Bellerophon patted his head, and spoke a few kind and soothing words, another look came into the eyes of Pegasus; for he was glad at heart, after so many lonely centuries, to have found a companion and a master.

While Pegasus had been doing his utmost to shake Bellerophon off his back, he had flown a very long distance; and they had come within sight of a lofty mountain by the time the bit was in his mouth. Bellerophon had seen this mountain before, and knew it to be Helicon, on the summit of which was the winged horse's abode. Thither Pegasus now flew, and, alighting, waited patiently until Bellerophon should dismount. The young man leaped from his steed's back, but still held him fast by the bridle. Meeting his eyes he was so affected by the gentleness of his aspect, and by his beauty, and by the thought of the free life which Pegasus had heretofore lived, that he could not bear to keep him a prisoner, if he really desired his liberty.

Obeying this generous impulse, he slipped the

enchanted bridle off the head of Pegasus and took the bit from his mouth.

"Leave me, Pegasus," said he. "Either leave me or love me."

In an instant, the winged horse shot almost out of sight, soaring straight upward from the summit of Mount Helicon. Being long after sunset, it was now twilight on the mountaintop, and dusky evening over all the country around about. But Pegasus flew so high that he overtook the departed day, and was bathed in the upper radiance of the sun. Ascending higher and higher, he looked like a bright speck, and, at last, could no longer be seen in the hollow waste of the sky. And Bellerophon was afraid that he should never behold him more. But the bright speck reappeared, and drew nearer and nearer, and Pegasus had come back! After this trial, there was no more fear of the winged horse making his escape. He and Bellerophon were friends, and put loving faith in one another.

That night they lay down and slept together, with Bellerophon's arm about the neck of Pegasus. And they awoke at peep of day, and bade one another good morning, each in his own language.

In this manner, Bellerophon and the wondrous steed spent several days, and grew better acquainted and fonder of each other all the time. Bellerophon was delighted with this kind of life, and would have liked nothing better than to live always in the same way, aloft in the clear atmosphere. But he could not forget the horrible Chimera, which he had promised King Iobates to slay. So, at last, when he had become well accustomed to feats of horsemanship in the air, and could manage Pegasus with the least motion of his hand, and had taught him to obey his voice, he determined to attempt the performance of this perilous adventure.

At daybreak, therefore, as soon as he unclosed his eyes, he gently pinched the winged horse's ear, in order to arouse him. Pegasus immediately started from the ground, and pranced about a quarter of a mile aloft, and made a grand sweep around the mountaintop, by way of showing that he was wide awake and ready for any kind of an excursion. During the whole of this little flight, he uttered a loud, brisk, and melodious neigh, and finally came down at Bellerophon's side, as lightly as ever you saw a sparrow hop upon a twig.

"Well done, dear Pegasus! Well done, my sky-skimmer!" cried Bellerophon, fondly stroking the horse's neck. "And now, my fleet and beautiful friend, we must break our fast. Today we are to fight the terrible Chimera."

As soon as they had eaten their morning meal, and drunk some sparkling water from a spring called Hippocrene, Pegasus held out his head, so that his master might put on the bridle. Then, with a great many playful leaps and airy caperings, he showed his impatience to be gone, while Bellerophon was girding on his sword, and hanging his shield about his neck, and preparing himself for battle. When everything was ready, the rider mounted, turned the head of Pegasus toward the east, and set out for Lycia. It was still early when they beheld the lofty mountains of Lycia, with their deep and shaggy valleys. If Bellerophon had been told truly, it was in one of those dismal valleys that the hideous Chimera had taken up its abode.

As they were so near their journey's end, the winged

horse gradually descended with his rider. Hovering on the upper surface of a cloud, and peeping over its edge, Bellerophon had a pretty distinct view of the mountainous part of Lycia, and could look into all its shadowy vales at once. At first there appeared to be nothing remarkable. It was a wild, savage, and rocky tract of high and precipitous hills. In the more level part of the country, there were ruins of houses that had been burned, and, here and there, the carcasses of dead cattle strewn about the pastures where they had been feeding.

"The Chimera must have done this mischief," thought Bellerophon. "But where can the monster be?"

There was nothing remarkable to be detected, at first sight, in any of the valleys and dells that lay among the precipitous heights of the mountains. Nothing at all; unless, indeed, it were three spires of black smoke, which issued from what seemed to be the mouth of a cavern, and clambered sullenly into the atmosphere. The cavern was almost directly beneath the winged horse and his rider, at the distance of about a thousand feet. The smoke, as it crept heavily upward, had an ugly, sulfurous scent, which caused Pegasus to snort and Bellerophon to sneeze.

But, on looking behind him, Bellerophon saw something that induced him first to draw the bridle, and then to turn Pegasus about. The winged horse sank slowly through the air, until his hooves were scarcely more than a man's height above the rocky bottom of the valley. In front, as far off as you could throw a stone, was the cavern's mouth, with the three smoke-wreaths oozing out of it.

There seemed to be a heap of strange and terrible

creatures curled up within the cavern. Their bodies lay so close together that Bellerophon could not distinguish them; but, judging by their heads, one of these creatures was a huge snake, the second a fierce lion, and the third an ugly goat. The lion and the goat were asleep; the snake was broad awake, and kept staring about him with a great pair of fiery eyes. But the three spires of smoke evidently issued from the nostrils of these three heads!

All at once Bellerophon knew it to be the Chimera. Pegasus seemed to know it, at the same instant, and sent forth a neigh that sounded like the call of a trumpet to battle. At this sound the three heads reared themselves erect, and belched out great flashes of flame. Before Bellerophon had time to consider what to do next, the monster flung itself out of the cavern and sprang straight toward him, with its immense claws extended. If Pegasus had not been as nimble as a bird, both he and his rider would have been overthrown by the Chimera's headlong rush, and thus the battle have been ended before it was well begun. But the winged horse was not to be caught so. In the twinkling of an eye he was up aloft, halfway to the clouds, snorting with anger. He shuddered, too, not with affright, but with utter disgust at the loathsomeness of this poisonous thing with three heads.

The Chimera, on the other hand, raised itself up so as to stand absolutely on the tip-end of its tail, with its talons pawing fiercely in the air, and its three heads spluttering fire at Pegasus and his rider. How it roared, and hissed, and bellowed! Bellerophon, meanwhile, was fitting his shield on his arm and drawing his sword.

"Now, my beloved Pegasus," he whispered in the

winged horse's ear, "thou must help me to slay this insufferable monster; or else thou shalt fly back to thy solitary mountain peak without thy friend Bellerophon. For either the Chimera dies, or its three mouths shall gnaw this head of mine!"

Pegasus whinnied, and, turning back his head, rubbed his nose tenderly against his rider's cheek. It was his way of telling him that, though he had wings and was an immortal horse, yet he would perish, if it were possible for immortality to perish, rather than leave Bellerophon behind.

"I thank, you Pegasus," answered Bellerophon. "Now, then, let us make a dash at the monster!"

He shook the bridle; and Pegasus darted down aslant, as swift as the flight of an arrow, right towards the Chimera's threefold head, which was poking itself as high as it could into the air. As he came within arm's length, Bellerophon made a cut at the monster, but was carried onward by his steed before he could see whether the blow had been successful. Pegasus continued his course, but soon wheeled around. Bellerophon then perceived that he had cut the goat's head of the monster almost off, so that it dangled downward by the skin, and seemed quite dead.

But, to make amends, the snake's head and the lion's head had taken all the fierceness from the dead one into themselves, and spat flame, and hissed, and roared, with more fury than before.

"Never mind, my brave Pegasus!" cried Bellerophon. "With another stroke like that, we will stop either its hissing or its roaring."

And again he shook the bridle. Dashing aslantwise as before, the winged horse made another arrow-flight toward the Chimera, and Bellerophon aimed another downright stroke at one of the two remaining heads as he shot by. But this time neither he nor Pegasus escaped so well as at first. With one of its claws the Chimera had given the young man a deep scratch in his shoulder, and had slightly damaged the left wing of the flying steed with the other. On his part Bellerophon had mortally wounded the lion's head of the monster. It now hung with its fire almost extinguished, and sending out gasps of thick black smoke. The snake's head, however (which was the only one left), was twice as fierce and venomous as ever before. It belched forth shoots of fire five hundred yards long, and emitted hisses so loud, so harsh, and so ear-piercing that King Iobates heard them fifty miles off, and trembled till the throne shook under him.

"Welladay!" thought the poor king. "The Chimera is certainly coming to devour me!"

Meanwhile Pegasus had again paused in the air, and neighed angrily, while sparkles of a pure crystal flame darted out of his eyes. How unlike the lurid fire of the Chimera!

"Dost thou bleed, my immortal horse?" cried the young man, caring less for his own hurt than for the anguish of this glorious creature, that ought never to have tasted pain. "The execrable Chimera shall pay for this mischief with his last head!"

Then he shook the bridle, shouted loudly, and guided Pegasus, not aslantwise as before, but straight at the monster's hideous front. So rapid was the onset, that it seemed but a dazzle and a flash, before Bellerophon was at close grips with his enemy.

The Chimera by this time, after losing its second head, had got into a red-hot passion of pain and rampant rage. It so flounced about, half on earth and partly in the air, that it was impossible to say which element it rested upon. It opened its snake jaws to such a width, that Pegasus might have flown right down its throat, wings outspread, rider and all! At their approach, it shot out a tremendous blast of its fiery breath, and enveloped Bellerophon and his steed in flame.

But this was nothing to what followed.

When the airy rush of the winged horse had brought him within a hundred yards, the Chimera gave a spring, and flung its huge awkward, venomous, and utterly destestable carcass right upon poor Pegasus, clung round him with might and main, and tied up its snaky tail into a knot! Up flew the aerial steed, higher, higher, higher, above the mountain peaks, above the clouds, and almost out of sight of the solid earth. But still the earth-born monster kept its hold, and was borne upward, along with the creature of light and air. Bellerophon, meanwhile, turning about found himself face to face with the ugly grimness of the Chimera's visage, and could only avoid being scorched to death, or bitten right in twain, by holding up his shield. Over the upper edge of the shield he looked sternly into the savage eyes of the monster.

But the Chimera was so mad and wild with pain, that it did not guard itself. In its efforts to stick its horrible iron claws into its enemy, the creature left its own breast quite exposed; and perceiving this, Bellerophon thrust his sword up to the hilt into its cruel heart. Immediately the snaky tail untied its knot. The monster let go its hold of Pegasus, and fell from that vast height, downward: while the fire, instead of being put out, burned fiercer than ever, and quickly began to consume the dead carcass. Thus it fell out of the sky, all aflame. At early sunrise, some cottagers were going to their day's labor, and saw, to their astonishment, that several acres of ground were strewn with black ashes. In the middle of a field there was a heap of whitened bones. Nothing else was ever seen of the dreadful Chimera.

And when Bellerophon had won the victory, he bent forward and kissed Pegasus, while the tears stood in his eyes.

"Back now," said he. "Back to the Fountain of Pirene!"

Pegasus skimmed through the air, quicker than ever he did before, and reached the fountain in a very short time. And there he found the old man leaning on his staff, and the country fellow watering his cow, and the pretty maiden filling her pitcher.

"Where is the child," asked Bellerophon, "who used to keep me company, and never lost his faith?"

"Here I am!" said the child softly.

For the little boy had spent day after day, on the banks of Pirene, waiting for his friend to come back; but when he perceived Bellerophon descending through the clouds, mounted on the winged horse, he had shrunk back into the shrubbery.

"Thou has won the victory," said he joyfully, running to the knee of Bellerophon, who still sat on the back of Pegasus. "I knew thou wouldst."

"Yes!" replied Bellerophon, alighting from the winged horse. "But if thy faith had not helped me, I should never have waited for Pegasus, and never have gone up above the clouds, and never have conquered the terrible Chimera. And now let us give Pegasus his liberty."

So he slipped off the enchanted bridle from the head of the marvelous steed.

"Be free forevermore, my Pegasus!" cried he. "Be as free as thou art fleet!"

But Pegasus rested his head on Bellerophon's shoulder, and would not be persuaded to take flight.

"Well, then," said Bellerophon, caressing the airy horse, "thou shalt be with me as long as thou wilt; and we will go together and tell King Iobates that the Chimera is destroyed."

Then Bellerophon embraced the child, and departed.

Bone of Contention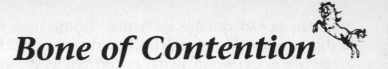

JOSEPHINE PULLEIN-THOMPSON

This is an exciting adventure story, in which ponies help villagers and prove their worth during a flood. Most riders will have met people who don't like horses, like Mr. Judd, and the fact that at the end of the story the children and Mr. Judd haven't really made friends seems realistic. Josephine Pullein-Thompson is one of three sisters all famous for writing pony stories. It must run in the family, for their mother, Joanna Cannan, was also well-known for hers.

Our quarrel with Mr. Judd over the path to the river began in the Easter holidays. It had been a wet spring and it was true that the ponies' hooves had cut up the path and made it muddy, but then if you live in the country you expect mud; Mr. Judd didn't.

He was a tall man, always neatly dressed, with watery eyes and a long, wandering nose. He had only moved to Hazebourne when he retired, and I think perhaps he thought of the country as a sort of dream place: thatched cottages and hollyhocks and just enough rain to water the garden. But Riverside Cottage was a real place, and his dream very nearly ended in disaster.

Anyway, when Mr. Judd first leaned over his new wrought-iron gate and complained about the state of the path, we explained politely that the mud was due to the exceptionally wet spring and that it would dry up as soon as the weather changed. When he began to shout at us that the path was a footpath and that horses weren't allowed, we had shouted back that it was a bridle path and had been for centuries. Steve had added cheekily that, anyway, Pumpkin wasn't a horse, but a pony.

My brother, Charles, and I had lived in Hazebourne since we were four and two, so naturally we knew quite a lot about the history of the village and we'd been told that our stretch of the river had once been an important link between two canals; in the old days, when the barges were moored along Riverside for the night, the towing horses had been led up the path, past the church, to the Ship Inn, which still has stables. So there was no doubt at all that it *was* a bridle path, and for all of us it was an important shortcut, taking us to the bridge and the towpath, where all our favorite rides begin, in a matter of minutes. Then there was another problem, for though Charles's speckled gray Sheikh and my dark brown Titus were wise and sensible animals, Georgie's Legend, a pretty-looking chestnut with white socks, was terrible in traffic. It would be a nightmare if we had to start our rides along the Seaton road, with huge trucks tearing past every twenty seconds, and then fight our way down the narrow village street, which is always jammed with cars and vans and pedestrians, so you can see that we had good reason to be alarmed and angry when we found that Mr. Judd had declared war over the path.

The Dawsons (Georgie and Steve) and the Cliftons (that's Charles and me) are the only two horsy families in Hazebourne, so it's natural that we ride together, but besides, Georgie and I go to the same school and she really likes Charles. I'm not sure if he's so keen on her; when I ask him he says she's OK. I think he prefers another friend of mine called Amanda, but she lives miles away and isn't horsy.

Anyway, we always ride together, and you can see at a glance that we're two separate families: the Dawsons are small with dark curly hair and brownish faces, and Charles and I are large and fair with dead-straight hair.

When we met for our first ride of the summer holidays we spent some time discussing where to go and exclaiming over our ponies' disgusting state of fatness—Pumpkin in particular looked fit to burst—before we set off down the path. We were amazed when we found the notice. It was a huge wooden board screwed to a stout post and in large red letters it stated:

FOOTPATH ONLY
NO HORSES ALLOWED

Our amazement soon turned to fury. We looked around for our enemy and thought we saw Mrs. Judd's anxious figure scuttle into the house. Their tiny Yorkshire terrier barked at us fiercely, but there was no sign of Mr. Judd so, after some more discussion, we decided to go on with our ride and deal with the notice later.

When we told our parents they were very angry, too, and my father immediately wrote letters to the parish, rural district, and county councils and sent me to post them. But, as Charles said, councils take months if not years to settle anything, and since Mr. Judd had no right to put up the notice we had every right to hack it down. We planned to wait until dusk and then set off with saws and choppers until someone thought of paint. Then it became the easiest thing in the world to change the meaning of Mr. Judd's notice. Giggling, we rushed down the path with our brushes and pot of paint, and in minutes the notice read:

PATH. ONLY

HORSES ALLOWED

And it stayed like that for several days until we all went off to camp. We came back from camp in the usual state of collapse and gave ourselves and the ponies a couple of days off. When we'd recovered enough to go for a hack we set off down the path and found the notice had gone, but a stout new stile blocked our way. Charles dismounted and tried to dismantle it with brute force, but it was well made and he said that he would need tools. As it was only about three feet high, the two of us were shrieking at him to get out of the way so that we could jump it, for even Pumpkin, who is one of those square ponies with a leg on each corner, can heave himself over three feet in slow motion if all his friends have gone first.

When we told our parents about this new development they all wrote another spate of letters to the various committees and councils, but of course nothing actually happened. We were rather enjoying jumping the stile; after a quick look to see that there were no pedestrians about, we would gallop down the path and fly over, giving war whoops as we passed Mr. Judd's cottage. I suppose he found that very irritating, because after about three days we found the stile festooned with barbed wire and had to go back for Mr. Dawson's wire cutters. As we were going to a rally and we were already late this was very frustrating; as we rode on, having cut and jumped our way through, we thought of horrible ends for Mr. Judd. We also tried to think up some practical form of vengeance that wasn't actually illegal, but we only got as far as planning to paint the wrought-iron gate and the rose pergola some really horrible color like mauve when we arrived at the rally. As it turned out the whole village rose up against the stile. It seemed that the elderly churchgoers and the pram-pushing mothers couldn't get over it, and even the able-bodied had torn their clothes on the wire.

When we found that Mr. Judd had cleared his fortifications away we were filled with triumph and felt that we had won a great victory until rumors began that he meant to start a legal battle. However, as Charles said, the law moves at a snail's pace and it's no use bothering about things that won't happen until you're ninety, so, apart from looking straight through Mr. Judd whenever we met him in the post office or on the village street we put the whole thing out of our minds and just went on as usual.

The whole summer had been a miserably wet one, and toward the end of the holidays there were several tremendous storms, which blew down trees and spoiled all the local shows and gymkhanas. One day it rained solidly from morning to night and we were so fed up with trying to clean pale, cardboard-texture tack that we didn't ride; the next morning the Dawsons burst in, full of excitement, to say that the river had burst its banks and flooded the water meadows and we must ride at once, before the floods went down, and cure Legend's neurotic horror of water. I knew that Georgie had been eliminated at the water in two junior horse trials, after doing a super dressage test, so I agreed and we went to find Charles. He was difficult; he said that *he* was neurotic about rain and we only persuaded him to come by offering to groom and saddle Sheikh. I do think elder brothers get spoiled. Younger ones aren't so bad—at least, Georgie hardly does anything for Steve.

We had an exciting ride splashing through the water meadows and we all thought Legend looked more confident. Steve fell in when Pumpkin stopped dead on the brink of some ditch or hole, but the weather was so hot he soon dried.

We didn't go straight home by the path but rode on along Riverside to inspect the floods by the bridge. The old quay, now just a roadway in front of the cottages, was all awash and the Haze, a biggish stream that runs into the river beside the bridge, could no longer get away, for the main river, so high and swollen, had become a watery barrier. The Haze, rising rapidly, had burst its banks and water was pouring down into Riverside on one side and making a great lake where the road dipped just before the bridge on the other.

The inhabitants of Riverside seemed to have retreated upstairs. Faces watched us from the dormer windows, and old Mr. Gold called down to us. "Terrible, isn't it? They ought to do something to stop this sort of thing happening. Mr. Judd rang the council and they're sending sandbags. Sandbags! And there's a foot of water on my kitchen floor already . . ."

The next window opened and old Mrs. Hastings's face appeared.

"Could one of you do me a favor?" she called down. "Post a letter for me? It's urgent and I daren't go wading through that lot, not with my rheumatism."

We all offered at once, but Charles on the tallest horse stood in his stirrups and stretched up to take the letter.

"Do you think anyone else wants shopping done?" I asked.

Mr. Gold remembered that he was almost out of matches, and he tapped on Mrs. Carpenter's window with a broomstick until her head appeared. She was in urgent need of cat food, and Mrs. Jacks beyond had run out of aspirin and was suffering from a terrible headache. We memorized the needs and were about to set off when someone called, "What about Mrs. Judd? Best give her a call."

I was trying to think of excuses when Steve answered: "We wouldn't shop for *them*. That mean old man can starve for all we care."

Georgie and I shushed him hastily, though I must say it was rather what I was feeling, too. Charles said, "I'm afraid we've fallen out with the Judds," in a very grown-up manner, but the row of elderly faces at the windows still looked shocked.

The Pearces at the shop seemed very pleased to have us as a sort of flood relief team. Mr. Pearce, who said the poor old souls had been on his conscience, produced a haversack and made up a parcel for each cottage, adding letters and newspapers and things that other people had failed to deliver to the shopping we'd been told to get. We felt rather like four Father Christmases as we rode back through the rain. Sheikh was very helpful about standing beneath the windows and handing things up and everyone seemed pleased with our efforts. We rode off promising to come again next day if the floods were still up.

They were. It rained all night and the watery waste began halfway down the path from the church. Mr. Judd's garden had vanished and we surveyed his drowned dahlias with relish. The water in Riverside was much deeper, well above Pumpkin's knees and hocks, and the Haze was flowing backward in a very eerie manner. The cottage doors had all been sandbagged, and the faces that appeared at the upper windows all looked quite cheerful. "Council wanted to move us out," said Mrs. Carpenter indignantly. "I'm not going to no old people's home. Lived in this house sixty years, I have, and never been driven out by floods before, so why should I go now?"

They had fixed up all sorts of convenient arrangements; baskets were lowered on cords, and a sort of aerial railway carried things from window to window.

In the village street the water was higher, too. The dip by the bridge had become a rushing waterway as the Haze poured over into the meadows on the other side of the road. A few damp, dispirited children stood on the bridge, looking at it gloomily. "Do you think they want to come across?" I asked, and then, since Georgie and Charles seemed inclined to deal with the post office and shop, Steve and I went and tested the water by the bridge for depth. It was well over children's gumboot height, so when we learned that most of the children had been sent to shop we decided to ferry them across on the ponies. We found that if we took our feet out of the stirrups the children could mount and sit in front of us, and as the flood was only a few meters wide it didn't matter that we were rather squashed and uncomfortable. I had trouble hauling up one small fat boy, but most of them scrambled up quite easily and booked a lift back again before running off to do their errands in the village. Quite a lot of cars and vans came up and their drivers, having inspected the flood, decided that it was too deep and they must go the long way around by one of the other bridges, so we felt very superior on the ponies.

We ran our ferry service until the others shouted that they had done Riverside; then we went for a ride in the woods for a change, all being fed up with the sight of gray expanses of water, but the woods dripped drearily and were boggy underfoot; it really was an awful summer.

It went on raining. Mummy had begun to fuss about school clothes and wanted to take me into Seaton to buy a blazer, but even she agreed that it was more important that we should ride down to the village and see if anyone wanted help. At the end of the path we found what looked like the river swirling by. It *was* the river. The low wall along the bank had been submerged and the old quay, right up to the cottage doors, had been incorporated into a great, wide torrent. It was quite frightening. The ponies saw the current and moved out into Riverside very cautiously, feeling for the ground at every step. All sorts of debris—chunks of wood, branches, broken plastic buckets, odd gumboots, cast-off tires—was being swept along and the water was almost up to the arches of the bridge. The Riverside water made a separate tributary, gushing over the road and into the water meadows beyond. Charles and I looked around anxiously.

"Keep close to the cottages," Charles told Steve, "and be ready to turn back if it gets too deep."

"I think he ought to go back now," I said, as Pumpkin wallowed in water up to his stomach and Steve took his feet out of the stirrups and put them forward just above the water.

"He'll be all right," said Georgie confidently.

"Of course I'll be all right; don't fuss, I can swim."

The inhabitants of Riverside were pleased to see us,

but rather gloomy. They seemed to be growing tired of their imprisonment. Mr. Gold wanted bread and cheese and asked if Charles could get him some beer. Mrs. Hastings wanted batteries for her radio, and Mrs. Jacks fish fingers and tomato ketchup. Mrs. Carpenter was the only cheerful one; she reported that two policemen had come round in a boat and offered to take her to the old people's home and the milkman hadn't made it through and she doubted whether the Meals on Wheels would. We agreed to get her milk and eggs and bread.

There was a mass of stuff for the flood-held prisoners. Everyone seemed to have brought them runner beans and huge squashes and windfall apples and some of their relations had left food parcels for us to deliver and there were letters and bottles of milk. Mr. Pearce was very efficient about packing it into parcels for each cottage, but some of his parcels were very awkward to carry on ponies. We gave Georgie the haversack for her load, as Legend was the most likely to be silly and shy; Steve carried a vast bag of vegetables and had a huge squash tucked in his anorak. I said, "I'm sure Pumpkin's going to sink under that lot," but Steve answered that she was so fat she would float. Just as we were starting, Mrs. Pearce came running out to say that Mrs. Judd had just telephoned an urgent order and Mr. Judd was going to come by for it. She'd told her to hold while she found out if they could send it.

"He's not a young man," said Mrs. Pearce reproachfully. "Don't you think you could take them, just this once?"

"No," said Steve firmly.

Charles looked around at us. "I don't see how we can. We're all laden up to the eyes already."

I felt guilty; I knew that we would have managed it somehow for anyone else, yet Mr. Judd was our enemy and the war hadn't been of our making. We splashed down the village street; children paddled in gumboots. One sailed a boat. The ponies wore purposeful expressions. I'm sure they knew that they were being really useful and were proud of themselves. Sheikh stood beneath the windows, nibbling at the roses that climbed the walls, as Charles handed up small things; I unloaded my groceries into baskets and Titus stood like a rock as I helped to heave them on their upward way. Steve and I were sorting out the vegetables when we saw Mr. Judd climbing stiffly out of a downstairs window. He was all dressed up in boots and mackintosh, which was madness; he would be waterlogged in a second.

"He'll drown in those boots," said Steve with satisfaction. Mrs. Jacks was telling Mr. Judd to stay at home: "Charles and Sarah will get whatever you need." We said nothing. Mr. Judd ignored her and us and let himself down slowly into the flood; the water came right up over his knees and he began to stagger forward uncertainly in his water-weighted boots. I put the rest of the beans into Mrs. Jacks's basket and called to her to pull it up when there was a loud splash. I looked around; Mr. Judd had tripped and fallen headlong into the water. Coughing and spluttering, he was trying to struggle up. Cries of horror followed by instructions and advice came from all the windows; then, as Georgie and Charles reached Mr. Judd and leaned down from their ponies to help him to his feet there was a cry of anguish, "Tess! Save Tess!" It was Mrs. Judd and she was pointing. I looked and saw that in falling, Mr. Judd had dropped his basket; and from

it had spilled the little Yorkshire terrier, and now she swam, a minute mat of wet hair, tiny paws paddling frantically as the current bore her away downstream.

"Save Tess!" screamed Mrs. Judd again.

I turned Titus. Despite her frantic paddling, Tess was being carried rapidly away—and the worst of it was that she was being carried toward the center of the river. I realized that in a moment she would be over the low wall and out in midstream. If I was going to grab her it had to be now.

I urged Titus forward; we both forgot to be cautious as we floundered toward the tiny dog. Suddenly Titus stopped, the submerged wall pressed against his legs. Leaning forward, I stretched and stretched to reach Tess. I touched the waterlogged hair, grabbed it, and at the same moment I overbalanced and tipped off Titus. Scraping my knees on the wall, I plunged headfirst into the river. As I came up, blinded and coughing, the current felt frighteningly strong, but I was still close to the wall. I put out a hand and found one of the big iron mooring rings and clung to it. Titus's worried brown face was above me. I looked around for Tess, but she was already meters away. I wasn't a strong enough swimmer to get her in this current. I began to haul myself up the submerged wall. Charles's outstretched hand appeared and helped. As I emerged dripping and stood on the wall, he said, "I'll see if there's any hope of saving the dog," and he and Sheikh floundered away through the water, toward the street.

Titus was still waiting for me, so I climbed on his back from the wall and followed. Georgie was trying to force Legend to jump down from the road through a cascade of foaming water into the meadows below. I pushed past and Titus slid down through the rushing water. From the bridge someone shouted at me to come back, that it was useless, that I would drown too. But Charles was out there and there might be something we could do. Titus was floundering through the water as fast as he could, hurrying to join Sheikh.

Charles shouted, "Sandy Bay?" above the noise our ponies made as they plunged through the water. I knew what he meant; we had been taken to paddle at the gravelly little bay when we were young. With a hard, shelving bottom, it was the only place where we could ride out into the river.

"The ashes!" I shouted back. "Opposite the clump of ash." I was watching the river intently, searching for the little brown-and-black mat, though I felt that it had probably already sunk. The water had more room to spread here and it was less deep. We galloped recklessly through it until we were level with the ash trees; then we turned toward the river. I hoped that I had remembered the position of the bay correctly. I had horrible visions of Sheikh and Titus plunging down a muddy bank into the depths of the river; they'd never be able to climb up again. I knew that bank, and there were no footholds for hooves in its steep, slimy side. The ponies recognized the danger, too, and proceeded cautiously, feeling for firm ground; I watched the river. Suddenly we saw the bedraggled little body floating toward us. It wasn't struggling or paddling anymore, but just being carried along on a small eddy with two pieces of wood and a torn-up tuft of grass. We both urged our ponies into the river, we both leaned forward, stretching out an arm. I missed again, by inches this time, but Charles, downstream of me, urged Sheikh forward one more reluctant step and grabbed. There was a terrible splash as horse and rider toppled into the water. Sheikh floundered helplessly for a moment, struggling for a footing on the muddy riverbed; then he turned and I was able to grab his rein. Titus and I steered him back to the graveled and shelving bank and he fought his way out of the mud and water with frantic heaves. "Charles!" I was calling. "Charles!" I couldn't see my brother anywhere. "Charles!" I called again as with a great lurch and a sucking noise Sheikh came out of the deep water and onto level ground. He stood trembling; his saddle and his ears were festooned with green weed.

"Charles!" I was almost screaming.

I was certain he had drowned, but then a voice answered, "It's all right, I'm here."

I looked downstream and there he was, climbing, out of the river with Tess's lifeless body in his arms. We moved into shallower water.

"Is Sheikh all right?" Charles asked.

"I think so—wet and frightened, but no legs broken."

"I'm afraid she's had it." He handed me the limp wet body and took Sheikh's reins and patted him. "Well, we did try," he said. Suddenly I began to cry. It seemed so sad that Tess was dead. If only we'd taken the Judds' shopping. Our quarrel had been with Mr. Judd, not with Tess, and yet it was Tess who'd died.

Charles was leaning against Sheikh's shoulder, he seemed exhausted. "Try holding her upside-down," he suggested. "You're supposed to let the water run out of the lungs."

I did as he said. It seemed insulting to hold the limp little body by its hind legs, but the water did come pouring out, and when it stopped I tried pressing gently on her rib cage. There was the kiss of life, but I didn't see how you could give it to a dog with a pointed nose. The tears were still running down my face, but I was so wet they didn't bother me much; in fact, I wouldn't have noticed them if they hadn't been so much hotter than rain and river water. "Are you OK?" I asked Charles, and when he nodded: "We'd better go back, then; it's no use, she's dead." I stuffed the little corpse inside my anorak. We mounted. Sheikh was still trembling.

Quite a few people had gathered on the bridge and in the street. Georgie and Steve waited at the gate. "Is she drowned?" asked Georgie. Charles nodded, and two huge tears began to slide down Steve's face.

But now, suddenly, I could feel a small stirring inside my anorak. When we had scrambled up the slippery and submerged bank onto the road I undid the zip and found that the little wet body was growing warmer and was no longer totally limp. "I think she's coming around!" I shouted, "I think she's still alive." Out of the crowd of faces Mr. Judd's, unsmiling, faintly purple, came closer. I handed him the damp body. "She's coming around," I repeated. "She seemed to be drowned but we got all the water out of her and now she's reviving."

"Brandy!" seemed to be the general cry, and there was a surge toward the White Hart, which stood in a private lake of water halfway up the street.

We looked at one another. "Let's go home," I suggested.

"Yes, you're both soaking," agreed Georgie.

As we sloshed along Riverside a row of faces appeared at the windows.

"She seemed to be drowned, but she's getting better," Steve shouted up to them. Charles stopped below Mrs. Judd's window. "Mr. Judd's taken her up to the White Hart for some brandy. I think she'll be all right," he said.

That night the rains stopped and next day the floods started to recede. Tess recovered, and it would be nice if I could report that we and Mr. Judd became firm friends, but we didn't. However, we did say good morning when we met on the street and he averted his eyes when we rode down the path. Then, quite soon a "For Sale" notice appeared outside Riverside Cottage and we heard that the Judds couldn't face the possibility of another flood and were moving to Worthing. I dare say that suited them better. The new people seem to like ponies and have made no trouble over the path. And Legend was third in a horse trial at Easter, jumping two streams with no trouble at all.

Across the Deserts of Peru

A. F. TSCHIFFELY

Aimé Félix Tschiffely was a Swiss schoolmaster who worked in Argentina. He wanted to show people how good the Argentinian Criollo horses were, so with two of them he rode ten thousand miles from Buenos Aires to Washington. His travels took him across grassy plains, through jungles, into deserts, and across frail rope bridges spanning mountain chasms; he had all sorts of adventures. His horses were Mancha (Spotty), who was sixteen when the journey began, and Gato (Cat), who was fifteen. The whole trip took two and a half years to complete. This extract is from Southern Cross to Pole Star: Tschiffely's Ride, *the book he wrote about his journey.*

The first day's ride was to take me to Ancon, some twenty-odd miles. Knowing that I would find no fodder there, I had sent a bale of hay ahead by train, for a railway connects this little bathing resort with the capital. About halfway I was stopped by a soldier of the *guardia civil* who demanded to see my license for firearms, a document I did not possess. He very politely asked me to accompany him to the local headquarters, where I explained to the *capitan* who I was, and this gentleman issued me a permit in order to prevent my being held up again.

This little incident proved to be a blessing in disguise, for the officer informed me that a river I had to cross a little farther ahead was high and therefore dangerous, and the *capitan* kindly sent a soldier with me to show the best place to cross. I never minded swimming rivers, but when I had to do this right alongside railway bridges that are impossible to cross with horses, I was none too pleased. If it was possible to swim the horses near the bridge I usually unsaddled the animals and carried everything over on foot, walking on the sleepers, and thus saving myself the trouble of having to wrap everything up in a waterproof sheet.

A few miles before we reached Ancon we entered the first sandy desert. Near here the last battle between Chile and Peru was fought, and the dead were buried in this stretch of desert where they fell. In time the winds shifted the sand, exposing a mass of skulls and bones. What a resting place for those who gave their lives for their country!

It was a good thing that I had sent some hay ahead, for otherwise the horses would have had to pass another night on empty stomachs. Water is very scarce in many places along the Peruvian coast, and even in this fashionable bathing resort it is sold at ten centavos a tin.

From Ancon north, practically to the border of Ecuador, I had planned to follow the coast. Rains are almost unknown in these regions; in fact, there are parts where people have never seen rain fall. A few towns and villages stand on the rivers that run down from the Andes and cross the dry coast to the sea, and when these rivers are high they are very wild and dangerous. Some of the valleys are watered by small irrigation canals, and where such irrigation exists, fine crops of sugar cane, cotton, and rice are grown. Between the distant rivers are the vast, sandy deserts where nothing grows and where the sand dunes rise one after another, like huge ocean billows. In such places the heat is terrific and there is absolutely no water. The ancient Mochica Indians, later the Chimus, and then the Incas, had irrigated many of the regions which are now empty deserts, and I saw the ruins of their towns, forts, canals, and burial grounds, which tell the sad story of the white man's invasion.

Contrary to the practice of most travelers in dry regions, I carried no water. For my own use I had a flask of brandy, and another filled with lemon juice mixed with a little salt. This concoction was very stimulating but tasted so bad that I was never tempted to drink much at a time. The juice of canned fresh tomatoes is probably the best thirst quencher, but then this article is rarely found when it is needed. As for the horses, I calculated that the energy wasted by them in carrying water would be greater than the actual benefit derived from drinking it, so they only drank when we came to a river or some village. I believe my theory was sound; with a light load we gained in speed, and avoided the horses getting sore, for water is the most uncomfortable and clumsy load a pack animal can carry. Only on rare occasions did the animals seem to suffer from excessive thirst.

After leaving Ancon we traveled over high sand dunes, and at eventide, in a fertile plain, we arrived at a big *hacienda* belonging to a Chinese man, whose hospitality I shall never forget. The next day's trip being a long one, we started long before daybreak. When I saddled up I thought my saddlebags were rather heavier than usual, and later I found out that my kind host had filled them with all sorts of good things during the night.

The first rays of dawn found us among sand dunes where the horses sank deep into the soft sand that had been blown about by the wind until it appeared like ripples on a lake. The imposing silence was broken only by the rolling of the waves that sounded like the snoring of some sleeping giant. The wind almost immediately covered our tracks, and soon the terrible heat rose in waves, making breathing uncomfortable. In some places I could follow the coast, riding along the wet sand, where I made the horses go at a fast trot or even at a slow gallop, for I knew that this would be impossible once the sun rose higher; and time was precious. Sometimes a wave, bigger than the average, would wash higher up the beach, and the moving foam would frighten the horses. The vastness of the ocean, and the regular roaring of the waves on the seemingly endless dunes, gave the impression of eternity. Thousands of seabirds hovered silently over our heads, and crabs of all sizes went running with amazing swiftness toward their holes in the sand as we approached. Their manner of walking sideways was almost comical, and often, while I gave the horses a few minutes to breathe, I amused myself trying to catch some of them. Once or twice I threw a dead one as far as I could, then watched the others come to devour it; the fights that ensued were fierce and terrible, and I could not help comparing these fighting crabs with human beings. The wet sand was white with seagulls waiting for the waves to wash up something to eat. The birds would only rise when we had almost reached them, fly in a small circle around us,

invariably toward sea, where the wind came from, and again settle behind us. Thousands of guanos (a kind of seabird) were flying in regular clouds, dashing and splashing into the water after fish, for all the world resembling airplanes in the moment of crashing; and every now and again a curious seal would come to the surface and look at us as if wondering what we were doing there. The hot and very bright sunlight reflected off the wet sand and the waves, and the snow-white gulls circling silently around us made my eyes smart, obliging me to wear the green goggles I had used in the mountains. Journeys through such deserts are trying in the extreme. At first the body suffers; then everything physical becomes abstract. Later on the brain becomes dull and the thoughts mixed; one becomes indifferent about things, and then everything seems like a moving picture or a strange dream, and only the will to arrive and to keep awake is left. All thinking ceases, and when one finally arrives and falls to sleep, even the will temporarily leaves the body.

Still following the hot, sandy coast, we came to a large sugar plantation, not far from which stands a fortress that was built by the ancient Chimu Indians. It is a colossal piece of work, entirely made of adobe and built in high terraces that appear like a square hill from the distance. Near the main fortress are high walls, and the way everything was built leaves no doubt that these ancients had a certain scientific knowledge of warfare. Some of the paint with which the walls were colored still remains, neither weather nor centuries having been able to make it fade or to destroy it. The colors that exist are red, black, and yellow, the same as are found in pottery that dates back to the Chimu period.

The fortress of Paramonga consists of two main strongholds. One of these is situated on a hill, the waves of the Pacific Ocean beating against its inaccessible cliffs which face west. The eastern side of that hill has a steep and sandy slope where numerous mummies, wrapped in colored cloths, were buried and have now become uncovered by the shifting and sliding sands. The main fortress is roughly half a mile east from there, and the two were probably separated by a swamp in former times, but today the low flat stretch of land between the two is dry, and sugar cane is successfully cultivated by a Japanese settler who entertained me splendidly when I happened to call at his place during my rambles among the ruins. Although subterranean passages and burial places exist here, the natives are afraid to explore them, for many strange tales and superstitions have been handed down from one generation to another. As I had not time enough, I could not do more than have a general look over these interesting relics of the past.

From Paramonga north there is a vast desert, close on a hundred miles from one river to the next, and as there is no water to be found there I was obliged to make the crossing in one journey. For this reason I had to wait for the full moon before I could, with a certain degree of safety, attempt this long ride.

There was an outbreak of bubonic plague while I was there, and quite a number of plantation workers died, while many more were ill. The authorities raided their filthy quarters, and it was a pathetic yet amusing sight to see their owners howling and wailing as they walked behind their filthy belongings which were being carted out to be burned, together with some ancient mummies that had been discovered near there in an old burial ground. I took every precaution against the horrible disease and was particularly careful never to lie down to rest unless I had previously sprinkled my bed with insect powder, for fleas and similar pests transmit the germs of bubonic plague. It was uncomfortable to have to remain in this place with the danger of catching the plague, but I was between the devil and the deep blue sea; for before attempting to cross the desert ahead of us I had to be careful to make my plans, and as I intended to start in the evening it was necessary to wait until the moon was at its brightest. I had heard many terrible stories about this sandy wilderness; its very name, "Matacaballo" (Horse Killer), gave me food for reflection.

After four days' waiting I was ready to start, and as I did not intend to carry water for the horses, I was careful not to give them anything to drink the day before we left, for I wanted them to be thirsty and therefore not likely to refuse a good drink immediately before starting out. For myself I packed two bottles of lemon juice in the saddlebags, and the only food I took with me was a few pieces of chocolate that had been in my pack for some days. Toward evening we were ready, and when the sun was setting we crossed the river, on the other side of which the rolling desert starts. I waited until the horses had finished their drink, and after they had pawed and played with the cool water I mounted, and soon we were on the soft and still-hot sands that made a peculiar hissing sound under the hooves of the animals. The indescribable colors of a tropical sunset were reflected on the glittering waves of the ocean, and the old Indian fortress assumed a tint of gold. Even the inhospitable sandy wastes had changed their dread and desolate appearance, for now the sand dunes and undulations were one mass of color, from golden brown to dark purple, according to light and shadows. A few belated seabirds were hurriedly flying toward their distant roosting places on some rocky island; everything seemed to be different now, except the regular, eternal rolling of the breakers on the shore. No sooner had the last clouds ceased to glow like fading beacon fires than darkness set in, and after a while the moon rose over the mountain ranges in the far east, slowly, majestically; and more than welcome to me.

The sensation of riding on soft sand is a peculiar one at first, until the body becomes used to the peculiar springless motion of the horse. Knowing that such conditions mean a great strain on the animal I could not help moving in the saddle, uselessly endeavoring to assist my mount. We were twisting and winding our way through among high sand dunes and, whenever it was possible, I guided the animals down to the wet sand on the beach where I would urge them into a slow gallop. Often we came to rocky places or to land points which stretched far out, and thus I was forced to make a detour inland again, frequently for considerable distances. For the first few hours I observed everything around me and admired the brilliance of the moon that made the ocean glitter like silver, and gave the often strange sand formations a ghostly appearance. Soon even all this became monotonous to me, and every time I stopped to rest the horses for a while or to adjust the saddles, I lit a cigarette to help pass the time away. Shortly before dawn I had to halt for quite a long time, for the moon had gone down behind some clouds and we were left in darkness; it would not have been wise to continue lest I should take the wrong direction or lead the horses into places where the sand is so soft that they would sink in up to their bellies.

My instinct for finding the direction had developed to a notable degree by this time, probably because I had not very much to think about besides keeping the horses' noses facing the right way, but even when I knew exactly which way to go, fogs or darkness on several occasions made me think it wiser to wait until I could see.

The first rays of the morning sun were hot, and I rightly anticipated that the day was going to be a scorcher. The horses plodded along as if they realized that they were in the midst of a serious test, and when it was about one hour after noon I noticed that they lifted their heads and sniffed the air. Immediately after they hurried their steps, and I believe they would have broken into a gallop if I had permitted them to do so. I was wondering why the horses were so keen to hurry along, and within an hour I knew the reason, for we arrived at the river, and I am certain that the animals had scented water long before I could see it; obviously Mancha and Gato still possessed the instincts of the wild horse.

Great were my feelings of relief when we left the Matacaballo desert behind us and, in spite of my already high opinion of the horses' resistance, I admired the splendid behavior they had shown during so long and trying a journey—a journey that would have killed most horses unaccustomed to such conditions. After I had unsaddled them they had a good drink, and then I gave them a much-needed bath. When this had been done I turned them loose in a small field with good grass, and after both had rolled, stretched, and shaken themselves, they started to eat, and anybody might have believed they had only just returned from a short canter. I only realized how tired and played out I was when I sat down on my saddles while a woman in a hut prepared some food for me, and I thought I had only dozed off to sleep for a few moments when I awoke in the evening. The good woman, knowing that I needed sleep more than food, had kept my meal warm for me, and once I had the first taste of it I did not stop until the last grain of rice and the last bean had disappeared. It had taken us exactly twenty hours to cross the desert, and I have no desire ever to make another such ride.

Fire!

ANNA SEWELL

Anna Sewell was lame and went about in a pony cart, never using a whip, but talking in a friendly way to the pony. She was troubled by cruelty to horses, especially the fashionable practice of using a bearing rein. This kept the horse from lowering its head. Anna Sewell started to write her only book, Black Beauty: the Autobiography of a Horse, *in 1871, "its special aim being," she said, "to induce kindness, sympathy, and an understanding treatment of horses." She died in 1878, the year after it was published.*

After this it was decided by my master and mistress to pay a visit to some friends who lived about forty-six miles from our home, and James was to drive them. The first day we traveled thirty-two miles; there were some long, heavy hills, but James drove so carefully and thoughtfully that we were not at all harassed. He never forgot to put on the drag as we went downhill, nor to take it off at the right place. He kept our feet on the smoothest part of the road, and if the uphill was very long, he set the carriage wheels a little across the road, so as not to run back, and gave us a breathing. All these little things help a horse very much, particularly if he gets kind words into the bargain.

We stopped once or twice on the road, and just as the sun was going down, we reached the town where we were to spend the night. We stopped at the principal hotel, which was in the marketplace; it was a very large one; we drove under an archway into a long yard, at the farthest end of which were the stables and coach houses. Two ostlers came to take us out. The head ostler was a pleasant, active little man, with a crooked leg, and a yellow-striped waistcoat. I never saw a man unbuckle harness so quickly as he did, and with a pat and a good word he led me to a long stable, with six or eight stalls in it, and two or three horses. The other man brought Ginger; James stood by while we were rubbed down and cleaned.

I was never cleaned so lightly and quickly as by that little old man. When he had done, James stepped up and felt me over, as if he thought I could not be thoroughly done, but he found my coat as clean and smooth as silk.

"Well," he said, "I thought I was pretty quick, and our John quicker still, but you do beat all I ever saw for being quick and thorough at the same time."

"Practice makes perfect," said the crooked little ostler, "and 'twould be a pity if it didn't; forty years' practice, and not perfect! Ha, ha! That would be a pity; and as to being quick, why, bless you! That is only a matter of habit; if you get into the habit of being quick, it is just as easy as being slow; easier, I should say; in fact, it don't agree with my health to be hulking about over a job twice as long as it need take. Bless you! I couldn't whistle if I crawled over my work as some folks do! You see, I have been about horses ever since I was twelve years old, in hunting stables and racing stables; and being small, ye see, I was jockey for several years; but at the Goodwood, ye see, the turf was very slippery and my poor Larkspur got a fall, and I broke my knee, and so, of course, I was of no more use there; but I could not live without horses, of course I couldn't, so I took to the hotels, and I can tell ye it is a downright pleasure to handle an animal like this, well-bred, well-mannered, well-cared-for; bless ye! I can tell how a horse is treated. Give me the handling of a horse for twenty minutes, and I'll tell you what sort of groom he has had; look at this one, pleasant, quiet, turns about just as you want him, holds up his feet to be cleaned out, or anything else you please to wish; then you'll find another, fidgety, fretty, won't move the right way, or starts across the stall, tosses up his head as soon as you come near him, lays his ears, and seems afraid of you; or else squares about at you with his heels. Poor things! I know what sort of treatment they have had. If they are timid, it makes them start or shy; if they are high-mettled, it makes them vicious or dangerous; their tempers are mostly made when they are young. Bless you! They are like children: train 'em up in the way they should go, as the Good Book says, and when they are old they will not depart from it—if they have a chance, that is."

"I like to hear you talk," said James; "that's the way we lay it down at home, at our master's."

"Who is your master, young man. If it be a proper question? I should judge he is a good one from what I see."

"He is Squire Gordon, of Birtwick Park, the other side the Beacon hills," said James.

"Ah! So, so, I have heard tell of him; fine judge of horses, ain't he? The best rider in the county?"

"I believe he is," said James, "but he rides very little now since the poor young master was killed."

"Ah! Poor gentleman; I read all about it in the paper at the time; a fine horse killed too, wasn't there?"

"Yes," said James, "he was a splendid creature, brother to this one, and just like him."

"Pity! Pity!" said the old man " 'Twas a bad place to leap, if I remember; a thin fence at top, a steep bank down to the stream, wasn't it? No chance for a horse to see where he is going. Now, I am for bold riding as much as any man, but still there are some leaps that only a very knowing old huntsman has any right to take; a man's life and a horse's life are worth more than a fox's tail; at least I should say they ought to be."

During this time the other man had finished Ginger and had brought our corn, and James and the old man left the stable together.

Later on in the evening a traveler's horse was brought in by the second ostler, and while he was cleaning him a young man with a pipe in his mouth lounged into the stable to gossip.

"I say, Towler," said the ostler, "just run up the ladder into the loft and put some hay down into this horse's rack, will you? Only lay down your pipe."

"All right," said the other, and went up through the trapdoor; and I heard him step across the floor overhead and put down the hay. James came in to look at us the last thing, and then the door was locked.

I cannot say how long I had slept, nor what time in the night it was, but I woke up very uncomfortable, though I hardly knew why. I got up; the air seemed all thick and choking. I heard Ginger coughing, and one of the other horses moved about restlessly; it was quite dark and I could see nothing, but the stable was very full of smoke, and I hardly knew how to breathe.

The trapdoor had been left open, and I thought that was the place it came through. I listened and heard a soft rushing sort of noise, and a low crackling and snapping. I did not know what it was, but there was something in the sound so strange that it made me tremble all over. The other horses were now all awake; some were pulling at their halters, others were stamping.

At last I heard steps outside, and the ostler who had put up the traveler's horse burst into the stable with a lantern, and began to untie the horses, and try to lead them out; but he seemed in such a hurry, and so frightened himself that he frightened me still more. The first horse would not go with him; he tried the second and third—they, too, would not stir. He came to me next and tried to drag me out of the stall by force; of course that was no use. He tried us all by turns and then left the stable.

No doubt we were very foolish, but danger seemed to be all around, and there was nobody we knew to trust in, and all was strange and uncertain. The fresh air that had come in through the open door made it easier to breathe, but the rushing sound overhead grew louder, and as I looked upward, through the bars of my empty rack, I saw a red light flickering on the wall. Then I heard a cry of "Fire!" outside, and the old ostler quietly and quickly came in; he got one horse out, and went to another, but the flames were playing around the trapdoor, and the roaring overhead was dreadful.

The next thing I heard was James's voice, quiet and cheery, as it always was.

"Come, my beauties, it is time for us to be off, so wake up and come along." I stood nearest the door, so he came to me first, patting me as he came in.

"Come, Beauty, on with your bridle, my boy; we'll soon be out of this smother." It was on in no time; then he took the scarf off his neck and tied it lightly over my eyes, and patting and coaxing he led me out of the stable. Safe in the yard, he slipped the scarf off my eyes, and shouted, "Here, somebody! Take this horse while I go back for the other."

A tall broad man stepped forward and took me, and James darted back into the stable. I set up a shrill whinny as I saw him go. Ginger told me afterward that whinny was the best thing I could have done for her, for had she not heard me outside, she would never have had courage to come out.

There was much confusion in the yard; the horses being got out of other stables, and the carriages and gigs being pulled out of houses and sheds, lest the flames should spread farther. On the other side of the yard, windows were thrown up, and people were shouting all sorts of things; but I kept my eye fixed on the stable door, where the smoke poured out thicker than ever, and I could see flashes of red light; presently I heard above all the stir and din a loud clear voice, which I knew was master's:

"James Howard! James Howard! are you there?"

There was no answer, but I heard a crash of something falling in the stable, and the next moment I gave a loud joyful neigh, for I saw James coming through the smoke leading Ginger with him; she was coughing violently and he was not able to speak.

"My brave lad!" said master, laying his hands on his shoulder, "are you hurt?"

James shook his head, for he could not yet speak.

"Aye," said the big man who held me, "he is a brave lad, and no mistake."

"And now," said master, "when you have got your breath, James, we'll get out of this place as quickly as we can," and we were moving toward the entry, when from the marketplace there came a sound of galloping feet and loud rumbling wheels.

" 'Tis the fire engine! the fire engine!" shouted two or three voices, "stand back, make way!" and clattering and thundering over the stones two horses dashed into the yard with the heavy engine behind them. The firemen leaped to the ground; there was no need to ask where the fire was—it was torching up in a great blaze from the roof.

We got out as fast as we could into the broad, quiet marketplace; the stars were shining, and except the noise behind us, all was still. Master led the way to a large hotel on the other side, and as soon as the ostler came he said, "James, I must now hasten to your mistress; I trust the horses entirely to you, order whatever you think is needed," and with that he was gone. The master did not run, but I never saw mortal man walk so fast as he did that night.

There was a dreadful sound before we got into our stalls; the shrieks of those poor horses that were left burning to death in the stable—it was very terrible, and made both Ginger and me feel very bad! We, however, were taken in and well done by.

The next morning the master came to see how we were and to speak to James. I did not hear much, for the ostler was rubbing me down, but I could see that James looked very happy, and I thought the master was proud of him. Our mistress had been so much alarmed in the night, that the journey was put off till the afternoon, so James had the morning on hand, and went first to the inn to see about our harness and the carriage, and then to hear more about the fire. When he came back we heard him tell the ostler about it. At first no one could guess how the fire had been caused, but at last a man said he saw Dick Towler go into the stable with a pipe in his mouth, and when he came out he had not one, and went to the tap for another. Then the under ostler said he had asked Dick to go up the ladder to put down some hay, but told him to lay down his pipe first. Dick denied taking the pipe with him, but no one believed him. I remember our John Manly's rule, never to allow a pipe in the stable, and thought it ought to be the rule everywhere.

James said the roof and floor had fallen in, and that only the black walls were standing; the two poor horses that could not be got out were buried under the burned rafters and tiles.

Winding-Up Time

JEAN INGELOW

Jean Ingelow was another writer who showed concern about the treatment of horses—though she devised a very unusual solution: at the ends of their lives on earth, the horses were looked after by servants powered by clockwork! This extract comes from Mopsa the Fairy, *which tells the story of Jack, a boy who finds a nest of fairies in a hollow thorn tree. He then travels on the back of an albatross and by boat to Fairyland. On the way, he has some extraordinary adventures. Jean Ingelow was a poet and children's author, but apart from* Mopsa the Fairy, *most of her work is now forgotten. She died in 1897.*

Jack looked at these hot brown rocks, first on the left bank and then on the right, till he was quite tired; but at last the shore on the right bank became flat, and he saw a beautiful little bay, where the water was still and where grass grew down to the brink.

He was so much pleased at this change that he cried out hastily: "Oh, how I wish my boat would swim into that bay and let me land!" He had no sooner spoken than the boat altered her course, as if somebody had been steering her, and began to make for the bay as fast as she could go.

"How odd!" thought Jack. "I wonder whether I ought to have spoken; for the boat certainly did not intend to come into this bay. However, I think I will let her alone now, for I certainly do wish very much to land here."

As they drew toward the strand the water got so shallow that you could see crabs and lobsters walking about at the bottom. At last the boat's keel grated on the pebbles; and just as Jack began to think of jumping on shore he saw two little old women approaching and gently driving a white horse before them.

The horse had panniers, one on each side; and when his feet were in the water he stood still; and Jack said to one of the old women: "Will you be so kind as to tell me whether this is Fairyland?"

"What does he say?" asked one old woman of the other.

"I asked if this was Fairyland," repeated Jack, for he though the first old woman might have been deaf. She was very handsomely dressed in a red satin gown, and did not look in the least like a washerwoman, though it afterwards appeared that she was one.

"He says "Is this Fairyland?" " she replied; and the other, who had a blue satin cloak, answered: "Oh, does he?" and then began to empty the panniers of many small blue and pink and scarlet shirts, and coats, and stockings; and when they had made them into two little heaps they knelt down and began to wash them in the river, taking no notice of him whatever.

Jack stared at them. They were not much taller than himself, and they were not taking the slightest care of their handsome clothes; then he looked at the cold white horse, who was hanging his head over the lovely, clear water with a very discontented air.

At last the blue washerwoman said: "I shall leave off now; I've got a pain in my works."

"Do," said the other. "We'll go home and have a

cup of tea." Then she glanced at Jack, who was still sitting in the boat, and said: "Can you strike?"

"I can if I choose," replied Jack, a little astonished at this speech. And the red and blue washerwomen wrung out the clothes, put them again into the panniers, and, taking the old horse by the bridle, began gently to lead him away.

"I have a great mind to land," thought Jack. "I should not wonder at all if this is Fairyland. So, as the boat came here to please me, I shall ask it to stay where it is in case I should want it again."

So he sprang ashore, and said to the boat: "Stay just where you are, will you?" and he ran after the old women, calling to them:

"Is there any law to prevent my coming into your country?"

"Wo!" cried the red-coated old woman, and the horse stopped, while the blue-coated woman repeated: "Any law? No, not that I know of; but if you are a stranger here you had better look out."

"Why?" asked Jack.

"You don't suppose, do you," she answered, "that our Queen will wind up strangers?"

While Jack was wondering what she meant, the other said:

"I shouldn't wonder if he goes eight days. Gee!" and the horse went on.

"No, wo!" said the other.

"No, no. Gee! I tell you," cried the first.

Upon this, to Jack's intense astonishment, the old horse stopped, and said, speaking through his nose:

"Now, then, which is to be? I'm willing to gee, and I'm agreeable to wo; but what's a fellow to do when you say them both together?"

"Why, he talks!" exclaimed Jack.

"It's because he's got a cold in his head," observed one of the washerwomen; "he always talks when he's got a cold, and there's no pleasing him; whatever you say, he's not satisfied. Gee, Boney, do!"

"Gee it is, then," said the horse, and began to jog on.

"He spoke again!" said Jack, upon which the horse laughed, and Jack was quite alarmed.

"It appears that your horses don't talk?" observed the blue-coated woman.

"Never," answered Jack; "they can't."

"You mean they won't," observed the old horse; and though he spoke the words of mankind it was not in a voice like theirs. Still Jack felt that his was just the natural tone for a horse, and that it did not arise only from the length of his nose. "You'll find out some day, perhaps," he continued, "whether horses can talk or not."

"Shall I?" said Jack very earnestly.

"They'll *tell*," proceeded the white horse. "I wouldn't be you when they tell how you've used them."

"Have you been ill used?" said Jack, in an anxious tone.

"Yes, yes, of course he has," one of the women broke in; "but he has come here to get all right again. This is a very wholesome country for horses; isn't it, Boney?"

"Yes," said the horse.

"Well, then, jog on, there's a dear," continued the old woman. "Why, you will be young again soon, you know—young, and gamesome, and handsome; you'll be quite a colt by and by, and then we shall set you free to join your companions in the happy meadows."

The old horse was so comforted by this kind speech that he pricked up his ears and quickened his pace considerably.

"He was shamefully used," observed one washer-woman. "Look at him, how lean he is! You can see all his ribs."

"Yes," said the other, as if apologizing for the poor old horse. "He gets low-spirited when he thinks of all he has gone through; but he is a vast deal better already than he was. He used to live in London; his master always carried a long whip to beat him with, and never spoke civilly to him."

"London!" exclaimed Jack. "Why, that is in my country. How did the horse get here?"

"That's no business of yours," answered one of the women. "But I can tell you he came because he was wanted, which is more than you are."

"You let him alone," said the horse in a querulous tone. "I don't bear any malice."

"No; he has a good disposition, has Boney," observed the red old woman. "Pray, are you a boy?"

"Yes," said Jack.

"A real boy, that wants no winding up?" inquired the old woman.

"I don't know what you mean," answered Jack; "but I am a real boy, certainly."

"Ah!" she replied. "Well, I thought you were, by the way Boney spoke to you. How frightened you must be! I wonder what will be done to all your people for driving, and working, and beating so many beautiful creatures to death every year that comes? They'll have to pay for it some day, you may depend."

Jack was a little alarmed, and answered that he had never been unkind himself to horses, and he was glad that Boney bore no malice.

"They worked him, and often drove him about all night in the miserable streets, and never let him have so much as a canter in a green field," said one of the women; "but he'll be all right now, only he has to begin at the wrong end."

"What do you mean?" said Jack.

"Why, in this country," answered the old woman, "they begin by being terribly old and stiff, and they seem miserable and jaded at first, but by degrees they get young again, as you heard me reminding him."

"Indeed," said Jack; "and do you like that?"

"It has nothing to do with me," she answered. "We are only here to take care of all the creatures that men have ill used. While they are sick and old, which they are when first they come to us—after they are dead, you know—we take care of them, and gradually bring them up to be young and happy again."

"This must be a very nice country to live in then," said Jack.

"For horses it is," said the old lady significantly.

"Well," said Jack, "it does seem very full of haystacks certainly, and all the air smells of fresh grass."

At this moment they came to a beautiful meadow, and the old horse stopped and, turning to the bluecoated woman, said: "Faxa, I think I could fancy a handful of clover." Upon this Faxa snatched Jack's cap off his head, and in a very active manner jumped over a little ditch, and gathering some clover, presently brought it back full, handing it to the old horse with great civility.

"You shouldn't be in such a hurry," observed the old horse; "your weights will be running down some day, if you don't mind."

"It's all zeal," observed the red-coated woman.

Just then a little man, dressed like a groom, came running up, out of breath. "Oh, here you are, Dow!" he exclaimed to the red-coated woman. "Come along, will you? Lady Betty wants you; it's such a hot day, and nobody, she says, can fan her so well as you can."

The red-coated woman, without a word, went off with the groom, and Jack thought he would go with them, for this Lady Betty could surely tell him whether the country was called Fairyland, or whether he must get into his boat and go farther. He did not like either to hear the way in which Faxa and Dow talked about their works and their weights; so he asked Faxa to give him his cap, which she did, and he heard a curious sort of little ticking noise as he came close to her, which startled him.

"Oh, this must be Fairyland, I am sure," thought Jack, "for in my country our pulses beat quite differently from that."

"Well," said Faxa, rather sharply, "do you find any fault with the way I go?"

"No," said Jack, a little ashamed of having listened. "I think you walk beautifully; your steps are so regular."

"She's machine-made," observed the old horse, in a melancholy voice, and with a deep sigh. "In the largest magnifying glass you'll hardly find the least fault with her chain. She's not like the goods they turn out in Clerkenwell."

Jack was more and more startled, and so glad to get his cap and run after the groom and Dow to find Lady Betty, that he might be with ordinary human beings again; but when he got up to them he found that Lady Betty was a beautiful brown mare! She was lying in a languid and rather affected attitude, with a load of fresh hay before her, and two attendants, one of whom stood holding a parasol over her head, while the other was fanning her.

"I'm so glad you are come, my good Dow," said the brown mare. "Don't you think I am strong enough today to set off for the happy meadows?"

"Well," said Dow, "I'm afraid not yet; you must remember that it is no use your leaving us till you have quite got over the effects of the fall."

Just then Lady Betty observed Jack and said: "Take that boy away; he reminds me of a jockey."

The attentive groom instantly started forward, but Jack was too nimble for him; he ran and ran with all his might, and only wished he had never left the boat. But still he heard the groom behind him; and in fact the groom caught him at last, and held him so fast that struggling was no use at all.

"You young rascal!" he exclaimed, as he recovered breath. "How you do run! It's enough to break your mainspring."

"What harm did I do?" asked Jack. "I was only looking at the mare."

"Harm!" exclaimed the groom. "Harm, indeed! Why, you reminded her of a jockey. It's enough to hold her back, poor thing!—and we trying so hard, too, to make her forget what a cruel end she came to in the old world."

"You need not hold me so tightly," said Jack. "I shall not run away again; but," he added, "if this is Fairyland, it is not half such a nice country as I expected."

"Fairyland!" exclaimed the groom, stepping back with surprise. "Why, what made you think of such a thing? This is only one of the border countries, where things are set right again that people have caused to go wrong in the world. The world, you know, is what men and women call their own home."

"I know," said Jack; "and that's where I came from." Then, as the groom seemed no longer to be angry, he went on: "And I wish you would tell me about Lady Betty."

"She was a beautiful fleet creature, of the racehorse breed," said the groom; "and she won silver cups for her master, and then they made her run a steeple-chase, which frightened her, but still she won it; and then they made her run another, and she cleared some terribly high hurdles, and many gates and ditches, till she came to an awful one, and at first she would not take it, but her rider spurred and beat her till she tried. It was beyond her powers, and she fell and broke her forelegs. Then they shot her. After she had died that miserable death we had her here, to make her all right again."

"Is this the only country where you set things right?" asked Jack.

"Certainly not," answered the groom; "they lie about in all directions. Why, you might wander for years and never come to the end of this one."

"I am afraid I shall not find the one I am looking for," said Jack, "if your countries are so large."

"I don't think our world is much larger than yours," answered the groom. "But come along; I hear the bell, and we are a good way from the palace."

Jack, in fact, heard the violent ringing of a bell at some distance; and when the groom began to run, he ran beside him, for he thought he should like to see the palace. As they ran, people gathered from all sides—

fields, cottages, mills—till at last there was a little crowd, among whom Jack saw Dow and Faxa, and they were all making for a large house, the wide door of which was standing open. Jack stood with the crowd and peeped in. There was a woman sitting inside upon a rocking chair, a tall, large woman, with a gold-colored gown on, and beside her stood a table, covered with things that looked like keys.

"What is that woman doing?" said he to Faxa, who was standing close to him.

"Winding us up, to be sure," answered Faxa. "You don't suppose, surely, that we can go forever?"

"Extraordinary!" said Jack. "Then are you wound up every evening, like watches?"

"Unless we have misbehaved ourselves," she answered; "and then she lets us run down."

"And what then?"

"What then?" repeated Faxa. "Why, then we have to stop and stand against a wall, till she is pleased to forgive us, and let our friends carry us in to be set going again."

Jack looked in, and saw the people pass in and stand close by the woman. One after the other she took by the chin with her left hand, and with her right hand found a key that pleased her. It seemed to Jack that there was a tiny keyhole in the back of their heads, and that she put the key in and wound them up.

"You must take your turn with the others," said the groom.

"There's no keyhole in my head," said Jack; "besides, I do not want any woman to wind me up."

"But you must do as others do," he persisted; "and if you have no keyhole, our Queen can easily have one made, I should think."

"Make one in my head!" exclaimed Jack. "She shall do no such thing."

"We shall see," said Faxa quietly. And Jack was so frightened that he set off, and ran back toward the river with all his might. Many of the people called to him to stop, but they could not run after him, because they wanted winding up. However, they would certainly have caught him if he had not been very quick, for before he got to the river he heard behind him the footsteps of those who had been first attended to by the Queen, and he had only just time to spring into the boat when they reached the edge of the water.

No sooner was he on board than the boat swung around, and got again into the middle of the stream; but he could not feel safe till not only was there a long reach of water between him and the shore, but till he had gone so far downriver that the beautiful bay had passed out of sight and the sun was going down. By this time he began to feel very tired and sleepy; so, having looked at his fairies, and found that they were all safe and fast asleep, he lay down in the bottom of the boat, and fell into a doze, and then into a dream.

The Magician's Horse

retold by Andrew Lang

*Some people think horses are magic; the horse in this story
is a magician. It is certainly very good fortune for the Prince
that he meets such a clever animal. The story comes from
Sicily, and was included in a German collection of folktales
from the island. Andrew Lang, who was extremely interested
in folktales and fairy tales himself, retold the story in* The
Gray Fairy Book. *This was one of twelve books of such
tales, all called after different colors, that Andrew Lang
retold. He also wrote several good fairy stories of his own
invention.*

Once upon a time, there was a King who had three
sons. Now it happened that one day the three
Princes went out hunting in a large forest at some
distance from their father's palace, and the youngest
Prince lost his way, so his brothers had to return home
without him.

For four days the Prince wandered through the glades
of the forest, sleeping on moss beneath the stars at
night, and by day living on roots and wild berries. At
last, on the morning of the fifth day, he came to a large
open space in the middle of the forest, and here stood a
stately palace; but neither within nor without was there
a trace of human life. The Prince entered the open door
and wandered through the deserted rooms without

seeing a living soul. At last he came on a great hall, and in the center of the hall was a table spread with dainty dishes and choice wines. The Prince sat down, and satisfied his hunger and thirst, and immediately afterward the table disappeared from his sight. This struck the Prince as very strange; but though he continued his search through all the rooms, upstairs and down, he could find no one to speak to. At last, just as it was beginning to get dark, he heard steps in the distance and he saw an old man coming toward him up the stairs.

"What are you doing wandering about my castle?" asked the old man.

To whom the Prince replied: "I lost my way hunting in the forest. If you will take me into your service, I should like to stay with you, and will serve you faithfully."

"Very well," said the old man. "You may enter my service. You will have to keep the stove always lit, you will have to fetch the wood for it from the forest, and you will have the charge of the black horse in the stables. I will pay you a florin a day, and at mealtimes you will always find the table in the hall spread with food and wine, and you can eat and drink as much as you require."

The Prince was satisfied, and he entered the old man's service, and promised to see that there was always wood on the stove, so that the fire should never die out. Now, though he did not know it, his new master was a magician, and the flame of the stove was a magic fire, and if it had gone out the Magician would have lost a great part of his power. One day the Prince forgot, and let the fire burn so low that it very nearly burned out. Just as the flame was flickering the old man stormed into the room.

"What do you mean by letting the fire burn so low?" he growled. "I have only arrived in the nick of time." And while the Prince hastily threw a log on the stove and blew on the ashes to kindle the glow, his master gave him a severe box on the ear, and warned him that if ever it happened again it would fare badly with him.

One day the Prince was sitting disconsolate in the stables when, to his surprise, the black horse spoke to him.

"Come into my stall," it said, "I have something to say to you. Fetch my bridle and saddle from that cupboard and put them on me. Take the bottle that is beside them; it contains an ointment which will make your hair shine like pure gold; then put all the wood you can gather together onto the stove, till it is piled quite high up."

So the Prince did what the horse told him; he saddled and bridled the horse, he put the ointment on his hair till it shone like gold, and he made such a big fire in the stove that the flames sprang up and set fire to the roof, and in a few minutes the palace was burning like a huge bonfire.

Then he hurried back to the stables, and the horse said to him: "There is one thing more you must do. In the cupboard you will find a looking glass, a brush, and a riding whip. Bring them with you, mount on my back, and ride as hard as you can, for now the house is burning merrily."

The Prince did as the horse bade him. Scarcely had he got into the saddle than the horse was off and away, galloping at such a pace that, in a short time, the forest and all the country belonging to the Magician lay far behind them.

In the meantime the Magician returned to his palace, which he found in smoldering ruins. In vain he called for his servant. At last he went to look for him in the stables, and when he discovered that the black horse had disappeared too, he at once suspected that they had gone together; so he mounted a roan horse that was in the next stall, and set out in pursuit.

As the Prince rode, the quick ears of his horse heard the sound of pursuing feet.

"Look behind you," he said, "and see if the old man is following." And the Prince turned in his saddle and saw a cloud like smoke or dust in the distance.

"We must hurry," said the horse.

After they had galloped for some time, the horse said again: "Look behind, and see if he is still at some distance."

"He is quite close," answered the Prince.

"Then throw the looking glass on the ground," said the horse. So the Prince threw it; and when the Magician came up, the roan horse stepped on the mirror, and crash! His foot went through the glass, and he stumbled and fell, cutting his feet so badly that there was nothing for the old man to do but to go slowly back with him to the stables, and put new shoes on his feet. Then they started once more in pursuit of the Prince, for the Magician set great value on the horse, and was determined not to lose it.

In the meanwhile the Prince had gone a great distance; but the quick ears of the black horse detected the sound of following feet from afar.

"Dismount," he said to the Prince; "put your ear to the ground, and tell me if you do not hear a sound."

So the Prince dismounted and listened. "I seem to hear the earth tremble," he said; "I think he cannot be very far off."

"Mount me at once," answered the horse, "and I will gallop as fast as I can." And he set off so fast that the earth seemed to fly from under his hoofs.

"Look back once more," he said, after a short time, "and see if he is in sight."

"I see a cloud and a flame," answered the Prince; "but a long way off."

"We must make haste," said the horse. And shortly after he said: "Look back again; he can't be far off now."

The Prince turned in his saddle, and exclaimed: "He is close behind us; in a minute the flame from his horse's nostrils will reach us."

"Then throw the brush on the ground," said the horse.

And the Prince threw it, and in an instant the brush was changed into such a thick wood that even a bird could not have got through it, and when the old man got up to it the roan horse came suddenly to a standstill, not able to advance a step into the thick tangle. So there was nothing for the Magician to do but to retrace his steps, to fetch an ax, with which he cut himself a way through the wood. But it took him some time, during which the Prince and the black horse got on well ahead.

But once more they heard the sound of pursuing feet. "Look back," said the black horse, "and see if he is following."

"Yes," answered the Prince, "this time I hear him distinctly.

"Let us hurry on," said the horse. And a little later he said: "Look back now, and see if he is in sight."

"Yes," said the Prince, turning around, "I see the

flame; he is close behind us."

"Then you must throw down the whip," answered the horse. And in the twinkling of an eye the whip was changed into a broad river. When the old man got up to it he urged the roan horse into the water, but as the water mounted higher and higher, the magic flame which gave the Magician all his power grew smaller and smaller, till, with a fizz, it went out, and the old man and the roan horse sank in the river and disappeared. When the Prince looked around they were no longer to be seen.

"Now," said the horse, "you may dismount; there is nothing more to fear, for the Magician is dead. Beside that brook you will find a willow wand. Gather it, and strike the earth with it, and it will open and you will see a door at your feet."

When the Prince had struck the earth with the wand a door appeared, and opened into a large vaulted stone hall.

"Lead me into that hall," said the horse. "I will stay there; but you must go through the fields till you reach a garden, in the midst of which is a King's palace. When you get there you must ask to be taken into the King's service. Good-bye, and don't forget me."

So they parted; but first the horse made the Prince promise not to let anyone in the palace see his golden hair. So he bound a scarf around it, like a turban, and the Prince set out through the fields, till he reached a beautiful garden, and beyond the garden he saw the walls and towers of a stately palace. At the garden gate he met the gardener, who asked him what he wanted.

"I want to take service with the King," replied the Prince.

"Well, you may stay and work under me in the

garden," said the man; for as the Prince was dressed like a poor man, he could not tell that he was a king's son. "I need someone to weed the ground and to sweep the dead leaves from the paths. You shall have a florin a day, a horse to help you to cart the leaves away, and food and drink."

So the Prince consented, and set about his work. But when his food was given to him he only ate half of it; the rest he carried to the vaulted hall beside the brook, and gave to the black horse. And this he did every day, and the horse thanked him for his faithful friendship.

One evening, as they were together, after his work in the garden was over, the horse said to him: "Tomorrow a large company of Princes and great lords are coming to your King's palace. They are coming from far and near, as wooers for the three Princesses. They will all stand in a row in the courtyard of the palace, and the three Princesses will come out, and each will carry a diamond apple in her hand, which she will throw into the air. At whosesoever feet the apple falls he will be the bridegroom of that Princess. You must be close by in the garden at your work. The apple of the youngest Princess, who is much the most beautiful of the sisters, will roll past the wooers and stop in front of you. Pick it up at once and put it in your pocket."

The next day, when the wooers were all assembled in the courtyard of the castle, everything happened just as the horse had said. The Princesses threw the apples into the air, and the diamond apple of the youngest Princess rolled past all the wooers, out onto the garden, and stopped at the feet of the young gardener, who was busy sweeping the leaves away. In a moment he had stooped down, picked up the apple

217

and put it in his pocket. As he stooped the scarf around his head slipped a little to one side, and the Princess caught sight of his golden hair, and loved him from that moment.

But the King was very sad, for his youngest daughter was the one he loved best. But there was no help for it; and the next day a threefold wedding was celebrated at the palace, and after the wedding the youngest Princess returned with her husband to the small hut in the garden where he lived.

Some time after this the people of a neighboring country went to war with the King, and he set out to battle, accompanied by the husbands of his two eldest daughters mounted on stately steeds. But the husband of the youngest daughter had nothing but the old broken-down horse which helped him in his garden work; and the King, who was ashamed of this son-in-law, refused to give him any other.

So as he was determined not to be left behind, he went into the garden, mounted the sorry nag, and set out. But scarcely had he ridden a few yards before the horse stumbled and fell. So he dismounted and went down to the brook, to where the black horse lived in the vaulted hall. And the horse said to him: "Saddle and bridle me, and then go into the next room and you will find a suit of armor and a sword. Put them on, and we will ride forth together to battle."

And the Prince did as he was told; and when he had mounted the horse his armor glittered in the sun, and he looked so brave and handsome, that no one would have recognized him as the gardener who swept away the dead leaves from the paths. The horse bore him away at a great pace, and when they reached the battlefield they saw that the King was losing the day, so many of his warriors had been slain. But when the warrior on his black charger and in glittering armor appeared on the scene, hewing right and left with his sword, the enemy were dismayed and fled in all directions, leaving the King master of the field. Then the King and his two sons-in-law, when they saw their deliverer, shouted, and all that was left of the army joined in the cry: "A god has come to our rescue!" And they would have surrounded him, but his black horse rose in the air and bore him out of their sight.

Soon after this, part of the country rose in rebellion against the King, and once more he and his two sons-in-law had to fare forth to battle. And the son-in-law who was disguised as a gardener wanted to fight, too. So he came to the King and said; "Dear Father, let me ride with you to fight your enemies."

"I don't want a blockhead like you to fight for me," said the King. "Besides, I haven't got a horse fit for you. But see, there is a carter on the road carting hay, you may take his horse."

So the Prince took the carter's horse, but the poor beast was old and tired, and after it had gone a few yards it stumbled and fell. So the Prince returned sadly to the garden and watched the King ride forth at the head of the army accompanied by his two sons-in-law. When they were out of sight the Prince betook himself to the vaulted chamber by the brook side, and having taken counsel of the faithful black horse, he put on the glittering suit of armor, and was borne on the back of the horse through the air, to where the battle was being fought. And once more he routed the King's enemies, hacking to right and left with his sword. And again they all cried: "A god has come to our rescue!" But when they tried to detain him the black horse rose in the air and bore him out of their sight.

When the King and his sons-in-law returned home they could talk of nothing but the hero who had fought for them, and all wondered who he could be.

Shortly afterward the King of a neighboring country declared war, and once more the King and his sons-in-law and his subjects had to prepare themselves for battle, and once more the Prince begged to ride with them, but the King said he had no horse to spare for him. "But," he added, "you may take the horse of the woodman who brings the wood from the forest, it is good enough for you."

So the Prince took the woodman's horse, but it was so old and useless that it could not carry him beyond the castle gates. So he betook himself once more to the vaulted hall, where the black horse had prepared a still more magnificent suit of armor for him than the one he had worn on the previous occasions, and when he had put it on, and mounted on the back of the horse, he bore him straight to the battlefield, and once more he scattered the King's enemies, fighting single-handed in their ranks, and they fled in all directions. But it happened that one of the enemy struck with his sword and wounded the Prince in the leg. And the King took his own pocket handkerchief, with his name and crown embroidered on it, and bound it around the wounded leg. And the King would fain have compelled him to mount in a litter and be carried straight to the palace, and two of his knights were to lead the black charger to the royal stables. But the Prince put his hand on the mane of his faithful horse, and managed to pull himself up into the saddle, and the horse mounted into the air with him. Then they all shouted and cried: "The warrior who had fought for us is a god! He must be a god."

And throughout all the kingdom nothing else was spoken about, and all the people said: "Who can the hero be who has fought for us in so many battles? He cannot be a man, he must be a god."

And the King said: "If only I could see him once more, and if it turned out that after all he was a man and not a god, I would reward him with half my kingdom."

Now when the Prince reached his home—the gardener's hut where he lived with his wife—he was weary, and he lay down on his bed and slept. And his wife noticed the handkerchief bound around his wounded leg, and she wondered what it could be. Then she looked at it more closely and saw in the corner that it was embroidered with her father's name and the royal crown. So she ran straight to the palace and told her father. And he and his two sons-in-law followed her back to her house, and there the gardener lay asleep on his bed. And the scarf that he always wore bound around his head had slipped off, and his golden hair gleamed on the pillow. And they all recognized that this was the hero who had fought and won so many battles for them.

Then there was great rejoicing throughout the land, and the King rewarded his son-in-law with half of his kingdom, and he and his wife reigned happily over it.

Dapplegrim

retold by G. W. Dasent

From the earliest times horses have been given magical powers in Scandinavian stories—the ancient sagas and Eddas name many, including eight-footed Sleipnir, the horse of Odin All-father, who carries his master across the rainbow bridge from heaven to earth. The ancient peoples of Germany kept white horses in their sacred woods and groves: they were regarded with great reverence and no one was allowed to ride them. The horse in this story, Dapplegrim, is clearly related to these magical and mysterious animals. This story comes from Popular Tales from the Norse, *collected by Sir George Dasent. "The Seven Foals," on p. 351, is another tale from this collection.*

Once on a time there was a rich couple who had twelve sons; but the youngest, when he was grown up, said he wouldn't stay any longer at home, but be off into the world to try his luck. His father and mother said he did very well at home, and had better stay where he was. But no, he couldn't rest; away he must and would go.

So at last they gave him leave. And when he had walked a good bit, he came to a King's palace, where he asked for a place and got it.

Now the daughter of the King of that land had been carried off into the hill by a Troll, and the King had no other children; so he and all his land were in great grief and sorrow, and the King gave his word that anyone who could set her free should have the Princess and half the Kingdom. But there was no one who could do it, though many tried.

So when the lad had been there a year or so, he longed to go home again and see his father and mother, and back he went; but when he got home his father and mother were dead, and his brothers had shared all that the old people owned between them, and so there was nothing left for the lad. "Shan't I have anything at all, then, out of Father's and Mother's goods?" said the lad. "Who could tell you were still alive, when you went gadding and wandering about so long?" said his brothers. "But all the same, there are twelve mares up on the hill which we haven't yet shared among us; if you choose to take them for your share, you're quite welcome."

Yes! the lad was quite content; so he thanked his brothers and went at once up on the hill, where the twelve mares were out at grass. And when he got up there and found them, each of them had a foal at her side, and one of them had besides, along with her, a big dapple-gray foal, which was so sleek that the sun shone from its coat.

"A fine fellow you are, my little foal," said the lad.

"Yes," said the foal; "but if you'll only kill all the other foals, so that I may run and suck all the mares one year more, you'll see how big and sleek I'll be then."

Yes! The lad was ready to do that; so he killed all the twelve foals and went home again.

So when he came back the next year to look after his foal and the mares, the foal was so fat and sleek that sun shone from its coat, and it had grown so big, the lad had hard work to mount it. As for the mares, they each had another foal.

"Well, it's quite plain I lost nothing by letting you suck all my twelve mares," said the lad to the yearling, "but now you're big enough to come along with me."

"No," said the colt, "I must bide here a year longer; and now kill all the twelve foals, that I may suck all the mares this year, too, and you'll see how big and sleek I'll be by summer."

Yes! the lad did that; and next year when he went up on the hill to look after his colt and the mares, each mare had her foal, but the dapple colt was so tall the lad couldn't reach up to his crest when he wanted to feel how fat he was; and so sleek he was, too, that his coat glistened in the sunshine.

"Big and beautiful you were last year, my colt," said the lad, "but this year you're far grander. There's no such horse in the King's stable. But now you must come along with me."

"No," said Dapple again, "I must stay here one year more. Kill the twelve foals as before, that I may suck the mares the whole year, and then just come and look at me when the summer comes."

Yes! the lad did that: he killed the foals, and went away home.

But when he went up next year to look at Dapple and the mares, he was quite astonished. So tall, and stout, and sturdy, he never thought a horse could be; for Dapple had to lie down on all fours before the lad could bestride him, and it was hard work to get up even then, although he lay flat; and his coat was so smooth and sleek, the sunbeams shone from it as from a looking glass.

This time Dapple was willing enough to follow the lad, and when he came riding home to his brothers, they all clapped their hands and crossed themselves, for such a horse they had never heard of nor seen before.

"If you will only get me the best shoes you can for my horse, and the grandest saddle and bridle that are to be found," said the lad, "you may have my twelve mares that graze upon the hill yonder, and their twelve foals into the bargain." For you must know that this year, too, every mare had her foal.

Yes, his brothers were ready to do that, and so the lad got such strong shoes under his horse that the stones flew high aloft as he rode away across the hills; and he got a golden saddle and a golden bridle, which gleamed and glistened a long way off.

"Now we're off to the King's palace," said Dapplegrim—that was his name; "but mind you ask the King for a good stable and good fodder for me."

Yes! the lad said he would mind; he'd be sure not to forget; and when he rode off from his brothers' house, you may be sure it wasn't long, with such a horse under him, before he got to the King's palace.

When he came there, the King was standing on the steps, and stared and stared at the man who came riding along.

"Nay, nay!" said he, "such a man and such a horse I never yet saw in all my life."

But when the lad asked if he could get a place in the King's household, the King was so glad, he was ready to jump and dance as he stood on the steps.

Well, he said, perhaps he might get a place there.

"Aye," said the lad, "but I must have good stable-room for my horse, and fodder that one can trust."

Yes! He should have meadow hay and oats, as much as Dapple could cram, and all the other knights had to lead their horses out of the stable that Dapplegrim might stand alone and have it all to himself.

But it wasn't long before all the others in the King's household began to be jealous of the lad, and there was no end to the bad things they would have done to him, if they had only dared. At last they thought of telling the King how he had said he was the man to set the King's daughter free—whom the Troll had long since carried away into the hill—if only he chose. The King called the lad before him, and said he had heard that the lad said he was good to do so and so; so now he must go and do it. If he did it, he knew how the King had promised his daughter and half the Kingdom, and that promise would be faithfully kept; if he didn't he should be killed.

The lad kept on saying he never said any such thing; but it was no good—the King wouldn't even listen to him; and so the end of it was he was forced to say he'd go and try.

So he went into the stable, down in the mouth and heavy-hearted, and then Dapplegrim asked him at once why he was in such dumps.

Then the lad told him all, and how he couldn't tell which way to turn—"For as for setting the Princess free, that's downright nonsense."

"Oh! But it might be done perhaps," said Dapplegrim. "I'll help you through; but you must first have me well shod. You must go and ask for twelve pounds of iron and twelve pounds of steel for the shoes, and one smith to hammer and one to hold."

Yes, the lad did that, and got for answer "Yes!" He got both the iron and steel, and the smiths, and so

Dapplegrim was shod both strong and well, and off went the lad from the courtyard in a cloud of dust.

But when he came to the hill into which the Princess had been carried, the pinch was how to get up the steep wall of rock where the Troll's cave was, in which the Princess had been hid. For you must know the hill stood straight up and down right on end, as upright as a house-wall, and as smooth as a sheet of glass.

The first time the lad went at it he got a little way up; but then Dapplegrim's forelegs slipped, and down they went again, with a sound like thunder on the hill.

The second time he rode at it he got some way farther up; but then one foreleg slipped, and down they went with a crash like a landslide.

But the third time Dapple said —

"Now we must show our mettle," and went at it again till the stones flew heaven-high about them, and so they got up.

Then the lad rode right into the cave at full speed, and caught up the Princess, and threw her over his saddlebow, and out and down again before the Troll had time even to get on his legs; and so the Princess was freed.

When the lad came back to the palace, the King was both happy and glad to get his daughter back; that you may well believe; but somehow or other, though I don't know how, the others about the court had so brought it about that the King was angry with the lad after all.

"Thanks you shall have for freeing my Princess," said he to the lad, when he brought the Princess into the hall and made his bow.

"She ought to be mine as well as yours; for you're a wordfast man, I hope," said the lad.

"Aye, aye!" said the King, "have her you shall, since I said it; but, first of all, you must make the sun shine into my palace hall."

Now, you must know there was a high steep ridge of rock close outside the windows, which threw such a shade over the hall that never a sunbeam shone into it.

"That wasn't in our bargain," answered the lad; "but I see this is past praying against; I must go and try my luck, for the Princess I must and will have."

So down he went to Dapple, and told him what the King wanted, and Dapplegrim thought it might easily be done, but first of all he must be new shod; and for that twelve pounds of iron and twelve pounds of steel, besides, were needed, and two smiths, one to hammer and the other to hold, and then they'd soon get the sun to shine into the palace hall.

So when the lad asked for all these things, he got them at once—the King couldn't say nay for very shame; and so Dapplegrim got new shoes, and such shoes! Then the lad jumped upon his back, and off they went again; and for every leap that Dapplegrim gave, down sank the ridge fifteen ells into the earth, and so they went on till there was nothing left of the ridge for the King to see.

When the lad got back to the King's palace, he asked the King if the Princess were not his now; for now no one could say that the sun didn't shine into the hall. But then the others set the King's back up again, and he answered the lad should have her of course, he had never thought of anything else; but first of all he must get as grand a horse for the bride to ride on to church as the bridegroom had himself.

229

The lad said the King hadn't spoken a word about this before, and that he thought he had now fairly won the Princess; but the King held to his own; and more, if the lad couldn't do that he should lose his life; that was what the King said. So the lad went down to the stable in doleful dumps, as you may well fancy, and there he told Dapplegrim all about it; how the King had laid that task upon him, to find the bride as good a horse as the bridegroom had himself, else he would lose his life.

"But that's not so easy," he said, "for your match isn't to be found in the wide world."

"Oh, yes, I have a match," said Dapplegrim. "But 'tisn't so easy to find him, for he abides in Hell. Still we'll try. And now you must go up to the King and ask for new shoes for me, twelve pounds of iron, and twelve pounds of steel; and two smiths, one to hammer and one to hold; and mind you see that the points and ends of these shoes are sharp; and twelve sacks of rye, and twelve sacks of barley, and twelve slaughtered oxen we must have with us. And mind, we must have twelve ox hides, with twelve hundred spikes driven into each; and, let me see, a big tar barrel—that's all we want."

So the lad went up to the King and asked for all that Dapplegrim had said, and the King again thought he couldn't say nay, for shame's sake, and so the lad got all he wanted.

Well, he jumped on Dapplegrim's back, and rode away from the palace, and when he had ridden far, far over hill and heath, Dapple asked—

"Do you hear anything?"

"Yes, I hear an awful hissing and rustling up in the air," said the lad. "I think I'm getting afraid."

"That's all the wild birds that fly through the wood. They are sent to stop us; but just cut a hole in the grain sacks, and they'll have so much to do with the grain, they'll forget us quite."

Yes! the lad did that; he cut holes in the grain sacks, so that the rye and barley ran out on all sides. Then all the wild birds that were in the wood came flying around them so thick that the sunbeams grew dark; but as soon as they saw the grain, they couldn't keep to their purpose, but flew down and began to pick and scratch the rye and barley, and after that they began to fight among themselves. As for Dapplegrim and the lad, they forgot all about them, and did them no harm.

So the lad rode on and on—far, far over mountain and dale, over sand hills and moor. Then Dapplegrim began to prick up his ears again, and at last he asked the lad if he heard anything. "Yes! Now I hear such an ugly roaring and howling in the wood all around, it makes me quite afraid."

"Ah!" said Dapplegrim. "That's all the wild beasts that range through the wood, and they're sent out to stop us. But just cast out the twelve carcasses of the oxen; that will give them enough to do, and so they'll forget us outright."

Yes! the lad cast out the carcasses, and then all the wild beasts in the wood, both bears, and wolves, and lions—all fell beasts of all kinds—came after them. But when they saw the carcasses, they began to fight for them among themselves, till the blood flowed in streams; but Dapplegrim and the lad they quite forgot.

So the lad rode far away, and Dapplegrim didn't let the grass grow under him, as you may fancy. At last Dapple gave a great neigh.

"Do you hear anything?" he said.

"Yes, I hear something like a colt neighing loud, a long, long way off," answered the lad.

"That's a full-grown colt then," said Dapplegrim, "if we hear him neigh so loud such a long way off."

After that they traveled a good bit. Then Dapplegrim gave another neigh.

"Now listen, and tell me if you hear anything," he said.

"Yes, now I hear a neigh like a full-grown horse," answered the lad.

"Aye, aye!" said Dapplegrim, "you'll hear him once again soon, and then you'll hear he's got a voice of his own."

So they traveled on and on, and then Dapplegrim neighed the third time. But before he could ask the lad if he heard anything, something gave such a neigh across the heathy hillside, the lad thought hill and rock would surely be rent asunder.

"Now, he's here!" said Dapplegrim. "Make haste now, and throw the ox hides, with the spikes in them, over me, and throw down the tar barrel on the plain; then climb up into that great spruce fir yonder. When it comes, fire will flash out of both nostrils, and then the tar barrel will catch fire. Now, mind what I say. If the flame rises, I win; if it falls, I lose. But if you see me winning, take and cast the bridle—you must take it off me—over its head, and then it will be tame enough."

So just as the lad had done throwing the ox hides, with the spikes, over Dapplegrim, and had cast down the tar barrel on the plain, and had got well up into the spruce fir, up galloped a horse, with fire flashing out of his nostrils, and the flame caught the tar barrel at once. Then Dapplegrim and the strange horse began to fight till the stones flew heaven high. They fought, and bit, and kicked, both with fore feet and hind feet, and sometimes the lad could see them, and sometimes he couldn't, for the blaze and smoke of the tar was blowing and whirling all ways about them. But at last the flame began steadily to rise; for wherever the strange horse kicked or bit, he met the spiked hides, and at last he had to yield. When the lad saw that, he wasn't long in getting down from the tree, and in throwing the bridle over its head, and then it was so tame you could hold it with a pack thread.

And what do you think? That horse was dappled, too, and so like Dapplegrim, you couldn't tell which was which. Then the lad bestrode the new Dapple and rode home to the palace, and the old Dapplegrim ran loose by his side. So when he got home, there stood the King out in the yard.

"Can you tell me now," said the lad, "which is the horse I have caught, and which is the one I had before? If you can't, I think your daughter is fairly mine."

Then the King went and looked at both Dapples, high and low, before and behind, but there wasn't a hair on one which wasn't on the other as well.

"No," said the King, "that I can't; and since you've got my daughter such a grand horse for her wedding, you shall have her with all my heart. But still we'll have one trial more, just to see whether you're fated to have her. First she shall hide herself twice, and then you shall hide yourself twice. If you can find out her hiding place, and she can't find out yours, why then you're fated to have her, and so you shall have her."

"That's not in the bargain, either," said the lad. "But we must just try, since it must be so."

And the Princess went off to hide herself first.

So she turned herself into a duck and lay swimming

on a pond that was close to the palace. But the lad only ran down to the stable, and asked Dapplegrim what she had done with herself.

"Oh, you only need to take your gun," said Dapplegrim, "and go down to the brink of the pond, and aim at the duck which lies swimming about there, and she'll soon show herself."

So the lad snatched up his gun and ran off to the pond. "I'll just take a pop at this duck," he said, and began to aim at it.

"Nay, nay, dear friend, don't shoot, it's I," said the Princess.

So he had found her once.

The second time the Princess turned herself into a loaf of bread, and laid herself on the table among four other loaves; and so like was she to the others, no one could say which was which.

But the lad went again down to the stable to Dapplegrim, and said how the Princess had hidden herself again, and couldn't tell at all what had become of her.

"Oh, just take and sharpen a good bread knife," said Dapplegrim, "and do as if you were going to cut in two the third loaf on the left hand of those four loaves which are lying on the dresser in the King's kitchen, and you'll find her soon enough."

Yes! the lad was down in the kitchen in no time, and began to sharpen the biggest bread knife he could lay hands on; then he caught hold of the third loaf on the left hand, and put the knife to it, as though he was going to cut it in two.

"I'll just have a slice off this loaf," he said.

"Nay, dear friend," said the Princess, "don't cut. It's I."

So he had found her twice.

Then he was to go and hide; but he and Dapplegrim had settled it all so well beforehand, it wasn't easy to find him. First he turned himself into a tick, and hid himself in Dapplegrim's left nostril; and the Princess went about hunting for him everywhere, high and low. At last she wanted to go into Dapplegrim's stall, but he began to bite and kick, so that she daren't go near him, and so she couldn't find the lad.

"Well," she said, "since I can't find you, you must show me where you are." And in a trice the lad stood there on the stable floor.

The second time Dapplegrim told him again what to do; and then he turned himself into a clod of earth and stuck himself between Dapple's hoof and shoe on the near forefoot. So the Princess hunted up and down, out and in, everywhere. At last she came into the stable, and wanted to go into Dapplegrim's box stall. This time he let her come up to him, and she pried high and low, but under his hoofs she couldn't come, for he stood firm as a rock on his feet, and so she couldn't find the lad.

"Well, you must show yourself, for I'm sure I can't find you," said the Princess, and as she spoke the lad stood by her side on the stable floor.

"Now you are mine indeed," said the lad; "for now you see I'm fated to have you." This he said both to the father and the daughter.

"Yes, it is so fated," said the King. "So it must be."

Then they got ready for the wedding in right down earnest, and lost no time about it. And the lad got on Dapplegrim and the Princess on Dapplegrim's match, and then you may fancy they were not long on their way to church.

Black Shadows of Palms

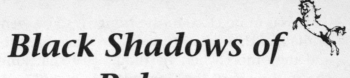

ELYNE MITCHELL

This story is taken from Light Horse to Damascus, *which tells of the Australian Light Horse during the First World War, and how they fought the Turkish army in Palestine. Karloo—a brown Thoroughbred from the Snowy Mountains of Queensland—and his rider, Dick Osborne, are fictional, but the events of the story are true. The author's father was General Sir Harry Chauvel, the general in the story.*

The currawongs mentioned in the story are a kind of bird. They have black or gray feathers, and are sometimes called "bell magpies."

Elyne Mitchell has also written a series of stories about the Silver Brumby, a wild horse of the Snowy Mountains.

The horse lines were quiet, every horse sleeping. The only animal that moved was a mule that had chewed through his rope and gone wandering—long-eared, grotesque in the fading moonlight.

Karloo was sound asleep and never felt *his* rope being chewed. When he woke he was loose and apparently had walked some distance in his sleep, because he was no longer in the lines.

He woke completely.

He was quite close to the troughs, so he went for a drink, and then was just going to make back to Silver and the others when he thought of that kind little chestnut mare of the General's. He would go to find her. He began walking carefully and rather quietly around the bivvy sheets that were tied up with guy ropes as shelters, and around the men who were simply sleeping in the open rolled in their rugs. Each section was together. He knew where Dick and his lot were.

There were, of course, sentries all around the camp, and yet no one seemed to see Karloo in that misted light between moonset and sunrise. He had quite a distance to go and he threaded his way so quietly with an unusual feeling of freedom, while the army slept around him. He stepped gently, ears listening this way and then that way. No one seemed to see him . . . no one after he had left his own regiment well behind, except one wakeful man whose horse had a shrapnel wound and had been sent back to the Canal or Hill 70.

Now, no man wanted to be left out of the pursuit of the retreating Turkish army, so a certain amount of fairly sporting horse thieving or "deflecting" of reinforcements had been tried since the Battle of Romani.

Karloo, walking loose, was almost the answer to the prayer of that wakeful, horseless Light Horseman.

Karloo soon realized he was being followed. He quickened his pace. The man spoke in a whisper. Karloo looked around suspiciously—and tripped over the guy rope of someone's bivvy. The man had his fingers on his headstall, and might have caught him if the owners of the bivvy tent had not woken up, cursing.

Karloo leaped away. There was some laughter from the men who came out from under the bivvy sheet.

They knew that the one following Karloo needed a horse. They began to encircle Karloo, all speaking quietly, kindly, but all of them ready to laugh.

Then Karloo caught sight of that chestnut mare in the distance. He jumped one bivvy, got away from his pursuers, and rushed into the lines by the pretty mare. They touched noses and for a moment he forgot the men who were after him. That moment was too long, and there was a strange hand gripping his headstall. He struggled briefly, but he knew he should not be loose, so he gave in, and was led away, two or three other men following behind, to make sure he did not pull back.

Sometime later a strange saddle was placed on his back by a strange man. Karloo danced away from the saddle, blew himself out when he was girthed up. He had been well broken in and well educated, so that he had never thought how he would get rid of a rider. Nor had anyone ever ridden him except Dick and Dick's father.

The stranger spoke gently to him and was kind, but he tried to swing away when the man went to mount. He was too tightly held to do much. The stranger was a good horseman, but the minute he was in the saddle, Karloo reefed, plunged, got the bit firmly in his teeth and sprang away at a gallop.

Already a long column of horsemen had ridden from the camp in the oasis. Perhaps Dick was there. . . . The chestnut mare was out in the lead, he knew, because he had seen her start off.

Just here, the desert was fairly firm, firm enough on which to gallop fast, but even so a cloud of sand flew up behind him. Karloo had won races at home and he was racing now. The man on his back was going to be difficult to unseat, but Karloo was determined to throw him somehow.

There had been laughter from all the stranger's mates, when Karloo had taken off. Now it was just a tussle between himself, the stranger—and the desert. If he hit a soft spot going at this speed . . .

Karloo wasn't thinking of the column of horsemen, but suddenly he realized he was getting closer to them; he could dimly hear cheers rippling along the lines.

The stranger on his back tried to pull him around in a circle. Karloo clamped his teeth tighter on the bit and fought with all the strength in his neck. It was then that he started to aim for the head of the column and that chestnut mare.

His off forefoot landed on a sharp stone: he faltered in his stride and felt the stranger lose his balance and his grip just for a second, and the girth was loose. In that second Karloo stretched his neck out farther and went even faster. It was a long time since he had galloped like this.

He half-heard another ripple of cheering. He was getting closer to the head of the column. The stranger was still on his back.

Perhaps if he propped and swung one way, that stranger—whose grip, he knew, was getting tired— might just fly off. Perhaps he could make it a real twist around, one way, and then if he did not go off, twist the other way.

Closer, closer, and the laughter and the cheering was quite clear. Then Karloo propped and swung, and suddenly kicked up his heels at the same time. He felt the strange rider go forward as he propped. The swing and the kick-up and the loose girth had him out of the saddle and onto the pommel. Karloo swung the other

way and kicked up again. Suddenly he started to enjoy himself. He could hear the yells and cheers, and a voice calling: "A fiver on the horse."

That chestnut mare could not be far off now. He had seen her go out in front of the red-and-white standard . . .

The stranger was still with him, but only just. Karloo galloped toward the head of the column, but not so fast that he could not give a few twisting kicks to keep

241

that stranger from getting back into the saddle.

There was the standard; the mare must be right in front of it. Karloo propped again, tucked his head down, and made the first real buck of his life.

The stranger shot off into the sand.

Karloo headed straight for that chestnut mare, and a cheer roared from hundreds of throats—louder and deeper than the noise made by any mob of white cockatoos in the gumtrees back at home.

"Well done, Karloo," the General said, having enjoyed the show as much as anyone. "We seem to be getting to know you rather well," and a trooper was detailed off to return him to Dick.

It was not till hours later, when the section had been sent off on a patrol, that Karloo's off forefoot began to feel sore where he had trodden on that sharp stone.

The four had done what they set out to do, and a little more, for they had amused themselves by examining some more oases and chasing a few Bedouin from one. Then they stopped to boil the quartpots and have a meal in the shade of some rather pretty palms.

Karloo, tethered very close to Dick, nibbled gently at a biscuit which Dick was just going to put into his own mouth.

"You are a devil." Dick grinned and gave it to him.

All four horses were tied to the palm trees against which their owners sat, and presently Joker's enquiring nose came around Roy's shoulder.

Joker rather liked bully beef.

They were well on their way back to camp when Karloo began to go lame.

"Karloo's going short!" Dick exclaimed and he dismounted quickly and picked up the brown forefoot.

There, unmistakably, was the cut and swollen frog of his foot. All the men clustered around to look—for a man and his horse could not be considered apart; they were one indivisible unit, and they had all shared in Dick's fear for Karloo early that morning.

"Must've hurt it in his gallop this morning," Jim said, and Roy was muttering: "What lousy luck." Bill looked anxiously across the desert.

The only thing for Dick to do was to walk, to save his horse as much as possible. So he and Karloo plodded side by side, wearily through the sand, and the others came slowly along with them.

That night the section went out on a skirmish without Karloo or Dick, and when they returned, Jim had a flesh wound in one leg.

That was how Karloo came to be looked after by Jim, while Dick went out on Silver.

Karloo liked Jim very well, and Jim kept his hoof cleaned out, and painted it with some liniment every few hours; he fed and watered him, he groomed him, and he talked to him all day. In spite of all this, Karloo was very restless. His foot was much better, and Jim was always close, but he felt a creeping coldness in his coat and behind his ears. Something was happening . . . something was wrong.

A small party of those who had been on the same patrol as Silver, Joker, and Snow, came back, but Jim and Karloo could see no sign of the rest of their section. Jim walked quickly toward those who had returned. Most of these, or their horses, were slightly wounded.

"Where are the others?" he called.

"Looking for Dick and Silver," came the answer.

Jim borrowed a horse—one that did not mind a strange rider. He stood thinking for a moment; then he untied Karloo.

"His horse will find him and Silver, if anyone can," he said to the others who stood around.

Someone handed him an extra water bottle.

"Dick could be pretty thirsty," he said.

Night was coming on, and the moon would not rise till later.

Jim had got his directions from the men who had come back. He had been told that there was a fair-sized oasis held by strong bodies of Turks where there had been quite a fight, and no one had seen Dick and Silver since. That they were missing was only discovered as the small force was mustering up to come back. Then Roy and Bill, with Joker and Snow, had gone off looking for him, and several others had gone too.

Jim, on a big, raking bay horse, Bosker, and with Karloo's reins in his hand, set off. He was not leading Karloo, for Karloo had known for hours that something was wrong, and now he knew exactly which direction he should go. He led.

In a few minutes they were joined by two other men.

"If you're going to let Karloo lead you, he may take you right to Jacko, if Dick's a prisoner," they said. "We'd best come along too."

So three men and four horses set forth, into that strange light when the air between sand and sky is already dark, yet the sky still holds a last light, and the sand catches this light so that every little ridge is touched with white and every hollow a dark pool. Sand dunes loomed against the sky, and they skirted around them, wove their way between them. Sometimes Karloo headed straight up a long sandy ridge toward the first pale, evening star, sometimes he went along a narrow strip of flat desert with high dunes on either side, and the men shivered, wondering whether the Turks could be high above them.

Karloo, with fine disregard for the possibility of Turks being close, threw up his head and neighed when they came out of one of these narrow defiles. It was not that he felt he was really close to Dick and Silver, it was that he knew he was heading toward them, and also he had a feeling that Joker and Snow must be somewhere in the vicinity.

He neighed again and stopped to listen. From far, far ahead he could hear an answer. It was Snow. He moved on briskly, even though the sand was making the frog of his foot sore again.

The men had all strained their ears to hear an answering neigh, but they had not heard that thin, faraway call.

Jim's leg was sore, too.

"We're heading straight for the oasis where the boys found Jacko," one man whispered.

"After every scrap since Romani, Jacko's fought like hell and then quietly withdrawn," Jim said. "They may have left this oasis by now."

"Hope you're right, but what if they've taken Dick with them?"

Yes, what? Karloo was filled with what was no more than an intense feeling that he was heading straight for Dick and Silver—and that something was wrong.

All light, except starlight, was gone now; there was just the faint radiance in the sand of that bright-starred sky, that cold, brittle sky.

The men were all alert for any faint sign or sound of

danger, but the only sound through the whole of that ice-cold desert night was the whisper of the horses' hooves. The utter silence that stretched around them for miles was only intensified by this whisper of the hooves.

Karloo did not notice the silence; he did notice the narrow defiles between the sand dunes, the shape of bushes, as though it were all drawn in black and white on his mind as they passed.

Quite suddenly, out of this intense silence there sounded Snow's neigh. Karloo threw up his head to reply, and stepped out even faster. There were horses coming toward them, Snow in the lead.

Karloo greeted Snow and Joker, but he was fretting to keep going. Jim tried to hold him for a moment or so while they all talked in whispers, but in the end he had to say to the others:

"Better come on. If you've not found them, maybe Karloo is our only hope."

Now there were nine men and ten horses going on through the night over the sand that whispered around their horses' hooves.

Ten horses and nine men getting closer and closer to the oasis where the Turks had put up such a strong defense the day before . . . ten horses, three of one section, and the main one, Karloo, that horse which even the great bushmen of the Light Horse called bush-wise.

Jim pulled Karloo to a halt while the other men unslung their rifles, and there was click, click, click, as three fixed bayonets. They would be ready for any-thing. Karloo could feel their tension, and it made him go more warily, his ears pricked forward. He for-got his sore foot—he was feeling and listening with every part of himself. He was sure that Dick and Silver were not so very far away, and he nearly called, but for so long now, Dick had quietened his wish to neigh whenever there was danger, that he was quiet. He knew by the tension in the other horses and the men, by the unslung rifles and the clicks of the fixed bayonets, that this was a time there could be danger.

Then he smelled water.

All the horses smelled water, and they strode out a little faster. After a while, the men pulled up so that they could sit and listen, peer into the cold starry night, and listen. There was just silence and the smell of water. Then ahead, on the eastern horizon, there came a radiance. Men and horses stayed quite still watching—the sinewy, strong horses, the lean, strong men, keen-faced, staring ahead—and the moon rose over the desert's rim. Now every sand ridge was eerily silvered. Some palm heads were etched in black, only about a quarter of a mile away.

A soft sigh sounded from the men. Instinctively they spread out in skirmishing order, so that they did not present one quite large dark mass in the moonlight.

One small dune rose on the left. It would provide a little cover behind which to creep up on that oasis. There were a few scrub bushes.

Jim made Karloo come with him, in line with the dune. These Light Horsemen had become so clever at using every little piece of cover that it seemed sometimes that they and their horses could melt into the desert and become ghosts of all those other great armies—but these men were in ragged shirts and breeches, not chain mail, like the Crusaders, and their chargers were not like the Greek horses ... they were strange ghosts ...

Nine men, ten horses, they edged their way forward to that oasis. One man with his rifle ready, one with fixed bayonet went ahead of Jim, who, leading Karloo, could not defend himself.

There was a deadly silence among the palm trees, and emptiness.

Karloo felt Jim's hand between his ears, as though Jim knew he would almost have to neigh. He kept quiet.

Snow had come up alongside him, and it was good to feel the warmth of him—the warmth of his body and the warmth of the old shared friendship.

The moon was still low on the horizon, its light coming obliquely through the palm trunks—these straight trunks throwing long, black shadows on the blanched sand, shadows so black, so straight.

They moved out into open desert. A string of oases ran southeast. The next one was some distance off and far larger. That was where the Turks might be, the one where the day's fighting had been.

There was very little cover, just a ridge here and there, and a few prickly bushes. Nine men and ten horses spread themselves out and made use of every depression, every rise, every piece of scrub. The moon slowly rose, and they moved forward.

Karloo saw the tracks before the men seemed to notice them, tracks of quite a few horses, both to and from the oasis. There was also a smell of blood. Soon there were empty cartridge cases lying on the sand. He knew that Jim had noticed the tracks when he felt himself pulled a bit closer to Bosker, made to go even more carefully.

Once again the men assembled together behind a little hillock of sand, before advancing on the oasis, and then two went ahead of Jim and Karloo, but this time there were men with rifles ready on either side of them, too.

They walked so slowly that even the horses seemed to be on tiptoes . . . slowly on through the unearthly silence.

They stepped across the first black shadow of a palm tree. No sound. The horses ahead flickered through the straight black shadows of more and more palm trunks. The sand through which they walked was all churned up. One horse shied at a dead Turk. The silence was still absolute.

The nine horsemen and ten horses did not go out into the open center of the oasis by the well, in case they made too good a target for hidden Turkish snipers. They went on around, flickering through the palm trunks.

Around the well there were more bodies. They all seemed to be in the yellowy-gray Turkish uniform. There were tins, bottles, ammunition boxes, all the dirt and untidiness that was usual at an oasis when the Turks had gone. Tough, courageous fighters though they were, their camps were filthy beyond bearing.

The Turks had gone. Their tracks led due east, and the string of oases wound around in a more southerly direction.

Karloo turned for the next clump of palms and stepped out well, even though his foot was getting very sore. They passed through one untracked oasis, and another was not far ahead. Suddenly Karloo felt sure he heard something, or smelled something—felt sure Dick and Silver were ahead—and he neighed loudly.

Clear on the night air came an answering neigh.

"Silver!" said Jim, enormous relief in his voice. He pressed Bosker into a canter, and the eight other horses were cantering behind them.

Even then, when it seemed most unlikely that any Turks were ahead, one with rifle and one with bayonet took the lead, and they all slowed to a walk as they came within a few yards of the palm trees. The first straight black shadow lay across the sand. They were entering the oasis.

Silver called again and every horse answered. The shadow horses and men went weaving, flickering through the palms toward the central open space.

It could be a trap. Turks could be there, with Silver and Dick held prisoner.

There was the small open space, all barred over with the palm shadows, and in the middle, tethered to something, beside a rough wall, the moon lighting up his mane and tail, stood Silver.

It was Dick to whom he was tethered.

In a second Jim was kneeling beside him. Karloo was sniffing at his face. There was a strong smell of blood, but he was breathing. Silver's reins were wound around his left wrist and clutched in his hand. He stirred as Karloo's whiskers moved over his chin.

"Drink," he muttered.

Jim undid the top of his water bottle, went to raise Dick's head, and withdrew his hand, sticky with clotted blood. He tried to trickle some water into Dick's mouth. It was difficult to do so, out of an army water bottle, without either wasting water or choking him.

Silver had started nudging Jim with his nose. Now Roy was behind Dick, raising him a little, feeling his head.

"Not a very deep cut," he said, "but a bump like an emu's egg."

"Butt of a rifle," Dick said thickly, after another sip of water. "Be all right . . . Silver . . . ?"

"He's here safely. Karloo's here, too; he found you both."

"Karloo," said Dick, but then he seemed to have fainted, or his mind wandered off somewhere else.

Jim washed his face with a wet handkerchief. It was essential to get him out of the oasis and back to camp before daylight, before the heat of the sun. After the next drink, Dick seemed rather more sensible. He put up a hand to Karloo's nose:

"Thought I heard a great mob of currawongs," he said, and grinned.

One of the men was feeling Silver all over for any wounds. Roy had already gone over Dick's legs and arms, and was gently testing out his ribs, his spine.

They decided to put him in front of Roy, but on Bosker, who had not had the whole day out in the desert, and who looked strong enough to carry three or four. They fastened Roy and Dick together, at the waist, with bandoliers.

Ten men and eleven horses started back over the moon-white desert.

The Fall of Troy

retold by James Reeves

One of the most exciting horse stories ever told is about a wooden horse. The story of the Trojan Horse has been enjoyed for thousands of years. It is part of the Iliad, *a long story-poem about the siege of Troy (or Ilium), thought to have been written by Homer, who lived some time between the eleventh and seventh century* B.C. *James Reeves was a poet and children's author, as well as a reteller of classic stories.*

For ten years the Greeks had been trying in vain to capture the city of Troy, which lay across the sea. Paris, the son of Priam, King of Troy, had carried off a Greek queen, the beautiful Helen. Her husband, Menelaus, had roused many of the Greek kings and chieftains to gather an army together. They collected many ships and sailed to the coast near Troy. Then they besieged the city and tried to force their way in. For ten long years the war went on. Many brave men were killed on both sides. The Greek warriors began to fear they could never win. But the war came to an end at last, and this is the story of how it happened.

The guardian goddess of Troy was Pallas Athena. There were many statues to her set up in temples in the city, and of these the most famous and the most precious was known as the Palladium. It was thought to have fallen from heaven and so to be a gift from the gods themselves. The Trojans believed that the city could never be taken so long as the Palladium was safe inside its walls.

Then one dark night when all Troy was asleep, and the towers and palaces were lit only by starlight, two bold Greeks, Odysseus and Diomedes, stole silently into Troy, carried off the precious statue, and took it back to their camp. The Greeks well knew how greatly their enemies prized the Palladium.

But in spite of the loss of the statue Troy still held out. The Greeks called a council of war and decided that, since they could not take the city by force, they must do it by trickery. This was the advice of the cunning leader Odysseus. They pretended that they were giving up the fight and sailing home. Some of the ships set sail and left the coast, only to anchor a short distance away behind a nearby island called Tenedos. Some of the Greeks remained behind in their camp on the plains between the sea and the city. Then they built from fir wood a gigantic horse, which they left well within sight of the Trojans. This done, they carried away their tents and equipment and sailed away to join the rest of the fleet moored behind Tenedos. Next morning the Trojan guards reported with amazement that the Greeks were nowhere to be seen. Their camp was broken up, the ships vanished. Great was the rejoicing as the gates of the city were opened and the citizens poured out. They wandered freely over the deserted battlefields of the past ten years, gazing with wonder at their enemy's old encampment. It all seemed too marvelous to be true.

What excited their liveliest curiosity was the wooden horse. Everyone tried to guess what it was for. Most thought it was a sign of surrender, or a peace offering,

or else perhaps an image for the gods to ensure a safe return for the Greek ships.

"Let us take it into the city!" cried some. "Let us set it up in our marketplace as a memorial to our dead and a sign of victory to be shown to our children and grandchildren."

"Yes," echoed others. "Into the city with the horse!"

"Fetch wheels and ropes and drag it in triumph through our gates!"

Then Laocoön, the priest of the sea god, Poseidon,

who was on his way to make a morning sacrifice to the god, raised his hand for silence and called out sternly:

"Are you mad, fellow Trojans? Never trust the Greeks. This is some trick. Have you fought them for ten years only to be beaten by cunning? I am no coward, but I am afraid of all Greeks, especially when they bring gifts."

With these words he aimed his spear at the horse's side.

The point pierced it, and a hollow sound came from within. It seemed as if Laocoön had persuaded the Trojans to his way of thinking, for some prepared to destroy the Greek offering there and then.

"He is right," said someone. "Let us burn the thing!"

But at that moment a group of Trojans appeared, dragging with them a terrified Greek who had been left behind and had been found hiding among the bushes near the seashore. The man, whose hands had been tied behind his back, was brought before King Priam and the other Trojan leaders.

"Spare my life, I beg," pleaded the prisoner. "Or if you will not, then give me a quick and merciful death."

"We will spare your life," said the king, "on condition that you answer our questions truthfully."

The man promised to tell them all they wanted to know, and his hands were untied.

"I am a Greek," he said in answer to their questions, "by name Sinon. The Greeks have sailed for home. The decision to give up the war was taken after long and bitter discussion. It was agreed to make a human sacrifice to the gods on their departure to make sure of a fortunate voyage. Because Odysseus hated me, he persuaded the leaders that I, Sinon, was to be the victim. However, last night I managed to escape and hide near the shore. My countrymen are now my enemies, as they have been yours. All I ask is to be allowed to live among you and become a citizen of Troy—or only a slave, if you so decide."

Sinon looked so humble and so piteous that no one doubted his words.

"And what," asked Priam, "is the purpose of this monstrous image?"

Sinon told the Trojans that the Greeks had left the horse as an offering to the goddess Athena.

"But why did it have to be of this enormous size?"

"Ah," replied the crafty Sinon, "it was made huge so that you would not be able to bring it inside your gates. One of our prophets said that if you managed to get the horse inside the city, no one would ever be able to conquer Troy. You would be safe as long as the wooden horse was within your walls."

All who heard the Greek were deeply impressed. Surely this unfortunate man was speaking the truth. They were beginning to think of ways by which they might drag the monster through the gates of the city when a terrible event occurred—an event which made them hesitate no longer.

Their priest Laocoön, with his two little sons, was on his way to the shore to make his offering to Poseidon when two huge serpents appeared from the sea and advanced directly toward him. All gasped with horror as the scaly creatures wound themselves around the bodies of the boys and crushed them to death. Their father, struggling hopelessly to free the boys, was himself wrapped around by the serpents' coils, so that he could no longer breathe and fell lifeless to the ground beside the bodies of the children. A cry of horror went up from the people.

"He has angered the gods," they said, "and this is their revenge. He struck the horse with his spear, and they sent the sea serpents to kill him. Now we know that the image is sacred, and the Greek is speaking the truth."

Some of the Trojans fetched wheels and ropes and hauled the wooden horse to the gates of the city. Others, meanwhile, took down one of the gateposts and part of the wall which supported it, so as to make room for its passage. Then, with songs of triumph, they pulled it right to the very heart of Troy, where it stood in the marketplace towering over the people. They danced about it, strewing flowers before it and throwing garlands about its neck. Then, as evening fell, the people prepared to feast and make merry. Drinking and singing, they roamed about the streets until, worn out with the day's excitements, they went home and slept a sounder sleep than they had enjoyed for ten years. Their enemies had gone, and the wooden horse would keep their city safe.

But Laocoön had been right to mistrust the Greeks, for the horse was no offering to the gods but a means of destruction. Inside its hollow side were a score or more of the bravest of the Greek warriors. They had been waiting there, fully armed, all that day and the whole of the night before. Sinon, who had taken care to hide near the horse, now crept out of the shadows, gave his friends the signal, and let them out of their hiding place. Swiftly they climbed down the rope ladder they had taken inside the horse and made their way to the city gates.

The breach in the wall had been repaired by the Trojans as soon as the horse was inside, and the gates had been closed and barred. But the sentries, fearing no ill, had fallen asleep after their merrymaking, and the Greek warriors had no difficulty in overpowering them. Meanwhile, under cover of night the main body of the Greeks had returned from their shelter behind the island of Tenedos, and were now gathered outside the gates, waiting for their friends to let them in.

Then began the utter destruction of Priam's beautiful city. As the terrified Trojans awoke from sleep, they heard the crackling of flames, the clash of arms, and the shouting of the exultant Greeks. Their enemies rushed from street to street, burning, looting, and pulling down. The men of Troy hastily buckled on their armor, helped by the women; they went out, sword in hand, to battle with the Greeks. Spears and lances flew through the air. Even the boys fought. As the flames took hold of the lofty buildings, roofs and gables caught fire, and stone towers toppled upon the heads of attackers and defenders alike. Dogs rushed shrieking through the streets, driven mad by the flames. Girls cowered inside the houses, trying to quieten their baby brothers and sisters, until driven out by fire or the enemy.

The Trojans, taken by surprise, were no match for the Greeks. They were put to the sword, while the women were carried off to be slaves. Yet many of the Greeks were slain too. Many of the sons of King Priam were killed or taken prisoner; Priam himself was slain as he took refuge in the temple of Athena.

So ended the great and proud kingdom of Troy, and the city became a smoking ruin, a scene of death and desolation. The Greeks withdrew to their ships and set sail for home, carrying away their slaves and their booty, the treasures of Troy's temples and palaces. Thus ended the ten years' war in a single night.

The Tale of the Ebony Horse

retold by Geraldine McCaughrean

Another story about a wooden horse—from the Arabian Nights. The stories in this book are told by Shahrazad (Scheherazade) to her husband, King Shahryar of Sasan. King Shahryar's first wife had betrayed him; and to avenge himself, he married a new woman each day and had her executed the following morning. During the night after their wedding, Shahrazad told her husband such a wonderful story that he decided to put off her execution until he had heard the end of it. She told him stories for a thousand and one nights, before her own story ended. . . .

Before the winds of Time blow, and every trace of Man is covered with Sahara sand, let me name the name of King Sabur, ruler of all Persia, who had one son and one daughter.

Every year King Sabur's birthday was celebrated more lavishly than the year before. The fame of the festivities spread like the circular sound of a gong echoing to the very rim of Persia: the dervishes who danced, the slave girls who served, the chefs who cooked, and the presents that were presented. But in the year of King Sabur's fifty-fifth birthday, the celebrations reached new splendors, and every road in the Kingdom was

littered with the presents that fell from the overfull
saddlebags of camel trains streaming into Tehran.

One gift surpassed all other gifts. It was brought by
an old Sage as twisted and stunted as a pollarded tree,
who lived in the mountain caves of Persia. The gift
was carried into the court under a white canopy with
curtains on all sides, and unveiled in front of the

King's throne. There stood a life-sized ebony horse. Its saddle was of red morocco with stirrups of chased gold, and its flanks were dappled with inlaid ivory in the shape of flower heads. Its mane and tail were of the finest strands of raw silk ever coaxed from the slow silkworm; and its eyes were many-faceted diamonds encasing brown- and black-striped tigereye.

"There is more wonderful artistry here than in any statue in my entire realm, sir," said the King. "You have honored me greatly."

"You see only its shape, and not its purpose, O best of Kings," said the Sage in a voice like safflower oil. "This horse has the power of flight: it can leap the rainbow and bring you safely to earth on the far shores of the sea."

"If this were true," said Sabur, "it would be the present to shame all other presents, and I would reward your generosity by granting as many wishes as your heart could think to express."

So the Sage demonstrated his magic ebony horse. Although it required six slaves to lift his twisted body into the saddle, once there the old man was little less than an angel. He flicked a key in the saddle's pommel, and the horse lifted its front hooves and plunged into the air, which buoyed it up as water buoys up a swimmer. Over the balcony rail and around the garden it flew, until the Sage brought it back to rest in front of the King's throne. The King was astonished:

"It is written that Alexander of Macedon had a flying horse called Bucephalus. With this horse I would be a second Alexander! Sabur the Great! Ask anything of me, gentle Sage, for if your wishes were as many as the grains of sand in a dune, I would grant them all!"

But the old man had only one wish. How then

could the King refuse him? He asked for the hand of the King's only daughter, and at once received permission from Sabur to marry her.

The Princess's cry could be heard throughout the palace when she was given the news and told to prepare herself for her immediate wedding. She ran distractedly to the eastern wing of the building and fell down at her brother's feet in a monsoon of tears.

"Whatever is the matter, little sister?" asked Kamar al-Akmar. "Nothing can be so terrible that your brother cannot remedy it."

"Then plead with my father, O brother among brothers, and beg him not to marry me to the foul, twisted old man who gave him the magic horse! I would rather die than marry a man whose face alone terrifies me!"

"What old man? What magic horse? Hush, little sister," said the Prince. "Our father will grant me anything, for I am his only son and heir. Put away your wedding clothes and do not think another thought concerning this repulsive suitor."

"Father!" said the Prince as he entered the throne room. "What is this I hear about you marrying my little sister to a baboon in return for some childish rocking horse?" He stopped short as he saw the horse in question, and walked around it admiringly. The King introduced the old Sage, who (can you wonder at it?) immediately hated Prince Kamar. He realized at once that Kamar al-Akmar would dissuade King Sabur from giving away his daughter in return for a birthday gift. But this hatred showed no more on his face than the sourness of a lemon shows on its skin. As the King explained how the magic horse flew, the Sage smiled and bowed and nestled close to the Prince.

"I must ride this wonderful beast!" exclaimed Kamar al-Akmar, and leaped into the saddle.

Still the Sage smiled and made little respectful bows toward him. "If you would raise it from the ground, simply flick the key on the right-hand side of the saddle, O delightful one, beat of your father's heart."

With a click and a whirring, a mechanical jolt, and a rushing slipstream, the magic horse bounded over the balcony rail and soared into the sky while Prince Kamar was still feeling for the stirrups. Half in and half out of the saddle, he was heaved up into the sky faster than an arrow aimed at the sun. The air thinned; he struck the separate sunbeams like a stick clattered along a fence; a little cloud fell past him on the right side like a lamb dropped from the claws of an eagle.

"Down, boy! Whoa!" he shouted. But the horse's ears were of solid ebony and deaf to all commands.

He was riding toward the sun as the moth rides on its wings toward the destruction of a candle flame.

"Fetch back my boy!" cried King Sabur, dragging on the Sage's clothes. "Bring down your horse or you will rob the whole kingdom of Persia of its Prince and heir!"

"As you would have robbed me of my rightful prize—the hand of your daughter. I know that it was already in your heart to withdraw your offer. Kamar al-Akmar had decided that the marriage was not to be. Well, now your son has gone to marry the world's sun, and may the warmth of that marriage char his skin!"

King Sabur threw the Sage into his deepest, most crawling dungeon, but revenge did nothing to ease his sorrow, for he was certain that Kamar al-Akmar was flying to his death. . . .

Kamar al-Akmar spoke severely to his quaking heart.

"Man was given mastery over all animals. Use those powers given you by Allah to control this mechanical beast, for as the poet might have said: *What flies up must fly down.*"

He searched the saddle for another key and, finally, as the silk mane of the horse began to shrivel in the sun's heat, found a switch, no larger than a pin, on the left-hand side. One flick, and the horse's climb slowed—stopped—reversed—and Kamar al-Akmar was plunging toward the open sea beyond the rivers of Tigris and Euphrates and the Shatt al-Arab. Having mastered both keys, Kamar was able to save himself from galloping into the sea, and crossed both water and land. His delight in the pleasures of flight had carried him to a land rich with many cities. And the fairest of these was Sana.

Seeing the palace of Sana amidst the tree-lined avenues of its surrounding city, Kamar al-Akmar thought to himself: "This seems like a place where a young Prince of blood royal might be offered meat and milk. But I shall land on the roof first and make certain that I am in a land friendly toward Persia, for I shall not eat off the table of my father's enemies."

The roof was not flat, as the roofs of Araby are flat. The ebony horse had to pick its way between a hundred minarets and sloping dormer windows, but was hidden from all eyes when the Prince dismounted and climbed into the palace attic through a small fanlight.

Below the palace dovecote and several storerooms, Kamar came to the uppermost staterooms of the royal apartments and accidentally walked into the bedroom of the kingdom's only Princess. (Believers in Love would say that Allah guided his footsteps.) There she lay, sound asleep on a satin bed hung with voile curtains and roofed with a carved rosewood canopy. Her golden hair covered all but her little white feet and her small white hands, and her face was turned toward him.

"This is how the sun must feel when the white and purple passionflower turns its face toward the light," thought Kamar al-Akmar, and his heart waded into the quicksand of love and was swallowed up wholly, completely, instantaneously.

"My heart is a swinging bell and you are its clapper," he said to the Princess Shams al-Nahar as she woke to his kisses.

"Your kisses are rain and I am a little parched flower," she said and wrapped him in the golden cloak of her hair as her soul cloaked him in love.

"You are my destiny, the reason for Allah's gift of sight," he said.

"You are my fate, and the reason for Allah's gift of hands," she replied.

"You are my sea, let me lay my shore alongside you," he said.

"You are my husband, let me lay my life beside yours," she said.

"You are a bee stealing the honey of the kingdom, and I shall wrench out your sting and crush you underfoot," said the King of Sana, entering the bedroom among a dozen armed and armored soldiers. The Princess hurriedly caught up a veil. "How did you come here past the hundred guards on the stairs and the twenty ferocious dogs in the palace garounds?"

After some moments, Prince Kamar al-Akmar managed to tear his eyes from the face of Shams al-Nahar and said, "Why do you offer such violence to your future son-in-law? For I am a Prince of the blood royal and I have decided to marry your daughter even if, for the bride-price, I must pay you a whole half-hemisphere of the world."

"Enough words from a miserable housebreaker. Get up, or your blood will dirty my daughter's bedspread when my soldiers kill you," said the King between his teeth. "This girl is promised to my cousin's third nephew's uncle—a venerable man of seventy-four respectable and noteworthy years. And what are *you*?"

The Princess Shams al-Nahar put her arms around Kamar al-Akmar and begged him not to rise and fight.

"I am the Prince Kamar al-Akmar and I am not a coward," he said, prizing himself free from her, "but I think your father is lacking in courtesy if he will not abide by the most basic rules of chivalry."

"How have I broken the rules of chivalry, runt of a thousand pig litters?" demanded the King (who was, in truth, a highly chivalrous man).

"Either you should offer to fight me in single combat, my lord, father of my lover," Kamar replied, "or you should send your whole army against me on a field of battle. But you insult me by sending a mere dozen against me like dogs set loose on a burglar."

The King of Sana looked the youth up and down as a woodcutter sizes up a tree for felling. He quickly decided that he could not fight such a leopard of a boy himself. "Very well, young civet cat. I shall range my army on the northern plain and place at your disposal a pitched tent, a horse, and some armor as soon as the midday heat has slackened."

"Armor is unnecessary," said Kamar, "and I have my own horse with me; I left it on your roof."

Then the King feared greatly for his daughter's honor: the young man who had seen her with her face uncovered and wearing only her hair was clearly as mad as a bareheaded man in a desert. "There are seventy stairs between each floor, and this is the topmost floor. Did your horse climb all those stairs or simply leap the two hundred feet to my roof? Come away, daughter, for this young man's wits have gone, and his wits will be followed shortly by his life."

When Prince Kamar al-Akmar was left alone, he climbed back to the roof and watched the army of Sana assemble on the field below. At a distance, the King had placed a pavilion and a horse, and a set of shining armor was laid out on the grass. Kamar mounted the ebony horse, flicked the key on the saddle, and together they leaped over the roof's parapet, somehow settling on the battlefield without being noticed by the milling soldiers.

"There he is!" one of them shouted. "Poor baby's only got a toy horse!" And wheeling their iron-shod horses toward Kamar, they galloped down on him like the unholy Turks when they stormed the Holy City.

As the first whirling sword shortened the hairs of the silken mane, Kamar flicked the key, and the ebony horse lifted into the air above the soldiers' heads and came to rest behind them. With a cry of astonishment, the whole army tried to turn, and some of the horses collided and fell over. Kamar met the return charge in just the same way, lifting out of reach of their lunging swords. Back and to, to and fro, the army rushed up and down the field with Kamar hovering a little above their heads on his magic, mechanical horse, teasing and enraging them. He never even drew his sword.

The Princess Shams al-Nahar watched spellbound from

a window, thinking she must be in love with the ghost of Alexander of Macedon, rider of Bucephalus. At last he rose so high into the air that the arch of the window prevented her from seeing his movements.

"What an amazing thing!" exclaimed the King, bustling into the room behind her among several soldiers who were red with heat and embarrassment. "A truly amazing thing! Did he tell you that his horse could fly, my dear? What an astounding young man! Send for the Royal Historian and have the story set down in writing."

"But where is Kamar al-Akmar?" his daughter interrupted. "Please tell me, Father, for he taught not only his horse to fly, but my heart also."

"Was that his name? Kamar al-Akmar?" asked the King. "Oh, well, he has gone, of course—flew away into the sun after he had shamed my fighting men sufficiently. Where's the Royal Historian?—Ah, there you are! Look now, you need not mention where we found him, but I want the story of this Kamar al-Akmar written down and . . ."

The King's voice grew fainter as he walked off along the corridor with his courtiers and officers, and Princess Shams al-Nahar found herself alone. But now she was alone as only ladies can be who have been unalone in the arms of Love. She vowed then and there that she would never marry any man but Kamar al-Akmar. And after a week of waiting, she had her maidservant burn the rosewood chest in which all her wedding clothes were stored. Little clouds came and went on the horizon, but the ebony horse and Kamar al-Akmar, it seemed, had ridden out of the whole realm of Sky.

*　　*　　*

Throughout the telling of the Tale of the Ebony Horse, Shahrazad stood to speak the words. When she had described the disappearance of Kamar al-Akmar from the life of Princess Shams al-Nahar, she said: "Does this conclusion please you, sir?"

"No, Shahrazad, of course not!" said the King, sitting up in bed.

"Then you may wish to hear the remainder of the story tomorrow night?"

"Certainly, if you will sit down to tell it," said Shahryar.

"I would rather stand, lord King," she said shortly, and then left the room and was not seen anywhere in the palace until the following evening.

When Prince Kamar al-Akmar returned to his father's kingdom, the whole countryside was grieving and the palace balcony, where he set down the ebony horse, was strewn with ashes of mourning.

"Who has died?" he asked anxiously when he found his mother, father, and sister all weeping in one room. At the sight of him they leaped up and danced with delight.

"Where have you been, core of my heart's fruit, son of my old age?" asked King Sabur. "For we saw you fly toward the sun and certain destruction, like a moth toward a candle flame. The sorcerer who made that evil horse is locked in my deepest dungeon, for he undoubtedly expected you to die."

"Oh free him, Father, for his evil intention brought me nothing but good." Then, Kamar told his story and begged his father to send ambassadors to Sana to ask for the hand of Shams al-Nahar.

"No, no, son. For you were received there like a

common burglar and entertained with violence. Besides, the daughter's tears will have long since dried, and your name will be to her nothing but a half-remembered sound heard through a wall. Woman's love is as short as the stride of a man standing still. No. We shall celebrate your return, select for you four of the fairest Persian brides, and lock away the ebony horse which so nearly robbed me and my kingdom of its most glorious Prince."

Kamar could not believe in his heart that the King's words were true.... But Sabur his father had great experience of the world, and the wisdom of an older man. So Kamar was obedient and allowed the celebrations to roll around him like an incoming sea. Seven whole days passed in festivities. Then the Prince spoke these words to himself:

"There is food on every table, and yet there is an emptiness inside me larger than hunger. There is laughter on all sides, and yet my throat is blocked with tears. There are presents given me with every passing hour, and yet I seem to have nothing." He went to the storeroom where the mechanical ebony horse was standing, dragged it to a landing at the head of the stairs, and climbed into its saddle.

"I must fetch back my Shams al-Nahar!" he called out as he swooped low over the heads of his family and relatives and out across the terrace. "I have starved my love but it will not die. I have denied my love but it will not set me free." As he crossed the palace moat, Kamar could see the wrinkled face of the old Sorcerer, newly released from prison, watching him with open hatred.

"I have told my heart what you say," said Shams al-Nahar to her father, "but it will not listen. I have argued with my heartbeat, but I lose every argument. I will not marry my cousin's third nephew's uncle, because he is not Kamar al-Akmar."

"Why shed tears for a boy who has forgotten you already?" said her mother. "The love of a man (and of foreigners in particular) is as short as your memory of tomorrow."

But the Princess had cried herself to sleep between her parents, and they left her sleeping, and went downstairs with much cursing of Love and of Kamar al-Akmar.

"There is salt water enough in the Seven Seas, Shams al-Nahar. Why weep more?" said Prince Kamar, stepping from his hiding-place behind a curtain to wake her with kisses.

"You are the songbird in my heart's cage," she said on waking and seeing his eyes.

"You are the crescent moon flying through my night sky," he said. "And I have come back for you."

She dressed, and braided her hair with the most valuable jewels, and climbed with him to the roof, where they mounted the ebony horse. She sat behind him in the saddle, her arms around his waist, and sang this love song as they flew:

> *I have been without my Kamar*
> *One long week, but not again;*
> *For without him I am summer*
> *Drought without the touch of rain.*
>
> *I am now without my mother—*
> *Father too—and far from home;*
> *But because I'm with my lover,*
> *Where in me shall tears find room?*

Shams al-Nahar did not unclasp her hands until they landed together in the water gardens of Tehran, a mile from the royal palace of King Sabur.

"Wait here: I shall go ahead and prepare the city to greet you as befits a Princess arriving to marry the Prince of Persia," said Kamar. "Look after the ebony horse."

"Do not be long," replied Shams al-Nahar, kissing his fingers, "for no civic welcome can make up for the time we shall be apart."

The Princess sat beside a fountain, singing love songs and holding the bridle of the ebony horse as if it might gallop away of its own accord. This was the sight which met the eyes of the foul-faced Sorcerer as he left Tehran city. (When King Sabur had released the horse-maker from prison, he had made it perfectly clear that the Sorcerer would not be given the Persian Princess for a bride: "Count yourself fortunate that Prince Kamar has begged me to free you!" Sabur had said. "That is reward enough for an ugly jackal like you!")

Imagine the mixture of passions that seethed in his chest as he walked through the water gardens. Imagine his joy at seeing the horse he had labored long years to create!

"Child! You must be the Princess Shams al-Nahar from the city of Sana in al-Yaman. Let me kiss the ground between your feet." (Shams al-Nahar let out a little scream as the twisted shadow of old ugliness sprang at her and huddled like a toad at her feet.) "The Prince has sent me to bring you to the city. For the streets have been strewn with catkins and yellow flowers, and there are ribbons flying from every lattice of every window in Tehran. Your wedding canopy has been made of watered-silk embroidered with diamonds. If you will help me up on to the flying horse and climb up behind me, I shall pilot you to your wedding feast."

Because she was sweet-natured and trusting, and because this grotesque stranger knew the secret of the ebony horse, she believed his every word. She steadied his buckled, knotty old legs as he climbed onto the fountain wall and then onto the horse. Vaulting daintily into the saddle behind him, she was glad when he knotted his belt around them both for safety, because she did not have to put her arms around his wizened waist.

A mile above the water gardens, where the first drops of dew were gathering along the colored rim of evening, Shams al-Nahar realized that they were turning away from the city. "Where are you taking me, father of all foulness? Where is my wedding feast? Why are you disobeying your master, Kamar al-Akmar?"

"Him my master? I who mastered the secret of flight am master of a thousand times more than that . . . that smudged painting of a boneless boy! I shall give you far less poetry and far more kisses when you are married to *me*!"

Shams al-Nahar screamed and tried to break the belt that tied her to the Sorcerer, and throw herself down through the snow-valleys of cloud. But the cloth was magic, and held her like a hoop of steel. "I am the grain and you are the millstone," she cried. "Will you crush me to dust with such unhappiness?" But her terror only delighted the Sorcerer, and the ebony horse bucked between his excited knees.

"I see a party of noblemen hunting in that wood."

He laughed. "I shall have them witness a marriage between you and me before the sun moves farther through the sky."

"You may have captured me, O murderer of joy," said Shams, "but you can never capture my heart. I gave that to Kamar, and he has it safe with him in Tehran." And her tears fell like rain out of the sky, and splashed the face of the King of Rums who was among the hunting party in the wood.

No sooner had the King wiped his face and looked around for rain clouds, than his men brought him word of a strange threesome standing in a clearing close by: an old man, a beautiful young woman, and a life-sized toy horse. The King of Rum combed his beard and went to meet them.

"King among huntsmen, inventor of grace and royalty," said the Sorcerer, screwing his detestable face into a yellow smile, "I have been searching for a man of breeding, chivalry, and rank to witness the marriage of two happy lovers. Will you be so good as to declare us married?" Turning to Shams, he said, "I take you for my wife, Shams al-Nahar."

"Well, I refuse you!" cried the bride. "For it is against Allah's will that a girl should be married by force to a deceitful barbarian who steals her away from family and fiancé!" She shut her eyes as the Sorcerer turned on her with his fists raised. Waiting for him to strike her down, she heard the whistle of a sword's blade and felt the belt fall from around her waist. Opening her eyes, she saw the body of the Sorcerer stretched out on the ground with the King's sword through him.

"Allah bless you with wealth and happiness," she said, bowing down to the King of Rum. "For I was promised already to a Prince of Persia who loves me as the sword loves its sheath—"

"Let him show his face in the land of Rum, and I shall kill him too," the King interrupted. "For your beauty was the downfall of this monstrous imitation of a man: I have decided to marry you myself." And he seized her bodily and threw her across his saddle. His courtiers followed him back to the Court of Rum, bringing with them the strange model of a horse.

When Kamar al-Akmar returned to the water gardens to fetch his bride into a city festooned with joy, his heart sickened inside him and almost died. He wandered through the countryside, calling out the name of Shams al-Nahar; asking everyone and everywhere for news of a priceless beauty and a horse of ebony and ivory. For months he searched the remotest places and busiest towns, singing in his soul the song:

> *Why have you left me, daughter of brightness,*
> *My dearest of girls?*
> *Before I believe that your loving proved faithless,*
> *I'll travel the world:*
> *Then if it's true that all women are heartless*
> *And most of all you,*
> *I'll marry and slaughter a wife every night, yes,*
> *For fear they leave too.*

One day his search brought him to the gates of Rum, and as he entered, the guards seized hold of him and demanded to know his name.

"I am Kamar, a simple Persian," he said. "I'm in search of a lady lost to me."

"A Persian, eh? Don't you realize that Rum has

sworn war against the empire of Persia? The police will want to question you in case you are a spy." And they dragged him away to prison.

As he sat in his cell, writing fragments of poetry on the wall, the jailer struck up a conversation with him. "Did you hear what the King did to the last Persian he found inside the realm of Rum? A gruesome-looking old man he was, with a beautiful young wife and a peculiar toy horse carved out of ebony and ivory. He ran the old man through with his very own sword— for kidnapping the girl—and then claimed her for himself! He would have married her, too, if she hadn't gone quite mad on the spot. A pitiful case. Now all the King has is a toy horse locked up in his treasure house, and a stream of doctors calling at the door every day to try and cure the girl."

Prince Kamar realized at once what had happened and, in his joy, wrote on the wall:

> *No, it is not true what some men say*
> *That love lasts no more than two days;*
> *For the fair Shams is beautiful*
> *And Allah is merciful;*
> *And I'll love them both longer than always.*

When the police came to question Kamar the next morning, he answered them in these words: "I am Kamar of Persia, a doctor specializing in the treatment of young ladies who have suddenly fallen into madness. You have doubtless heard my name for my successes are past numbering. Indeed, many lovely maidens have been restored to their happy parents when their minds had seemed as broken as twelve eggs in a basin."

Naturally, the police hurried Kamar al-Akmar to the King's private chamber and introduced him as a doctor.

"If you can cure this wild beauty from al-Yaman," said the King, "you will never have to work again, for I shall make you as rich as chocolate cake."

Shams al-Nahar was tearing herself and rolling on the floor as though her skin was on fire, but at first sight Kamar knew that his beloved fiancée was only *pretending* to be mad to save herself from a marriage to the King of Rum. She threw herself at him, snarling and snapping as if she would bite and scratch him to death, but she whispered in his ear: "I am sick with the sickness which cures all sicknesses, for I am sick with love for the Prince Kamar al-Akmar."

"If I am correct, this cure will be easier than any of my previous cases. This child seems to be suffering from woodworm-to-the-brain. Has she by chance been in contact with a wooden carving of any kind—a cradle or a rocking horse?"

"Indeed she has!" exclaimed the King, greatly impressed. "For she was found in the company of a life-sized ebony horse."

"Good, good, good," said Kamar. "Bring the horse and the girl to an open place where I can treat them both; for the spirit of the horse has obviously entered her head along with the woodworm, and I must return it to the horse."

You may be able to imagine the plan in Kamar's mind. You may also be able to imagine the fright in his heart when he saw the King of Rum make ready wedding garments and a feast, so that he could marry the Princess immediately after her cure.

In the center of the palace polo-grounds, Kamar set

to work. He bound Shams hand and foot and tied her across the saddle of the ebony horse. Then he circled the beast, uttering imprecations and chants and all the names of medicines he had taken as a boy. Just as the King of Rum gave his first yawn of boredom, Kamar leaped into the saddle and flicked the key for flight.

When the horse filled itself with a parcel of wind and lifted its front hooves in the air, the King of Rum and all his courtiers threw up their hands in amazement. The King rushed forward to seize his bride, and his hands snatched at her sandals as the ebony horse pounced over his head and soared into the sky.

"Come back, you Persian horse thief!" he bellowed. "Bring back my woman!"

Arrows as thick as a locust swarm clipped the horse's flanks, but soon the two riders were so high that they strummed the separate sunbeams as a hand strums the strings of a guitar.

"You are all the music I have ever heard," said Shams al-Nahar as they flew.

"You are all the poetry that was ever written," Kamar replied.

In that era, there was only one thing happier than the wedding of Shams al-Nahar and Kamar al-Akmar, and that was the married life which followed it. In all the realms of Time, there was only one thing greater than the love of Shams al-Nahar and Kamar al-Akmar—and that was the love of Shahrazad of Sasan for Shahryar, ruler of Sasan and destroyer of all love.

When Shahryar looked up with astonishment at this last sentence of the story of the ebony horse, his bedroom was empty and Shahrazad was gone. Even night had paused in its passing to hear the love story of Shams and Kamar, and it was still dark outside. A cold draft blew through the heart of Shahryar, even though no windows stood open, and even though the doors of his heart had stood shut for several thousand days.

Jane, Betsy, and Blanche

THÉOPHILE GAUTIER

Théophile Gautier was born in 1811, and tried to train as an artist, but he had to give this up because of his bad eyesight. He turned to writing, and became well-known as a poet, novelist, and journalist. He loved animals, and in his book Ménagerie Intime *he told the stories of the cats, dogs, horses, and other animals he had owned. In this extract about some of his horses, Théophile Gautier mentions a revolution. This isn't the famous French Revolution of 1789—France has experienced several revolutions! There was an important uprising in 1848, and another, less important, in 1851.*

After Théophile grew to be a man, he wrote a great many books, which are all delightful to read, and everybody bought them, and Théophile got rich and thought he might give himself a little carriage with two horses to draw it.

And first he fell in love with two dear little Shetland ponies who were so shaggy and hairy that they seemed all mane and tail, and whose eyes looked so affectionately at him that he felt as if he should like to bring them into the drawing room instead of sending them to the stable. They were charming little creatures, not a bit shy, and they would come and poke their noses into Théophile's pockets in search for sugar, which was always there. Indeed their only fault was that they were so very, very small, and that, after all, was *not* their fault. Still, they looked more suited to an English child of eight years old, or to Tom Thumb, than to a French gentleman of forty, not so thin as he once was, and as they all passed through the streets, everybody laughed, and drew pictures of them, and declared that Théophile could easily have carried a pony on each arm, and the carriage on his back.

Now Théophile did not mind being laughed at, but still he did not always want to be stared at all through the streets whenever he went out. So he sold his ponies and began to look out for something nearer his own size. After a short search he found two of a dapple gray color, stout and strong, and as like each other as two peas, and he called them Jane and Betsy. But although, to look at, no one could ever tell one from the other, their characters were totally different, as Jane was very bold and spirited, and Betsy was terribly lazy. While Jane did all the pulling, Betsy was quite contented just to run by her side, without troubling herself in the least, and, as was only natural, Jane did not think this at all fair, and took a great dislike to Betsy, which Betsy heartily returned. At last matters became so bad that, in their efforts to get at each other, they half kicked the stable to pieces, and would even rear themselves upon their hind legs in order to bite each other's faces. Théophile did all he could to make them friends, but nothing was of any use, and at last he was forced to sell Betsy. The horse he found to replace her was a shade lighter in color, and therefore not quite so good a match, but luckily Jane took to her at once, and lost no time in doing the honors of the stable. Every day the affection between the two became greater: Jane would lay her head on Blanche's shoulder—she had been called Blanche because of her fair skin—and when they were turned out into the stable yard after being rubbed down, they played together like two kittens. If one was taken out alone, the other became sad and gloomy, till the well-known tread of its friend's hoofs was heard from afar, when it would give a joyful neigh, which was instantly answered.

Never once was it necessary for the coachman to complain of any difficulty in harnessing them. They walked themselves into their proper places, and behaved in all ways as if they were well brought up, and ready to be friendly with everybody. They had all kinds of pretty little ways, and if they thought there was a chance of getting bread or sugar or mellow rind, which they both loved, they would make themselves as caressing as a dog.

Nobody who has lived much with animals can doubt that they talk together in a language that man is too stupid to understand; or, if anyone *had* doubted it, they would soon have been convinced of the fact by the conduct of Jane and Blanche when in harness. When Jane first made Blanche's acquaintance, she was afraid of nothing, but after they had been together a few months, her character gradually changed, and she had sudden panics and nervous fits, which puzzled her master greatly. The reason for this was that Blanche, who was very timid and easily frightened, passed most of the night in telling Jane ghost stories, till poor Jane learned to tremble at every sound. Often, when they were driving in the lonely alleys of the Bois de Boulogne after dark, Blanche would come to a dead stop or shy to one side as if a ghost, which no one else could see, stood before her. She breathed loudly, trembled all over with fear, and broke out into a cold perspiration. No efforts of Jane, strong though she was, could drag her alone. The only way to move her was for the coachman to dismount and to lead her, with his hand over her eyes, for a few steps, till the vision seemed to have melted into air. In the end, these terrors affected Jane just as if Blanche, on reaching the stable, had told her some terrible story of what she had seen, and even her master had been known to confess that when, driving by moonlight down some dark road, where the trees cast strange shadows, Blanche would suddenly come to a dead halt and begin to tremble, he did not half like it himself.

With this one drawback, never were animals so charming to drive. If Théophile held the reins, it was really only for the look of the thing, and not in the least because it was necessary. The smallest click of the tongue was enough to direct them, to quicken them, to make them go to the right or to the left, or even to stop them. They were so clever that in a very short time they had learned all their master's habits, and knew his daily haunts as well as he did himself. They would go of their own accord to the newspaper office, to the printing office, to the publisher's, to the Bois de Boulogne, to certain houses where he dined on certain days in the week, so very punctually that it was quite provoking; and if it ever happened that Théophile spent longer than usual at any particular place, they never failed to call his attention by loud neighs, or by pawing the ground, sounds of which he quite well knew the meaning.

But alas, the time came when a Revolution broke out in Paris. People had no time to buy books or to read them; they were far too busy in building barricades across the streets, or in tearing up the paving stones to throw at each other. The newspaper in which Théophile wrote, and which paid him enough money to keep his horses, did not appear anymore, and sad though he was at parting, the poor man thought he was lucky to find someone to buy horses, carriage, and harness, for a fourth part of their worth. Tears stood in his eyes as they were led away to their new stable; but he never forgot them, and they never forgot him. Sometimes, as he sat writing at his table, he would hear from afar a light quick step, and then a sudden stop under the windows.

And their old master would look up and sigh and say to himself, "Poor Jane, poor Blanche, I hope they are happy."

A Wayside Adventure

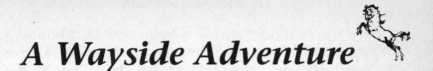

C. S. LEWIS

The seven books that make up C. S. Lewis's Chronicles of
Narnia *have been very popular with readers of all ages
since they were first published. This story comes from* The
Horse and His Boy. *When Shasta learns that the fisherman he has always thought is his grandfather plans to sell
him as a slave to a Tarkaan, a great lord of Calormen, he
does not know what to do. To his great surprise, the
Tarkaan's horse can talk—and the horse knows exactly
what to do. He wants to escape to his own country, Narnia,
but he needs a rider so that people who see him won't try to
catch him. Bree, the horse, persuades Shasta to escape with
him . . . and that is where the adventure starts.*

I t was nearly noon on the following day when Shasta
was wakened by something warm and soft moving
over his face. He opened his eyes and found himself
staring into the long face of a horse; its nose and lips
were almost touching his. He remembered the exciting events of the previous night and sat up. But as he
did so he groaned.

"Ow, Bree," he gasped. "I'm so sore. All over. I can
hardly move."

"Good morning, small one," said Bree. "I was afraid
you might feel a bit stiff. It can't be the falls. You
didn't have more than a dozen or so, and it was all

lovely, soft, springy turf that must have been almost a pleasure to fall on. And the only one that might have been nasty was broken by that gorse bush. No: it's the riding itself that comes hard at first. What about breakfast? I've had mine."

"Oh, bother breakfast. Bother everything," said Shasta. "I tell you I can't move." But the horse nuzzled at him with its nose and pawed him gently with a hoof till he had to get up. And then he looked about him and saw where they were. Behind them lay a little copse. Before them the turf, dotted with white flowers, sloped down to the brow of a cliff. Far below them, so that the sound of the breaking waves was very faint, lay the sea. Shasta had never seen it from such a height and never seen so much of it before, nor dreamed how many colors it had. On either hand the coast stretched away, headland after headland, and at the points you could see the white foam running up the rocks but making no noise because it was so far off. There were gulls flying overhead and the heat shivered on the ground; it was a blazing day. But what Shasta chiefly noticed was the air. He couldn't think what was missing, until at last he realized that there was no smell of fish in it. For of course, neither in the cottage nor among the nets, had he ever been away from that smell in his life. And this new air was so delicious, and all his old life seemed so far away, that he forgot for a moment about his bruises and his aching muscles and said:

"I say, Bree, didn't you say something about breakfast?"

"Yes, I did," answered Bree. "I think you'll find something in the saddlebags. They're over there on that tree where you hung them up last night—or early this morning, rather."

They investigated the saddlebags and the results were cheering—a meat pasty, only slightly stale, a lump of dried figs and another lump of green cheese, a little flask of wine, and some money; about forty crescents in all, which was more than Shasta had ever seen.

While Shasta sat down—painfully and cautiously— with his back against a tree and started on the pasty, Bree had a few more mouthfuls of grass to keep him company.

"Won't it be stealing to use the money?" asked Shasta.

"Oh," said the horse, looking up with its mouth full of grass, "I never thought of that. A free horse and a talking horse mustn't steal, of course. But I think it's all right. We're prisoners and captives in enemy country. That money is booty, spoil. Besides, how are we to get any food for you without it? I suppose, like all humans, you won't eat natural food like grass and oats."

"I can't."

"Ever tried?"

"Yes, I have. I can't get it down at all. You couldn't either if you were me."

"You're rum little creatures, you humans," remarked Bree.

When Shasta had finished his breakfast (which was by far the nicest he had ever eaten) Bree said, "I think I'll have a nice roll before we put on that saddle again." And he proceeded to do so. "That's good. That's very good," he said, rubbing his back on the turf and waving all four legs in the air. "You ought to have one too, Shasta," he snorted. "It's most refreshing."

But Shasta burst out laughing and said, "You do

look funny when you're on your back!"

"I look nothing of the sort," said Bree. But then suddenly he rolled round on his side, raised his head, and looked hard at Shasta, blowing a little.

"Does it really look funny?" he asked in an anxious voice.

"Yes, it does," replied Shasta. "But what does it matter?"

"You don't think, do you," said Bree, "that it might be a thing *talking* horses never do?—a silly, clownish trick I've learned from the dumb ones? It would be dreadful to find, when I get back to Narnia, that I've picked up a lot of low, bad habits. What do you think, Shasta? Honestly, now. Don't spare my feelings. Should you think the real, free horses—the talking kind—do roll?"

"How should I know? Anyway, I don't think I should bother about it if I were you. We've got to get there first. Do you know the way?"

"I know my way to Tashbaan. After that comes the desert. Oh, we'll manage the desert somehow, never fear. Why, we'll be in sight of the northern mountains then. Think of it! To Narnia and the North! Nothing will stop us then. But I'd be glad to be past Tashbaan. You and I are safer away from cities."

"Can't we avoid it?"

"Not without going a long way inland, and that would take us into cultivated land and main roads; and I wouldn't know the way. No, we'll just have to creep along the coast. Up here on the downs we'll meet nothing but sheep and rabbits and gulls and a few shepherds. And by the way, what about starting?"

Shasta's legs ached terribly as he saddled Bree and climbed into the saddle, but the horse was kindly to him and went at a soft pace all afternoon. When evening twilight came they dropped by steep tracks into a valley and found a village. Before they got into it Shasta dismounted and entered it on foot to buy a loaf and some onions and radishes. The horse trotted around by the fields in the dusk and met Shasta at the far side. This became their regular plan every second night.

These were great days for Shasta, and every day better than the last as his muscles hardened and he fell less often. Even at the end of his training Bree still said he sat like a bag of flour in the saddle. "And even if it was safe, young 'un, I'd be ashamed to be seen with you on the main road." But in spite of his rude words Bree was a patient teacher. No one can teach riding so well as a horse. Shasta learned to trot, to canter, to jump, and to keep his seat even when Bree pulled up suddenly or swung unexpectedly to the left or the right—which, as Bree told him, was a thing you might have to do at any moment in a battle. And then of course Shasta begged to be told of the battles and wars in which Bree had carried the Tarkaan. And Bree would tell of forced marches and the fording of swift rivers, of charges and of fierce fights between cavalry and cavalry, when the war-horses fought as well as the men, being all fierce stallions, trained to bite and kick, and to rear at the right moment so that the horse's weight as well as the rider's would come down on an enemy's crest in the stroke of sword or battle-ax. But Bree did not want to talk about the wars as often as Shasta wanted to hear about them. "Don't speak of them, youngster," he would say. "They were only the Tisroc's wars and I fought in them as a slave and a dumb beast. Give me the Narnian wars where I shall fight as a free horse among my own people! Those will be wars worth talking about. Narnia and the North! Bra-ha-ha! Broo Hoo!"

Shasta soon learned, when he heard Bree talking like that, to prepare for a gallop.

After they had traveled on for weeks and weeks past

more bays and headlands and rivers and villages than Shasta could remember, there came a moonlit night when they started their journey at evening, having slept during the day. They had left the downs behind them and were crossing a wide plain with a forest about half a mile away on their left. The sea, hidden by low sand hills, was about the same distance on their right. They had jogged along for about an hour, sometimes trotting and sometimes walking, when Bree suddenly stopped.

"What's up?" said Shasta.

"S-s-ssh!" said Bree, craning his neck around and twitching his ears. "Did you hear something? Listen."

"It sounds like another horse—between us and the wood," said Shasta after he had listened for about a minute.

"It *is* another horse," said Bree. "And that's what I don't like."

"Isn't it probably just a farmer riding home late?" said Shasta with a yawn.

"Don't tell me!" said Bree. "*That's* not a farmer's riding. Nor a farmer's horse either. Can't you tell by the sound? That's quality, that horse is. And it's being ridden by a real horseman. I tell you what it is, Shasta. There's a Tarkaan under the edge of that wood. Not on his warhorse—it's too light for that. On a fine blood mare, I should say."

"Well it's stopped now, whatever it is," said Shasta.

"You're right," said Bree. "And why should he stop just when we do? Shasta, my boy, I do believe there's someone shadowing us at last."

"What shall we do?" said Shasta in a lower whisper than before. "Do you think he can see us as well as hear us?"

"Not in this light so long as we stay quite still," answered Bree. "But look! There's a cloud coming up. I'll wait till that gets over the moon. Then we'll get off to our right as quietly as we can, down to the shore. We can hide among the sand hills if the worst comes to the worst."

They waited till the cloud covered the moon and then, first at a walking pace and afterward at a gentle trot, made for the shore.

The cloud was bigger and thicker than it had looked at first and soon the night grew very dark. Just as Shasta was saying to himself, "We must be nearly at those sand hills by now," his heart leaped into his mouth because an appalling noise had suddenly risen up out of the darkness ahead: a long snarling roar, melancholy and utterly savage. Instantly Bree swerved around and began galloping inland again as fast as he could gallop.

"What is it?" gasped Shasta.

"Lions!" said Bree, without checking his pace or turning his head.

After that there was nothing but sheer galloping for some time. At last they splashed across a wide, shallow stream and Bree came to a stop on the far side. Shasta noticed that he was trembling and sweating all over.

"That water may have thrown the brute off our scent," panted Bree when he had partly got his breath again. "We can walk for a bit now."

As they walked Bree said, "Shasta, I'm ashamed of myself. I'm just as frightened as a common, dumb Calormene horse. I am really. I don't feel like a Talking Horse at all. I don't mind swords and lances and arrows but I can't bear—those creatures. I think I'll trot for a bit."

About a minute later, however, he broke into a gallop again, and no wonder. For the roar broke out again, this time on their left from the direction of the forest.

"Two of them," moaned Bree.

When they had galloped for several minutes without any further noise from the lions Shasta said, "I say! That other horse is galloping beside us now. Only a stone's throw away."

"All the b-better," panted Bree. "Tarkaan on it—will have a sword—protect us all."

"But Bree!" said Shasta. "We might just as well be killed by lions as caught. Or *I* might. They'll hang me for horse stealing." He was feeling less frightened of lions than Bree because he had never met a lion; Bree had.

Bree only snorted in answer, but he did sheer away to his right. Oddly enough the other horse seemed also to be sheering away to the left, so that in a few seconds the space between them had widened a good deal. But as soon as it did so there came two more lions' roars, immediately after one another, one on the right and the other on the left, and the horses began drawing nearer together. So, apparently, did the lions. The roaring of the brutes on each side was horribly close and they seemed to be keeping up with the galloping horses quite easily. Then the cloud rolled away. The moonlight, astonishingly bright, showed up everything almost as if it were broad day. The two horses and the two riders were galloping neck to neck and knee to knee just as if they were in a race. Indeed Bree said (afterward) that a finer race had never been seen in Calormen.

Shasta now gave himself up for lost and began to

wonder whether lions killed you quickly or played with you as a cat plays with a mouse and how much it would hurt. At the same time (one sometimes does this at the most frightful moments) he noticed everything. He saw that the other rider was a very small, slender person, mail-clad (the moon shone on the mail) and riding magnificently. He had no beard.

Something flat and shining was spread out before them. Before Shasta had time even to guess what it was, there was a great splash and he found his mouth half full of salt water. The shining thing had been a long inlet of the sea. Both horses were swimming and the water was up to Shasta's knees. There was an angry roaring behind them, and looking back Shasta saw a great, shaggy, and terrible shape crouched on the water's edge; but only one. "We must have shaken off the other lion," he thought.

The lion apparently did not think its prey worth a wetting; at any rate it made no attempt to take the water in pursuit. The two horses, side by side, were now well out into the middle of the creek and the opposite shore could be clearly seen. The Tarkaan had not yet spoken a word. "But he will," thought Shasta. "As soon as we have landed. What am I to say? I must begin thinking out a story."

Then, suddenly, two voices spoke at his side.

"Oh, I *am* so tired," said the one.

"Hold your tongue, Hwin, and don't be a fool," said the other.

"I'm dreaming," thought Shasta. "I could have sworn that other horse spoke."

Soon the horses were no longer swimming but walking, and soon, with a great sound of water running off their sides and tails and with a great crunching of pebbles under eight hoofs, they came out on the farther beach of the inlet. The Tarkaan, to Shasta's surprise, showed no wish to ask questions. He did not even look at Shasta but seemed anxious to urge his horse straight on. Bree, however, at once shouldered himself in the other horse's way.

"Broo-hoo-hah!" he snorted. "Steady there! I *heard* you, I did. There's no good pretending, ma'am. *I* heard you. You're a Talking Horse, a Narnian horse just like me."

"What's it got to do with you if she is?" said the strange rider fiercely, laying hand on sword hilt. But the voice in which the words were spoken had already told Shasta something.

"Why, it's only a girl!" he exclaimed.

"And what business is it of yours if I am *only* a girl?" snapped the stranger. "You're only a boy: a rude, common little boy—a slave probably, who's stolen his master's horse."

"That's all *you* know," said Shasta.

"He's not a thief, little Tarkheena," said Bree. "At least, if there's been any stealing, you might just as well say I stole *him*. And as for its not being my business, you wouldn't expect me to pass a lady of my own race in this strange country without speaking to her? It's only natural I should."

"I think it's very natural, too," said the mare.

"I wish you'd held your tongue, Hwin," said the girl. "Look at the trouble you've got us into."

"I don't know about trouble," said Shasta. "You can clear off as soon as you like. We shan't keep you."

"No, you shan't," said the girl.

"What quarrelsome creatures these humans are," said Bree to the mare. "They're as bad as mules. Let's try to talk a little sense. I take it, ma'am, your story is the same as mine? Captured in early youth—years of slavery among the Calormenes?"

"Too true, sir," said the mare with a melancholy whinny.

"And now, perhaps—escape?"

"Tell him to mind his own business, Hwin," said the girl.

"No, I won't, Aravis," said the mare, putting her ears back. "This is my escape just as much as yours. And I'm sure a noble warhorse like this is not going to betray us. We are trying to escape, to get to Narnia."

"And so, of course, are we," said Bree. "Of course you guessed that at once. A little boy in rags riding (or trying to ride) a warhorse at dead of night couldn't mean anything but an escape of some sort. And, if I may say so, a high-born Tarkeenha riding alone at night—dressed up in her brother's armor—and very anxious for everyone to mind their own business and ask her no questions—well, if that's not fishy, call me a cob!"

"All right then," said Aravis. "You've guessed it. Hwin and I are running away. We are trying to get to Narnia. And now, what about it?"

"Why, in that case, what is to prevent us all going together?" said Bree. "I trust, Madam Hwin, you will accept such assistance and protection as I may be able to give you on the journey?"

"Why do you keep talking to my horse instead of me?" asked the girl.

"Excuse me, Tarkheena," said Bree (with just the slightest backward tilt of his ears), "but that's Calormene talk. We're free Narnians, Hwin and I, and I suppose, if you're running away to Narnia, you want

to be one too. In that case Hwin isn't *your* horse any longer. One might just as well say you're *her* human."

The girl opened her mouth to speak and then stopped. Obviously she had not quite seen it in that light before.

"Still," she said after a moment's pause, "I don't know that there's so much point in all going together. Aren't we more likely to be noticed?"

"Less," said Bree; and the mare said, "Oh, do let's. I

should feel much more comfortable. We're not even certain of the way. I'm sure a great charger like this knows far more than we do."

"Oh, come on, Bree," said Shasta, "and let them go their own way. Can't you see they don't want us?"

"We do," said Hwin.

"Look here," said the girl. "I don't mind going with *you*, Mr. Warhorse, but what about this boy? How do I know he's not a spy?"

"Why don't you say at once that you think I'm not good enough for you?" said Shasta.

"Be quiet, Shasta," said Bree. "The Tarkheena's question is quite reasonable. I'll vouch for the boy, Tarkheena. He's been true to me and a good friend. And he's certainly either a Narnian or an Archenlander."

"All right, then. Let's go together." But she didn't say anything to Shasta and it was obvious that she wanted Bree, not him.

"Splendid!" said Bree. "And now that we've got the water between us and those dreadful animals, what about you two humans taking off our saddles and our all having a rest and hearing one another's stories."

Both the children unsaddled their horses and the horses had a little grass and Aravis produced rather nice things to eat from her saddlebag. But Shasta sulked and said no thanks, and that he wasn't hungry. And he tried to put on what he thought very grand and stiff manners, but as a fisherman's hut is not usually a good place for learning grand manners, the result was dreadful. And he half knew that it wasn't a success and then became sulkier and more awkward than ever. Meanwhile the two horses were getting on splendidly. They remembered the very same places in Narnia— "the grasslands up above Beaversdam"—and found that they were some sort of second cousins once removed. This made things more and more uncomfortable for the humans until at last Bree said, "And now, Tarkheena, tell us your story. And don't hurry it—I'm feeling comfortable now."

A Horse Called Terror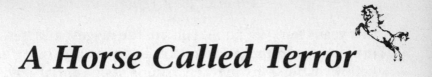

retold by Felicity Trotman

Horses are loved and admired all around the world, but one country where they are thought of especially highly is India. Many Indian stories feature horses; this one is particularly enjoyable because there is a strong sense of humor in it. It's also nice to find a small girl succeeding where larger and more important people have failed!

The horse trader could not understand it. He had come to the great horse fair of Mathura as he usually did, with a large string of horses. He had done well, they had all been sold, and he was about to return to his home at Gandhara, when he had received the summons. The Prime Minister of the Kingdom of Anga wanted to see him! Why?

He did deal with nobles sometimes, he thought, but young ones, who wanted racehorses and chargers on which they could go to war. The more important older nobles usually left their masters of horse to deal with traders like himself. Now here was a Prime Minister – and from another kingdom, too—asking to see him. What could he possibly want?

He soon found out. "A hallowed horse," said the Prime Minister, into whose dignified presence he had been taken. "Anga needs a hallowed horse for our Crown Prince. There was nothing that met our need at this year's fair. We know you are the biggest and best horse trader in the land, so I am asking you to bring a hallowed horse to me at Champa, our capital city, next year. For this, you can name your own price."

The horse trader stood, speechless, for a moment. He had never heard of a hallowed horse. Then he plucked up his courage. "Please, sir," he said nervously, "what is a hallowed horse? I have been in the horse trade since I was a lad, but I have never heard of such a thing."

"A hallowed horse!" said the Prime Minister of Anga. "A hallowed horse is a pure bay, a stallion. It treads the earth lightly, and its hooves raise no dust. Happiness lies on its forehead, and there is joy in its possession." He went through a list of thirty-two points by which the very special horse might be recognized, ending with "Its coat is as smooth as a moonstone, the surge of the ocean is in its tossing mane, its neighing stirs like a trumpet call, and its feet are shod with fountains of fire."

"Stop!" cried the unhappy horse trader. "I am only a plain man from the hills, and I do not understand the poetry of the plains. But I can promise you this. Next year I shall bring five hundred of the finest horses to Champa, and you can choose the one you like best."

When the horse dealer had gone, the Prime Minister told his staff that he himself had never seen a hallowed horse. "The experts are quite clear," he said. "A hallowed horse understands human speech, and can talk if it wants to. It will give its rider intelligence and wisdom, and maybe even foresight. Who knows? Maybe there is such a wonderful horse in our midst already, but we have not been able to identify it."

When the Prime Minister had returned to Champa,

he reported to the King: "Sire, there were no horses of the right description at the Mathura horse fair. We must wait until next year, when the Gandhara horse dealer will come here, with five hundred horses to choose from, and hope that one of them will be the right animal for the Crown Prince."

The King sighed. "If we must wait, we must wait. But a hallowed horse we must have. I am very old now, and cannot live much longer. The Crown Prince is my grandson; he is young; we have talked often of the danger he will be in if he comes to the throne without this protection. There are nobles in this kingdom who will band together to make trouble. They'll seize the throne if they get the chance."

The Prime Minister nodded. They had indeed often discussed the perilous future. What would happen to the young Prince, and to the Kingdom of Anga?

It was late in the season when, the following year, the horse dealer from Gandhara arrived at Champa with a string of five hundred magnificent horses. "My deepest apologies," he said to the Prime Minister. "I was held up for three months at Pujita because of the monsoon."

The Prime Minister at once began to check through the horses. He inspected every one, speaking to each animal that appeared to have the thirty-two special characteristics of the hallowed horse. But none of the horses replied.

"None of these is the right horse," the old man told the horse dealer. "We must try again, next year." He felt very depressed and worried that the plan had not worked.

The horse dealer sold all five hundred horses and returned home. Twice more the dealer brought strings of animals to Champa, but there was no hallowed horse among them. The next year, the old King died. The young Crown Prince came to the throne—and the trouble foreseen and feared by his grandfather and his minister began.

"Why should we acknowledge this boy?" the powerful Rajah Ganesha asked the other nobles. "He is young, and has no experience. Let us take him prisoner when he goes out hunting. Then we shall decide which one of us shall be King."

News of this came to the Prime Minister. He went at once to the King.

"Sire," he said, having told the King what he had heard, "you must stay in your palace, with a strong guard, so that you may be safe until the hallowed horse comes."

The King understood the need to keep himself safe, but was angry at being kept in. He did not really believe in the Prime Minister's talk of hallowed horses. "What you mean is, I must live like a prisoner!" cried he. "Does this amazing horse live anywhere except your imagination? How long do you expect me to wait until you find one? Can't you find someone expert enough to go through the royal stables? There are hundreds of horses there—maybe one of them is this fabulous creature."

"I will do what I can, Sire," the Prime Minister said with a sigh.

So he summoned experts—experts in history, experts in reading the stars, experts in horses; they all came to the royal stables. They studied every one of the King's horses. At last they discovered a mare who showed all the signs of having had a foal and that foal should have had all thirty-two marks of a hallowed horse.

"But where is the foal?" they asked.

The Prime Minister sent for the horse master and the record books. He went through the books with the greatest care, but there was no record of the foal.

He was in despair. He went through the books one more time—and he noticed that the mare was one of the horses brought in by the horse dealer from Gandhara. He sent at once for the man.

"Have you sold any foals in the last four years?" the Prime Minister questioned him.

"No," replied the horse dealer. "You can check in my record books—you'll find not one sale before I brought my horses to Anga."

That seemed to be the end of the matter. But, just as he was about to dismiss the dealer, the Prime Minister had an idea. It seemed unlikely, but he would try. "Did you give any foals away?" he asked.

The horse dealer went pale. "That terror!" he whispered.

Faced with the Prime Minister's anger and his urgent questioning, the story came out. Four years ago, the horse dealer had been delayed at Pujita—but it was not because of the monsoon, as he had claimed. Before he had gotten near Pujita, all the horses in the string had suddenly started to move very slowly.

"What is the matter?" he had asked the men who helped him. "Have the horses gone lame, or been struck down by some illness? We should be much farther along the road than this."

"We don't know what is wrong," the men told him. "But it seems to be something to do with that mare who has foaled recently. We have noticed that the other horses have stopped neighing. We have also noticed that they will not drink until the mare and the foal have drunk, and they will not eat until the mare and the foal have had all they want. And as for the slow pace you mention—that is because the horses will not go faster than the foal. When he is tired, they stop until he is rested and ready to go on."

"So the problem is the foal, not the mare," said the horse dealer, who had listened carefully to what his men had told him. "We all know that some horses are troublemakers. I don't want one in my string. This foal is upsetting five hundred good horses; we will get rid of him when we come to Pujita."

The horses and men had been delayed so long on the road that when they arrived at Pujita they were caught by the monsoon. Traveling was impossible: the roads were like rivers, and the fords were too dangerous to cross. So the horse dealer was forced to spend three months in lodgings. During this time he tried to sell the terrible foal, but no one would buy it. When the monsoon was over, he got ready to start his journey again. When he saw the size of his bills for both horses and men, he cursed the colt that had caused all the trouble.

"Won't you take this colt in part payment?" he asked.

"No, thank you," was the answer from the owner of the lodgings. "I do not want my ears bitten off."

"Certainly not," the merchant who had provided hay and straw said, "Everyone in Pujita knows about your colt. No one in this town would want him. He bites and kicks—take him away. He's a terror."

The last man to be paid was the potter. He was more interested in making beautiful things from clay than in collecting money, so he was late in bringing his bill.

The string of horses was already moving out of the town.

"I'm so sorry," the horse dealer said. "I sent my cashier on ahead. You should have come earlier. But I would not like to leave you unpaid. I will give you this beautiful colt. Terror is worth more than your bill. Otherwise you will have to wait for six months, until I come back this way on my homeward journey."

The potter was the one man in the town who had not heard about the colt. But he knew that a lively foal in a potter's home was not a good idea. There were too many things to break.

But the foal came right up to the potter and nuzzled him. The horse dealer watched in horror, expecting the animal to bite or kick as usual—but instead he licked the potter's feet, like a dog. The potter stroked the foal and scratched his ears. He liked the foal—and the foal clearly liked him.

"I'll take him," the potter decided.

The horse dealer, delighted that at last he had gotten rid of the troublemaker, hurried off on his journey to Champa.

"That must be the foal we are looking for!" cried the experts, when they had heard the horse dealer's story. "Do you know the date he was born? Can you tell us what stars were in the sky? What time was it? And where exactly did it happen?"

"I don't know," the dealer confessed. "All I can tell you was that the foal was born somewhere between Gandhara and Pujita—and that he brought me nothing but bad luck."

"We are not surprised!" the experts said. "He is a hallowed horse. You did not blow conch shells to

welcome him into the world. You didn't garland him
with marigolds or paint his forehead with vermilion.
All these things should have been done to honor him.
The other horses knew what he was, and treated him
with respect—but you treated him like a common
horse. No wonder he showed his displeasure."

The Prime Minister issued orders at once. "Go to
Pujita," he told twelve of the experts. "Find the colt
and buy him back—whatever the price! We must have
him here, and as fast as possible!"

So the experts set out, carrying silver horseshoes for
the colt. When they reached Pujita, they found a
potter who owned a horse.

"Where did you get that horse?" they asked.

"It was in payment of a debt," the potter told them.
He told them what had happened when he had gone
to the horse dealer with his bill.

"When I got back home, my wife was furious," he
said, remembering. "'What have you done?' she
demanded. 'Don't you know that is Terror, the wild
colt that cannot be controlled? Send it to the knackers
at once—at least you will get some of the money you
are owed.'

"But Terror went up to her, and licked her hand. She
could not resist him, and began to pat him. I told her I
would like to keep him, and at last she agreed.

"'Let it stay,' she said. 'But take care that it does not
get near your bowls and jars.'"

"So what has happened since then?" asked the team
of experts.

"He has grown into a fine horse," the potter told
them. "He is the greatest help to me in my work. Just
after we got him, I had to go and get a sack of clay. He
followed me, and when I put the load of clay on his

back, he carried it home. He has done this ever since. And he steps very gently among all my wares; he has never broken a thing."

The potter even took the experts out of his house, and showed them the stable he had built for Terror.

"We would like to buy this horse," the experts said. "We will give you a good donkey and a bag of gold for him."

"No," said the potter. "Terror helps me, and he is my friend. I will not sell him."

"It is a good offer," they said. "Think it over. Discuss it with your wife. We'll call again in the morning."

The experts did not want the potter to guess that they thought his horse was valuable. They thought that they could buy it back cheaply—especially since the potter's neighbors were still frightened of it.

The potter sat down at his wheel and started to work.

"Don't miss this opportunity! You should ask for a very high price," a voice behind him said.

"Don't talk rubbish," said the potter without turning around. He thought it was his wife speaking. "It would be like selling your son for money."

"What if your son were destined to be Prime Minister?" he was asked. "Would it be fair to keep him tied to your potter's wheel because you liked to have him at home?"

"All right!" said the potter. "I am no good at arguing. Just let me get on with my work."

"Think of this!" the potter heard. "A pure bay, finely bred born under a lucky star should only serve kings and feed on the finest hay from a golden manger. Where will you find money to buy a manger made of gold? Strike a bargain with the men from Anga. Say,

'Give me the price of a hallowed horse for my Terror,' and you will get a hundred thousand rupees."

The potter's wife came into his workshop. "That is a bargain worth making at once," she said.

The potter turned from his wheel. "Who was I talking to just now?" he asked his wife, bewildered. "I thought it was you!"

"You were talking to me," said Terror. "I can talk. This is another sign that I am no ordinary horse. Sell me to the men from Anga. Tell them that you ask for me as much gold as I can scatter with a single kick."

The potter was speechless with amazement to hear his horse speak. He could only nod in agreement.

In the morning, the men from Anga came back.

"I will sell Terror to you," the potter told them. "But he is a hallowed horse, and I will only let him go for as much gold as he can scatter with a single kick."

The band of experts were shocked. "How did he find out?" they whispered to themselves. "Someone must have told him. But the Prime Minister said we must get the horse at any price. We will have to accept the potter's terms."

So the experts agreed to pay what the potter asked. Lakh upon lakh of gold was piled up outside Terror's stable, in the field where the potter dug his clay. The potter brought Terror out. The horse turned away from the glittering mass, and gave a great kick with one powerful hoof.

There was an explosion of gold. It filled the sky, and all the air was thick with shining metal. When it had finished falling, the whole enormous mound had been scattered. Gold covered the potter's house, it filled Terror's stable, and it carpeted the field. The potter and his wife were clothed in brilliant, shimmering

garments. Terror had ensured that his friends, the potter and his wife, would be rich beyond imagining for the rest of their lives.

Now that Terror was safely in their possession, the experts shod him with the silver horseshoes they had brought with them, and took him back to Anga. When they reached Champa, the Prime Minister and the young King both rejoiced, for the king's enemies, led by Rajah Ganesha, were massing together. The horse had arrived just in time!

But then news came that filled them with horror. Terror would not eat! Neither would he speak, so they could not find out what was wrong. The hallowed horse was losing weight, reported the King's horse master, and no one could find anything wrong with the animal. "Perhaps the horse dealer of Gandhara was right, and he is a troublemaker. All the other horses in the stables have stopped eating, too."

The King was angered by what he heard, and the Prime Minister summoned back the experts who had found Terror. They went to look at the horse, and quickly came back.

"You have treated Terror as though he were an ordinary horse!" they said accusingly. "He should have been greeted like an ambassador, with banners in the streets when he arrived! Were there musicians to play to him when he was brought to his stable? And why does he not have a gold manger to eat from?" And, to the shame and embarrassment of King and Prime Minister, they listed many things that should have been done to welcome Terror, and which had not been done.

"What shall we do?" said the Prime Minister. He was almost in despair, for that morning the army of Rajah Ganesha had camped outside the city walls.

"You must do all the things that we have told you," the experts said. "You must also get the first lady in the land to apologize, and to beg Terror to eat."

When the experts had gone, first the King and then the Prime Minister went to the stable and apologized deeply to Terror for failing to welcome him to the country with the honor due him. But the horse still refused to eat.

"Where is my cousin, the Princess Sweetness?" demanded the King. "She is the first lady in the land. She must come and speak to the horse."

A search was made, and the Princess was found. She

had climbed up a tree in the palace gardens, and was eating unripe mangoes. She did not want to come down, but at last the King managed to persuade her to do so. Princess Sweetness was taken off by her servants to be bathed and dressed in her best. While the King had nervously explained yet again what the problem was, she was led to Terror's stall.

Princess Sweetness waited until the bustling crowd had all gone. When she was alone, she opened the door and went in.

"Oh!" she said. "You are beautiful!" At the sight of Terror, she had forgotten the formal, polite greeting she had been told to give.

"I am Princess Sweetness," she went on. "I'm the King's cousin. They said I should come, because I'm the first lady, but that won't last long. As soon as the King gets married, I shan't be first lady anymore. Would you like a mango?"

Terror turned his head to look at the speaker. He saw a small girl, dressed very finely, but with a mossy smudge on her dress and hair escaping from her plaits. She was holding out a mango toward him.

"I thought you might like mangoes," the princess said. "I like sweets best, and that's why I'm called Sweetness. My real name is much longer, and I can't spell it."

Terror bent his head and licked her cheek.

"Oh, Terror!" she said, putting her arms around his neck and resting her cheek against his silky mane. "Please eat! We didn't mean to offend you. We just didn't understand. And if you don't eat, Rajah Ganesha will turn my cousin off his throne and kill him, and I shall have to marry Ganesha and never eat sweets again!"

"Cheer up!" said Terror. "For your sake, I will eat."

"You can talk!" cried Sweetness. "They told me you could, but I have never met a talking horse before. Do eat plenty, and grow strong, so that you can bite off one of Rajah Ganesha's ears."

Terror made a low, whickering noise, as though he were laughing.

"I'll bite both ears off for you tomorrow, if you like," he said.

"No, only one ear," said Princess Sweetness. "He is a very bad man, but he might go deaf if you bit off both ears, and I would not like that to happen to him."

"He is a very bad man," Terror agreed. "I know all about him. He plans to starve the King to death, kill all the King's ministers, and take the throne for himself. He would be a harsh and cruel ruler. I shall save you from that dreadful fate."

"Can you do that?" Sweetness asked. "In that case, why wait for tomorrow? And please, may I come with you when you go off to deal with him?"

"Certainly," said Terror. "I would be pleased if you came too. But first, you must go to the Prime Minister and tell him to get ready to put five thousand horses in the stables—and five thousand prisoners into safekeeping in the fort."

Princess Sweetness was rather frightened of the Prime Minister. She thought he would laugh at her if she went and told him what Terror had said. She was also afraid that he might stop her going with Terror. So she wrote him a letter, giving him Terror's instructions about the horses and the prisoners, before putting on her riding clothes and going back to Terror.

As soon as she was on his back, Terror galloped straight out of the stable, and set off at high speed right into the heart of the enemy's camp. Standing outside Rajah Ganesha's own tent, he neighed loudly—and at once all five thousand horses in the rebel army neighed back, for they recognized Terror as their leader.

Rajah Ganesha and the other nobles came out of their tents at once to see what was happening. They could hardly believe what they saw—Princess Sweetness alone in the middle of the camp! Rajah Ganesha was delighted, for capturing Sweetness was an important part of his plan.

"Look, my friends!" he cried. "Luck is on our side! Now we can march straight to Champa and capture the stupid boy who calls himself King of Anga! Get off that horse, Sweetness, and come with me. I shall marry you at once."

But Rajah Ganesha had spoken too soon. Terror neighed again, once. At the sound, all the horses in the rebel army neighed in turn, reared up on their hind legs, then turned on their dismounted riders and picked them up by their belts with their teeth. Ganesha was picked up in the same way by his own horse. Within minutes, Terror was leading a procession of five thousand horses toward the capital, with five thousand very unhappy soldiers dangling from the horses' mouths. Ganesha, minus an ear, was among them.

When the cavalcade reached the city, the King was waiting. "You are truly the most wonderful horse," he said, as conch shells blew and he placed a magnificent wreath of marigolds aaround Terror's neck. "There is nothing too good for you. I wish I knew how to thank you."

That night there was feasting in Champa to celebrate Terror, the hallowed horse who had saved the King and the kingdom. Bonfires blazed, bands played, and at midnight there was a splendid display of fireworks. And Princess Sweetness was full of pride for her friend as she heard the King lead the crowds as they cheered, "Long live Terror, the hallowed horse!"

The Ghost Horse

CHIEF BUFFALO CHILD LONG LANCE

The horse in "A Horse Called Terror" behaved fiercely because he wasn't treated properly. In this story the horse is terrifying because that is his nature. This is a thrilling account of a horse hunt, which tells of the capture of a wild and dangerous steel-gray stallion—and what happened afterward. This true story, which happened when the author was a boy, is taken from Long Lance, *the autobiography of Chief Buffalo Child Long Lance. A member of the Blackfoot people of western United States and Canada, he was a sportsman, soldier (he fought in the First World War) and writer.*

With the first touch of spring, we broke camp and headed southwest across the big bend of the upper Columbia, toward the plateau between the Rockies and the Cascades. It was on this lofty plateau that the world's largest herd of wild horses had roamed during the last hundred and fifty years. Several hundred head of them are still there, where every summer efforts are being made to exterminate them by the provincial government of British Columbia. It was these horses that we were after, to replace the herd which the storm had driven away from our camp.

We struck the herd in the season of the year when it was weakest: early spring, after the horses had got their first good feed of green grass, and their speed had been slowed by dysentery. Since these wild creatures can run to death any horse raised in captivity, it is doubly a hard job to try to ensnare them on foot. But, like wolves, wild horses are very curious animals; they will follow a person for miles out of mere curiosity. And, when chased, they will invariably turn back on their trails to see what it is all about; what their pursuers look like, what they are up to.

The big timber wolves would do the same, when we were traveling in the north country. They would trot along behind us all day. When we would stop, they would stop, and stand motionless and look at us with one foot raised; and when we would start again, they would continue to follow us. If we made a noise at them, they would jump back and hide behind the nearest bush. From then on, they would keep out of sight, but whenever we looked back we would see them peeping at us from behind the farthest bush.

They used to scare us children, but our fathers told us not to be scared, the wolves would not hurt us; they were just curious about us—although, they said, if the wolves followed us all day, they might try to snatch off our dogs when we camped at night. So they told us boys who were traveling in the rear to keep trying to shoo them away before we should make camp for the night. Wolves like dog meat better than any other, though male wolves will never harm a female dog.

But with the wild horses it was different. They always traveled ahead of us, but they had a way of turning back on their own trails and coming upon us from the side or the rear, to keep watch on us. It was this never-satisfied curiosity of the wild horse that enabled our braves to capture them on foot.

The method of our warriors was to locate a herd and then follow it unconcernedly for hours, and maybe for days, before making any attempt to round it up. This was to get the horses used to us, and to show them that we would not harm them.

We had been trailing fresh manure for five days before we finally located our first herd away up on the expansive Couteau Plateau of central British Columbia. There they were: a herd of about five hundred animals, grazing away over there on the side of a craggy little mountain on top of the plateau. Their quick, alert movements, more like those of a deer than those of a horse, showed they were high-strung beings that would dash off into space like a flock of wild birds on the slightest cause for excitement. There was one big, steel-dust stallion who grazed away from the rest, and made frequent trips along the edge of the herd. It was obvious to our braves that this iron-colored fellow with the silver mane was the stallion who ruled the herd; and our warriors directed all of their attention to him, knowing that the movements of the entire herd depended on what he did.

When we had approached to within about five hundred yards of the herd, our braves began to make little noises, so that the horses could see us in the distance, and would not be taken by surprise and frightened into a stampede at seeing us suddenly at closer range.

"Hoh! Hoh!" our braves grunted softly. The steel-dust stallion uttered a low whinny, and all the herd raised their heads high into the air and, standing perfectly still as though charmed, looked intently over at us with their big, nervous nostrils wide open. They stood that way for moments, without moving a muscle, looking hard at us. Then, as we came too near, the burly stallion tried to put fear into us by dashing straight at us with a deep, rasping roar.

Others followed him, and on they came like a yelling war party, their heads swinging wildly, their racing legs wide apart, and their long tails lashing the ground like bundles of steel wire. But before they reached us the speeding animals stiffened their legs and came to a sudden halt in a cloud of dust. While they were close, they took one more good look at us, and then they turned and scampered away with the rest of the herd, which had already begun to retreat over the brow of the mountain.

But the big steel-dust stood his ground alone for a moment and openly defied us. He dug his front feet into the dirt far out in front of him, wagged his head furiously, and then stopped long enough to look and see what effect his mad antics were having upon us. Around and around he jumped gracefully into the air, swapping ends like a dog chasing its tail. Then again he raised his head as high as his superb stature would carry him; and with his long silver tail lying over his back, he blazed fire at us through the whites of his turbulent flint-colored eyes. Having displayed to us his courage, his defiance, and his remarkable leadership, he now turned and pranced off, with heels flying so high and so lightly that one could almost imagine he was treading air.

Our braves laughed and said:

"Ah, Ponokamita, vain Elk-dog, you are a brave warrior. But trot along and have patience. We shall yet ride you against the Crows."

For five days we chased this huge herd of horses,

traveling along leisurely behind them, knowing that they would not wander afar, that they would watch us like wolves as long as we were in the vicinity.

By the fifth day they had become so used to us that they merely moved along slowly when we approached them, nibbling the grass as they walked. All during this time our braves had been taming them by their subtle method. At first they just grunted at them. But now they were dancing and shouting at them. This was to let the horses know that, although man could make a lot of noise and act fiercely, he would not harm them, that no injury could come to them through closer contact with man.

Nothing scares a horse quicker than a quiet thing that moves toward him and makes no noise. He will jump and break his neck at the noiseless movement of a rodent in the grass or a falling twig, while roaring buffalo or a steaming train will pass him unnoticed. That is because he has the same kind of courage that man has: real courage; the courage to face any odds that he can see and hear and cope with, but a superstitious fear of anything ghostlike. The mountain lion and most other animals of prey have courage of a different kind. A slight, unexpected noise will bring them to a low, crouching, waiting position, while a loud noise will send them scurrying for cover. They have more discretion and less valor than man or the horse.

On the tenth night of our chase, our warriors made their final preparations to capture the herd. They had maneuvered the horses into the vicinity of a huge half-natural, half-artificial corral which they had built of logs against the two sides of a rock-bound gulch. From the entrance of this corral they had built two long fences, forming a runway, which gradually widened as it left the gate of the corral. This funnel shaped entrance fanned out on to the plateau for more than a half-mile, and it was covered over with evergreens to disguise its artificiality. It was a replica of the old buffalo corral which we used to build to round up the buffalos when they were plentiful on the plains.

The mouth at the outer end of this runway was about one hundred yards wide. From this point on, the runway was further extended and opened up by placing big treetops, stones, and logs along the ground for several hundred yards. This was to direct the herd slowly into the mouth of the fenced part of the runway, where, once wedged inside, they would neither get out nor turn around and retrace their steps. They would be trapped; and the only thing left for them to do would be to keep on going toward the corral gate.

Subdued excitement reigned in our hidden camp on this tenth night of our chase; for it was the big night, the night that we were going to "blow in" the great, stubborn herd of wild horses. No one went to bed that night. Shortly before nightfall, more than half of our braves, comprising all of our fastest-traveling scouts, and young men, quietly slipped out of our camp and disappeared. According to prearranged directions, they fanned out to the right and left in a northerly route and crept noiselessly toward the place where the herd had disappeared that afternoon. All during the early night we heard wolves calling to one another; Arctic owls, nighthawks, and panthers crying out moanfully in the mystic darkness of the rugged plateau. They were the signals of our men, informing one another of their movements.

Then, about midnight, everything became deathly

quiet. We knew that they had located the herd and surrounded it, and that they were now lying on their bellies, awaiting the first streaks of dawn and the signal to start the drive.

One of our subchiefs, Chief Mountain Elk, now went through our camp, quietly giving instructions for all hands to line themselves along the great runway to "beat in" the herd. Every woman, old person, and child in the camp was called up to take part in this particular phase of the drive. We children and the women crept over to the runway and sprawled ourselves along the outside of the fence, while the men went beyond the fenced part of the runway and concealed themselves behind the brush and logs—where it was a little more dangerous.

Thus we crouched on the ground and shivered quietly for an hour or more before we heard a distant "Ho-h! . . . Ho-h!" It was the muffled driving cry of our warriors, the cry which for ten days they had been uttering to the horses to let them know that no harm could come to them from this sound. Thus, the horses did not stampede, as they would have done had they not recognized this noise in the darkness.

We youngsters lay breathless in expectancy. We had all picked out our favorite mounts in this beautiful herd of wild animals; and to us as we lay there, it was like the white boy lying in bed waiting for Santa Claus. Our fathers had all promised us that we could have the ponies that we had picked, and we could hardly wait to get our hands on them. My favorite was a beautiful calico pony, a roan, white, and red pinto—three different colors splashed on his shoulders and flanks like a crazy-quilt of exquisite design. He had a red star on his forehead between his eyes, and I had already named him Naytukskie-Kukatos, which in Blackfoot means One Star.

Presently we heard the distant rumble of horses, hooves—a dull booming which shook the ground on which we lay. Then, "Yip-yip-yip, he-heeh-h-h," came the night call of the wolf from many different directions. It was our braves signaling to one another to keep the herd on the right path. From out of this medley of odd sounds, we could hear the mares going, "Wheeeeeh-hagh-hagh-hagh"—calling their little long-legged sons to their sides that they might not become lost in the darkness and confusion.

Our boyish hearts began to beat fast when we heard the first loud "Yah! Yah! Yah!" We knew that the herd had now entered the brush portion of the runway, and that our warriors were jumping up from their hiding places and showing themselves with fierce noises, in order to stampede the horses and send them racing headlong into our trap.

Immediately there was a loud thunder of pattering hooves. Horses crying and yelling everywhere, like convulsive human beings in monster confusion. Above this din of bellowing throats and hammering feet, we heard one loud, full, deep-chested roar which we all recognized, and it gave us boys a slight thrill of fear. It sounded like a cross between the roar of a lion and the bellow of an infuriated bull. It was the massive steel-dust stallion, furious king of the herd. In our imagination we could see his long silver tail thrown over his back, his legs lashing wide apart, and stark murder glistening from the whites of those terrible eyes. We wondered what he would do to us if he should call our bluff and crash through that fence into our midst.

But, now, here he came, leading his raging herd,

and we had no further time to contemplate danger. Our job was to do as the others had done all along the line: to lie still and wait until the lead stallion has passed us, and then to jump to the top of the fence and yell and wave with all the ferocity that we could command. This was to keep the maddened herd from crashing the fence or trying to turn around, and to hasten their speed into our trap.

"Therump, therump, therump." On came the storming herd. As we youngsters peeped through the brush-covered fences, we could see their sleek backs bobbing up and down in the starlit darkness like great billows of raging water. The turbulent steel-dust stallion was leading them with front feet wide apart and his forehead sweeping the ground like a pendulum. His death-dealing heels were swinging alternately to the right and left with each savage leap of his mighty frame.

Once he stopped and tried to breast the oncoming herd, but these erstwhile slaves of his whims struck and knocked him forward with terrific force. He rose from his knees; and like something that had gone insane, he shot his nostrils into the air and uttered a fearful bellow of defiance at any and everything. He seemed to curse the very stars themselves. Never before had he tasted defeat, helplessness. The loyal herd that had watched his very ears for their commands was now running wildly over him.

I believe that, if at that moment there had been a solid iron wall in front of that stallion, he would have dashed his brains out against it. I remember looking backward into the darkness for a convenient place to hop, if he should suddenly choose to rush headlong into the noise that was driving him wild with helpless rage. But, even as I looked back, I heard a whistling noise, and my eyes were jerked back to the runway just in time to see the steel-dust king stretching himself past us like a huge greyhound. With each incredible leap, he panted a breath that shrieked like a whistle.

No one will ever know what was in his brain, why had he so suddenly broken himself away from his herd. But on he went, leaving the other horses behind like a deer leaving a bunch of coyotes. A few seconds later the rest of the herd came booming past us. As we went over the fence, shouting and gesticulating, we looked into a blinding fog of sweat and breath, which fairly stung our nostrils with its pungency.

I thought that herd would never stop passing us. I had never seen so many horses before, it seemed. We stuck to our posts until it was nearly daylight, and still they came straggling along; now mostly colts limping and whining for their mothers.

When we climbed down from the fence and went down to the corral at daylight, the first thing we saw was four of our warriors lying on pallets, bleeding and unconscious. They were four of the best horsemen in our tribe: Circling Ghost, High Hunting Eagle, Wild Man, and Wolf Ribs. When our mothers asked what was the matter, someone pointed to the corral and said: "Ponokomita—akai-mahkahpay!" ("That very bad horse!")

We looked and saw a dozen men trying to put leather on that wild steel-dust stallion, who, with his heavy moon-colored mane bristling belligerently over his bluish head and shoulders, looked now more like a lion than a horse. He was splotched here and there with his own blood, and his teeth were bared like a wolf's. Four men had tried to get down into the corral and throw rawhide around his neck. While the other wild horses had scurried away to the nethermost corners of the corral, this ferocious beast of a horse had plunged headlong into them and all but killed them before they could be dragged away.

He had proved to be one of the rarest specimens of horse known to man—a killer—a creature that kicked and bit and tore and crushed his victims until they were dead. One might live a hundred years among horses without ever seeing one of these hideous freaks of the horse world, so seldom are they produced. He had already killed two of his own herd, young stallions, right there in our corral. Little did we wonder, now, that he was the leader.

Our braves were taking no more chances with him. They were high up on top of the seven-foot corral fence, throwing their rawhide lariats in vain attempts to neck the murderous monstrosity. But this devil disguised as a horse had the reasoning of a human being. He would stand and watch the rawhide come twirling through the air, and then just as it was about to swirl over his head he would duck his shaggy neck and remain standing on the spot with his front feet spread apart, in devilish defiance of man and matter. None of our oldest men had ever seen anything like him.

It was finally decided to corner him with firebrands and throw a partition between him and the rest of the herd, so that our braves could get busy cutting out the best of the other animals, before turning the rest loose. This was done, and by nightfall we had captured and hobbled two hundred of the best bottoms anywhere in the Northwest.

The next day our braves began the arduous task of breaking the wild horse to the halter. They used the Indian method, which is very simple and methodical. While four men held onto a stout rawhide rope which was noosed around the animal's neck, another man would approach the horse's head gradually, "talking horse" to him and making many queer motions and sounds as he went nearer.

"Horse talk" is a low grunt which seems to charm a horse and make him stand perfectly still for a moment or so at a time. It sounds like "Hoh—hoh," uttered deep down in one's chest. The horse will stop his rough antics and strain motionless on the rope for a few seconds; while he is doing this and looking straight at the approaching figure, the man will wave a blanket at him and hiss at him—"Shuh! Shuh!" It takes about fifteen minutes of this to make the horse realize that the man is harmless; that no motion which he makes, no sound that he utters, will harm him in any way.

It is a strange fact that a wild horse, of either the ranch or the open ranges, will not react to quiet kindliness at first. He must first be treated gruffly—but not harshly—and then when he is on a touching acquaintance with man, kindness is the quickest way to win his affections.

When the man has reached the head of the horse, his hardest job is to give him the first touch of man's hand, of which the horse seems to have a deathly fear. The man maneuvers for several minutes before he gets a finger on the struggling nose, and rubs it and allows the horse to get his smell or scent. When this has been done, the brave loops a long, narrow string of rawhide around the horse's nose and then carries it up behind his ears and brings it down on the other side, and slips it under the other side of the nose loop, making something like a loose-knotted halter, which will tighten up on the slightest pull from the horse.

This string is no stronger than a shoelace, yet, once the warrior has put it on the horse's head, he tells the other men to let go the strong rawhide thong, and from then on he alone handles the horse with the small piece of string held lightly in one hand. The secret of this is that whenever the horse makes a sudden pull on the string, it grips certain nerves around the nose and back of the ears, and this either stuns him or hurts him so badly that he doesn't try to pull again.

With the horse held thus, the warrior now stands in front of him and strokes the front of his face and hisses at him at close range. It is the same noise that a person makes to drive away chickens—"Shu, shu"—and perhaps the last sound an untrained person would venture to use in taming a wild, ferocious horse, yet it is the quickest way of gaining a horse's confidence and teaching him not to be afraid.

When the warrior has run his fingers over every inch of the horse's head and neck, he now starts to approach his shoulders and flanks with his fingers. The horse will start to jump about again at this, but a couple of sharp jerks on the string stop him; and as he stands trembling with fear, the warrior slowly runs his hand over his left side. When this is finished, he stands back and takes a blanket and strikes all of the portions of his body that he has touched, and shouts, "Shu!" with each stiff stroke of the blanket.

When he has repeated these two operations on the other side of the horse, he now starts to do his legs. Each leg, beginning with his left front leg, must be gone over by his hand, with not an inch of its surface escaping the touch. This is the most ticklish part of the work; for his feet are the horse's deadly weapons. But two more jerks on the string quiet the horse's resentment; and within another fifteen minutes every square inch of the horse's body has been touched and rubbed, even down to his tail and the ticklish portions of his belly and between his legs.

Now the job of breaking the horse is all but finished. There is just one other thing to do, and that is to accustom the horse to a man hopping on his back and riding him. This is done very simply, and within about five minutes.

The warrior takes the blanket and strikes the horse's back a number of blows. Then he lays the blanket on his back very gently. The horse will at first start to buck it off, but another jerk on the string, and he is quieted. The warrior picks the blanket up and lays it across his back again. The horse will jump out from under it perhaps twice before he will stand still. When he has been brought to this point, the man throws the blanket down and walks slowly to the side of the horse and places both hands on his back, and presses down lightly. He keeps pressing a little harder and harder, until finally he places his elbows across his back and draws his body an inch off the ground, putting his full weight on the back of the animal. A horse might jump a little at the first experience of this weight, but he will stand still the next time it is tried.

After the warrior has hung on his back by his elbows for several periods of about thirty seconds each, he will now very gradually pull himself up, up, up, until he is ready to throw his right foot over to the other side. It is a strange fact that few horses broken in this manner ever try to buck. He will stand perfectly still, and the man will sit there and stroke him for a moment and then gently urge him to go; and the horse will awkwardly trot off in a mild, aimless amble, first this way and that—so bewildered and uncertain in his gait that one would think it was the first time he had ever tried to walk on his own feet.

The reason a horse can be broken in the above manner is that he is a remarkably intelligent being with rationality. A chicken has no reason; therefore it goes through its life running away from "Shuhs" that never harm it. This keeps it from getting many extra crumbs that it could leisurely eat if it only had the reason to learn from experience as the horse does.

Four months later we were again back on our beloved plains in upper Montana. Our horses were the envy of every tribe who saw us that summer. They all wanted to know where we got them. Our chief told the story of this wild horse hunt so many times that it has since become legend among the Indians of these prairies.

But at the end of the story, our venerable leader would always look downcast, and in sadly measured words, he would tell of the steel-dust stallion with the flowing moon-colored mane and tail, which he had picked out for himself. He would spend many minutes describing this superb horse, yet he would never finish the story, unless someone should ask him what became of the spectacular animal.

Then he would slowly tell how our band had worked all day trying to rope this beast, and how that night they had decided to leave him in the little fenced-off part of the corral, thinking that two or three days' contact with them might take some of the evil out of him. But the next morning when they visited the corral, he had vanished. The horse had literally climbed over more than seven feet of corral fence, which separated him from the main corral, and there, with room for a running start, he had attacked the heavy log fence and rammed his body clear through it. Nothing was left to tell the tale but a few patches of blood and hair and a wrecked fence.

That should have ended the story of the steel-dust beast, but it did not. On our way out of the camp on the wild horse plateau, we had come across the bodies of seven wild stallions and a mare, which this fiend of the plateau had mutilated in his wake. He had turned killer through and through, even unto the destruction of his own kind. Our old people said that he had been crazed by the fact that he had lost control of his herd in that terrible dash down the runway. This blow to his prowess and pride of leadership had been too much for him; it had turned him into a destructive demon, a roaming maniac of the wilds.

This horse became famous throughout the Northwest as a lone traveler of the night. He went down on to the plains of Montana and Alberta, and in the darkest hours of the night he would turn up at the most unexpected points in the wilderness of the prairies. Never a sound from him; he had lost his mighty bellow. He haunted the plains by night, and was never seen by day. His sinister purpose in life was to destroy every horse he came across.

This silent, lone traveler of the night was often seen silhouetted against the moon on a butte, with his head erect, his tail thrown over his back like a statue, his long moon-colored mane and tail flowing like silver beneath the light of the stars. Owing to his

The Ghost Horse

peculiar nocturnal habits and to the fact that his remarkable tail and mane gave off in the moonlight something like a phosphorescent glow, he became known throughout the Northwest as the Shunka-tonka-Wakan—the Ghost Horse. The steel-blue color of his body melted so completely into the inky blueness of the night, that his tail and mane stood out in the moonlight like shimmering threads of lighted silver, giving him a halo which had a truly ghostly aspect.

Taming the Colt

LOUISA M. ALCOTT

Here's another story from America that describes the break-ing in of a horse. Little Women *is Louisa M. Alcott's most famous book, but there are three more that tell of the further adventures of the March girls and their friends. In* Little Men, *from which this extract comes, we read of the school set up by Jo and her husband, and the doings of the boys who went to it. Dan Kean is a wild and restless boy who has been in and out of trouble since he arrived at the school. In this story he finds a good way to harness his energy.*

"What in the world is that boy doing?" said Mrs. Jo to herself as she watched Dan running around the half-mile triangle as if for a wager. He was all alone, and seemed possessed by some strange desire to run himself into a fever, or break his neck; for, after several rounds, he tried leaping walls, and turning somersaults up the avenue, and finally dropped down on the grass before the door as if exhausted.

"Are you training for a race, Dan?" asked Mrs. Jo from the window where she sat.

He looked up quickly, and stopped panting to answer, with a laugh:

"No; I'm only working off my steam."

"Can't you find a cooler way of doing it? You will be

ill if you tear about so in such warm weather," said Mrs. Jo, laughing also as she threw him out a big palm-leaf fan.

"Can't help it. I *must* run somewhere," answered Dan, with such an odd expression in his restless eyes that Mrs. Jo was troubled, and asked quickly:

"Is Plumfield getting too narrow for you?"

"I wouldn't mind if it was a little bigger. I like it though; only the fact is the devil gets into me sometimes, and then I do want to bolt."

The words seemed to come against his will, for he looked sorry the minute they were spoken, and seemed to think he deserved a reproof for his ingratitude. But Mrs. Jo understood the feeling, and though sorry to see it she could not blame the boy for confessing it. She looked at him anxiously, seeing how tall and strong he had grown, how full of energy his face was, with its eager eyes and resolute mouth; and remembering the utter freedom he had known for years before, she felt how even the gentle restraint of this home would weigh upon him at times when the old lawless spirit stirred in him. "Yes," she said to herself, "my wild hawk needs a larger cage; and yet, if I let him go, I am afraid he will be lost. I must try and find some lure strong enough to keep him safe."

"I know all about it," she added aloud. "It is not 'the devil,' as you call it, but the very natural desire of all young people for liberty. I used to feel just so, and once, I really did think for a minute that I would bolt."

"Why didn't you?" said Dan, coming to lean on the low window ledge, with an evident desire to continue the subject.

"I knew it was foolish, and love for my mother kept me at home."

"I haven't got any mother," began Dan.

"I thought you had *now*," said Mrs. Jo, gently stroking the rough hair off his hot forehead.

"You are no end good to me, and I can't ever thank you enough, but it isn't just the same, is it?" and Dan looked up at her with a wistful, hungry look that went to her heart.

"No, dear, it is not the same, and never can be. I think an own mother would have been a great deal to you. But as that cannot be, you must try to let me fill her place. I fear I have not done all I ought, or you would not want to leave me," she added sorrowfully.

"Yes, you have!" cried Dan eagerly. "I don't want to go, and I won't go, if I can help it; but every now and then I feel as if I must burst out somehow. I want to run straight ahead somewhere, to smash something, or pitch into somebody. Don't know why, but I do, and that's all about it."

Dan laughed as he spoke, but he meant what he said, for he knit his black brows, and brought down his fist on the ledge with such force that Mrs. Jo's thimble flew off into the grass. He brought it back, and as she took it she held the big brown hand a minute, saying, with a look that showed the words cost her something:

"Well, Dan, run if you must, but don't run far; and come back to me soon, for I want you very much."

He was rather taken aback by this unexpected permission to play truant, and somehow it seemed to lessen his desire to go. He did not understand why, but Mrs. Jo did, and, knowing the natural perversity of the human mind, counted on it to help her now. She felt instinctively that the more the boy was restrained the more he would fret against it; but leave him free, and the mere sense of liberty would content him, joined to the knowledge that his presence was dear to those whom he loved best. It was a little experiment, but it succeeded, for Dan stood silent a moment, unconsciously picking the fan to pieces and turning the matter over in his mind. He felt that she appealed to his heart and his honor, and owned that he understood it by saying presently, with a mixture of regret and resolution in his face:

"I won't go yet awhile, and I'll give you warning before I bolt. That's fair, isn't it?"

"Yes, we will let it stand so. Now, I want to see if I can't find some way for you to work off your steam better than running about the place like a mad dog, spoiling my fans, or fighting with the boys. What can we invent?" And while Dan tried to repair the mischief he had done, Mrs. Jo racked her brain for some new device to keep her truant safe until he had learned to love his lessons better.

"How would you like to be my express-man?" she said as a sudden thought popped into her head.

"Go into town, and do the errands?" asked Dan, looking interested at once.

"Yes; Franz is tired of it, Silas cannot be spared just now, and Mr. Bhaer has no time. Old Andy is a safe horse, you are a good driver, and know your way about the city as well as a postman. Suppose you try it, and see if it won't do most as well to drive away two or three times a week as to run away once a month."

"I'd like it ever so much, only I must go alone and do it all myself. I don't want any of the other fellows bothering round," said Dan, taking to the new idea so kindly that he began to put on business airs already.

"If Mr. Bhaer does not object you shall have it all your own way. I suppose Emil will growl, but he cannot be trusted with horses, and you can. By the way, to-morrow is market-day, and I must make out my list. You had better see that the wagon is in order, and tell Silas to have the fruit and vegetables ready for Mother. You will have to be up early and get back in time for school, can you do that?"

"I'm always an early bird, so I don't mind," and Dan slung on his jacket with dispatch.

"The early bird got the worm this time, I'm sure," said Mrs. Jo merrily.

"And a jolly good worm it is," answered Dan, as he went laughing away to put a new lash to the whip, wash the wagon, and order Silas about with all the importance of a young express-man.

"Before he is tired of this I will find something else, and have it ready when the next restless fit comes on," said Mrs. Jo to herself as she wrote her list with a deep sense of gratitude that all her boys were not Dans.

Mr. Bhaer did not entirely approve of the new plan, but agreed to give it a trial, which put Dan on his mettle, and caused him to give up certain wild plans of his own, in which the new lash and the long hill were to have borne a part. He was up and away very early the next morning, heroically resisting the temptation to race with the milkmen going into town. Once there, he did his errands carefully, and came jogging home again in time for school, to Mr. Bhaer's surprise and Mrs. Jo's great satisfaction. The Commodore did growl at Dan's promotion, but was pacified by a superior padlock to his new boathouse, and the thought that seamen were meant for higher honors than driving market-wagons and doing family errands.

* * *

So Dan filled his new office well and contentedly for weeks, and said no more about bolting. But one day Mr. Bhaer found him pummeling Jack, who was roaring for mercy under his knee.

"Why, Dan, I thought you had given up fighting," he said as he went to the rescue.

"We ain't fighting, we are only wrestling," answered Dan, leaving off reluctantly.

"It looks very much like it, and feels like it, hey, Jack?" said Mr. Bhaer, as the defeated gentleman got upon his legs with difficulty.

"Catch me wrestling with him again. He's 'most knocked my head off," snarled Jack, holding onto that portion of his frame as if it really was loose upon his shoulders.

"The fact is, we began in fun, but when I got him down I couldn't help pounding him. Sorry I hurt you, old fellow," explained Dan, looking rather ashamed of himself.

"I understand. The longing to pitch into somebody was so strong you couldn't resist. You are a sort of berserker, Dan, and something to tussle with is as necessary to you as music is to Nat," said Mr. Bhaer, who knew all about the conversation between the boy and Mrs. Jo.

"Can't help it. So if you don't want to be pounded you'd better keep out of the way," answered Dan with a warning look in his black eyes that made Jack sheer off in haste.

"If you want something to wrestle with, I will give you a tougher specimen than Jack," said Mr. Bhaer; and leading the way to the wood-yard, he pointed to certain roots of trees that had been grubbed up in the spring, and had been lying there waiting to be split.

"There, when you feel inclined to maltreat the boys, just come and work off your energies here, and I'll thank you for it."

"So I will"; and, seizing the axe that lay near, Dan hauled out a tough root, and went at it so vigorously that the chips flew far and wide, and Mr. Bhaer fled for his life.

To his great amusement, Dan took him at his word, and was often seen wrestling with the ungainly knots, hat and jacket off, red face, and wrathful eyes; for he got into royal rages over some of his adversaries, and swore at them under his breath till he had conquered them, when he exulted, and marched off to the shed with an armful of gnarled oak-wood in triumph. He blistered his hands, tired his back, and dulled the axe, but it did him good, and he got more comfort out of the ugly roots than anyone dreamed, for with each blow he worked off some of the pent-up power that would otherwise have been expended in some less harmless way.

"When this is gone I really don't know what I *shall* do," said Mrs. Jo to herself, for no inspiration came, and she was at the end of her resources.

But Dan found a new occupation for himself, and enjoyed it some time before anyone discovered the cause of his contentment. A fine young horse of Mr. Laurie's was kept at Plumfield that summer, running loose in a large pasture across the brook. The boys were all interested in the handsome, spirited creature, and for a time were fond of watching him gallop and frisk with his plumy tail flying, and his handsome head in the air. But they soon got tired of it, and left Prince Charlie to himself. All but Dan, *he* never tired of looking at the horse, and seldom failed to visit him each day with a lump of sugar, a bit of bread, or an apple to make him welcome. Charlie was grateful, accepted his friendship, and the two loved one another as if they felt some tie between them, inexplicable but strong. In whatever part of the wide field he might be, Charlie always came at full speed when Dan whistled at the bars, and the boy was never happier than when the beautiful, fleet creature put his head on his shoulder, looking up at him with fine eyes full of intelligent affection.

"We understand one another without any palaver, don't we, old fellow?" Dan would say, proud of the horse's confidence, and so jealous of his regard, that he told no one how well the friendship prospered, and never asked anyone but Teddy to accompany him on these daily visits.

Mr. Laurie came now and then to see how Charlie got on, and spoke of having him broken to harness in the autumn.

"He won't need much taming, he's such a gentle, fine-tempered brute. I shall come out and try him with a saddle myself someday," he said, on one of these visits.

"He lets me put a halter on him, but I don't believe he will bear a saddle even if *you* put it on," answered Dan, who never failed to be present when Charlie and his master met.

"I shall coax him to bear it, and not mind a few tumbles at first. He has never been harshly treated, so, though he will be surprised at the new performances, I think he won't be frightened, and his antics will do no harm."

"I wonder what he *would* do," said Dan to himself as Mr. Laurie went away with the Professor, and Charlie returned to the bars, from which he had retired when the gentlemen came up.

A daring fancy to try the experiment took possession of the boy as he sat on the topmost rail with the glossy back temptingly near him. Never thinking of danger, he obeyed the impulse, and while Charlie unsuspectingly nibbled at the apple he held, Dan quickly and quietly took his seat. He did not keep it long, however, for with an astonished snort, Charlie reared straight up, and deposited Dan on the ground. The fall did not hurt him, for the turf was soft, and he jumped up, saying, with a laugh:

"I did it anyway! Come here, you rascal, and I'll try it again."

But Charlie declined to approach, and Dan left him resolving to succeed in the end; for a struggle like this suited him exactly. Next time he took a halter, and having got it on, he played with the horse for a while, leading him to and fro, and putting him through various antics till he was a little tired; then Dan sat on the wall and gave him bread, but watched his chance, and getting a good grip of the halter, slipped onto his back. Charlie tried the old trick, but Dan held on, having had practice with Toby, who occasionally had an obstinate fit, and tried to shake off his rider. Charlie was both amazed and indignant; and after prancing for a minute set off at a gallop, and away went Dan heels over head. If he had not belonged to the class of boys who go through all sorts of dangers unscathed, he would have broken his neck; as it was, he got a heavy fall, and lay still collecting his wits, while Charlie tore around the field tossing his head with every sign of satisfaction at the discomfiture of his rider. Presently it seemed to occur to him that something was wrong with Dan, and, being of a magnanimous nature, he went to see what the matter was. Dan let him sniff about and perplex himself for a few minutes; then he looked up at him, saying, as decidedly as if the horse could understand:

"You think you have beaten me, but you are mistaken, old boy; and I'll ride you yet—see if I don't."

He tried no more that day, but soon after attempted a new method of introducing Charlie to a burden. He strapped a folded blanket on his back, and then let him race, and rear, and roll, and fume as much as he liked. After a few fits of rebellion Charlie submitted, and in a few days permitted Dan to mount him, often stopping short to look around, as if he said, half patiently, half reproachfully: "I don't understand it, but I suppose you mean no harm, so I permit the liberty."

Dan patted and praised him, and took a short turn every day, getting frequent falls, but persisting in spite of them, and longing to try a saddle and bridle, but not daring to confess what he had done. He had his wish, however, for there had been a witness of his pranks who said a good word for him.

"Do you know what that chap has ben doin' lately?" asked Silas of his master, one evening, as he received his orders for the next day.

"Which boy?" said Mr. Bhaer, with an air of resignation, expecting some sad revelation.

"Dan, he's ben a breaking the colt, sir, and I wish I may die if he ain't done it," answered Silas, chuckling.

"How do you know?"

"Wal, I kinder keep an eye on the little fellers, and most gen'lly know what they're up to; so when Dan kep going off to the paster, and coming home black and blue, I mistrusted that *suthing* was goin' on. I didn't say nothin', but I crep up into the barn chamber, and from there I see him goin" through all manner of games with Charlie. Blest if he warn't throwed time and agin, and knocked round like a bag o' meal. But the pluck of the boy did beat all, and he 'peared to like it, and kep on as ef bound to beat."

"But, Silas, you should have stopped it—the boy might have been killed," said Mr. Bhaer, wondering what freak his inexpressibles would take into their heads next.

"S'pose I oughter; but there warn't no real danger, for Charlie ain't no tricks, and is as pretty a tempered horse as ever I see. Fact was, I couldn't bear to spile sport, for ef there's anything I do admire it's grit, and Dan is chock-full on't. But now I know he's hankerin' after a saddle, and yet won't take even the old one on the sly; so I just thought I'd up and tell, and maybe you'd let him try what he could do. Mr. Laurie won't mind, and Charlie's all the better for't."

"We shall see"; and off went Mr. Bhaer to inquire into the matter.

Dan owned up at once, and proudly proved that Silas was right by showing off his power over Charlie; for by dint of much coaxing, many carrots, and infinite perseverance, he really had succeeded in riding the colt with a halter and blanket. Mr. Laurie was much amused, and well pleased with Dan's courage and skill, and let him have a hand in all future performances; for he set about Charlie's education at once, saying that he was not going to be outdone by a slip of a boy. Thanks to Dan, Charlie took kindly to the saddle and bridle when he had once reconciled himself to the indignity of the bit; and after Mr. Laurie had trained him a little, Dan was permitted to ride him, to the great envy and admiration of the other boys.

"Isn't he handsome? And don't he mind me like a lamb?" said Dan one day as he dismounted and stood with his arm round Charlie's neck.

"Yes, and isn't he a much more useful and agreeable animal than the wild colt who spent his days racing about the field, jumping fences, and running away now and then?" asked Mrs. Bhaer from the steps where she always appeared when Dan performed with Charlie.

"Of course he is. See, he won't run away now, even if I don't hold him, and he comes to me the minute I whistle; I have tamed him well, haven't I?" and Dan looked both proud and pleased, as well he might, for, in spite of their struggles together, Charlie loved him better than his master.

"I am taming a colt too, and I think I shall succeed as well as you if I am as patient and persevering," said Mrs. Jo, smiling so significantly at him that Dan understood and answered, laughing, yet in earnest:

"We won't jump over the fence and run away, but stay, and let them make a handsome, useful span of us, hey, Charlie?"

The Seven Foals

retold by G. W. Dasent

*Every country in the world has its own folktales, and no
matter how different the countries are, in folktales those
who are good do well, and those who are bad come to grief.
In this story the poor youngest son does what he's told,
which is sometimes more difficult than you might think!
The story, which comes from Norway, was translated by
Sir George Dasent, who worked for a time at the British
embassy in Stockholm. His* Popular Tales from the Norse
*allowed English-speaking readers to enjoy some of the rich
and exciting stories that come from Scandinavia. In that
part of the world, "Boots" is a traditional name for an idle
or stupid boy.*

Once on a time there was a poor couple who lived
in a wretched hut, far, far away in the wood.
How they lived I can't tell, but I'm sure it was from
hand to mouth, and hard work even then; but they
had three sons, and the youngest of them was Boots—
he did little else than lie in the ashes and poke about.

So one day the eldest lad said he would go out to
earn his bread, and he soon got leave, and wandered
out into the world. There he walked and walked the
whole day, and when evening drew in, he came to a
King's palace, and there stood the King out on the
steps, and asked whither he was bound.

"Oh, I'm going about, looking after a place," said the lad.

"Will you serve me?" asked the King, "and watch my seven foals? If you can watch them one whole day, and tell me at night what they eat and what they drink, you shall have the Princess to wife, and half my kingdom; but if you can't, I'll cut three red stripes out of your back. Do you hear?"

Yes! that was an easy task, the lad thought; he'd do that fast enough, never fear.

So next morning, as the first peep of dawn came, the King's coachman let out the seven foals. Away they went, and the lad after them. You may fancy how they tore over hill and dale, through bush and bog. When the lad had run so long a time, he began to get weary, and when he had held on a while longer, he had more than enough of his watching, and just there, he came to a cleft in a rock, where an old hag sat and spun with a distaff. As soon as she saw the lad, who was running after the foals till the sweat ran down his brow, this old hag bawled out,

"Come hither, come hither, my pretty son, and let me comb your hair."

Yes! the lad was willing enough; so he sat down in the cleft of the rock with the old hag, and laid his head on her lap, and she combed his hair all day while he lay there, and stretched his lazy bones.

So, when evening drew on, the lad wanted to go away.

"I may just as well toddle straight home now," said he, "for it's no use my going back to the palace."

"Stop a bit till it's dark," said the old hag, "and then the King's foals will pass by here again, and then you can run home with them, and then no one will know that you have lain here all day long, instead of watching the foals."

So, when the foals came, she gave the lad a flask of water and a clod of turf. Those he was to show to the King, and say that was what his seven foals ate and drank.

"Have you watched true and well the whole day, now?" asked the King, when the lad came before him in the evening.

"Yes, I should think so," said the lad.

"Then you can tell me what my seven foals eat and drink," said the King.

"Yes!" And so the lad pulled out the flask of water and the clod of turf, which the old hag had given him.

"Here you see their meat, and here you see their drink," said the lad.

But then the King saw plain enough how he had watched, and he got so wrath, he ordered his men to chase him away home on the spot; but first they were to cut three red stripes out of his back, and rub salt into them. So when the lad got home again, you may fancy what a temper he was in. He'd gone out once to get a place, he said, but he'd never do so again.

Next day the second son said he would go out into the world to try his luck. His father and mother said no, and bade him look at his brother's back; but he held to his own, and at last he got leave to go, and set out. So when he had walked all day, he, too, came to the King's palace. There stood the King out on the steps, and asked whither he was bound. And when the lad said he was looking about for a place, the King said he might have a place there, and watch his seven foals. But the King laid down the same punishment, and the same reward, as he had settled for his brother.

Well, the lad was willing enough; he took the place at once, for he thought he'd soon watch the foals and tell the King what they ate and drank.

So, in the gray of the morning, the coachman let out the seven foals, and off they went again over hill and dale, and the lad after them. But the same thing happened to him as had befallen his brother. When he had run after the foals a long, long time, till he was both warm and weary, he passed by the cleft in a rock, where an old hag sat and spun with a distaff, and she bawled out to the lad,

"Come hither, come hither, my pretty son, and let me comb your hair."

That the lad thought a good offer, so he let the foals run on their way, and sat down in the cleft with the old hag. There he sat, and there he lay, taking his ease, and stretching his lazy bones the whole day.

When the foals came back at nightfall, he, too, got a flask of water and a clod of turf from the old hag to show to the King. But when the King asked the lad,

"Can you tell me now, what my seven foals eat and drink?" The lad pulled out the flask and the clod and said,

"Here you see their meat, and here you see their drink."

Then the King got wrath again, and ordered them to cut three red stripes out of the lad's back, and rub salt in, and chase him home that very minute. And so when the lad got home, he also told how he had fared, and said he had gone out once to get a place, but he'd never do so anymore.

The third day Boots wanted to set out; he had a great mind to try and watch the seven foals, he said. The others laughed at him, and made game of him, saying,

"When we fared so ill, you'll do it better—a fine joke! You look like it—you, who have never done anything but lie there and poke about in the ashes!"

"Yes!" said Boots. "I don't see why I shouldn't go, for I've got it into my head, and can't get it out again."

And so, in spite of all the jeers of the others, and the prayers of the old people, there was no help for it, and Boots set out.

So after he had walked the whole day, he, too, came at dusk to the King's palace. There stood the King out on the steps, and asked whither he was bound.

So Boots said he was brother to those two who had watched the King's seven foals, and ended by asking if he might try to watch them next day.

"Oh, stuff!" said the King, for he got quite cross if he even thought of them. "If you're brother to those two, you're not worth much, I'll be bound. I've had enough of such scamps!"

"Well," said Boots; "since I've come so far, I may just as well get leave to try, too."

"Oh, very well, with all my heart!" said the King. "If you *will* have your back flayed, you're quite welcome!"

"I'd much rather have the Princess," said Boots.

So next morning, at gray of dawn, the coachman let out the seven foals again, and away they went over hill and dale, through bush and bog, and Boots behind them. And so, when he, too, had run a long while, he came to the cleft in the rock, where the old hag sat, spinning at her distaff. So she bawled out to Boots,

"Come hither, come hither, my pretty son, and let me comb your hair."

"Don't you wish you may catch me?" said Boots. "Don't you wish you may catch me?" as he ran along, leaping and jumping, and holding on by one of the foal's tails. And when he had got well past the cleft in the rock, the youngest foal said, "Jump up on my back, my lad, for we've a long way before us still."

So Boots jumped up on his back.

So they went on and on, a long, long way.

"Do you see anything now?" said the foal.

"No," said Boots.

So they went on a good bit farther.

"Do you see anything now?" asked the foal.

"Oh, no," said the lad.

So when they had gone a great, great way farther—I'm sure I can't tell how far—the foal asked again,

"Do you see anything now?"

"Yes," said Boots, "now I see something that looks white—just like a tall, big birch trunk."

"Yes," said the foal, "we're going into that trunk."

So when they got to the trunk, the eldest foal took and pushed it on one side, and then they saw a door where it had stood, and inside the door was a little room, and in the room there was scarce anything but a little fireplace and one or two benches; but behind the door hung a great rusty sword and a little pitcher.

"Can you brandish the sword?" said the foals. "Try!"

So Boots tried, but he couldn't; then they made him take a pull at the pitcher; first once, then twice, and then thrice. And then he could wield that sword like anything.

"Yes," said the foals, "now you may take the sword with you, and with it you must cut off all our seven heads on your wedding day, and then we'll be Princes again as we were before. For we are brothers of that Princess whom you are to have when you can tell the King what we eat and drink; but an ugly troll has thrown this shape on us. Now mind, when you have hewn off our heads, take care to lay each head at the tail of the trunk which it belonged to before, and then the spell will have no more power over us."

Yes! Boots promised all that, and then on they went.

And when they had traveled a long, long way, the foal asked,

"Do you see anything?"

"No," said Boots.

So they traveled a good bit still.

"And now?" asked the foal.

"No, I see nothing," said Boots.

So they traveled many, many miles again, over hill and dale.

"Now then," said the foal, "do you see anything now?"

"Yes," said Boots, "now I see something like a blue stripe, far, far away."

"Yes," said the foal, "that's a river we've got to cross."

Over the river was a long, grand bridge; and when they had got over it to the other side, they traveled on a long, long way. At last the foal asked again, if Boots didn't see anything?

Yes, this time he saw something that looked black, far, far away, just as though it were a church steeple.

"Yes," said the foal, "that's where we're going to turn in."

So when the foals got into the churchyard, they became men again, and looked like Princes, with such fine clothes that it glistened from them. And so they went into the church, and took bread and wine from the priest who stood at the altar. And Boots, he went in too. But when the priest had laid his hands on the Princes, and given them the blessing, they went out of the church again, and Boots went out too. But he took with him a flask of wine and a wafer.

As soon as ever the seven Princes came out into the churchyard, they were turned into foals again, and so Boots got up on the back of the youngest, and they all went back the same way that they had come; only they went much, much faster. First they crossed the bridge, next they passed the trunk, and then they passed the old hag, who sat at the cleft and spun, and they went by her so fast, that Boots couldn't hear what the old hag screeched after him; but he heard so much as to know she was in an awful rage.

It was almost dark when they got back to the palace, and the King himself stood out on the steps and waited for them.

"Have you watched well and true the whole day?" said he to Boots.

"I've done my best," answered Boots.

"Then you can tell me what my seven foals eat and drink," said the King.

Then Boots pulled out the flask of wine and the wafer, and showed them to the King.

"Here you see their meat, and here you see their drink," said he.

"Yes," said the King, "you have watched true and well; and you shall have the Princess and half the kingdom."

So they made ready the wedding feast, and the King said it should be such a grand one, it should be the talk far and near.

But when they sat down to the bridal feast, the bridegroom got up and went down to the stable, for he said he had forgotten something and must go and fetch it. And when he got down there, he did as the foals had said, and hewed their heads off, all seven, the eldest first, and the others after him; and at the same time he took care to lay each head at the tail of the foal to which it belonged. And as he did this, lo! they all became Princes again.

So when he went back into the bridal hall with the seven Princes, the King was so glad he both kissed Boots and patted him on the back, and his bride was still more glad of him than she had been before.

"Half the Kingdom you have got already," said the King; "and the other half you shall have after my death; for my sons can easily get themselves lands and wealth, now they are Princes again."

And so, like enough, there was mirth and fun at that wedding. I was there too; but there was no one to care for poor me; and so I got nothing but a bit of bread and butter. And I laid it down on the stove, and the bread was burned and the butter ran, and so I didn't get even the smallest crumb. Wasn't that a great shame?

Sure Magic

MONICA EDWARDS

Many readers will sympathize with Paul in this story—he wants a pony, but can only afford a goat. This story, which is based on a true incident, is by one of the most popular and highly esteemed writers of pony stories. Her Romney Marsh and Punchbowl Farm series are particularly well-known.

"When I were eleven I didn't have three pound in my money box; no, nor I didn't have one." Old Tim Terrell leaned on his spade for a moment and got his breath while looking at Paul reflectively.

"I've been saving for two years," Paul pointed out. "But now I almost think I shall have to give up," he added sadly. "It's funny, but when I started I thought I'd only have to save very hard and carefully, and I'd soon have enough to buy a pony. But of course, I was very young then."

Old Tim took a whetstone out of his pocket, upended his spade, and began sharpening the edge of it. "Thass a thing I wholly do believe in," he said, "an edge to a spade." He suddenly looked up again for a moment, the whetstone poised. "You could get yourself a real nice nanny goat with that. Chap what sold me mine, he got another up for sale I do know. Now thass a useful animal, is a nanny goat. Usefuller nor what riding a pony would be, I will say. All that milk. Your mum'd be pleased, I lay."

"But I don't want a goat."

"Ah well, that do make a difference," the old man admitted, resuming the digging, which he was doing for Paul's father. And then he added persistently: "Some folks do drive 'em in a liddle cart, and that."

"What I'm in two minds about," said Paul, "is spending it on a secondhand air gun. Roy Boley's got one at Partridge Farm that he said I could have for three pounds. I thought I'd go and look at it this afternoon. Of course I'd much rather have a pony, even if it meant waiting another two or three years, but I'd only have six or seven pounds then, at this rate. It's pretty hopeless, isn't it, Tim?"

Mr. Terrell looked at his watch and then he looked at the heavy sky. "Thass full of snow," he said, "for all it's near the end of March. If you fare to go out to Partridge and back I lay you better start now. That'll get dark early, see, with all that cloud, and your mum'll worry."

"If I had a pony," Paul said, "I'd be there and back in no time, galloping across the fields."

"If wishes was horses," said Tim Terrell, "beggars would ride. Now mind my pea rows—troddlin' all over 'em." He glanced up again at a sky that looked like suspended London fog and shook his head. "I tell you, spring ain't what it used to be, nor it ain't. I call to mind when I were a tiddler—" but Paul, apologetically waving his hand, was already out of earshot.

Partridge Farm had several attractions for Paul, the air gun being one of the least. For one thing, there was Roy, a good friend and wonderful company on ferreting expeditions, though quite incredibly uninterested in horses. Oh, the waste of it! Paul thought as he strode across the fields: here was a boy whose father kept and rode such a splendid hunter mare as Calluna was, a boy who could have kept a pony of his own if he had wanted to, but who was much more interested in the two farm tractors and the cowman's motorcycle.

A further attraction for Paul was the Ayrshire dairy herd. He liked to help in the cowsheds when he could, and Roy often joined him there, though with him the tractors always took first place. But the greatest attraction of all at Partridge was Calluna, and Mr. Boley had a special liking for Paul because of this. He would dearly have liked his own son, Roy, to share his interest in horses and hunting, but failing this it was nice to have Paul about the stable, being useful and absorbed in all that happened there.

Calluna was shortly expecting a foal and so had not been hunted through the winter just finished. The sire was a very fine premium stallion and Calluna herself was an excellent type of hunter mare, so that Paul and Mr. Boley expected great things of the foal. In about a fortnight it would be born. Feeling snow suddenly brush his cheeks, Paul wondered what sort of a world it would be born to. Winter, with east winds and snow? Or spring, with mild sunshine? Anything, it seemed, could happen in an English spring. This time last year they had been picnicking. Now it looked as if they might be sleighing in the morning.

Once started, the snow began to fall fast, like plum petals in a sudden wind, and by the time Paul reached the farm the ground was white. They were already milking in the long cowshed, but Paul stopped to look over the box stall at Calluna, talking to her and offering her the quartered apple he had brought for her. But she was restless, staring past him at the snow and then walking around her box and staring out again. She took the apple politely but crunched it as if her mind was not on it.

"I expect it does look queer to you, old girl," said Paul, rubbing his hands down the old corduroy shorts that he wore in school holidays, "when you thought it was spring." And he went across to the cowshed, shaking the snow from his hair as he hurried inside.

It was the usual thing that, whenever Roy and Paul were at each other's houses around a mealtime, they stayed there for it, unless it was going to be dark before they could get home again. "And tonight, even with the snowy sky, it ought to be light till half past six," Mr. Boley said.

"And there's cherry cake for tea," said Roy, "and we can look at the air gun after."

But somehow, they never did look at the air gun. At tea, the talk turned to Calluna and her great expectations, and Paul mentioned how restless she had seemed when he had looked in at her.

"That's the snow, I dare say," said Mr. Boley. "We haven't had much this winter, for all it's been so cold, and I expect it looked strange to her, coming down so fast and swirly. Anyway, we'll have a look at her after tea, and I always go around last thing, too. You never know with mares in foal, though really she ought to go another fortnight."

"What I'm wondering about," said Mrs. Boley, glancing through the window a little anxiously, "is Paul getting home safely. I wonder if you ought to start early, Paul? I don't want to hurry you, but it does seem to be getting thicker."

"It is jolly thick," said Roy. "You can't even see where the path is anymore."

"Oh, I'll be all right," said Paul. "It can't be really deep before I get home, and I can go back by the road."

"Tell you what," said Mr. Boley. "We'll go out and have a look at the old girl, shall we, and then I'll see you back as far as the signpost?"

Mr. Boley's hands were deep in his pockets as they trudged through the snow to the stable. "It's already up to the ankles," he said. "Pity the poor wretches who have their dairy herds lying out!"

Because their heads were tucked down against the blizzard they did not notice the open stable door until they were nearly in front of it. Then, for a moment, they stood staring in horrified disbelief at the empty box stall. Mr. Boley swung around, peering through the snow into the corners of the yard. "She can't be far off," he muttered in a shocked voice, adding as if to himself, "in this weather, and growing dusk, and so near to foaling. Did you notice if the door was properly shut when you looked in at her, Paul?" They were hurrying across to the cowshed now.

"It seemed quite firm when I leaned on it," panted Paul, hurrying too. "How on earth could she have got out?"

"Heaven only knows," said Mr. Boley, staring into the shadows of the cowshed. But Calluna wasn't there, and the double row of white-splashed cows looked up curiously, clanking their chains. "She used to be a bit of a devil at getting out when she was younger," he added. "Used to pull the bolt back with her lips. But we thought she'd grown out of that, these three years past."

"How about tracks?" Paul asked anxiously, peering now at the snowy ground.

"No, it's falling too thick for that, son. You can hardly see our own tracks from the house. We'll have to send out searchers. With lanterns, too; it'll be dark in an hour. But I'll get out the car and run you to the signpost before I join them."

"Oh—couldn't I help to look for Calluna?" Paul's voice went up in an urgent appeal. "You could telephone Mother: she wouldn't mind, I'm sure. I could get back all right if you lent me a flashlight."

"Sorry, old chap." Mr. Boley looked at him regretfully. "I couldn't have the responsibility. Job enough finding the mare, I dare say—it may take us all night, in this—without keeping an eye on chaps of Roy's and your age. Come along to the house for a minute while I get the search started, and then I'll soon have you on the road. You can come straight out again in the morning," he added, seeing Paul's forlorn face. "But we want grown men on this job."

The next ten minutes for Mr. Boley were a whirl of telephoning, and sending one person to fetch another, and someone else to search the farm buildings, until he was satisfied that four were about to set out seeking Calluna, and that the police were on the lookout as well. Roy brought out the air gun, to fill up the time usefully, but Paul hardly felt so interested in it now. He kept looking up, out of the dusky window where snowflakes flew before the wind, and imagining Calluna out in it, probably foaling in it; because, as Mr. Boley said, you never knew with mares in foal.

That night the snow fell heavily until dawn. The telephone wires were down in many places, so that, when Paul got up in the morning, he could not get through to Partridge Farm to inquire about the search. But news came very quickly, of its own accord, on the legs of old Tim Terrell. Tim was postman as well as jobbing gardener in Paul's village, and he stood on the doorstep stamping his feet and sorting letters while Paul looked out past him at the amazing snow of spring. "Treating you well, this morning," Tim was saying. "Five letters, and not a bill among them."

"Have you heard anything about the Boley's search party, Tim?"

"I have that. Just been talking to the chap what's driving the snowplow, and he says their cowman told him as they found the mare in Merlin Wood." He was talking through the fingers of a glove that he held in his mouth while handling letters.

"Oh, I am glad they found her!" cried Paul, taking the letters. "Was she all right?"

"Right enough," said Tim, "but what do you think? With a foal at foot! In all that snow."

"Tim! Really? Is the foal all right, too? Oh, Mr. Boley will be pleased!"

"The little 'un's good as new, he say," said Tim. "Funny, ain't it, the things they'll stand? Sometimes you hear of 'em digging out sheep what have been buried days and days in them deep hill drifts. I reckon they got air and warmth down in that snow—must have, mustn't they? Oh well, this won't do." Mr. Terrell swung his bag around his back again and then set off on his way.

Paul would have thrown his coat and rubber boots on and trudged to Partridge Farm at once, if his mother hadn't reminded him that he had not made his bed or dried the breakfast things, which were his holiday tasks, but he was out there before the morning was half over. He found Mr. Boley in the box stall with Calluna, and there, walking experimentally about in the straw on long stilty legs, was the most beautiful but quite the tiniest colt he had ever seen.

"Oh, I say!" Paul stared in rapturous awe. "Isn't he small?"

"Fortnight premature, of course," said Mr. Boley. "Lucky to find him when we did. It was close on dawn; we'd been trudging all the countryside. No tracks, you see, until the snow began to clear. Still, he seems well enough for all his bitter welcome. It's his mother that worries me."

"She looks all right to me," said Paul, studying her anxiously.

"Won't settle," said Mr. Boley. "She doesn't seem to care about the little fellow at all. Seems to want to get out in the snow again. Look at her fretting! I can't make it out. I've been trying to get her to stand for feeding him, off and on, ever since we brought her in. But you can see for yourself how it is."

Paul could see very easily now, for Calluna fussed around her box with her swinging stride, throwing her head up at the doorway and staring out over the snow with strange restless eyes. And this was the way she went on behaving through all of that day. Paul stayed for lunch, but not for tea because of the snow, and most of his time he spent with Mr. Boley in Calluna's box, trying to get the mare to settle quietly with her foal.

"She's always been such a good mother before," the farmer said in a baffled voice. "And this little chap— he's so small, being premature, he wants a good start. I don't reckon he's had a proper meal yet. Now, see if

she'll stand quietly while you hold her, and I'll help the colt."

But Calluna swung her quarters this way and that, and stared out at the snow as if it were a green summer meadow and she was starving.

The next morning, with the snow still deep on the ground and no birds singing, Paul went to the door in answer to Tim Terrell's knock. "Moldy old lot I brought you this morning," said Tim, who always took a great interest in the letters. "Four circulars and a postcard."

"How's Calluna, Tim? Have you seen her this morning? Has she settled down yet, do you know?"

"Cor! That's a case, that is," said Tim, shaking his head. "Rumbusting around her box all night, whinnying and that, so Mr. Boley says. Don't know what to do with her, they don't, and that's a fact, 'cept padlock her door. Nice little tiddler, too, the colt. But she don't seem to take to him nohow. Just fussing to get out."

"Oh, Tim!" Paul stared at the letters without seeing them. "How awful for the colt. I wish—oh, I wish that he were my colt! I think he's quite the loveliest thing I ever saw. So small, and yet so—sort of perfect."

"You wouldn't be able to ride him now, not for years," Tim pointed out, straightening his shoulders under the heavy bag.

"I know. But it isn't only riding that's such fun. It's having a horse, and being able to look after it, and all that."

"Telly what, then," said Mr. Terrell helpfully. "You wanter find out where the old mare dropped her foal, son; then go there and wish, see. Sure magic, that is— to wish where a foal been newly born. But he must be a colt foal, mind, or it doesn't work out."

"This one is," said Tim, his eyes suddenly lighting up with interest. But in a moment they had darkened again. "Magic, and all that, isn't really true of course," he said wistfully.

"Telly what Parson said in the pulpit Sunday—since you was at home with your cold," said Tim Terrell. "He said: 'There's more things in heaven and earth than this world dreams of.' Well this won't do; I must be getting along down the lane, now. Cheerybye, son. So long."

Paul took the letters in and shut the door. He made his bed and dried the breakfast things, and then fetched in some logs for the sitting-room fire. Then he put on his rubber boots and coat and set off for Partridge Farm.

Merlin Wood, wasn't it, where Calluna's foal had been born? It lay between Paul's house and the farm, as near as mattered. At a pinch, he might say it was almost on his way. Of course, no one believed in magic in these days, but all the same, it wouldn't do any harm just to trudge about inside the wood for a bit. No one need know, least of all Roy Boley, who was exceedingly practical with his carburetors and alternators and overhead drive and the like—good chap though he was.

The snow on the edges of the wood was thicker than in the fields. It reached nearly to the top of Paul's rubber boots in places, and drifts of it were so deep that he had quickly to step out of them, though none had fallen since the night of Calluna's escape. Paul saw her tracks here and there, in sheltered places, and the tracks of men. Some of the prints were half hidden by the snow that had fallen during the search, some stopped and turned back, and others were criss-crossed and lost in muddle. Trudging through deep drifts, Paul began to think he would never find the place. And for how long could one still consider the colt "newly born," as Tim had said he must be? Nearly a day and a half had passed already. . . .

Suddenly Paul stared, opening his eyes wider, hurrying faster though the snow lipped into his boot tops. Here, many tracks came together; the snow was trampled, pawed and scattered. Hoofprints and shoeprints overlapped—and there, sure enough, was the smoothed hollow in the snow where the mare had lain down. Paul stopped, puffing from his struggle through the drifts and flushed with the cold damp of snowy woods. This was the place. Here was where the small colt had first opened his eyes, not to daylight but to clouded starlight.

Oh well, Paul decided to himself in an offhand manner, now that he was here he might as well make a wish. After all, anything could happen, especially in a wood called Merlin. . . .

He never could be certain, afterward, whether he

had, in fact, wished at all before, suddenly, he saw the two small brown leaf things sticking up from the snow. Like leaves, they were, but not quite like leaves; and they stood in the top of a drift against the hedge, not ten yards away. He could almost imagine that one of them had moved. Then something seemed to pull tight in Paul's chest as he floundered forward. He bent and scrabbled at the snow with wet-gloved hands; the small leaf-brown things shook and flickered under his eyes, and—really, yes, there was no doubt what-ever about it, but—impossible though it might seem—he knew he was looking at the damp dark ears of a newborn foal.

Gently now, but tense with horrified anxiety, the gloved hands scraped and swept and felt their way. And under them the curled form of the foal was gradu-ally revealed. It looked at him with vague, heavy-lidded eyes, snuffling a little at the snow around its nostrils and shivering at the sudden cold air on wet skin. It was alive—a twin foal of Calluna's! Buried in the snow for a day and a half and still alive—though smaller, even, than the little one already at the farm.

Thinking quickly, Paul pulled off his coat and bent to rub the wet furry coat with the sleeves of it. He rubbed the ears, too, because he knew how important this was from having helped with Calluna after hunting; and he lifted the thin, incredibly long forelegs to rub down the narrow little chest. Then, wrapping his coat carefully around the tiny creature, he lifted it into his arms. The foal took little notice, being weak beyond caring, and accepted all things as it found them. Its weight was quite considerable for an eleven-year-old to carry, small though it was; and through deep snow the task was doubly hard. But Paul trudged on, leaning back to balance the weight. The long legs dangled against his knees as he staggered down the hidden field paths, and often he had to stop and sit down in the snow to get his breath and stretch his arms, the foal lying across his knees like a big, tired dog, and not moving anything except its small leaflike ears.

So this was why Calluna swung fretting around her box; why she stared out over the snow across the door that was now padlocked as well as bolted. She knew—though no one else had guessed—that one of her foals lay out in Merlin Wood, desperately needing warmth and milk and dryness.

"I'm bringing it, Calluna. I'm bringing it, Calluna," Paul was saying over and over in his mind as he stumbled along, as if his thoughts might reach the mare and reassure her.

When at last he came to the farm, and people rushed around him, and the foal was lifted from him, he could hardly straighten his stiff arms.

"Well, bless my soul!" Mr. Boley kept saying, as they strode to the stable. "The old girl knew, all along."

"It looks pretty far gone, Dad," said Roy, in the matter-of-fact tone that Paul could never understand.

"A bit weak," agreed his father, "and small wonder. But it's marvelous how they can pull around, sometimes."

"Listen! She's whinnying," said Paul, as they came into the yard. "She knows we've brought him!"

Calluna's lovely head was stretched over the door toward them as they came; and then she was licking the little foal all over its head and ears, and all over Paul's coat, too, wherever it came in her way. Mr. Boley laid the twin in the straw beside her, and Paul thought that he would never see anything in the whole of his life so moving as the mother's reunion with the lost one.

"Another little colt, too," said Mr. Boley. "Twin sons! Well, I'd sooner it'd been a single; twins don't often do so well. But, bless my soul, Paul, you're a hero if ever I've met one! Look, you can see her settling down already. She knew. My word, it's wonderful what they do know, isn't it?"

But all was not entirely as well as it seemed, for the second twin was very small and weak, and Calluna proved not to have enough milk to feed both of her foals. The bigger colt took well to mixed feeding, with cows' milk addition, but the small one drowsed in the straw and seemed only to hold onto his frail life by the lightness of a thread. For some days there was much anxiety about him, but no anxiety was greater than Paul's. All kinds of things were tried, such as boiling the milk to make it more digestible, and diluting it with water and adding fresh yolk of egg, but nothing seemed to make any difference.

Mr. Boley tried to comfort Paul with common sense and praise. "Well, look at it like this, son; if you've done nothing more than get Calluna to settle, that's enough for anyone to be proud of. I shouldn't set too much store on the little one living, if I were you. He doesn't seem to get on with cows' milk, and—well, even if he does pull through, I doubt if he'll ever be much good, you know."

"But, in a way, he's almost as if he were my colt," Paul said wistfully. "I mean, more especially mine than any other horse ever was. If he died, I don't think I could ever be interested so much in anything, ever again."

"Tell you what," said Mr. Boley, trying to cheer him up; "if he pulls through, you shall have him! There, what about that? Mind you, I doubt if he will—or that he'd be a credit to you when he grew up, either. More likely to grow up a weed, the way he's started. But there it is—yours, if you want him!"

Paul simply couldn't find a word to say, except, some minutes later, "Mine? Really? Oh—I say! Thank you!"

After that, the only thing that mattered to him was the saving of his colt. He spent most of every day in the box with it, offering small bottles of warm milk mixture after the little that was available from Calluna. But the colt seemed, somehow, to grow frailer, more dreamy, more often with the long sweeping lashes lowered over his eyes; though by now his brother was bucking wickedly around the box and biting their mother's tail. In the mornings, Paul talked over these things with old Mr. Terrell.

"Well now," said Tim thoughtfully one day, settling his postman's cap, "you might try a bit of goats' milk, p'raps. Wonderful, that is, for rearing delicate young things—animal or human, the both. Very digestible, is goats' milk, see."

Paul stared at him, thinking away backward. "Mr. Terrell—that nanny goat you told me about —"

Old Tim nodded. "I reckon she's still available. But Will Fletcher he don't reckon to sell no milk. Says it pays him better to feed it to his pigs. 'Sides, he's a good long way from Partridge Farm, son."

"I know. I don't want to buy the milk, but the goat," said Paul. "I want to have it at the farm, near the colt, so that he can have a little often, and really fresh."

Tim Terrell looked at him doubtfully for a moment,

although it had really been his own idea in the first place. Then he said, "Well, it's your money, old son. And, after all, as I said before, a goat's a useful thing to have."

Paul went out to Will Fletcher's smallholding that same morning. The snow had all thawed away now, and blackbirds were singing in softly greening hedges. Will Fletcher fetched out the nanny to show Paul, and expressed himself willing to take three pounds for her, without guarantee (because he was a cautious man) except for his word that she was giving half a gallon a day and was quiet to milk and handle, her name being Milkmaid. She was a nice, intelligent-looking creature with a white coat as white as the snow the colt had been born in, and Paul led her away gratefully, at once, with the promise of sending out his money by Mr. Terrell the next day.

He took the nanny straight to Partridge Farm, though it was nearly four miles from Will Fletcher's place, and she trotted along willingly enough on the end of her rope, though plainly much astonished at all this tramping. Mr. Boley was quite agreeable to Paul's establishing her in a spare box stall near Calluna's, and, until he managed to teach himself to hand milk, the cowman came along and milked a bottleful when needed, as well as supplying a pile of hay and roots and dairy-nuts, which were things Paul had somehow not thought about, in the emergency.

It was even as Tim Terrell had said. Where all else failed, the goat's milk seemed to agree with the small one, and slowly he began to look less dreamy and shadowy, taking a growing interest in the things around him. When, after a day or two, Paul brought his goat right into the box stall and taught the colt to suckle properly, the real recovery began. Folding down loosely on his knees to reach the low udder, and wriggling his bushy little tail, the colt took to feeding from Milkmaid at once. As Mr. Boley said, from that day you could almost see him growing. Within a week, he also was bucking round the box stall, and Mr. Boley came and watched him one morning when Paul was leading Milkmaid out to her tether in the orchard.

"Bless my soul!" he said, laughing at the twin colts' antics, "I half regret saying I'd give him to you. Getting on fine, now, isn't he? You'd never credit it."

"Let me put Milkmaid out," begged Roy. "I know about moving her tether."

"All right," said Paul happily, handing over the head rope. He was so happy, now, that he would have agreed to almost anything. Realizing this, Roy suddenly said, "When the colt's weaned, I'll swap you my air gun for Milkmaid. I think she's rather nice. And I could sell her kids, too."

"I'll think about it," said Paul, leaning over the stable door to look at his colt—his very own colt.

"Time you named him, isn't it?" asked Mr. Boley.

"I have," said Paul. "His name is Sure Magic."

"Sure what? Magic? Funny name, that. Why Magic?"

"Oh well—it just suits him, I think."

Mr. Boley suddenly laughed. "Oh, I see! Of course—because he was born in Merlin Wood!"

"Well, partly," said Paul evasively. Then: "I don't suppose there really is any magic, do you, Mr. Boley?" He sounded half doubtful, trying again to remember if he had wished before he saw those leaflike ears in the snowdrift.

"Well—not quite magic, perhaps," said Mr. Boley thoughtfully. "Funny thing, though. Parson was talking about it, one Sunday in the snow time. He was quoting someone, and he said, 'There are more things in heaven and earth than this world dreams of.' But I took it he was thinking of miracles."

"I know," said Paul slowly, remembering old Tim Terrell. And then he added, "Perhaps that's just what magic means."

The Perfect Partnership

CAROLINE PLAISTED

The problem of wanting to ride but having no horse of one's own has cropped up before in this collection, in Sandy Ransford's "Show Time." Here, Caroline Plaisted finds one solution to the difficulty for her heroine, Jo, who makes very good use of it. And like Monica Edward's "Sure Magic" (among others) this story is based on a real incident!

"I'm sorry, Jo, but we haven't got that kind of money. There's nothing we can do about it." Jo's eyes were stinging with tears as she realized the truth. However much she loved riding, however good she was at it, there was a limit to how far she could without a decent pony of her own. Oh, she loved Baffle, her dear little Shetland, who'd come with her to Pony Club camps and was so brilliant at Pony Club rallies. But even she knew that his conformation wasn't great and, anyway, he was too small for her now. After all, her feet practically touched the ground when she was in his saddle! So now Jamie, her younger brother, had Baffle. Thank goodness they hadn't had to sell him— Jo would have hated that. They'd solved Jamie's and Baffle's problem, but what about hers?

Jo's parents weren't rich, and the only reason they'd

been able to buy Baffle in the first place was because he'd belonged to a local farmer who was prepared to sell him for very little in order to keep him close by. Jo had always been obsessed with horses and her dad always laughed when he told people that one of his daughter's first words as a baby was "horses." Jo had learned to ride as soon as she was big enough to wear a riding hat and hold on properly to the reins.

Now Jo was thirteen and she spent every weekend at the local riding school and livery stable. In exchange for helping muck out the horses at livery, Jo was allowed a free riding lesson once a week. But Mrs. Ashby, her teacher, was concerned.

"We've got to think of a way to get you on a good pony, Jo," she said one week. "We've got some nice horses here, and you can practice on them. Without a horse of your own, though, one that you can develop a perfect partnership with, you'll soon have got as far as you can go."

Jo had moped around for the next few weeks as Mrs. Ashby's words went around and around her head. Then, one Friday night, Mrs. Ashby telephoned Jo's mother.

"Tell Jo to come in wearing her best jodhpurs and boots. I've got a silk she can wear over her hat to smarten it up a bit. I want her to look her best, because there's going to be someone at the yard tomorrow that I want her to impress!"

Jo had no idea what it could all mean, but she did as she was told. That night, she polished her boots so hard she nearly rubbed through the leather. She brushed down her jodhpurs and laid them out neatly on the chair before falling into bed. The next morning, she reported to the riding school office at eight o'clock, prompt as usual.

"Ah, excellent, Jo," said Mrs. Ashby, putting down her mug of tea.

"Look, I've got someone coming in today who says she saw you at the county show on Baffle last year. She's looking for someone to take on her daughter's pony, but she doesn't want to sell him. She wants to keep him in competition. I've seen him, Jo. He's gorgeous, just the thing for you. I can't promise anything but . . . it's the best chance you're likely to get."

Jo was almost breathless with excitement as she hugged Mrs. Ashby. "Oh, thanks! Thanks so much!"

"As I said, I can't promise anything. But just do your best and you won't let us down! Now, go out and warm up on Cinders." Mrs. Ashby took another slurp of tea. "I've got her ready for you. Mrs. Henry will be here at nine, so you haven't any time to lose. Well—go on, then!"

Jo did her best—and within the week the handsome Danbury Romeo arrived at her parents' house.

"Hello, Danbury Romeo," Jo whispered as she stroked the pony's nose. "Welcome to your new home."

"Danbury Romeo's a bit of a mouthful, isn't it? We call him B.J. at home, on account of the fact that once upon a time he broke his jaw. B.J.—Broken Jaw," said Mrs. Henry as she helped to settle him into his new stable. "He loves apples, so it's fortunate that we've got some apple trees at home. I've brought a couple of buckets of them with me today and I'll bring as many as I can every time I visit."

Mrs. Ashby and Mrs. Henry had explained carefully to Jo and her parents the terms of B.J.'s loan to them. B.J. was to live with them at their expense, but Mrs. Henry would pay any competition entry fees and would

loan them her box whenever they went to a show.

"I've seen you, Jo, and I think you could go far on B.J." Mrs. Henry said. "So that's why I've lent him to you. You can have him for six months initially. But if things go as well as I hope, we'll extend the loan for the rest of the year. And then, who knows? In the meantime, I want you both to go to a show next month and see how you get on."

The first show had really been a test, Mrs Henry said afterward, a chance for them to get used to each other at competitions. And they hadn't done too badly, after all—they were placed fifth in a class of twenty-five.

Jo worked hard over the next six months—harder than she ever had before. She had B.J. to muck out every morning before school; then, after school, before she did her homework, she took him around the sand ring that her father had made out of the paddock behind their house. On the weekends, Jo hacked B.J. to the riding stables for their weekly lesson.

B.J. and Jo did get used to each other. Jo groomed the pony to shiny perfection and, after all their practicing—of dressage, show jumping, and cross-country—the pair managed to collect some rosettes. At first they got yellow third-place ones, but it wasn't long before they progressed to red seconds and, better still, blue firsts. Jo's mum was so proud that she stuck the rosettes to the fridge door.

But it was on the day they won a first at the county show that Jo and B.J. proved that they really were a winning team. They were being led by Jo's mother back to the box in the parking lot as Mrs. Henry came racing up to them.

"Jo! Jo!" Mrs. Henry screamed. "You've done it. You have! I've just been speaking to the selector for the British junior team. He wants you and B.J. for the team!"

Jo was both excited and terrified as she and the other British team members arrived at the Country Park for the European competition. She'd spent weeks being coached by Mrs. Ashby, and on weekends, she'd been along to the special training sessions organized by Mr. Smythe, the *chef d'équipe*, or captain, of the British team. Mr. Smythe was in charge of them all—the horses and the riders—and Mrs. Henry had told Jo to make sure she did everything he said. Jo and her teammates were eager to have a peek around the stables being used by the other teams. But, by the time they had helped unbox their own ponies and given their tack a last brush, the competition was ready to begin. The dressage section wasn't too bad, although it was Jo's least favorite. By the end of it, the British and Irish teams were tied for second, with the German team in first place. After the show jumping, the British team had slipped down to third—Jo had knocked off part of a jump and Robert, one of the two boys on the team, took two jumps in the wrong order, so they'd lost some valuable points. After her round, Jo couldn't even look her teammates in the face. How could she have been so stupid? If it hadn't been for her, the British team might have kept its second place.

Of course, no one said anything to her, but that didn't stop Jo from feeling so anxious. The *chef d'équipe* had organized a barbecue for everyone to help them relax that evening. Jo had hardly been able to eat anything. All she could think about was tomorrow's round of the competition—and that just made her feel sick. When she went to bed that night, Jo found it difficult to sleep. Supposing she knocked down another jump tomorrow? Imagine if it was her fault that the team didn't do well . . .

Now it was the second day and the cross-country, which was Jo's favorite. She loved being able to race against the clock on B.J., with the wind ruffling his mane. Midway through the day, the *chef d'équipe* came to talk to his team.

"Sadly for them," Mr. Smythe said seriously, "the Germans have lost a lot of points this morning. The Irish team is still doing well, though. There's a lot to be done by you all—but I'm sure you'll all do what you can. Good luck."

Robert and Paula, another team member, both did better than they were expected to—after all, the cross-country wasn't the best section for either of them.

"And now, representing Great Britain, here is Jo riding Danbury Romeo."

Jo's stomach butterflied as she heard the announcement. This was it: Jo and her beautiful pony were the last in the team to compete—and everyone was relying on them.

"Keep calm, Jo," she told herself as she checked B.J.'s girth. "Go for it, B.J. You've got to get me through this." She tickled the handsome pony behind his right ear.

B.J. whinnied, almost as if he was trying to tell her that she could rely on him; he'd do the ride for both of them.

The bell went and the pair of them headed off around the course. Jo knew that, as the last rider in her team, everyone was depending on her. She and B.J. would make the difference between a medal or a fourth place. The water jump was wider than Jo had remembered from when she'd walked the course with the rest of the team earlier that morning. But B.J. cleared it with ease. Honestly, thought Jo, you'd think B.J. had wings, he was so light on his feet. The steep bank was horrid, and Jo was quite frightened as she and B.J. launched themselves from the top. They got to the bottom so quickly that Jo hardly caught her breath. Then the pair raced through some woods. Almost too late, Jo spotted a large branch which had fallen from a tree, perhaps knocked by one of the other riders. Quickly, she maneuvered B.J. around it. It was a relief when he was through and heading out of the woods.

Only two more jumps to go. B.J. clipped the top of the first with his front legs. The pole wobbled dangerously . . . and then settled back into its slot. At the last fence, Jo gripped at the reins tightly, asking B.J. to jump—too soon, she realized. Surely the whole thing would come crashing down now? But, as ever, it was B.J. who helped her out. Somehow he just knew what to do, and he cleared the jump in his own timing.

As Jo, hot and exhilarated, just like B.J., led the trusty pony back to the stables, Mrs. Henry came racing up to her.

"Jo! B.J.! You were brilliant. There's another rider to go for the German team, but I think you've helped us to get a third place."

Jo couldn't bear to watch the German rider. Anyway, she had B.J. to clean up. After all his hard work, she didn't want him to catch a chill because she hadn't looked after him. Jo was just giving B.J. slices of apple as a treat when she heard the announcer.

"Ladies and gentlemen. After the points have been worked out, we are able to announce that Ireland has won the gold, Great Britain the silver, and Germany the bronze."

The *silver*? Jo could hardly believe it. She'd been hoping to make it to the bronze. She and B.J. had helped to win a silver medal!

Happier than she remembered ever being before, Jo wrapped her arms around B.J.'s neck.

"Oh, B.J.," she said. "You're the best!"

The Valiant Chattee-Maker

retold by M. Frere

What do you do if you have never ridden a horse in your life, and the king appoints you commander-in-chief of his army, sending a magnificent charger for you to ride as you lead his army into battle? This is the situation the chattee-maker in this story finds himself in! The story comes from Southern India. A chattee-maker is a potter, and the king is called by the Indian title, "Rajah."

Once upon a time, in a violent storm of thunder, lightning, wind, and rain, a tiger crept for shelter close to the wall of an old woman's hut. This old woman was very poor, and her hut was but a tumble-down place, through the roof of which the rain came drip, drip, drip on more sides than one. This troubled her much, and she went running about from side to side, dragging first one thing and then another out of the way of the leaky places in the roof, and as she did so she kept saying to herself, "Oh dear! oh dear! how tiresome this is! I'm sure the roof will come down! If an elephant, or a lion, or a tiger were to walk in, he wouldn't frighten me half so much as this perpetual dripping." And then she would begin dragging the bed and all the other things in the room about again, to get them out of the way of the wet.

The tiger, who was crouching down just outside, heard all that she said, and thought to himself, "This old woman says she would not be afraid of an elephant, or a lion, or a tiger, but that this perpetual dripping frightens her more than all. What can this 'perpetual dripping' be?—it must be something very dreadful."

And hearing her immediately afterward dragging all the things about the room again, he said to himself, "What a terrible noise! Surely that must be the *'perpetual dripping'*."

At this moment a chattee-maker, who was in search of his donkey, which had strayed away, came down the road. The night being very cold, he had, truth to say, taken a little more toddy than was good for him, and seeing, by the light of a flash of lightning, a large animal lying down close to the old woman's hut, he mistook it for the donkey he was looking for. So, running up to the tiger, he seized hold of it by one ear, and commenced beating, kicking, and abusing it with all his might and main. "You wretched creature!" he cried, "is this the way you serve me, obliging me to come out and look for you in such pouring rain and on such a dark night as this? Get up instantly, or I'll break every bone in your body"; so he went on scolding and thumping the tiger with his utmost power, for he had worked himself up into a terrible rage.

The tiger did not know what to make of it all, but he began to feel quite frightened, and said to himself, "Why, this must be the 'perpetual dripping'; no wonder the old woman said she was more afraid of it than of an elephant, a lion, or a tiger, for it gives most dreadfully hard blows."

The chattee-maker, having made the tiger get up, got on his back and forced him to carry him home, kicking and beating him the whole way, for all this time he fancied he was on his donkey; and then he tied his forefeet and his head firmly together, and fastened him to a post in front of his house, and when he had done this he went to bed.

Next morning, when the chattee-maker's wife got up and looked out of the window, what did she see but a great big tiger tied up in front of their house, to the post to which they usually fastened the donkey; she was very much surprised, and running to her husband, awoke him, saying, "Do you know what animal you fetched home last night?"

"Yes, the donkey to be sure," he answered.

"Come and see," said she, and she showed him the great tiger tied to the post.

The chattee-maker at this was no less astonished than his wife, and felt himself all over to find if the tiger had not wounded him. But no! there he was safe and sound, and there was the tiger tied to the post, just as he had fastened it up the night before.

News of the chattee-maker's exploit soon spread through the village, and all the people came to see him and hear him tell how he had caught the tiger and tied it to the post; and this they thought so wonderful that they sent a deputation to the Rajah, with a letter to tell him how a man of their village had, alone and unarmed, caught a great tiger and tied it to a post.

When the Rajah read the letter, he also was much surprised, and determined to go in person and see this astonishing sight. So he sent for his horses and carriages, his lords and attendants, and they all set off

together to look at the chattee-maker and the tiger he
had caught.

Now the tiger was a very large one, and had long
been the terror of all the country around, which made
the whole matter still more extraordinary; and all this
being represented to the Rajah, he determined to confer all possible honor on the valiant chattee-maker. So
he gave him houses and lands, and as much money as
would fill a well, made him a lord of his court, and
conferred on him the command of ten thousand
horse.

It came to pass, shortly after this, that a neighboring
Rajah, who had long had a quarrel with this one, sent
to announce his intention of going instantly to war
with him; and tidings were at the same time brought
that the Rajah who sent the challenge had gathered a
great army together on the borders, and was prepared
at a moment's notice to invade the country.

In this dilemma no one knew what to do. The Rajah
sent for all his generals, and inquired of them which
would be willing to take command of his forces and
oppose the enemy. They all replied that the country
was so ill-prepared for the emergency, and the case
was apparently so hopeless, that they would rather
not take the responsibility of the chief command. The
Rajah knew not whom to appoint in their stead. Then
some of his people said to him, "You have lately given
the command of ten thousand horse to the valiant
chattee-maker who caught the tiger: why not make
him commander-in-chief? A man who could catch a
tiger and tie him to a post must surely be more courageous and clever than most."

"Very well," said the Rajah, "I will make him commander-in-chief."

So he sent for the chattee-maker and said to him, "In your hands I place all the power of the kingdom; you must put our enemies to flight for us."

"So be it," answered the chattee-maker; "but, before I lead the whole army against the enemy, suffer me to go by myself and examine their position, and, if possible, find out their numbers and strength."

The Rajah consented, and the chattee-maker returned home to his wife, and said: "They have made me commander-in-chief, which is a very difficult post for me to fill, because I shall have to ride at the head of all the army, and you know I never was on a horse in my life. But I have succeeded in gaining a little delay, as the Rajah has given me permission to go first alone and reconnoiter the enemy's camp. Do you therefore provide a very quiet pony, for you know I cannot ride, and I will start to-morrow morning."

But, before the chattee-maker had started, the Rajah sent over to him a most magnificent charger richly caparisoned, which he begged he would ride when going to see the enemy's camp. The chattee-maker was frightened almost out of his life, for the charger that the Rajah had sent him was very powerful and spirited, and he felt sure that even if he ever got on it, he should very soon tumble off; however, he did not dare to refuse it, for fear of offending the Rajah by not accepting his present.

So he sent back to him a message of thanks, and said to his wife, "I cannot go on the pony, now that the Rajah has sent me this fine horse; but how am I ever to ride it?"

"Oh, don't be frightened," she answered; "you've only got to get upon it, and I will tie you firmly on, so that you cannot tumble off, and if you start at night, no one will see that you are tied on."

"Very well," he said.

So that night his wife brought the horse that the Rajah had sent him to the door. "Indeed," said the chattee-maker, "I can never get into that saddle, it is so high up."

"You must jump," said his wife. So he tried to jump several times, but each time he jumped he tumbled down again.

"I always forget when I am jumping," said he, "which way I ought to turn."

"Your face must be toward the horse's head," she answered.

"To be sure, of course," he cried, and giving one great jump he jumped into the saddle, but with his face toward the horse's tail.

"This won't do at all," said his wife as she helped him down again; "try getting on without jumping."

"I never can remember," he continued, "when I have got my left foot in the stirrup, what to do with my right foot or where to put it."

"That must go in the other stirrup," she answered; "let me help you."

So, after many trials, in which he tumbled down very often, for the horse was fresh and did not like standing still, the chattee-maker got into the saddle; but no sooner had he got there than he cried, "Oh, wife, wife! tie me very firmly as quickly as possible, for I know I shall jump down if I can."

Then she fetched some strong rope and tied his feet firmly into the stirrups, and fastened one stirrup to the other, and put another rope around his waist and another around his neck, and fastened them to the horse's body and neck and tail.

When the horse felt all these ropes about him he could not imagine what queer creature had got upon his back, and he began rearing and kicking and prancing, and at last set off full gallop, as fast as he could tear, right across country. "Wife, wife!" cried the chattee-maker, "you forgot to tie my hands."

"Never mind," said she; "hold on by the mane." So he caught hold of the horse's mane as firmly as he could.

Then away went horse, away went chattee-maker—away, away, away, over hedges, over ditches, over rivers, over plains—away, away, like a flash of lightning—now this way, now that—on, on, on, gallop, gallop, gallop—until they came in sight of the enemy's camp.

The chattee-maker did not like his ride at all, and when he saw where it was leading him he liked it still less, for he thought the enemy would catch him and very likely kill him. So he determined to make one desperate effort to be free, and stretching out his hand as the horse shot past a young banyan tree, seized hold of it with all his might, hoping that the resistance it offered might cause the ropes that tied him to break.

But the horse was going at his utmost speed, and the soil in which the banyan tree grew was loose, so that when the chattee-maker caught hold of it and gave it such a violent pull, it came up by the roots, and on he rode as fast as before, with the tree in his hand.

All the soldiers in the camp saw him coming, and having heard that an army was to be sent against them, were sure the chattee-maker was one of the vanguard. "See," cried they, "here comes a man of gigantic stature on a mighty horse! He rides at full speed across the country, tearing up the very trees in his rage! He is one of the opposing force; the whole army must be close at hand. If they are such as he, we are all dead men."

Then, running to their Rajah, some of them cried again, "Here comes the whole force of the enemy" (for the story had by this time become exaggerated); "they are men of gigantic stature, mounted on mighty horses; as they come they tear up the very trees in their rage; we can oppose men, but not monsters such as these."

These were followed by others, who said, "It is all true," for by this time the chattee-maker had got pretty near the camp; "they're coming! they're coming! let us fly! let us fly! fly, fly for your lives!"

And the whole panic-stricken multitude fled from the camp (those who had seen no cause for alarm going because the others did, or because they did not care to stay by themselves), after having obliged their Rajah to write a letter to the one whose country he was about to invade to say that he would not do so, and propose terms of peace, and to sign it and seal it with his seal.

Scarcely had all the people fled from the camp when the horse on which the chattee-maker was came galloping into it, and on his back rode the chattee-maker, almost dead from fatigue, with the banyan tree in his hand: just as he reached the camp the ropes by which he was tied broke, and he fell to the ground.

The horse stood still, too tired with his long run to go farther. On recovering his senses, the chattee-maker found, to his surprise that the whole camp, full of rich arms, clothes, and trappings, was entirely deserted. In the principal tent, moreover, he found a letter addressed to his Rajah, announcing the retreat of the invading army and proposing terms of peace.

So he took the letter, and returned home with it as fast as he could, leading his horse all the way, for he was afraid to mount him again. It did not take him long to reach his house by the direct road, for whilst riding he had gone a more circuitous journey than was necessary, and he got there just at nightfall.

His wife ran out to meet him, overjoyed at his speedy return. As soon as he saw her, he said, "Ah, wife, since I saw you last I've been all around the world, and had many wonderful and terrible adventures. But never mind that now: send this letter quickly to the Rajah by a messenger, and send the horse also that he sent for me to ride. He will then see, by the horse looking so tired, what a long ride I've had; and if he is sent on beforehand, I shall not be obliged to ride him up to the palace door to-morrow morning, as I otherwise should, and that would be very tiresome, for most likely I should tumble off."

So his wife sent the horse and letter to the Rajah, and a message that her husband would be at the palace early next morning, as it was then late at night. And next day he went down there, as he had said he would; and when the people saw him coming, they said, "This man is as modest as he is brave; after having put our enemies to flight, he walks quite simply to the door, instead of riding here in state, as another man would." For they did not know that the chattee-maker walked because he was afraid to ride.

The Rajah came to the palace door to meet him, and paid him all possible honor. Terms of peace were agreed upon between the two countries, and the chattee-maker was rewarded for all he had done by being given twice as much rank and wealth as he had before, and he lived very happily all the rest of his life.

Beach Ponies

LINDA JENNINGS

*Many people, especially those who live in cities, only see
ponies on vacation. So they will understand the horror felt by
Laura and Jacob in this story when they find their beloved
beach ponies have gone. A little detection mixed with a
seaside holiday brings this collection to an end. Linda Jennings
works as a children's book editor, but has recently also
turned to writing, and in particular writing pony stories.*

"Can you see them?" Laura stood on tiptoe beside
her brother, trying to peer through the tangled
hedge.

Jacob shook his head. "No, I can't—I don't think
they're there."

Laura pushed him aside and stuck her head right
through the hedge. From here she could look all the
way down from the garden to the beach below, where
a few families were sitting with their coats on in the
weak April sun. But of the beach ponies there was no
sign.

"Perhaps it's too early for them," said Jacob. "They'll
probably be brought out in May, when the visitors
start arriving."

Laura looked at him scornfully. "You *know* they're
always down there, from Easter through October. They
always have been."

It was true. Laura and Jacob had been coming to the seaside cottage every holiday for years. And for as long as they could remember, the beach ponies would be down there on the beach, plodding backward and forward with children on their backs. And now there was not one pony in sight.

Jacob and Laura ran indoors, calling out to Mum and Dad, who were still busily unpacking.

"They've gone! The ponies have gone!" cried Laura as she rushed into the kitchen. Dad looked up from unpacking a box of provisions.

"I expect they're around somewhere," he said. "Now let's see—we still need sugar and some Slimline spread for your mum. . . ."

Laura gave a big sigh. Parents were hopeless. They never cared about the important things in life. "Let's go down to the stables," she suggested to Jacob. "Perhaps you're right, and they haven't come out yet. Easter's early this year, after all."

Both children ran out of the cottage before Mum and Dad could ask them to help unpack. They walked across the road and down a footpath that led to the back of the stables where the beach ponies had their winter quarters. "Stables" was really rather a grand word for them. They were just a line of tumbledown sheds standing at the edge of a field. Old Greg, who owned the ponies, didn't care about all the trimmings, even though he loved the ponies dearly. They were fed and watered well, and the sheds didn't leak. They were simple beach ponies, everyone loved them, and they didn't need any posh stables or tack to keep them happy.

"Oh!" Jacob stood stock-still by the field gate. Where the sheds had once stood there were now a few brown earthy patches. Nothing to suggest that ponies had ever lived there at all.

A woman walked by with her dog. Laura thought she was probably local, judging by her old mac and muddy wellies.

"Excuse me," she asked. "Do you know what's happened to the ponies who used to live in this field?"

"Old Greg's ponies?" said the woman. "They've been gone about four months. The old man had a nasty fall and went off to live with his niece. The ponies were bought by Mr. Parrish down the lane. He's building up a posh new riding school there." The woman called her dog and walked away down the footpath.

"I know the place," said Jacob. "Remember, last summer we asked about riding lessons? All frightfully expensive and fancy."

"So we went on riding the beach ponies instead," continued Laura. "Even though we were getting a bit big for them." She stood leaning over the gate, looking dejectedly at the bare patches of earth. "What's worrying me," she said, "is whether Mr. Parrish took *all* the ponies. Some were pretty old, remember, and not the sort of animals that would fit into an expensive setup like that."

Jacob nodded, biting his lip. In his mind's eye he could see all of them—old Ragbag, Dulcie, Peppermint, Jinty, Periwinkle, and Fred. Ragbag was the oldest, and Jinty a bit lame. Fred, too, was a rather ugly pony, even though he had the sweetest nature. What would have happened to them?

"Come on," said Laura, suddenly springing into action. "Let's go down to Parrish's and try to find out."

*　*　*

"Can I help you?" A blond girl in immaculate jodhpurs was walking across Parrish's stableyard as Laura
and Jacob came in.

"We're looking for Mr. Parrish."

"He's away at the horse trials this week," said the
girl. "Won't be back till Monday."

"Then perhaps you *can* help," said Jacob. "We're
looking for the ponies that Mr. Parrish bought from
old Mr. Gregory a few months back."

The girl smiled. "Oh yes, they're here. They need a
bit of schooling, so he didn't take any of them with
him."

She led the two children across the yard to a brand-
new block of stables. Jacob smiled. "They'll be
OK here," he said in relief. "Better than those old
sheds."

Laura was standing by the row of stable doors. Several familiar and friendly heads looked out at her,
bright-eyed. There was Dulcie, Ragbag, Peppermint,
and Periwinkle.

But where were Jinty and Fred?

When Laura asked about the missing ponies, the stable girl shook her head vaguely.

"I've only been here a couple of months. I knew Mr. Parrish had taken on the beach ponies, so I assumed these four were all there were. I don't know anything about the other two."

"I expect someone else bought them," said Jacob, who always liked looking on the bright side.

Laura didn't answer. Visions of the lame bay and the ugly little piebald came to her mind. She had been especially fond of Fred. "Stop it," she said to herself. "You're talking as though they're dead."

"Come on," she said to Jacob. "We must find out what's happened to them."

They walked down to the beach and asked at the ice cream kiosk, but the woman there couldn't help them.

"I miss them," she said. "So do the kids."

The car-park attendant was more helpful. "Poor old boy," he said. "He loved those ponies. He was delighted when Parrish decided to buy most of them."

"But the other two—what about them?" Laura almost shouted. "I've heard that Parrish took them over to Pilchester to a horse sale," he said.

A horse sale! Laura felt that she shouldn't ask any further. It would be lovely to think that the two little ponies had each gone to loving homes, but she feared the worst. What nearly always happened to decrepit or ugly ponies was too awful to contemplate.

"That's that, then," said Jacob. "Nothing else we can do."

Laura nodded miserably. "Yes, it's too late now," she said. "We'd best forget all about them."

*   *   *

For the next few days Laura and Jacob tried to put the beach ponies from their minds. It was too early in the year for swimming, but they went on lots of trips, to working farms and bird sanctuaries and craft centers. Laura bought a little carved wooden rocking horse from one of them. It was piebald, like Fred. She blinked back a tear.

"Let's have a cream tea," said Mum one day, after they'd all walked over the cliffs to the neighbouring village.

The family sat down thankfully in the dark little oak-beamed tearoom. Their feet ached from all the walking.

"We've come across from Mariner's Bay," Dad told the plump, fresh-faced woman who brought them their teas.

"Mariner's Bay, eh?" said the woman. "My old uncle lived there. Had a whole string of beach ponies, he did, till he sold 'em and came to live here with me."

Jacob and Laura opened their mouths in astonishment. Old Greg? Here! "We knew him," said Laura.

"He's having a nap at the moment," said his niece, "otherwise I'd call him down to meet you."

"Sad that he had to give up the ponies," said Mum.

Old Greg's niece smiled and sighed at the same time. "Not all of them," she said. "When Parrish said he'd take two of them to the horse sale in Pilchester, Uncle nearly went mad. "Horse fodder!" he yelled—so what could I do, softie that I am!"

"You mean—" said Laura.

Old Greg's niece beckoned the two children, and they went with her through a dark passageway and out into the garden beyond. It wasn't a large garden, and it was terribly overgrown, but it was big enough for two small, friendly ponies. They trotted over to Laura and Jacob, and nuzzled in their pockets for pony nuts.

"Fred!" said Laura happily. "And Jinty."

Acknowledgments

Grateful acknowledgment is made for permission to reprint previously published material.

"The Ghost Horse" from *Long Lance* by Chief Buffalo Child Long Lance (New York: Henry Holt and Company, Inc., 1928). Copyright © 1928 by Chief Buffalo Child Long Lance. Reprinted by permission of Henry Holt and Company Inc.

"Sure Magic" by Monica Edwards from *Pony Club Annual 1954* (London: Max Parrish, 1954). Copyright © 1954 by Monica Edwards. Reprinted by kind permission of Monica Edwards.

"Bonnie's Big Day" from *Bonnie's Big Day* by James Herriot (New York: St. Martin's Press, 1972). Copyright © 1972, 1987 by James Herriot. Reprinted by permission of St. Martin's Press Incorporated.

"Beach Ponies" copyright © 1996 by Linda Jennings.

"A Wayside Adventure" from *The Horse and His Boy* by C. S. Lewis (London: Geoffrey Bles Ltd., 1954). Copyright © 1954 by C. S. Lewis. Reprinted by permission of HarperCollins *Publishers* Limited, London.

"For 'Cow,' Read 'Horse'" copyright © 1996 by Donald Lightwood.

"One of Those Funny Little Mishaps" copyright © 1996 by Elizabeth Lindsay.

"The Tale of the Ebony Horse" from *One Thousand and One Arabian Nights*, retold by Geraldine McCaughrean (Oxford: Oxford University Press, 1982). Copyright © 1982 by Oxford University Press. Reprinted by permission of Oxford University Press.

"Black Shadows of Palms" from *Light Horse to Damascus* by Elyne Mitchell (Oxford: Oxford University Press, 1971). Copyright © 1971 by Elyne Mitchell. Reprinted by permission of Curtis Brown Ltd.

"The White Horse of Zennor" from *The White Horse of Zennor and Other Stories* by Michael Morpurgo (London: Kaye & Ward, 1982). Copyright © 1982 by Michael Morpurgo. Reprinted by kind permission of Reed Books.

"The Pony Club Camp" from *Ponies Plot* by C. Northcote

Acknowledgments

Parkinson (London: John Murray (Publishers) Ltd., 1965). Copyright © 1965 by C. Northcote Parkinson. Reprinted by permission of John Murray (Publishers) Ltd with arrangements through Singer Media Corp., California.

"The Perfect Partnership" copyright © 1996 by Caroline Plaisted.

"Bone of Contention" copyright © 1996 by Josephine Pullein-Thompson.

"Show Time" copyright © 1996 by Sandy Ransford.

"The Fall of Troy" from *Heroes and Monsters* by James Reeves (London: Pan Books Ltd., 1969). Copyright © 1969 by James Reeves. Reprinted by permission of the Estate of James Reeves.

"The Wild White Horses" by Joyce Stranger, from *The Noel Streatfeild Christmas Holiday Book* (London: J. M. Dent and Sons Ltd., 1973). Copyright © 1973 by Joyce Stranger Ltd. Reprinted by kind permission of Aitken & Stone Ltd.

"A Horse Called Terror" retelling copyright © 1996 by Felicity Trotman.

"Across the Deserts of Peru" from *Southern Cross to Pole Star: Tschiffely's Ride* by A. F. Tschiffely (London: William Heinemann, 1933). Copyright © 1933 by A. F. Tschiffely. Reprinted by kind permission of John Johnson Ltd.

"The Splendid Reality" from *I Own the Racecourse!* by Patricia Wrightson (London: Hutchinson Children's Books, 1968). Copyright © 1968 by Patricia Wrightson. Reprinted by permission of Random House UK Ltd.

400 PAGES OF FANTASTIC STORIES
BY SOME OF THE WORLD'S BEST WRITERS

☐ **The Random House Book of Dance Stories**
Including stories by Joan Aiken, Louisa May Alcott, Hans Christian Andersen, Alexandre Dumas, Rudyard Kipling, Margaret Mahy, E. Nesbit, Noel Streatfeild, and Oscar Wilde
(0-679-88529-3) $9.99

☐ **The Random House Book of Fantasy Stories**
Including stories by Joan Aiken, Neil Gaiman, Diana Wynne Jones, Tanith Lee, C. S. Lewis, George Macdonald, E. Nesbit, J. R. R. Tolkien, and Jane Yolen
(0-679-88528-5) $9.99

☐ **The Random House Book of Science Fiction Stories**
Including stories by Piers Anthony, Arthur C. Clarke, John Christopher, H. B. Fyfe, Douglas Hill, Samantha Lee, and William Temple
(0-679-88527-7) $9.99

Available wherever books are sold ...

OR

You can send in this coupon (with check or money order)
and have the books mailed directly to you!

Subtotal ....$ _____
Shipping and handling ....$ ___3.00___
Sales tax (where applicable) ....$ _____
Total amount enclosed ....$ _____

Name _____

Address _____

City _____ **State** _____ **Zip** _____

Make your check or money order (no cash or C.O.D.s)
payable to Random House, Inc., and mail to:
Random House Mail Sales, 400 Hahn Road, Westminster, MD 21157.

Prices and numbers subject to change without notice. Valid in U.S. only.
All orders subject to availability. Please allow 4 to 6 weeks for delivery.

Need your books even faster? Call toll-free 1–800–795–2665
to order by phone and use your major credit card.
Please mention interest code 049–13 to expedite your order.